Praise for Tiffany McDaniel's *Betty*

'This book will break your heart open, in the best way'
Good Housekeeping

'A brilliant, expansive exploration of family and grief. An innovative coming-of-age story filled with magic in language and plot, it is beautiful and devasting. McDaniel continues to be someone to watch'
Daisy Johnson, *Observer*

'Breathtaking'
Vogue

'A brutal and moving story. . . With its troubling subject matter, emotional punch and the backdrop of racism in mid-century America, *Betty* has echoes of Alice Walker's *The Color Purple*'
Irish Times

'There's a good chance you haven't read a family saga like *Betty* . . . Their story is simultaneously extraordinary (they are subjected to unthinkable racism, financial hardships, and untimely deaths) and run-of-the-mill (at the heart, they are a family like any other). Each day in their life is supplanted with the mysticism and interconnectedness of their father's traditions, offering a light at the end of a very dark plot tunnel'
Entertainment Weekly

'The book is rich with the texture of everyday living. It's these details that sing *Betty* to life and bring readers fully into the Appalachian landscape and the social milieu of Breathed'
Los Angeles Times

'So engrossing! Tiffany McDaniel's *Betty* is a page-turning Appalachian coming of age story steeped in Cherokee history, told in undulating prose that settles right into you'
Naoise Dolan, *Sunday Times* bestselling author of *Exciting Times*

'I loved *Betty*. I fell for its strong characters and was moved by the story it portrayed. McDaniel deals with the passage of time with subtlety and skill and descriptions of the rolling hills of Ohio were really beautiful'
Fiona Mozley

'I felt consumed by the ambitious enormity and sadness of this book. *Betty* is about the power of works and the language it is written in rings with this. I loved it, you will love it'

Daisy Johnson, Booker Prize shortlisted author of *Everything Under*

'*Betty* is woven of many things, light and dark, and most of all it is life in all its shades: all its brilliances and disappointments, sadnesses and hopes. Vivid and lucid, *Betty* has stayed with me'

Kiran Milwood Hargrave, author of *The Mercies*

'Tiffany McDaniel has given us a vivid and haunting portrait of the writer as a young girl. Betty Carpenter survives the brutality of her childhood through her father's stories and his steadfast belief in her own. A novel of tragedy and trouble, poetry and power, not a story you will soon forget'

Karen Joy Fowler, Booker Prize shortlisted author of *We Are All Completely Beside Ourselves*

'Magical, densely lyrical and often disturbing. Tiffany McDaniel follows the tradition of *The Color Purple* with her unflinching portrayal of the generational ripples of racism, poverty, and abuse. Shot through with moonshine, Bible verses, and folklore, *Betty* is about the cruelty we inflict on one another, the beauty we still manage to find, and the stories we tell in order to survive'

Eowyn Ivey, author of *The Snow Child*

ALSO BY TIFFANY MCDANIEL

Betty
The Summer That Melted Everything

ON THE

SAVAGE

SIDE

ON THE SAVAGE SIDE

Tiffany McDaniel

WEIDENFELD & NICOLSON

First published in the United States 2023 by Alfred A. Knopf,
a division of Penguin Random House LLC, New York
First published in Great Britain in 2023 by Weidenfeld & Nicolson,
an imprint of The Orion Publishing Group Ltd
Carmelite House, 50 Victoria Embankment
London EC4Y 0DZ

An Hachette UK Company

1 3 5 7 9 10 8 6 4 2

ISBN (Hardback) 978 1 3996 0607 3
ISBN (Trade paperback) 978 1 3996 0608 0
ISBN (eBook) 978 1 3996 0610 3
ISBN (Audio) 978 1 3996 0611 0

Printed in Great Britain by Clays Ltd, Elcograf S.p.A.

MIX
Paper from
responsible sources
FSC
www.fsc.org   FSC® C104740

www.weidenfeldandnicolson.co.uk
www.orionbooks.co.uk

Dedicated to the Chillicothe Six victims:

Charlotte Trego, 27.
Disappeared May 3, 2014.
Still missing.

Tameka Lynch, 30.
Disappeared May 2014.
Body discovered in river.

Wanda Lemons, 37.
Disappeared November 4, 2014.
Still missing.

Shasta Himelrick, 20.
Disappeared December 2014.
Body discovered in river.

Timberly Claytor, 38.
Disappeared May 2015.
Found shot to death in weeds May 29, 2015.

Tiffany Sayre, 26.
Disappeared May 11, 2015.
Body found near river.

You are not forgotten.

ON THE
SAVAGE
SIDE

The little girl woke up, certain she'd been dreaming. And then the little girl woke up, certain it'd been a dream.

Prologue

THE LOCALS CALLED THE RIVER IN AUTUMN THE EYE OF GOD. THE way the yellow, burgundy, and crimson leaves released from the branches overhead and landed on the surface, leaving a small circle where the muddy water appeared. The legend was, if you were to peer into this circle, you would be staring into the pupil of God and you would know your future. The river, though, knew what she was. And though she was flattered by the mythology, she did not think of herself as anything but another woman, like the ones who came and stood on her banks or dove beneath her waters.

The river had known the women from the time they were little girls. Her water had washed over them in baptisms, been the cool relief on hot summer days, and served as the view to first kisses and dares off the tall tree. The river came to think of the women as her own daughters, watching them come of age in a town of factories and men.

It was late when the river felt the splash. She thought maybe a limb had broken off. Or perhaps someone had thrown in a rock to see if it would skip against her. It was a heavy splash. The river thought of all heavy things. Then she saw the woman's face as her body floated. The river had lived long enough, it was not the first dead body to have been dumped in her waters. But as the old river stared into the eyes of the young woman, she couldn't help but feel a restless sorrow at having known her and the way she had splashed her feet in the water when she was a little girl.

The river knew there was a good distance to go before the woman would be seen. What the river did not know was that there would be more of them, floating facedown, as if they had no names at all.

P
A
R
T

I

The power of a flower is that she can tower.

—*Daffodil Poet*

THE FIRST SIN WAS BELIEVING WE WOULD NEVER DIE. THE SECOND sin was believing we were alive in the first place.

When a woman disappears, how is she remembered? By her beautiful smile? Her pretty face? The drugs in her system? Or by the johns who all have dope breath and graceless desires?

In Chillicothe, Ohio, there is the familiar quarrel. The same quarrel that is known through once-pastoral fields, where industry was made and generations were supported by grandfathers and fathers working in the paper mill until they came home at night to become the captains of the dinner table while our mothers were women of immortal hands who picked up our dropped prayers and answered them.

But it was all a myth, these gods in ordinary folk. No more real than the heroes of ancient Greece. Chillicothe, Ohio, it turned out, was full of mortals.

The land had once been called Chala-ka-tha by the Indigenous tribes who had lived there for thousands of years before European settlers came to steal it and rename it something the white tongue could own. Chillicothe.

In their white ways, they industrialized the land. Chillicothe rose in building and pitched roof, competing with the surrounding hills. In her newfound kingdom, she had been the first capital of Ohio, before that, too, was taken away. Remnants were found in the presence of a couple of department stores, the aisles married to the turning wheel of shopping carts and Sunday coupons. Beneath the harsh breath of development and asphalt, there existed the rounded tops of the trees blowing in the wind and the traces of those who had come centuries before.

Home to what had been the rich culture of the First Peoples, Chillicothe was a primal place of geometric earthworks and burial mounds. Ripe with fossilized shark teeth, obsidian, and shells from the faraway ocean, the earthworks were magic to someone like me. As a child, I would dig, beneath the seething beetles and below the earthworms, into the deep cool and native soil, hoping to uncover the buried trace of the beautiful and the hidden.

Some folks look at a place by how it is. I like to look at a place by how it would be discovered in the future. What artifacts would Chillicothe, Ohio, leave in the dark ground if it were lost to time? There would be leather straps from the purses of the women who visited the cosmetic counters every Easter sale, plastic straws from the never-ending selection of fast-food joints, camo jackets from the predators, feathers from the nests of the prey. There would be old Tecumseh brochures, family photos from fabric-covered albums, earmarked pages from the Bible, and used needles to remind us we were not perfect.

Most of all, there would be layers. Layers of fury, of beauty, of the hours that shrivel like dry grass. On top of that, as the crowning deposit, there would be the sawdust from the paper mill. Maybe there would even be the smell, mixed into the soil, hardened with the rocks, renewed with each inhale. Locals called the odor coming from the paper mill the smell of money. But for the ones who were not born and raised in Chillicothe, they held their noses and said, "Damn this town stinks."

There our entire lives, my sister Daffy and me figured it was what the whole world smelled like. A mixture of rotten eggs, hot garbage, and the toxic fumes that wood makes when it is forced to become paper. This odor would spew from the red-and-white-striped stacks, up into the sky, choking the birds. It would fall back down like a blanket upon us and cling to our clothes, hair, and homes.

It was in the shadow of the paper mill that Daffy and me lived with our mother Adelyn and her sister Clover in the part of town not visible when looking down Main Street with its brick and concrete, the works of old men. We lived on the south side, where slum landlords rented out small cinderblock houses. Ours was painted a brown that Daffy said was the color of watered-down Pepsi cola. I thought it was the color of sand from the riverbank, left to dry on the bottoms of our feet and get dusty in the light. The house had a little front porch that had black metal rails my sister and me would slip notes back and forth through when we pretended we were on opposite sides of the world.

"I wrote my note in purple unicorn ink," Daffy would always say, her pen as black as mine.

The houses had an uncomfortable nearness to one another. If there was an argument next door, you heard it. If there was dinner on the stove, you smelled it. If there was a woman sitting down at her kitchen table with her face in her hands, you saw it.

Perhaps when the houses had first been built, the concrete had been carefully poured on the porches in anticipation of the welcome mats. But as the nights tightened against the wasted time of those who slept their days away, it became the part of Chillicothe that the rats would chew their own legs off to be free of the hellhole falling in on them. A hellhole my sister and me would try to escape on our bikes.

We didn't think it could get much worse, but in 1979, when we were six years old, our father died and our mother screamed while my sister and me held hands, our backs pressed against the wall.

I thought our mother had hung our father's clothes on the windows out of anger. She seemed furious he had died, the way she banged on the walls with her fists.

"If he wasn't already dead, I'd kill him," she said as she kicked in and dented the kitchen cabinet. She pulled out a junk drawer and let it spill out on the floor as she headed for the hammer and nails.

"I'll show that son of Chillicothe." She yanked one of Dad's flannel shirts up off the floor by its sleeve and jerked it toward the window like she was jerking the man himself out of the grave. Then she dragged the old upholstered chair across the floor and climbed up on its brown floral cushion, falling no less than five times.

The thin strap of her red camisole had slid down, exposing herself. My mother wore camisoles as shirts year-round. Even during the months when the ground froze. Sometimes she paired them with loose cutoff shorts. Other times just satin panties, worn so many days, they were stretched and baggy in the rear and crotch. Come winter it was elastic band sweatpants, mostly the peach- or teal-colored ones, pushed up over the sores on her calves. That day in 1979 was late spring, and it was the satin panties, baby blue but faded to gray.

Daffy and me watched our mother nail our father's clothes to the wall, hammering with such force, there'd always be little cracks in the plaster around his ripped and dirty jeans, his yellowed underwear, even his army uniform, which was charred from the time he had tried to burn it, only to decide he didn't want to do that after all.

"Goddamn lizard dick," Mom grumbled as she stepped up on the wide armrest to balance.

"You better not fall off that chair, Addie." Aunt Clover kept her eyes on the image of the Danube River in Hungary flowing across the TV. "We'll have to throw your body into the tall weeds and let the animals drag you away. Spittle, spittle, spider, where you gonna hide her?" Aunt Clover spit into her palm and smacked it against the sofa's arm. "In the blood. That's where."

Whenever Aunt Clover said the word *blood,* which she often did, she would say it like she was from a people who had shed more of it than any other. She was sitting slumped on the old sofa, the same color as the rust ring in our bathroom sink. Her feet were up on the coffee table, spaced far enough apart that the empty cigarette cartons, beer bottles, and small squares of foil could pile between her ankles, the bracelets on them sliding down to her dirty heels.

She used the nightie wrapped around her shoulders to dab the sweat on her forehead. The satin was a creamy blue. Nearly as old as she was, which to Daffy and me at the time seemed an hour younger than the dust in our house. Truth be told, Aunt Clover wasn't more than a week into being thirty. She just wore the hardness of life a little too early.

"You think you could be any fucking louder with that hammer?" she asked, her head tossing with each word.

Even though Aunt Clover never watched TV with the sound on, she was always screaming about someone being so loud, she couldn't hear the damn program.

"Stuff your fist in your mouth and choke on it, Clover." Mom hammered even louder.

After every window was covered, I started to doubt Mom's fury because all she did then was cry as she walked down the hall to her bedroom, dropping the hammer along the way.

"Your mom's the wife to a ghost now, girls," Aunt Clover said as she leaned forward, managing to find her blue eyeliner rather quickly amid the trash on the coffee table. "She'll never be young again."

Without using a mirror, Aunt Clover circled her eyes with the eyeliner and drew it out to each of her temples. On these straight lines, she crossed tiny *x*'s until it looked like the barbs on the wire fence by the railroad tracks.

"Aunt Clover?" Daffy watched her. "How come you always wear blue eyeliner?"

Daffy sang out the word *blue* until I joined her.

"Because when our skin drops off," Aunt Clover said, "blue is the color we'll be beneath. How's my barbed wire look?" She turned her head side to side, showing the tiny *x*'s. "Will it protect me from the nine-eyed monsters who try to feast on a woman's blood?"

We nodded as she stood, slipping her black fringed vest over her crop top, cut low enough to see the lace of her bra. No matter what she wore, she always had her faux fur leopard collar on. It had rounded flaps and a snap in the front, like the collars I'd seen on sailors in the paintings in the books I got from the library.

She took the collar off her neck to knock it against her leg. The puffs of dirt kicked up in the air. It would be the most cleaning it would see. When she wrapped the collar back around her neck, she curled her tongue into a purr as she clicked the snap.

I stood up on the sofa cushion to pet the collar myself. "Where'd you get it from again, Aunt Clover?"

"I got it from the time I visited the jungle," she said. "It was my only souvenir. Now get your sticky fingers off it."

"How'd you get it in the jungle, Aunt Clover?" Daffy crossed her arms. "You ain't ever been outta Chillicothe."

"There's jungles here, too, child."

She'd never called either of us "child" before. It sounded soft in her accent, like she'd said it a hundred times over boiling soup.

"Now, hand me my scarf." She pointed to the nightie on the sofa.

After I gave it to her, she draped it over her shoulders. She called it her nighttime scarf. "Because," as she'd tell you, "only women who carry the river on their backs get to wear it. And I've been carrying the river on my back since I was old enough to know you either carry the river or it carries you. My nighttime scarf is the ripple of the water. The type of ripple that only comes in the moonlight."

We followed behind her into the bathroom, her long, stringy red hair grazing the back pockets on her denim skirt. We sat on the edge of the tub and watched her use the pink brush to feather her bangs. Then we stared at the white leather belt she wore. It had a bloody fingerprint by the gold-toned buckle and more in the area over her right hip. The blood was from a busted lip she'd once gotten. Another time, from a fist to the nose. A time after that, a cut to the back of her hand. Always she would rub the fresh blood into the tiny swirls on her finger and press it hard into the leather, blowing on it to help it dry faster.

"You think I'll make a lot of money tonight, girls?" She laid the hairbrush down to push up both of her boobs. "Enough to go to Brazil?" She shook her hips. "Or Morocco? Yeah, that's where I'm going."

We watched as she brushed what teeth she had left with her finger. After she spit, she looked up into the mirror. There were small pieces of clear tape in a few places on the glass. As she studied her reflection, she leaned closer to it with a frown, her eyes on her right shoulder.

"There's another one," she said, picking up the small roll of tape from the sink. "Another crack."

She tore off a piece of tape and put it over the reflected image of her shoulder.

"You've got to seal the cracks," she said, pressing down on the tape. "If you don't, they'll keep getting bigger and bigger until they break open completely and steal your name from you. Remember this, girls. One day your skin will crack, too. Your skin will crack even more because you're twins and you both have witches' marbles for eyes."

She stared at the tape on the glass, checking to make sure its edges were tightly sealed.

"Help me," she said. "Help me make sure the cracks are sealed good."

We hopped up from the tub and stood on our toes, pressing our fingers into the tape, the glass cold behind it.

"Press hard now," she said. "Give it all you've got. You don't want your aunt cracking to pieces, do you?"

We pressed so hard, the three of us grunted. That seemed to satisfy Aunt Clover as she smiled at her reflection.

"Spittle, spittle, spider, where you gonna hide her?" She spit into her palm and smacked it against the mirror glass. "Right there," she said, turning out the light.

"There's frozen dinners in the freezer." She grabbed her purse on her way to the front door, her nighttime scarf trailing after her. "It's a good thing we live in a cinderblock house."

"Why's that, Aunt Clover?" I asked.

"You can't burn it down." She winked, then slammed the door.

Once she was gone, Daffy and me mimicked her walk, sashaying our hips side to side. We giggled and fell back against the window. When one of Dad's pant legs fell over Daffy's shoulder, she stopped laughing and asked, "Why you think Momma didn't throw Daddy's clothes in the mud like she did his shoes? Or cut 'em up like she did his belts?"

"Maybe it's for the wind," I said. "When it blows in through the window, it'll get to wear the clothes. Get to wear his old shirts and pants. Maybe that's why she did it. To give the wind some clothes, so it don't come in our house naked all the time."

"Let's get her to say that in a whisper," Daffy herself whispered. "And then we'll keep it like a secret."

We raced each other to our mother's bedroom. It was at the very end of the narrow hall. The white door was closed. Daffy stuck her finger into the keyhole and turned it, like she was unlocking it. Inside, the room was dark. The bulb in the ceiling fan had not been replaced after burning out. The only source of light came from a green lamp sitting on the floor in the corner, but the shade was so dirty, the light had little chance.

"Momma?" Daffy called from the doorway. "You in here?"

We stepped slowly, using our bare toes to feel around the items littered on the floor. There was no bed frame any longer, just the gray mattress, printed with big blue flowers, pressed against the wall. The remaining furnishings were bare. An oak dresser, the drawers open and the clothes spilling out. The pink side table had legs at one time, but Mom broke them off, so the drawer sat directly on the floor, the tabletop within easy reach of the mattress.

I ran my fingers along the walls of the room, painted mint green years earlier and graffitied in marker with the words two addicts made together. I could tell my father's handwriting from my mother's. He always wrote with a slant to the right. She always wrote with a slant to the left. Their words never fully touching. In some places, their writing looked like drawn birds flying away from one another.

"Momma?" Daffy called again.

We saw her move on the mattress. She was using Dad's canvas bag from the army as a blanket.

"Who is it?" Our mother's voice came in a husky whisper. "Who's in my room?"

"Hi, Momma." Daffy stepped over to the mattress and sat down on the drift of dirty clothes there. "Why'd you put Daddy's clothes up on the windows?"

"What?" Mom's eyes rolled as she felt around the cluttered bedside table.

"His things. Mommmma." Daffy had to repeat the question not once, but three times more. "Listen to me."

"Oh, I hung his clothes, Daffy. It was me," Mom said. "I did it." Her words sounded like they had glue on them, each one sticking together.

"We know you did, Momma," I said. "But why? Was it to dress the wind?"

"He's gone now, babies." She turned over. "Your daddy's dead."

"We know that," I shouted. "We already know that."

She sat up, blinking, Dad's army bag sliding down to her waist.

"Well, why the fuck didn't you say so?" She ran her fingers through her greasy hair. "Ya little shits. Is Clover already gone?"

"Yep," Daffy said. "She wore her barbed wire. She'll be gone all night."

"Fuck." Mom laid her hand on her head.

I nudged Daffy and pointed down to the mattress. There was a new hole in the side of it, a couple of inches across, the edges frayed. I could see the end of a lighter sticking out of it, a few rubber bands, and what appeared to be the cap off a pen.

"Leave me alone, girls." Mom turned over, the smell of body sweat drifting out to us.

We held our noses as Daffy asked, "But why'd you put Daddy's clothes on the windows?"

"Well, goddamn." Mom wiped the dribble off her chin. "So the world will think a man still lives here. If they know we're a house of women now, they'll make us sit naked on gravel until it embeds in the backs of our legs. We'll never be able to swim in the river then. We'll sink like stones. Do you know what will happen? We'll walk so heavy we lose our breath. The rest of our lives will be us trying to find it again. Now leave me alone." She slapped the mattress, the smell of urine rising up in the air. "I can't think with you two on me all the damn time."

"C'mon, Daffy." I pulled her up. "Let's go get something to eat."

On our way out, Daffy grabbed the sleeve of the plaid shirt on the window. She yanked it so hard, the fabric ripped and tore off the nail. The sound took over the room and caused our mother to rise up as quickly as we'd ever seen her do.

"I'm sorry, Momma." Daffy stood there shaking as she dropped the shirt. "I didn't mean to—"

"No." Mom cried as she crawled off the mattress, her knees banging hard against the floor and making a thumping sound. "Why would you do this, you endlessly stupid girl?"

"I'm sorry, Momma," Daffy said in a small voice.

Mom grabbed Daffy by the arm. When I tried to step in, she yanked me into her, too.

"I'm gonna sell you both to the paper mill," Mom said as she threw us down onto the floor. "They're gonna put you up on the big conveyor belt like you're logs and the saw is gonna come for you. *Whosh, whosh.*" She made the sounds of a saw as she ran her nails up and down our skin. "It's gonna cut you into thin paper. *Whosh, whosh.* You ain't gonna be no girls no more. You're gonna be quiet. Quiet as paper."

"No, Momma, no." We both screamed.

"Oh, yes Momma, yes." She dug her nails deeper into our skin. "After you're turned into paper, I'm gonna burn you until you're nothing but ash."

"No." I reached up and slapped my mother across the face. As Daffy scooted back and cried against the wall, I stayed pinned beneath Mom. I frowned up at her, and she looked down at me. Growling, she picked up Dad's shirt from the floor and held it to her heaving chest.

"Bad girls, very bad girls." She hugged the shirt and crawled across the floor to the lamp, where she checked the fabric under the light as if searching for tears or holes. She held the shirt close as the light caught on her face.

Someone had once told her she had beautiful cheeks, so she cut her red hair in a short shag that was so common in the magazines she looked at in those late 1970s. She would bleach and spike her tips, leaving the roots to show. Maybe at one time she'd had beautiful cheeks, but by then her hooded eyes were sunken and watery, the green irises having disappeared more and more until she looked to have nothing but black pupils, a reflection of the shadows around her.

Her nose constantly ran, the nostrils red because of it. She had marks on her skin from her endless picking that got worse at night, the scratch lines connecting the old sores with the new ones. The sweat on her forehead always made the hair at her crown wet, and the dirt she didn't wash off every day collected in the wrinkles she was too young to have. Even at six years old, I wanted to take her and put her into the tub because I thought I could wash it all away as if it were nothing more than the filth of having fallen down.

"Why would you do this to your daddy?" she asked as she cradled her pointy chin into the shirt. "Why would you yank him off the window like that? Huh? Why would you do this to him? I hate you both. You're half of the same rotten apple. I wish the two of you'd never been born."

She ran toward us on all fours, screaming. We jumped out of the room. Our hiding place wasn't very good. It was in the kitchen, in the narrow space between the green refrigerator and the paneled wall where the old calendars were thrown. We piled them on top of us and waited.

"You're breathing too loud, Arc," Daffy said in a whisper. "She'll find us and feed us to the needle monster."

But we knew when we heard Mom shout "Stay the fuck out of my room" and slam her bedroom door that she would not emerge for the rest of the night.

"We'll be okay now," I said to my trembling sister. "I'll make us something to eat and we can invite anyone we want to have dinner with us."

"Even Daddy?" she asked.

"Even Daddy," I said.

We crawled back out of our hiding place, the calendars sliding out with us.

"Sometimes Momma is scary," Daffy said as she took a bowl and filled it with water from the sink. She cleared a spot on the table and set it down. She tapped the side of the bowl until the water rippled, then she said, "Hi, Daddy. Arc's gonna make us something to eat." She tapped the bowl again, the ripples answering her. "Daddy, you're so funny." She laughed like the ripples had told her a joke.

While I opened the freezer and grabbed the box of macaroni and cheese, Daffy pushed the stool across the floor and stood up on it to reach the phone on the wall. As her tears fell on the buttons, she dialed Mamaw Milkweed's number, counting the seconds before she answered.

"Hi, hi, Mamaw? Mamaw Milkweed, you hear me?" Daffy shouted into the phone. "It's me. Daffy. Mom's a mad rat, Mamaw. She put Daddy's shirts and pants on all the windows and she tried to turn me and Arc into paper."

"Don't worry, honey." Mamaw Milkweed's voice filled the kitchen as I peeled the plastic back on the macaroni and cheese and set the container in the oven. "I'll take care of it."

The next morning Mamaw Milkweed came wearing her sheer scarves in three shades of fuchsia. She had a bolt of bright yellow fabric beneath her arm.

"You can't drape your house in a dead man's clothes," she said to Mom. "I don't know what gets in your head at times, Adelyn."

"It's so shiny," Daffy said as she reached out toward the yellow fabric. "It's the prettiest thing we'll ever have, Arc. I bet it's the stuff butterflies use for their wings."

"That fabric ain't gonna look right 'round here, Momma," Mom said as she looked into a small mirror on the kitchen table. She was getting ready to go out somewhere and was dragging blue liner across her eyelids. She kept circling them until she had to sharpen the pencil again, using a knife to do so.

"Where's Clover?" Mamaw Milkweed made room for the bolt on the table by gathering up the dirty dishes. The sink was full, so she had to set them on the floor. She used her foot to slide them out of sight.

"She went to Paris," Mom said, pushing her lips out and making kissy noises toward her reflection. "I don't know why you've got your mind set on new curtains anyways, Momma. Our curtains are fine. In fact, they're marvelous."

"Think about the children, Adelyn." Mamaw Milkweed put her hands on her hips.

"Mamaw Milkweed?" Daffy reached up and tugged on her sleeve.

"Oh, I almost forgot. Here ya go, babies." Mamaw unzipped her fanny pack and handed my sister and me a new set of markers.

The flooring of our house wasn't wood, it wasn't linoleum, it wasn't carpeting. It was cold hard concrete that'd been painted white by someone who I suppose had been trying to cover up the cold hard fact of the ground they walked on. Through the dirt and grime, my sister and me drew. Houses with stick figure families. Dogs and cats. A clown or two. Horses we wished were ours and flowers we wished we had.

It was Mamaw Milkweed who brought us markers to make sure we'd always have enough red to color the ladybug's back, enough blue for the sky, enough green to bring the hills to life. We even drew our mother and father. We gave them smiles because it was a drawing, and in drawings you don't have to tell the truth.

"Thank you, Mamaw Milkweed," Daffy said as she beamed up at her.

We always called her Mamaw Milkweed, named after the plant the Monarch butterflies laid their eggs on. I can't tell you how often we would reach up to the flat moles on her neck and say they were eggs left behind by the passing butterflies that swarmed the flowers out by the back door.

"You're welcome, honey." Mamaw Milkweed patted Daffy on the head. "Now you and your sister go play. I've gotta speak to your momma."

We ran out into the hall but didn't go any farther, as we laid our ears against the wall.

"Hanging their father up like that," Mamaw Milkweed was saying. "Shame on you, Adelyn. How the hell are they supposed to get over his death if it's his clothes that block the very light they should be seeing? Now I meant what I said over his grave. If you don't clean up, I mean you, the house, everything, I'm gonna take 'em again."

"Momma, don't start." Mom groaned. "Clover's here. Everything's fine. The girls are happy."

"Who do you think you're talking to?"

"You're not gonna take my kids, Momma. I'll kill myself if you do. You hear me? If they're not here, what reason do I have to be better? I love them. Please, Momma. I swear, I'll kill myself. You wanna clean up your daughter's blood? You wanna bury her? You better pick me out one hell of a nice coffin, Momma. 'Cause it's gonna be all your fault if you take my babies."

"Oh, Adelyn." Mamaw Milkweed's sigh was deep and weary.

When I heard the chair's legs scrape against the floor, I knew my mother had gotten up to hug Mamaw Milkweed. It was something she always did so she could reach into Mamaw's fanny pack and take what money was up for grabs.

Silence followed until Mamaw Milkweed *tsk-tsked* and said, "All this blocking of light. You'll love yellow curtains, Adelyn. Make ya happier to see such a bright color. You need more yellow in your life, honey."

"She's coming," I whispered into Daffy's ear.

We grabbed hands and ran outside, flopping down in the grass like we'd been there all along as Mamaw Milkweed came out to go to her car. She smiled at us as she reached into the back seat and got her workhorse of a sewing machine.

I cupped my hands over my mouth and hollered, "You gonna sew something, Mamaw Milkweed?"

"I'm gonna sew you some new curtains, honey." She carried the sewing machine with both hands and a series of grunts.

"New curtains, Arc." Daffy beamed. "I hope she makes them for my room first."

Within minutes of the front screen door closing, we could hear the steady hum of the sewing machine. We also heard the arguing. Daffy sat down and covered her ears.

I grabbed one of her hands and asked, "You wanna see something cool, Daffy?"

I pulled her up, and we ran into the backyard.

"Look there." I pointed to the hornets' nest balanced in the branches of a dying maple.

"Oh." Daffy sighed. "It's so pretty, Arc. *Bzzz, bzzz, bzzzz.* You think them hornets will be our friends?"

"Maybe not. The nest is high. Means it'll be a hard winter," I said as Mamaw Milkweed would have.

Daffy clapped at the nest, while I sat down and used a rock to scrape back layers of ground at the base of the maple's trunk. I tried not to listen to Mom's yells coming from inside the house, getting louder and louder all while the sewing machine continued. Mamaw Milkweed's voice was like a distant echo.

"Clap with me, Arc." Daffy buzzed around.

"Can't," I said. "Busy digging. I'm gonna find something nice to make Momma happy again."

We both looked up at the sound of Mom running out the back screen door. She was naked except for a bright yellow scrap of fabric she wore around her hips like a fallen sash. She gripped a vodka bottle in her hand and had white powder around her nostrils.

"Mamaw Milkweed is gonna be mad," Daffy said as I stood up from the hole I'd dug.

"Momma?" I yelled at her. "Put your clothes on. Put your clothes on, Momma."

I wished for camisoles and cutoff shorts to rain down from the sky at that very moment.

"She's so sweaty," Daffy said as we stared at how our mother's body glistened.

"Momma, stop." I screamed. "Please. What you doing?"

"She's dancing." Daffy giggled.

"Dancing?" I thought she was jerking away from something, like a bee or a fly. It took me a second to see my mother was swaying in tempo. When she fell down to the ground, she didn't stop. It was as though she didn't recognize her back was against the grass. She kept swinging her arms and kicking her legs through the air.

"Not everyone's momma can dance on the ground, Arc," Daffy said, laughing louder.

Mom's orange lipstick had smeared. Her electric blue mascara ran in lines over the boils in her cheeks. She was a thin woman. This thinness gave her body hard lines akin to corners struggling to make what should be curved, like her waist and hips. My sister and me silently stared at those narrow hips of our mother, curious how we could have been born from between them.

"I'm free," Mom screamed as she got back up.

When she ran by us, Daffy reached out, her fingers grazing the trailing end of the yellow sash.

"I'm free," Mom screamed again. "I'm—"

The hiccups came for our mother just as Mamaw Milkweed stepped out of the house, her reading glasses down on her nose and a measuring tape still in her hand. She gripped the curtain panel she had already sewn as her eyes widened at the sight of her daughter.

"Adelyn, where are your clothes?" Mamaw Milkweed shouted.

"I'm so-rry, Mom-ma."

As if to prove the empty vodka bottle in her hand was nothing more than a vase, Mom began to pick dandelions from the yard.

"For goodness' sake. The children, Adelyn." Mamaw Milkweed looked at Daffy and me. She worked hard for a smile as she shook out the curtain in her hand and chased after her daughter. "Come here, Adelyn. Stop this very instant."

But Mom wouldn't. She kept running, picking dandelions and shoving them down into the bottle until the opening was sealed with stems. Only then did she hold the bottle up to her mother and say, "I picked—you flo-wers."

"I see." Mamaw Milkweed quickly wrapped the curtain around Mom's body that was shaking with each and every hiccup. "Come inside now, honey. Let's get you dressed and calmed down."

The two women walked inside the house. My mother staring at the dandelions and her mother staring at the bright yellow curtain. A minute later Mom returned to run around the yard, the curtain sliding down her back like a falling cape. As she skipped and hopped, Mamaw Milkweed cried loudly in the kitchen, saying the curtains had been "a goddamn mistake."

"Arc?" Daffy leaned against my side.

"Yeah?" I leaned back against hers.

"Mamaw Milkweed's cries sounds like apples falling from a tree."

"Yeah," I said. "We'll probably sound like that one day, too."

We watched Mom lie in the grass, this time not moving except for the blinking in her eyes and the slight rise of her chest each time a hiccup came.

"Momma's gonna lay here so long," Daffy said, "she's gonna turn into a town. We'll live there and nothing bad will happen. No Daddys will die, and no rivers will freeze, except when we want to skate on top of them with cats."

"Where's my blue-eyed girl?" Mom asked. Whenever she did that, I would close my left eye and Daffy would shut her right one, until only our blue eyes were showing. "Where's my green-eyed girl?" Mom asked. We each closed our one blue eye, leaving our green eyes open.

Mom smiled as Daffy stepped over and began to pick the remaining dandelions from the yard. I joined her. Together we laid them upon our mother.

"You're bu-bury-ing me?" she asked.

"I'll dig you up later," I said.

"I kno-ow you will, kiddo." She smiled up at me. "You di-ig up everything."

This was something she would say over a decade later, when a journalist from New York came to interview her.

"My Arc dug it all up," she would tell them. "My Arc likes digging. She digs up everything."

"Why?" they would ask as if they really cared, but it was just their job.

"Because she was an archaeologist," my mother would answer.

"Where is she at now? This archaeologist daughter of yours?"

"In the dirt." Mom's eyes would light up with hope. "In the dirt digging something else up. Whatever she digs up, she'll bring home to me. She always did. She always will. When she was a kid, she'd bring home bottle caps. Another time, a piece of old rope. A time after that, someone's retainer that'd been in the ground a long time. You could tell from the way the wire had rusted. Can you imagine? I wonder what she'll bring home to me this time."

Then my mother will sit and wait, getting high enough to know there is little space between the past and the present. In that space, maybe I really will come back home to her. She will think this because it was my promise.

But I will never come back home. I'm too dead to do a thing like that.

ALMOST EVERYTHING THE RIVER KNEW WAS ABOUT FISH AND CUR-
rents and the organic matter that settles in her waters. She therefore
understood decomposition of the human body the best way she knew
how. Erosion. What she herself does to the land around her. Taking
more and more of it away, until it is less than what it once was.

The decay of the body would happen slower in the cold temperature
of her water than it would in the warm grass. Long days and nights of
floating would be the last the world would inflict as the skin softened,
preparing to disappear. The river watched the long strands of hair
float out on her surface like worms the fish tried to eat.

The river knew what she had to do. She entered the lungs, making
the body heavy enough to sink to the mud at the bottom while the
hawks flew away over the hills. As the eyes bloated, and the heart
soaked, the river smelled it. The heart smelled at times like something sweet and bitter. Other times, it smelled so much like her own
water, the river could not tell them apart. She became possessed by
the moment of the body saying *I am*.

Under these Ohio clouds, a river will keep flowing and a mother will
cry out. In the currents forced by rain and fog, how far will a body
drift from home?

CHAPTER 2

I am in the span of time, a rhyme.

—*Daffodil Poet*

1993

MY NAME IS ARCADE. I WAS NAMED AFTER THE BRIGHT FLASHING lights of the game my mother played with my father when they were sober enough to remember how. Later I was called Arc. My mother would say I was her little archaeologist. For all the things I have dug up, no one has come close to digging up me.

There is distance in the afterlife. There are also horses. Dark brown like burnt souls. Their manes black. The stars on their chest white. They gallop past me so fast, I can only reach out to graze them with the tips of my fingers. Their bodies are warm, their breathing is smooth. Their hooves dig into the ground and kick the red dust up until I close my eyes and see the autumn of 1993.

It was October. The leaves had changed, but not yet fallen. The pumpkins had ripened, but not yet been carved. Cold air had arrived, but fires had yet to blaze. Daffy and me were turning twenty. The skies hung heavy with slow-moving clouds. We had been at our friend's place. Her name was Thursday. She lived in a trailer she said was the color of a barking dog. To me, it just looked tan.

It was near the river, a drive through the fields and hills outside town. Her parents had bought the trailer for her a few years prior when she had refused to come home. Both professors, they couldn't stand the idea of their daughter out on the streets. They gave her a place they hoped she would outgrow so she would come home to the life she'd had before, of carefully kept schedules and long-dreamed plans. She told them that would never happen. She even got a stamp tattooed on the back of her right hand that read PAID. The type of stamp you get at a nightclub. She told her parents when she showed it to them, "See? I'll always stay out late."

Her parents paid the bills and brought her groceries a couple times a week, as they were that day. The dad in his khakis and pastel shirt. The mom wore dark blue and kept rubbing her thumb over the face of her wristwatch. Daffy and me stood in the yard, watching the dad hand over a paper bag full of things like apples and a box of bran cereal poking out of the top. They stared at Thursday, but instead of saying she could do with a shower, they said she'd let the grass get too tall. And instead of saying she was too thin and her teeth were too rotten, they said don't forget to take your vitamins.

"They're in the bottom of the bag," the mom was sure to add.

Thursday was short like her mother and brunette like her father. Her eyes were like neither's. They were the color of deep water. Her crimped hair was piled over to one side. It fell crooked above her wide brows, both pierced, like her nose. The small stud was fake, but she told everyone it was a fallen star she'd found on the night the sky remembered her, even if she had stopped remembering it.

"You know," her dad said, "your telescope is still in your room." He cleared his throat. "If you came home, we could take it out to the backyard, finish following time across the universe. Find new moons and name them anything you want. What do you say?"

"I don't know, Dad." Thursday searched through the grocery bag. "You see one fucking star, you've seen 'em all, am I right? Hey, you didn't get me no candy." She looked up from the bag.

"We got you fruit," her mom said as she reached into her back pocket and pulled out some cash. She handed it to the dad, who gave it to Thursday.

"Some pizza money," he said, then cleared his throat again.

That's what they called it, even though they knew the money wouldn't be going to cheese and mushrooms.

"Thanks." Thursday took it and moved the bag of groceries to her hip. "Well, I guess I'll see ya later, alligators."

"See you, alligator." The dad held his hands up like chomping teeth. Something I knew he had done since she was a child. Her mother, meanwhile, was already halfway to the car. The dad lingered to look at the holes in his daughter's clothes, then followed his wife with his head down.

They weren't even free of the gravel driveway before Thursday held the money out to me. "My birthday gift to you," she said. "Get our crowns, and we'll all be queens."

She let Daffy and me use her small red car to drive into town. On the way, Daffy rolled deodorant under her arms and reached into my purse. The lipstick she got out was a dark burgundy. She put it only on her top lip, leaving her bottom bare.

"Two halves of the same mouth," she said as she reached over and put the lipstick on my bottom lip.

I never wore lipstick on my top lip, and she never wore it on her bottom. Each of us, with only half of our mouths colored.

"Two halves of the same." I pulled into the parking lot of the discount store, where I got out and exchanged Thursday's money for a baggie.

"You get enough?" Daffy asked when I got back into the car.

"There's never enough," I said, reaching into my purse and getting a needle out.

"Make me a gold crown, Arc," she said, holding the spoon for me. "The goldest crown in history with red jewels that I'll say are the still-beating hearts of small birds."

She breathed heavy as I stuck the needle into her vein. When it was my turn, I counted to ten, lost my eyes for a moment, then found them again on the road in front of me. With the town disappearing behind us, I sped up on the curves, the trees' leaves a study in yellow, crimson, and bright orange. The dry dust of the fields came in through our open windows. Daffy held her fingers up and pretended to smoke the falling particles all the way back to the trailer.

When we got there, Thursday was sitting on the bottom step, scratching the scabs open on her ankles. The weeds were growing up in between the porch steps, just above her white socks pushed down against the tops of her dirty sneakers. Midnight blue was her favorite color, and the sweater she wore was striped with it, though it, like the rest of her clothing, had tiny holes everywhere.

It was Thursday herself who'd made them with the scissors she kept in her pocket. Her parents never asked her why she cut her clothes. They simply drove to the store and bought her new shirts and pants and socks, but only when the other ones got ruined enough that you saw more of her skin than the fabric.

"I like her parents," Daffy said as we pulled into the drive. "Must be nice to have a daddy above ground and a momma who don't want you to die."

Despite the gravel crushing beneath our tires, Thursday didn't seem to hear us driving up. She ran her fingers down the bracelets on her wrists. Sometimes she was more jewelry than woman. She wore multiple necklaces, her ears were pierced all the way to the top, and even her belt was a metal chain with charms hanging down from it. It was all cheap beads and plastic gems she had strung together herself.

"Thursday always gives you bracelets," Daffy said as we got out of the car. "But never me."

"That's because I give all of mine to you." I reached back inside the car and honked the horn.

Thursday finally looked up.

"You get our crowns?" she asked, standing, the tattoos of stars showing on her legs through the holes in her black jeans, splashed with bleach stains.

"I got 'em," I said.

"Get your ass out here," she yelled into the trailer.

A few moments later a thin figure appeared behind the screen door. She was wearing a faded red sweatshirt with Greek sorority letters sewn into white satin on the front of it. Her name was Nell, but we all called her Sage Nell because of the sweatshirt. For the time I'd known her, she was never without it. Stretched out, it fell above her knobby knees. Sometimes she'd be wearing it and nothing else, like she was that day despite the cool breeze. The sweatshirt was what remained from her year in college. She bought it not because she was in a sorority but because of the Greek letters.

Greece, as she would tell you, was the birthplace of philosophy. That'd been her major, with a minor in theology, before she dropped out.

"Like a rock," she'd say. "Just like a falling rock."

It was her who told us what a sage was.

"In classical times," she had said, "when they built all them columns to hold up all that stone, a sage wasn't just a garden plant. A sage was a person. Someone who is wise. Spends their time thinking about infinity and space and frosted windowpanes and cracked glass."

When she told us that, Thursday said, "Well, hell, Nell, I guess that makes you one of them sages."

The name stuck ever since.

Sage Nell smiled as she pushed the screen door open, her bare feet sitting atop one another.

"Why is it when you get our crowns, Arc," she said, her voice soft and low, "they're never as shiny as I imagine they'll be?" She sighed as she stepped down the porch steps into the grass. "I suppose what is good is easy to get."

"Who said that?" I asked.

"I did." She tapped her finger to her chin. "And Epicurus might have said something similar."

Her teased bangs were stiff with hairspray. She was wearing a wide padded headband, one of the cheap velvet ones, holding her thick curls out of her face, the rest kept back with a scrunchie. Her bare feet were dirty and rough. The nail on her big toe, blackened and bruised.

Inside her hand was the magnet she made a habit out of passing back and forth between her fingers. It was a fish, shaped like the bass Dad once brought home from the river. The fins dark green. The body, a muddy brown. The eyes, small and black. On the side of the fish she had written "ripples of my soul" inside a heart shape drawn in red marker.

"What the hell are we waitin' for?" Thursday asked. "Let's wear our crowns on top of our greasy heads and be queens."

Sage Nell pushed her wire-rimmed eyeglasses up on her nose as she said quietly, "We are shiny and ride among the stars."

"We are shiny and ride among the stars," we all shouted together. The words had become our way of telling the world something different than it was telling us.

"To our kingdom we go," Sage Nell said as she draped her arm across me. "Our hearts full of mud."

I could smell her apple-scented gum. She was constantly chewing it, when she wasn't chewing her fingernails.

"Wait, a hot second," Thursday said, running back inside the trailer. She returned with her large purse on her shoulder and a bag of chips in her hand. She didn't offer us any, and we knew they weren't for us. They were for the squirrels or the raccoons or the opossums Thursday said were always as hungry as she would be if she were left to the wilderness.

She dropped some chips into the weeds in the yard, leaving none in the crossing of the dirt road. She picked back up when we got into the field on the other side, where the corn had since been harvested, leaving behind blonde and bluntly cut stalks. As the blackbirds flew down to grab the cobs left behind, Daffy slipped her hand into mine, but only to escape with the baggie and a growing grin on her face as she skipped ahead. Watching her, I wished she had something better in her hand.

My sister was born Farren Doggs. From an early age, we called her Daffodil Poet because of the way she'd stand in the daffodils in the spring at Mamaw Milkweed's. The white and yellow flowers reached up to her hips as she always said something that rhymed. The rhyme would be enough for Mamaw to clap and call Farren her Daffodil Poet.

"Daffodil Poet! Daffodil Poet!"

Most folks called her Daffy for short. Years after Mamaw Milkweed died, when Daffy first started wearing crowns, she'd often say something of no great value, but still it rhymed and reminded me of Mamaw Milkweed's warm hands and the flowers we used to know.

Daffy was older than me by a single minute. I often wonder about that minute. I see it in color. Dark blue in its center, light blue on its edges, silvered in between our mother's burning thighs. Was that minute Daffy's way of being early? Or was it my way of being late?

In death, I've come to the conclusion that the minute between us was nothing more than sisters lying as close to one another as they could without bearing a wider birth upon their mother. Twins, who in the womb decided on sixty seconds. It was as much as we would allow ourselves to be separated. Just enough for our mother to rest after the big push, but brief enough that we would not be long from each other in the new world outside the warm walls of her glistening body.

The firstborn is done so to applause. Her red, frightened figure risen, screaming, into the glow of the lights above her head, then laid on the table to be cleaned of that which had kept her safe for two hundred and eighty days. I would be the second born and less remarkable in the difference a single minute can make.

One nurse picked up Daffy and made certain to say, "This is your first," as she handed Daffy to our mother.

They watched Mom coo at her daughter, wiggling her tiny fingers and toes.

"Who's my baby?" she said, staring down into the eyes of the child who had stopped screaming in her arms. "Who's my 'ittle baby? It's you. I love you. Yes, I do."

They would give her a minute to hold Daffy, waiting the same time it took me to be born. Then they handed me off, making sure to say, "This is your second daughter."

"Oh, my." Mom accepted me into her left arm, for Daffy lay in the crook of her right. "You must be my other 'ittle baby. Yes, you are. Yes, you are." And then she would look from my pink smile to Daffy's and back again. "Two little baby girls." She nuzzled her nose against each of ours. "And you're all mine."

Two girls of fiery red hair and strange eyes. My right eye was blue. My left was green. It was reversed on Daffy. We were both born with complete heterochromia iridis. That's what the doctors called our different-colored eyes. But in the shadow of the paper mill, we knew them as witches' marbles.

"There are four elements in the universe," Mamaw Milkweed told Daffy and me. "Earth, air, fire, and water. You've got fire in your red hair. You've got the air in your lungs. And you've got the earth in your green eye and the water in your blue eye."

"But how, Mamaw Milkweed?" Daffy asked.

"Do you know what happens to the shadows of the birds when they fly? The shadows are caught between the tree branches and taken by the witches. And do you know what happens to the shadows of the fish when they swim above the rocks?"

"Their shadows are caught and taken by the witches?" I asked.

"That's right, Arc. And then the edges of the shadows are made smooth when the witches roll them in their hands. They roll and roll the shadows until they become marbles. The wisest of the old witches took four of these marbles and she gave one of each to the both of you to be your eyes, so you'd always be half of the other one. A blue eye for the girl who loves swimming." She tapped Daffy on top of the head. "A green eye for the girl who loves digging." She next tapped my head.

"But why can't I have both blue eyes?" Daffy asked her. "If I love the water? And why can't Arc have two green eyes if she loves the ground?"

"Because," Mamaw said, "the old witch knew that earth and water are bound to one another, girls, just like the two of you. And do you know the best thing about witches' marbles? They're inflammable."

"What does that mean?" Daffy asked.

"They can never be burned. Which means that even in fire, you will see."

It was because of our eyes that our mother would come to say, "You're two halves of the same." We had the same laugh. The same smile. The same love of Mamaw Milkweed's grape jelly. We even wore our hair the same ever since Daffy went crying into Mamaw Milkweed's arms after school one day shouting, "They're so mean to me and Arc. Like rabid dogs."

"Who?" Mamaw Milkweed asked.

"The other kids. They say we drink nothing but ketchup. So much of it that it comes outta the top of our heads and stains our hair. They say we got dirt on our faces, even though they know it's our freckles. They say we oughta wear paper bags. Arc makes it worse when she kicks at 'em and spits. They say she's both ugly and mad in the head like Momma."

That night as Mamaw Milkweed brushed our hair, she began to section it off.

"We have hair the color of the witches," she said. "The color of the fire they tried to burn us with. A stick here." She weaved the strands. "And a stick here. Enough to make a pile of wood outta your hair."

When she got to the tail of the braid, she pinned it on top of our heads, the undone hair sticking up. She pretended to have a match and light the tail of our braid into a flame.

"Anyone makes fun of you again," she said, "you lean your heads down and burn 'em with your fire."

That day as Daffy skipped ahead with the baggie through the cornfield, I stared at the flame on top of her head, flickering in the sunlight.

"Ow," Sage Nell cried out and grabbed her foot.

Thursday bent over to pick up the plastic bottle Nell had stepped on.

"Get a handful of Ohio," Sage Nell said, "and what you'll find with the dirt is more garbage than rocks."

Sage Nell took the chips from Thursday and dumped them out in the spot the plastic bottle had lain.

"Whenever you find something that takes away from the earth," she said, crumpling the bag and stuffing it down inside Thursday's purse, "you should give it something back that at least the birds can eat."

"You're my favorite fucking philosopher, you know that, Sage Nell?" Thursday said. "The great philosopher of Chillicothe, Ohio."

Sage Nell only smiled as she grabbed a chip off the ground, crunching on it as she walked forward and into the woods.

"The leaves here are still," she said, "because she lives alone."

"The ground is uneven," Thursday said, "because she lives alone."

Daffy turned to me as I touched the nearest tree trunk and added, "The bark is sweet, because she lives alone."

It was something we always did when walking through those woods because the first time we'd ever been there, Sage Nell had dropped her red lipstick. When she couldn't find it on the ground, she said, "That's okay. I'll let the woods have it. Because she lives alone."

From then on, we spoke of the woods like she was a woman we were merely passing by.

"She will outlive us all," Sage Nell said. "Because she lives alone."

We heard the river before we saw it. The little ripples the water made over the fallen log. Our place was a flattened area on the sandy bank where the thin weeds grew tall at the base of a large oak whose branches extended over the brown water. We called our spot the Distant Mountain. Something that rose in the great expanse with a rocky peak, so different from the soft hills of Ohio. A place we imagined was out of reach for everyone but us.

A few feet up the bank was a mound of dirt, out of which stuck the top of a 1950s convertible. It had been buried with only the edge of its windshield showing from the ground when we first found it. As we came back, time and again, to the Distant Mountain, we dug the car out, exposing the frayed seats, bent steering wheel, and blue painted metal.

"Look at all them rusty holes in it," Thursday said. "The number of holes there are will be the number of times we'll all end up married." She started to count the holes but stopped to say, "Well, shit, we'll have ourselves a new husband just about every day of the week with all these holes."

We called the car Cleopatra's Time Machine and imagined it'd been to the future as much as it had the past. It seemed it was always our present we were trying to escape.

Daffy sat behind the steering wheel, making sure to hand Thursday the small baggie before she did. Thursday was the one who prepared the crowns when we were in our group.

"Because," as she said, "I've been wearing 'em longer than any of you, bitches."

As she sang a rock song from the 1970s, she opened her purse, the fake leather peeling off the straps and sides.

"Do you have my pen for my sins?" Sage Nell asked, holding her hand out.

Thursday searched her purse, finally finding the black felt-tip marker that she handed over to Sage Nell. While Daffy pretended to drive the car, I watched Sage Nell take her marker and climb the oak, using the large rock beneath it as her starting point.

"You're gonna fall out of that damn thing one of these days," Thursday said as she carried the plastic bottle over to the river's edge and filled it with water.

"If I do fall," Sage Nell said as she straddled the lowest branch, "and I don't get back up again, promise you'll bury me facedown, so the dirt won't fall in on my eyes, and I can be the only dead dreamer not half blind."

She reached out and turned one of the golden leaves over, writing on the underside of it, the marker bleeding through and revealing the words, *I stopped knowing.*

On the crimson leaf, she wrote, *Wasted the hours.*

"I don't know why you bother with that leaf writing of yours." Thursday rolled her eyes.

"Soon these leaves will fall off the tree," Sage Nell said. "And my sins will fall with them. Mark my words, ladies, 1993 is the last year I'll be a dope queen."

While Sage Nell continued to write her sins on the leaves and

Thursday sat on the ground to mix the water, I bent down and removed the flat piece of sandstone I had placed at the bottom of the oak the last time we were there. Beneath it was the hole I had started.

"That one's climbing trees, and you're digging in the ground like an old rat." Thursday shook her head. "I don't know what you expect to find, Arc. Chillicothe ain't got no treasures left. What you digging for?"

"A horse," Daffy said, her voice quiet.

"A what?" Thursday asked

"A horse," I repeated louder.

"Our mother lost one a long time ago." Daffy looked away, her hands still on the steering wheel but slipping off.

I felt my own hands slide deeper into the hole as Sage Nell stared at the way I dug into the ground, then she jumped down from the tree, capping the marker. The leaves she had written on blew in the breeze above our heads. I thought she would say something to me, but she only met my eyes before sitting down beside Thursday, who was holding the lighter beneath the spoon.

"Because you mixed it with river water," Sage Nell told her, "we'll have the river inside us. We'll live forever."

"Who the hell cares about forever?" Thursday watched the mixture boil inside the spoon. "I want right now."

Sage Nell reached into Thursday's purse and pulled out the leather belt. She couldn't get it wrapped tight around her thin arm, so she took her pocketknife out and used it to add another homemade notch in the leather.

"What is good is easy to get," Thursday said as Sage Nell tightened the belt.

I covered the hole in the ground back up with the sandstone and crawled over to Daffy, who had already sat down on the other side of Thursday. When she took the belt from Sage Nell's arm to wrap around my own, she said, "I like your freckles, Arc."

"They're from the devil," I told her. "He grabbed the dust of the earth and blew it back into my face."

"Why?" She found a vein. "Why would the devil do that?"

"Because I told him he couldn't fly," I said, feeling the cold steel push into my skin.

I closed my eyes, her words following, "Happy birthday, Arc Doggs."

After Thursday injected herself, she pulled air back up inside the needle and stuck it down into the ground.

"A little for you, mother earth," she said, her head spiraling down until her chin rested on her chest, "so you can forget you are not loved either."

We sat there, staring out at the water. None of us got high anymore. That wasn't why we woke up and got dope. Fucked to get more dope. All afternoon hustling for that next hit of dope, dope, dope. Panicking when we couldn't get enough money for the *dope, dope, dope*. Get enough to last until the two hours later we would need more. Enough to endure.

No. We took it to keep outrunning the keyhole. It was what Daffy called the pain that came in the absence of the crowns. When I first asked her why she called it that, she said, "Remember when we were kids and we'd stick our fingers into the keyholes, the metal cutting into our skin? We could only push our fingers halfway through before it hurt too much to go farther. Imagine if we'd kept going, only not with our fingers but with our whole bodies being pushed through the keyhole, our skin scraping off on the metal. Our faces crushed. Our bodies broken, our identities as mangled as our bones until we remember everything we wanna forget. Women ain't meant to be pushed through keyholes, Arc. We come out the other side, less than we were."

Sage Nell laid her head on my shoulder and whispered, "We are shiny. We ride among the stars." She got up and grabbed Thursday's purse. She found the small bottle of nail polish inside. It was a blue that we'd all chipped in and bought because it was the closest color to the original shade of Cleopatra's Time Machine. We always did our best to cover the rust spots with the nail polish, as Sage Nell started to do then, but it seemed that no matter how many layers we put on, the rust belonged.

As Thursday lay down on the river's bank and hummed, Daffy elbowed me and pointed out at the river as she said, "There it is. The eye of God."

"They say it always comes in the autumn." Sage Nell's voice sounded distant as she covered a trio of rust spots on the hood of the car with the nail polish.

"I double-dog-dare you to look into it, Arc." Thursday sat up. "See your future. Or are you afraid?"

I climbed up to my feet and stepped down the bank into the cold water. So cold, it took my breath away. The water filled my socks and made my shoes heavier. Still I continued on until the water was up to my waist, and I stood over the leaves floating on the surface. I looked down into the darkness of the muddy water. It swirled with the currents, the sunlight like pieces of static lighting up in one-second flashes each time the branches above moved a certain way in the breeze. When I stepped forward to take a closer look, I lost the ground. Water fell in on my head, the sunlight disappearing as I sank deeper and deeper. I screamed underwater and my throat filled until I found the surface, gasping for air.

"Arc? What are you doing?" Thursday's voice reached me from the bank.

I had drifted so far out into the river, I could no longer find the bottom with my feet. The leaves that had created the eye of God were being carried on the ripples made by my splashes. The leaves moved farther away from me, past something pale floating on top of the water close to the bank on the other side.

"Arc, you crazy thing," Thursday shouted. "Get the fuck out of the water."

"There's something over there," I said. I trod out so far, the coldness wrapped around me. Still I kicked the water up, swimming toward the other side.

"It's a branch." Sage Nell's voice echoed off the trees. "That's all."

The closer I got, the more I found the bottom of the river again, sinking my feet down into the mud. I stood over the floating figure and saw the pale red hair moving out in thin wisps.

"Daffy?" I screamed my sister's name.

"I'm back here, Arc." She was standing on the bank with Sage Nell beside her. Thursday had walked out into the river, the water rippling up her calves.

"What is it, Arc?" Thursday asked, her voice high and tight.

I turned the body over.

"Arc?" Sage Nell called. "What is it?"

"A woman," I said, staring down into the two holes where her eyes should have been. "It's a woman."

THE RIVER HAS NO ARMS OR HANDS OF HER OWN. SHE FEELS WITH her water.

What she felt was the woman's body rising from the bottom, the gases building up, pushing the dead to the surface.

In fast-moving currents, the body may be carried for some time and some distance. If clothed, the fabric has a mind to snag on jagged rocks. Sometimes on fallen tree limbs. The naked ones, the river knows, are ruined the most.

If the gods insist, the body can be thrown into brush, leaving cuts and scrapes. Worst of all are the rocks that tend to favor breaking against the rib cage. These new wounds bleed. All the animals will head toward the scent, their noses up in the air, hoping the current comes close enough, they need not get their paws wet.

CHAPTER 3

You can only soar so much and no more.

—Daffodil Poet

1980

WE WOULD WATCH HER HANDS MOVE, MY SISTER AND I. WE WOULD watch her hands move and think they were the two oldest things in the world. Even older than the woman herself. As if in the beginning, there was the earth, there was the light, there was the dark, and there were Mamaw Milkweed's hands made in the very same second.

"You think our hands will get that old?" Daffy asked when we were seven and sitting at Mamaw Milkweed's feet, watching her crochet. Daffy had asked in a whisper so Mamaw wouldn't hear how we talked about the blue-green veins on the backs of her hands and how the skin was as thin as the pages of the Bible that sat on the table by her bed.

"Her hands may be old," I said, "but they're strong as boot heels."

How could they not be? They scrubbed pots and folded sheets, pulled weeds up from the ground and planted flower bulbs in the same hole. They built things, cleaned things, cooked things, tore things apart, and put them back together again in better ways. They moved things, lifted things, and bandaged them, like the cuts my sister and me got when we decided to fly off the tree in the backyard.

In the quiet moments, her hands would hold our faces as she gave us ten kisses apiece. "Enough for you to always find your way back home," she'd say.

There was little at the time that Daffy and me didn't believe was made by a woman or out of her. That was because of Mamaw Milkweed.

"The rain is a woman explaining time," she told us. "The grass is one growing through the years, and the river is another who had not laughed in life, her tears something that carves the land. All of Chillicothe, Ohio," she said, opening her arms wide, "is a woman lying in the grass on her side, a town built upon her from fingertip to ankle. A woman convincing herself she is on the right side of the cross and staying still enough to believe it. All the roads here are not graveled in rock, girls, but with the woman's scars, because only a woman's scars are strong enough to bear something driving over them, again and again."

Mamaw Milkweed had a wavy mane of red hair that was going white. She wore it long down her strong back, cutting the strands by her ears short, trying to hide the jowls that hung lower than her jawline. She wore several layers of mascara and lipstick, leaving the rest of her thin face scrubbed. Sometimes Daffy would point out the stiff hairs that grew out of Mamaw Milkweed's chin. Mamaw would laugh, the wrinkles forming at the corners of her face.

She wore scarves every day, hanging from around her neck, or tied into her hair, or wrapped around her wrists. They were light and sheer, some with images of flowers, others with fruit or insects like bees or butterflies. She would tell Daffy and me, "One day you too will wear scarves and be like women who ride the backs of trains."

Mamaw Milkweed always sported a tapestry fanny pack with large pink roses set against a black background. She clamped it over her long shirts that had motifs. Sometimes of angels, other times frogs, with messages like SAVE THE RAINFOREST and THANK GOD FOR GRANDDAUGHTERS. They were paired with spandex biker shorts and compression socks that she wore with green sandals, the same color of the beads on the chain of the reading glasses hanging around her neck.

"The noose of old ladies," she'd say with half a grin.

She lived in an Amish-built house that had two storeys and was on acreage that used to be a farm but was no longer. It was a home of simple build but sturdy doorways in which we could carry forth the knowledge Mamaw Milkweed passed to us, like how to can tomatoes and how to sew a cotton dress in an afternoon.

"Patience, my dears," Mamaw would say as she gave us her old woman's wisdom. "For without patience, you will always be at odds with the task before you."

Then she would break a jar of her homemade jam against the rock in the backyard and say it was a sacrifice to our own selves.

"In ancient times, they would spill the blood of a goat upon a rock," she told us. "But we spill the blood of the fruit, knowing we have claimed what is ours. That of our labor and that of our choosing."

She always laid a white towel down at the base of the rock, so the jam and glass collected there. As I watched the jam seep into the terry, Mamaw would wipe the sweat off her forehead. My mother, aunt, and grandmother were women of hot skin who seemed to sweat even in the middle of a blizzard. Women who always put on mascara to the radio, talking with pride about our centuries-dead mamaw who was hung as a witch, not once, but twice. She was burned when the noose broke.

"It is from her that we get our hot skin," Mamaw Milkweed would say, telling my sister and me that we had a touch of the witch in us. "You can't put a woman to fire and expect the flesh of the women after her not to feel that very heat. It is also from her that we dream the future."

"I don't wanna be a witch," Daffy said. "They have warts."

"My dear." Mamaw cupped Daffy's face in her old hands. "A witch is not a pointy hat or a broom or warts. A witch is merely a woman who is punished for being wiser than a man. That's why they burned her. They tried to burn away her power because a woman who says more than she's supposed to say, and does more than she's supposed to do, is a woman they'll try to silence and destroy. But there are some things that not even fire can destroy. One of those things is the strength of a woman. Don't you want to be a woman like that? A woman with *power?*"

"Won't they burn me, too?" Daffy asked, her cheeks still cupped by Mamaw's hands.

Mamaw lowered herself so she could be eye level. In a deep, dark tone, she said, "Not if you burn them first."

"Come over here, Arc." Mamaw turned to me. "You need to hear this, too." She pushed us head to head, then cupped one of each of our cheeks as if we were of the same face. "Listen to me now, girls." Mamaw spoke as seriously as ever. "Power is not only physical. It's not some muscleman lifting all the weights. It's much more than that. It's being smart. It means you endure."

"What does *endure* mean, Mamaw?"

I can't remember if I was the one who asked this or if it was Daffy.

"It means you suffer something, toward a greater end," Mamaw Milkweed said. "Because in this world you must be smart and you must endure. Most importantly, you must be ready to be treated like a woman. If you are not ready for that, you'll break wide open."

"How is a woman treated?" I asked.

"Not like a person," she said.

Perhaps seeing the fear in our faces, she said, "But you two are powerful. You two are witches. Like me."

That was one reason we thought the land Mamaw Milkweed lived on looked as though gasoline had been poured upon it and lit.

"Someone tried to burn her," I told Daffy.

There, on the brown and burnt ground, Mamaw planted flower bulbs ordered from catalogs that she piled in towers on the front porch outside the screen door.

"When I grow up, Mamaw Milkweed," Daffy would say, "I'm gonna have my own flower bulb catalog and mail them to you so you can buy from me. Every flower that blooms will be because I gave 'em to the world."

Mamaw would grab Daffy in a hug and ask her, "Did you see my new stack of catalogs? I got 'em for you."

"Where?" Daffy slid out of Mamaw's arms and ran to the front porch.

Mamaw Milkweed ordered from every bulb company she could find so she would get on their mailing list. She knew how much Daffy loved to pore over the catalogs, dog-earing the pages of full-color photographs of her favorite flowers.

"I love this one and this one and this one." She had started to cut the photographs out to glue them down on the construction paper Mamaw got us.

"I'll put your name on the catalogs, too, Arc," Daffy said.

She made several that she would send in the mail to Mamaw. The front cover always had "Daffodil Poet, Best Bulbs in the World" written across it. My name was just below Daffy's.

Mamaw would look through Daffy's handmade catalogs, writing her order down on a pad of paper.

"Will you give me a good price?" she asked Daffy. "Sell 'em to me cheap?"

"All they'll cost you is an afghan," Daffy told her.

An afghan because out of all the things Mamaw Milkweed's hands did, it was crocheting that Daffy and me liked best. Out of a single strand of yarn, Mamaw Milkweed could move her fingers like they were a rippling surface.

"My hands have the river in them," she told us. "Because I held them in the water for the year I disappeared."

"You disappeared, Mamaw Milkweed?" I asked.

"All women do, my dear, from time to time," she said. "It's not that we disappear, it's how we find ourselves that matters."

Mamaw Milkweed would make circles and swirls out of the yarn. It was as if she knew how God had done it and was showing us the way in secret by crocheting dish towels and placemats, pot holders and doilies for her glass cat collection. She would crochet socks for mine and my sister's feet, and hats for our heads come the cold winter months.

"Come be my yarn, girls," she would say to Daffy and me.

We would sit on the floor by her feet that smelled of the homemade bluebell and peony perfume she would spritz her compression socks with. She would lay the skein of yarn down on the floor by us, then direct us to hold the strand of it between our palms.

"Be my yarn," she would say again as we held our hands up.

While she crocheted, the strand would pull between our flat hands and rub against our palms, as she would sing a song she said had once filled the rooms of the farmhouse she had grown up in. Sometimes during these moments, Daffy would call Mamaw "Mom," and Mamaw would harshly say, "Don't." After a moment of silence, Mamaw would pat Daffy gently on the head.

"You should feel closer to God when you crochet," she said. "It's nun's work. That's how it started. The nuns would sit there all the way back in those dark and damp times, in churches that were lit only by candles, and they would crochet using their fingers. They didn't use hooks like we use now because the nuns understood you don't need more than your own two hands to work something beautiful."

"If the nuns didn't crochet with a hook," Daffy asked, "why do we use one, Mamaw?"

"Because we are not nuns, dear." She studied us. "It wouldn't be a terrible idea if you both considered becoming nuns. You'd be safer in this world, and your old Mamaw Milkweed wouldn't have to worry about you."

"What does a nun have to do?" Daffy tilted her head to the side.

"Oh, you'd pray mostly, dear," Mamaw Milkweed said, "and stay off the edge for the Lord Jesus Christ. You'll have a basket full of sisters."

"But we're already sisters," Daffy said with a nudge into my side.

"Oh, I mean other women will be your sisters, too. You'll call each other *sister* this and *sister* that." Mamaw Milkweed bit her tongue. "I think you have to be Catholic, but they'd teach ya how to be one and how to eat the flesh of Christ, which they seem so fond of doing. I doubt there's more to the life than that."

She paused long enough for us to fancy the idea, then asked, "Will you become nuns, girls? For your old Mamaw Milkweed?"

"I don't think so, Mamaw Milkweed," I said.

"No." She sighed. "I don't suppose either of you will become nuns. Your laugh is too wild like your mother's. And you, Arc, your hands are too dirty. If you must dig in the dirt, please clean your fingernails after, like I showed you, with an old toothbrush. Remember?"

I nodded, knowing I wouldn't scrub my fingernails. Sometimes I even pretended there were tiny artifacts under them and if I washed, I'd be losing the smallest shard of pottery down the drain.

"At least you can think about becoming nuns," Mamaw Milkweed said. "Maybe if you think long enough, you'll like the idea of praying and of having more than one sister. You're only seven. I'll give it some time."

"Okay, Mamaw." Daffy smiled wide.

"You're a little bug, aren't you?" Mamaw pulled Daffy up onto her lap and started to show her how to do the chain stitch, paying special attention to the spaces. "Very good, my little Daffodil Poet."

Mamaw handed a crochet hook to me and gave the same instructions.

"Did you know," she said, "that crocheting is also what peasants did in the past because they couldn't afford the lace of the rich kings?"

"Lace? I like lace," Daffy said.

"You've never seen lace," I told her as I frowned at my stitches. They were so loose, I could slip my whole finger through.

"Yes, I have," she said. "Mamaw Milkweed's got lace in the corners of her house."

"Those are spiderwebs, honey." Mamaw lifted my sister off her lap and came over to me, where she took my work into her hands as she said, "The poor people, envious of the wealthy man's lace, decided to make their own fancy things." She pulled out my bad stitches. "And you know what? It was better than the rich man's lace. Your tension is off, Arc."

"That's 'cause I'm no good." I threw the hook down.

Mamaw Milkweed turned my face to hers. "You can't give up because things get a little hard, or you'll never get through. Believe me, Arc, life gets a whole hell of a lot harder than loose yarn. Come on, now. Me and you." She placed the crochet hook and yarn back into my hands. "We're gonna learn this together. You and me."

Little by little, I got better with my stitches. As a reward, Mamaw said we were going to buy more yarn so Daffy and me could make our very first granny square afghan.

"Black will be your background," she told us at the store. "For the squares, pick colors you like, because they will be multicolored."

She pushed the cart down the yarn aisle while Daffy and me ran ahead to the shelves. We grabbed enough skeins to spill out of our arms.

"Make sure it's the same dye lot now." Mamaw put on her reading glasses and used her pinkie to point out the small numbers on a label. "That ensures it's the same color."

"But they're all purple, Mamaw Milkweed," I said.

"Yes, dear, but when they were dyed purple is what matters." She grabbed a skein from Daffy. "Some of these are early purples. Some are later purples. You want to get the purples that are at the very same time purple."

After our lesson on dye lots, we headed back to Mamaw Milkweed's house with our chosen skeins. On the way, she gripped the steering wheel tightly as she said, "I taught your momma and your aunt Clover how to crochet. They were wonderful, but they found other things to focus on. Your momma, she could crochet with anything. Hell, she used to use a spoon."

"Momma loves spoons," Daffy said as she looked out the window.

Mamaw Milkweed leaned up and stared at us through the rearview mirror.

"Don't you go loving spoons like your momma," Mamaw said as she turned her attention back out on the road before us. "Ain't nothing in this world for a woman who lives with difficult loves. Loving spoons is at the top of that list."

Once at the house, we unloaded the yarn onto the table. While Mamaw stepped into the kitchen to make us lunch, Daffy and me began crocheting our squares.

"This will take us forever," she said.

"Forever and a day." I nodded.

What was eternity to two little girls was four months. You could tell which squares Mamaw had crocheted because they were better than either mine or Daffy's. In the end, that was what made the afghan special.

My sister and me were so proud of it that we held the afghan up between us and smiled as Mamaw grabbed the camera. The afghan was larger than we were tall, so we had to stand on two chairs in order to keep enough of it off the floor to be seen in the photo. Mamaw Milkweed eventually framed that photo and hung it on the wall by her HOME SWEET HOME sampler. Before she did, she laid the afghan across her large dining table and said, "Listen up, girls, I'm gonna tell you something very important. Something my mother told me. In life, there is a savage side and a beautiful side."

"What do you mean, Mamaw Milkweed?" I asked.

She spread her hands over the neat rows of squares on the afghan. "This is the beautiful side. Come, girls, rub your hands over this side."

"But what's on the beautiful side?" I asked as I felt the stitches.

"What makes you happiest?" Mamaw Milkweed asked.

"I know." Daffy raised her hand as if we were in school. "You and yarn and flower bulbs and turtles and dancing cats and Arc."

"What about you, Arc?" Mamaw turned to me.

"Feathers and dirt and shovels to go deep into the earth with." I pretended I was digging right then. "And goddesses who are lions, July year-round—"

"Yeah." Daffy nodded. "I'm adding that one to mine, too."

"And you, Mamaw Milkweed," I said. "And Daffy and Momma's horse."

"Then that is what is on the beautiful side." Mamaw Milkweed smiled. "All the things that make you the happiest. All the things that are far from the fires of men."

As the three of us felt the granny squares, their multicolored rows bright against the black background, Mamaw said, "Beautiful things happen on this side. But on this side."

She flipped the afghan over, the wrinkles out to the sides of her eyes bearing the frown there.

"Look here, girls." She ran her fingers through the yarn ends dangling from the backs of the squares. "This is the savage side. See how the strands hang loose?"

"What's on the savage side?" Daffy asked, raising her eyes to Mamaw Milkweed's.

"It is empty of your flowers, your horses, your beautiful goddesses. What are the most terrible things you can think of?" Mamaw Milkweed asked.

Daffy turned to me and said, "The things Momma and Aunt Clover stick in their arms."

"And Daddy under the white sheet," I added.

"Cold nights." Daffy shivered. "Sound of Aunt Clover crying."

"Momma, too," I said.

"That is the savage side," Mamaw Milkweed said. "The side that is kind to the mood of monsters and all the things they play with. Do you see, girls? Do you see how wild these strings are?"

"But they're only the ends of the yarn sticking out, Mamaw Milkweed," I said.

"No, dear, no. They are more than that." Mamaw's voice was firm. "They are dangling fangs. Do you know what dangling fangs are?

They are teeth so sharp, not even the monsters' mouths can bear them. They must dangle below the lips of evil, like spiders dropped down from their webs, so far dropped, they ride the ripples of rolling thunder and cursed winds."

"But they're so soft." Daffy held the strings.

"Soft is the snake, but hard is the hiss," Mamaw said. "We live on the savage side, girls. That's why I'm telling ya this, so you can survive it."

She stepped over to the cabinet that held her crafting supplies and picked up a large needle with an eyehole big enough for things thicker than thread. Starting with one of the squares along the edge of the afghan, she began to weave the loose strands of yarn back into the squares.

"See what I do?" she asked. "I tuck the ends up into the square and turn the savage side beautiful. I want you both to try it now."

She handed the needle to me and showed how to tuck the loose yarn up into the square so it couldn't be seen again.

"When the savage side gets too much," she said, "you take a needle and weave the strands in."

"A needle?" My sister looked at it.

"You can make the savage side beautiful with a needle." Mamaw Milkweed took it back from me and started to work the ends in herself.

We didn't say anything as her tears fell quietly down her old cheeks. Nor did we say anything as the light outside started to dwindle, because all the lights in the house were on and we took comfort in knowing the rooms in Mamaw Milkweed's house would never be dark.

THE DROWNED POSITION IS WHEN THE BODY IS FACEDOWN. IF THIS was poetry, the body would roll over and say a word or two about being a creature of ripples, of something that floats toward the whirling earth. But this is brown water and mud, and in those places that water is not deep, the body may drag, the hands left to hang, the knuckles left to scrape. The skin is no longer skin. The lips are no longer lips. The face is one that has survived a change.

Should the river be with the swells of the gods, the body may be thrown so forcefully against the rocks that it lies there, unidentifiable. At these times, the river says, *I remember you. Who you were. I will listen to what you have to say. I will return your name to you, even as you disappear.*

The body slips in and out, the veins melting, and the collarbone a reflection of the whole sky.

CHAPTER 4

In a moment she is taken. We are forever shaken.

—*Daffodil Poet*

1981

MAMAW MILKWEED HAD BEEN SUCKING ON A LEMON DROP WHILE standing at her mailbox. She opened the little door and reached inside to pull out her mail, which included one of Daffy's homemade bulb catalogs. We had written, *Have a happy day, Mamaw,* in marker above our names and the drawings of ourselves on the front cover. *We love you,* we signed the back page in our best writing, surrounding it with drawn hearts and bunnies because we knew she liked them.

Hop, hop, hop, we wrote alongside.

Mamaw must have been flipping through the catalog when the car slammed into her, throwing her into the milkweed by the side of the road. I imagined she lay there on her back and watched the butterflies fluttering through the sunlight above her, landing from plant to plant as she closed her eyes. She died within minutes of impact.

The driver hadn't been drinking. No drugs were found in his system. He'd simply been looking out his driver's-side window at the hills. He failed to realize his car had been edging farther and farther to the right.

"Do you think the faucet upstairs still leaks in her house?" Daffy asked me later at home after the cops had come to deliver Mom and Aunt Clover the news.

"Don't know," I said. We never would because the county got her house.

"Damn Momma for not paying her taxes," our mother shouted when she found out.

Mamaw Milkweed couldn't keep up with all the bills, not with Mom and Aunt Clover taking her money and selling her things like her glass cat collection that slowly disappeared until all that endured was a shelf of crocheted doilies and nothing more.

Mom and Aunt Clover took the cheapest route of disposing of their mother's remains. They had her burned.

"Your Mamaw would like this." Mom tried to wrap her arms around Daffy and me, but we stepped away from her and into each other's arms instead. "Remember our great-great-great-great, a million greats, Mamaw?" she asked. "Who was burned for being a witch?"

We shook our heads, not liking the way our mother told the story.

"Now Momma gets to be burned like her," Mom said.

"I don't want Mamaw Milkweed burned," Daffy cried out.

"Well, I don't mean burned." Mom wrung her hands. "She won't feel it. She's dead, for chrissake. Think of it as her being turned into something light enough to fly."

"Fly?" I asked.

"We'll give her ashes to the wind, and she'll fly," Mom said. "Won't that be nice? Now, c'mon. Where's my blue-eyed girl?"

When Daffy and me just stood there, Mom said, "C'mon. Where is she?"

We both slowly closed our green eyes, showing only our blue ones.

"Now, where's my green-eyed girl?" Mom asked. We closed our blue eyes until she said, "There she is. There she is."

The person who burned Mamaw put her ashes in an old coffee can because Mom and Aunt Clover wouldn't buy one of the urns the old man showed us. The can of ashes sat on the kitchen counter. Every day Daffy would ask Mom and Aunt Clover when we were going to take Mamaw out to the wind to fly.

"Soon" was all our mother would say as she disappeared into her room.

Each morning Daffy would open the can and say hello to Mamaw Milkweed, telling her all about the dreams she had overnight.

"You should talk to her, too, Arc," Daffy told me, but I would sleep in, folding the pillow over my ears so I couldn't hear Daffy or her fingernails rapping against the side of the can as she held it. The morning Daffy went into the kitchen and found the can was no longer on the counter, she cried out and ran into my room.

"Arc, did you take Mamaw Milkweed?" She shook me hard by the shoulders.

"What?" I sat up in bed, wiping my eyes and yawning.

"Mamaw Milkweed." She tightened her grip on my shoulders. "Did you take her off the counter?"

"Why would I?"

"Arc, you're no help." She raced down the hall and into Mom's bedroom.

"I didn't do nothing." I could hear our mother's rough voice.

Daffy ran past the doorway while I got out of bed, the blanket slipping down to the floor.

Yawning, I followed Daffy into the living room. She was waving her arms and standing in front of Aunt Clover.

"I ain't done shit with them dirty ashes," Aunt Clover said. She was sitting on the sofa, watching another one of her travel documentaries and using a knife to drill a hole in the bottom of an empty can that still had the creamed corn label on it.

"Then where is Mamaw Milkweed?" Daffy asked. She let loose a high-pitched scream. She stopped only when she heard the flush of the toilet coming from the bathroom. A shirtless man emerged. He scratched his genitals on his way into the kitchen.

"Did you take the coffee can?" She tailed him. "The coffee can that was right here." She slammed her tiny fist against the counter in the spot the ashes had sat.

"That coffee was expired or something," he said. "Tasted terrible. I flushed it."

"You what?" Daffy's voice was as high as the ceiling.

"Easy little girl." He ran his hand through his slimy hair. "Shit, you're young to be a coffee head. I'll get ya some more later."

"It wasn't coffee, you ugly giant." She ran into the bathroom, coming out seconds later with the now-empty coffee can.

"What'd I do?" the man asked as Daffy escaped past him, through the front door.

He sat on the sofa with Aunt Clover. Mom was coming out of her room, struggling to open her eyes as she felt her way down the hall toward them.

"Mom, you stink," I said as she passed me.

"Fuck you . . ." Her words slurred together as she fell onto the sofa between her sister and the man who had flushed her mother down the toilet with his morning piss.

I sighed as I looked at the three of them, then slammed the front door behind me and stepped out onto the porch. Daffy was sitting on the bottom step, wiping tears on her sleeve.

"You should stop crying," I told her as I sat down beside her. "Remember how Mamaw Milkweed said we had oceans in our eyes? And that every tear we lost was letting a mermaid or a fish out? You don't wanna lose any mermaids or whales or any spectacular fish, do ya?"

She cried harder.

"It's not so bad, Daffy," I said, putting my arm around her.

"Not so bad?" She turned her wet eyes on me. "Mamaw Milkweed's in the toilet with poop and pee and things I don't even wanna think about."

"No." I wiped Daffy's cheeks with my own sleeve. "She's in the river."

"What are you talking about?" she asked.

"When the toilet gets flushed," I said, "it ends up in the river. Everyone and their dumb brother knows that. Mamaw Milkweed is with the fish and the turtles and all the sparkly things she loved. And one day she might even end up in the great big Nile River, because every river in the world is connected. Then she'll be one of the goddesses, forever. And someone will build her a pyramid, and she'll wear shiny crowns with jewels the colors of all her scarves. That's not so bad, is it?"

As Daffy stared down into the empty can, a shadow crossed over our heads.

When we looked up, we saw a figure. The sunlight at his back blinded us to his face, but we could see he had narrow shoulders and was about the height our father had been.

"Daddy?" Daffy's voice was small.

"Daddy's dead, Daffy," I said, shielding my eyes from the light. "It's just another man."

"You two look like you're the same girl," he said.

"We're twins." We spoke at the same time.

He turned and walked around the yard, staring down at the holes dug in it. No longer a halo of light, we saw his face. The lenses in his brown eyeglasses were of a thick prescription, enlarging his blue eyes. Blue like the glories that grew up the posts of Mamaw Milkweed's house. He looked to be in his thirties. His hairline was starting to recede. Soon he would have to make the choice whether to dye it or let it go completely gray. He was wearing a button-up shirt with a brown tie, matching his suede shoes.

"Looks as though someone's been busy," he said as he squatted, looking into one of the holes.

"She did it." Daffy pointed at me. "She digs."

"What are you digging for?" He raised his eyes to mine. I thought he could do with a mustache. His face seemed too big without one.

"All kinds of things," I said as Daffy and me stood. "Mostly I dig for something Mom lost a long time ago. But that's hard to find. Probably the hardest thing there is."

He stared at us as he stepped away from the hole. "I've never seen eyes like yours before."

"They're witches' marbles," Daffy told him. "Arc stole my blue eye in the womb and I stole her green, so we'd each have one eye that belonged to the other one. What you here for anyway?"

"I was told her family lived here," he said. "Eloise Milkweed's family."

"Eloise?" Daffy turned to me.

"He means Mamaw," I said.

"You're her granddaughters?" he asked.

We nodded.

"Oh." He laid his hand on the back of his neck. "Well, I'm . . . sorry."

"What do you have to be sorry about?" Daffy asked.

"He's the guy," I whispered into her ear. "Don't you recognize his picture from the paper? The one we drew the mustache on?"

She turned back to the man who had started to avoid our eyes. She studied him, then frowned.

"You're the one who killed Mamaw Milkweed?" she asked.

He slowly nodded as his hand dropped from the back of his neck and slid into his pant pocket.

"Is that the car you hit her with?" I looked at the four-door he'd parked in front of our house. The car was the color of the smoke from the paper mill.

"It's got to be the car," Daffy said. "It's still got the dent in it. C'mon, Arc."

She set down the coffee can and grabbed me. Together we ran toward the car. Daffy let go of my hand so she could use both of hers to feel the grooves and ridges of the distorted metal.

"The dent kind of looks like Mamaw Milkweed, don't it, Arc?" she asked.

I stared back at the man who was slowly walking up behind us.

"Our mom says if we'd had money for a decent attorney, you'd be in jail," I told him, "and Aunt Clover says someone should cut off your head and boil it in a large pot and feed it to your momma on her birthday, then feed her to the hungriest hog in the county."

"That's right." Daffy nodded. "That's what Aunt Clover says you deserve."

"How old are you two?" he asked, looking from me to Daffy, then back again.

"Eight," Daffy said. "But we'll be nine soon in October. Unless someone runs us over."

"Then we won't be anything," I added.

"It was an accident," he said as if he was already in the courtroom.

I kicked the car's tire while he stared off into space, and my sister kept her hand on the dent. Dragging my fingers and making lines through the road dust on the doors, I walked around the car. I stopped to stand on my toes and press my face against the cool glass of the back window. There on the back seat, among the empty fast-food cups and a suit in a dry-cleaning bag, was a long-necked case.

"What's that?" I asked the man.

He laid his face against the glass beside mine. "That's my violin," he said, then opened the car door and lifted out the case.

He set it on top of the trunk and released its brass locks, revealing a gold velvet lining that was partially fallen.

"It's a very old violin," he said as he held the tattered lining up. "It was my grandfather's."

"Did someone run him over, too?" Daffy asked, sticking her tongue out through the hole of the tooth she'd just lost.

"No one ran him over." He carefully removed the violin from its velvet bed.

"It's pretty like a hundred bees at once," Daffy said, buzzing as he held the instrument above our heads.

"It is pretty, ain't it?" The man started to smile, but frowned instead.

He let us touch the wood, which was the color of the honey in the jar Mamaw Milkweed would sip from as she read the Bible.

"You girls ever hear a violin?" he asked as he picked up the bow from the case.

"Don't know." Daffy turned to me. "Have we, Arc?"

"We heard a guitar on the radio," I said. "And drums and whatever else they play on there. Sure, might have been a violin."

"It sounds like this." He took the instrument and placed it on his shoulder.

He pressed his chin against the black rest and moved the bow over the strings. He played a melody that made me think of the smoke from the paper mill. Made me think of things expanding and swelling. Of everything overgrown, until I thought of the nights at Mamaw Milkweed's farmhouse. Tall grass. Crickets like a massive thrum. Bullfrogs in even voice. Clouds at midnight, and there amid it all, a staircase, old and painted white but chipping like it doesn't want to be.

The music put me there in the blue grass at the foot of the stairs. I started thinking my father could have built the stairs. The way they were so uneven. No straight lines. No good-job finish. I worried if I took a step, the whole thing would come crashing down. I worried if I didn't, I'd miss the last great truth of my life.

As the man played, I started to climb the steps, and it seemed like me and those stairs were the only things in existence. There were no trees around. No ground below. Neither Daffy nor the man existed. There were merely the steps I was climbing against the blue night sky and the stars so close I could embed them into my palm. I got to the top, where there was an old wooden door open to an even older room a man was tap-dancing in. I felt he must be handsome from the way the bones in his hands were. Lean, strong bones that expanded like a wonder. He was in a black tuxedo, and I thought there was magic in its cuffs, in his black top hat. His shoes were so very shiny, I reckoned the universe was in them. The whole universe fitting inside a pair of size-eleven shoes.

I couldn't see this man's face but I felt certain I knew him. I think I loved him even. I think he was my father. And yet my father never owned a tuxedo, a top hat, or shiny black shoes. He never owned magic or the universe. He never tap-danced. There was never a staircase leading to a room that had no walls. There was never a night so blue in color I was proved only by it.

Yet the music came, and I saw something blue in the smoke from the paper mill. Something sparkling, a man dancing there. I ended the thought, though. The smoke wasn't as nice as all that, after all.

Daffy nudged me. "Remember the sound of a violin, Arc. You can add it to the beautiful side."

The man stopped playing to ask, "Is there any particular song you'd like to hear?"

Daffy and me glanced at each other, then stared at the dent.

"What was that song Mamaw Milkweed loved, Arc?" Daffy asked.

"'Amazing Grace,'" I said.

The man once more rested his chin on the violin. He closed his eyes as he moved the bow slowly across the strings.

My sister silently waved goodbye to the dent, then grabbed my hand.

Before we stepped back into the house, Daffy picked up the coffee can. Once inside, we found Mom and the man lying on the floor, while Aunt Clover pulled a string through the hole she'd made in the bottom of the creamed corn can. When she looked up, her eyes landed on Daffy's hand.

"Give me that," she said.

Daffy stared down at the can. She turned it over, as if to check that it was completely empty. When nothing more fell out, she handed it to Aunt Clover.

We ran down the hall into Daffy's room, where we pulled back our father's clothes so we could push up the window and stare out at the man. Only after he finished the last note did he open his eyes. He searched for us around the front of the car, inside, and even under it. I suppose it finally occurred to him where we had gone, for he looked at the house.

"Draw the violin before we forget it, Arc," Daffy said as she sat down on the floor. "I'll draw him."

I got down beside her, grabbing a marker. As Daffy started to draw his hair on the floor, we heard a car door shut, followed by the sound of an engine.

"Is he leaving?" Daffy asked.

I rose enough to see out of the window and say, "Yes."

"Is he gone yet?" she asked.

I waited until he pulled out on the road, then said, "He's gone."

"Put the strings up into the square, Arc. Make the savage side beautiful."

I lay down on my stomach and drew a violin as I said, "Mamaw Milkweed got up that morning, feeling the happiest she'd ever felt. She made a persimmon pie and decided to paint the whole house yellow, just as she always said she wanted. A yellow house with green shutters. She was still thinking of this as she went out to the mailbox to get the mail. There was the bulb catalog we'd made for her. She was so happy to get it that she flagged down the car headed her way.

" 'Look at the beautiful catalog my grandbabies made for me.' She held it up for the man in the suede shoes to see.

"He thought it was such an amazing catalog that he got his violin out and played her favorite song. She told him she'd love to have a violin all her own, but he told her she'd have to go away to learn how to play first. She knew she would miss us if she left, but she also knew that if she went away and learned the violin, then when she came back, she could play for us. So she got in the car, holding our catalog tight as he drove them away. She only left us so she could learn how to play the violin. We can't be sad about that because when she comes back, she'll teach it to us, like she taught us how to crochet."

My sister was silent as the tears slipped down her cheeks and landed on the man's hair she had drawn and was still coloring brown, even though there was no more white space in it.

"I miss her, Arc," she said.

"I know." I pressed my marker harder into the floor until it squeaked.

When I finished coloring the violin, she laid her ear down on top of it.

"Put yours here, too," she said.

She moved her head over enough for me to lay mine beside hers. As I felt the cold, hard concrete against my ear, she asked, "Do you hear it, Arc? Do you hear Mamaw Milkweed playing the violin?"

"Yes," I said against the silence. "I hear her."

AS THE BLOOD INSIDE THE BODY BREAKS DOWN, IT ENTERS THE TIS-
sue, darkening it to black. The color of the blowflies that start to land.
The insects have been called.

The river watches them tunnel inside the body, hears the bones break
as the snapping turtle goes for a toe or two.

For a moment, the river turns her eyes to a feather falling toward her
from the bird's wing flying high above. The river catches the feather,
lets it float beside the body. She holds her breath, and the surface goes
still. When she exhales, the ripples cast, but the feather is no more
flying than the body is swimming.

She abandons the dream and instead holds the light of the sun before
breaking it in a current, scattering the flies.

For a second, the river tells the truth when she says, the woman is
left alone.

CHAPTER 5

If I look close enough, I will see that she is me.

—*Daffodil Poet*

THE FIRST AUTUMN WITHOUT MAMAW MILKWEED, THE LEAVES changed colors the way they always had. The temperatures dropped, as the autumns before, and the deep blue of the sky settled into a fine gray. Life had not stopped just because hers had.

Daffy and me dragged a stool around the house, standing on it to check the pockets of our father's clothes on the windows.

"What you two doing?" Aunt Clover asked as she came in from Mom's room. She was laying a long strand of string down through the hall.

"Checking to make sure," I said as Daffy stuck her hand all the way into Dad's jeans pocket, feeling around.

"Make sure about what?" Aunt Clover stopped behind us and peeked into the pocket.

"That Mamaw Milkweed ain't trapped," Daffy said.

We thought Mamaw would come back to us. No larger than a crochet hook, something we could hold in our hands or get lost in a pocket, but the only things we found were cigarette butts and lint.

"If you two don't stop trying to conjure the ghosts, they'll have your *blood* and keep themselves amused by it," Aunt Clover said as she put the string down in a continuous path to the sofa. "Spittle, spittle spider, where you gonna hide her?"

"Whatcha doing, Aunt Clover?" Daffy asked as we hopped down from the stool.

"Making a telephone," Aunt Clover said.

She had the old coffee can that had once held Mamaw Milkweed's ashes. She pushed the string through the hole she'd made in the bottom of it, tying a knot. As Aunt Clover flopped back onto the sofa with the can up to her ear, Daffy and me followed the string into Mom's room. She was covered up in Dad's old army bag, lying on the mattress, the hole in its side bigger. Mom's eyes were shut, but she was holding on to the creamed corn can, the string knotted inside it.

"Go back to Aunt Clover," I told Daffy as I took the can from Mom. "See if you can hear me on the other end."

Daffy ran out. I could hear her and Aunt Clover fighting over the can.

"Let me try it, Aunt Clover," Daffy was shouting. "I ain't gonna hurt it none."

"You stupid little river hag. It ain't a toy," Aunt Clover was yelling back.

Finally, I heard Daffy's voice through the can.

"Can ya hear me, Arc?" she asked.

"I can hear you," I spoke into my end. "You hear me?"

"You sound like you're in the same room. Do you—"

Daffy's voice was replaced by Aunt Clover's.

"You hear me, Addie?" she asked.

I looked down at Mom. Her eyes were still shut. I knew not even shaking her would wake her. I laid the can back down in her hand and returned to the living room where Aunt Clover was still talking in the can with the hope Mom would listen. Daffy was sitting beside her on the sofa, watching TV.

The screen was bright with the cathedrals of Europe. As I passed by, I stopped at the shelf that had our family photos on it. I stood in front of the one of Dad. Second Lieutenant Flood Doggs.

A handsome man of blue eyes and dark hair. Though he was young in the photo, I was certain he'd saved a million people by the time the camera flashed in his eyes. I did what I always did when I looked at his photo. I saluted it, the way I'd seen officers get saluted on TV and in the movies. I thought, *This is the man I love.* I saluted him for this reason and more.

My father was named Flood because he was born in one. The great flood of 1950 that saw the waters rise high enough for people to remember it for decades. As the oars of the boat dipped into the brown water, my father was born from his mother who screamed loud enough for the flooded river to ripple.

"He looks like a savior in the photo, don't he?" Aunt Clover had stopped talking in the can. She laid it down on the sofa. "And yet he never saved anyone in this house. I can tell ya that and damn near to it." She pet the leopard collar around her neck and said, "Reach me that bag." She nudged Daffy and pointed to the plastic bag on her side of the coffee table.

"Tell us about Daddy," Daffy said as she set the bag on Aunt Clover's lap. Inside it were receipts. Clover called it fishing. She'd dive in dumpsters or cruise parking lots to find them. Then she'd go into the store, steal the item on the receipt, and take it to the counter saying she wanted to return it to get the money back.

"Tell you about your daddy?" she asked. "Ha." She dug through the receipts like a many-armed centipede. "Well, he wasn't no treasure, I can tell ya that. He was an asshole."

"Asshole?" Daffy frowned. "No, he wasn't, Aunt Clover."

"Biggest asshole in the state of Ohio." Aunt Clover spit on the floor.

Daffy stood up on the sofa cushion as she slammed her fists against Aunt Clover's head. "You take it back." Daffy let out a scream as I grabbed her down from off the sofa.

"You crazy little bitch." Aunt Clover started to collect the receipts that had fallen to the floor. She didn't say anything for a few moments, and all that could be heard was Daffy's heavy breathing, her small chest quickly rising and falling as she glared at our aunt. Then as Clover kept her eyes on the TV, she said, "Both of you go ride your bikes for a while. Get outta my fucking hair."

"C'mon, Daffy." I pulled her along behind me. She frowned at Aunt Clover the whole way out to the porch.

"She don't know nothing," Daffy said as she ran down the porch steps to the side of the house where we kept our bikes. We hid them beneath a tarp with other trash pushed against the house so no one would steal them. Mamaw Milkweed had gotten the bikes for us before she died. Mine was burgundy, with navy blue tassels hanging from the shiny chrome of the handlebars. Daffy's was the color of rust, the orange vibrant against the tar of the road.

"We better put on some shoes," I told her as we pulled the bikes out from beneath the tarp. "And a jacket. It's chilly today."

"Naw, I don't wanna go back inside," she said. "Not with that witch." She yelled toward the house. "C'mon, let's go. We'll warm up once we start pedaling."

We hopped onto our bikes, riding over the gravel and onto the asphalt. As we passed by the paper mill, Daffy asked if I remembered what Dad had said about it. "Say it, Arc. Say it the way he did."

"There's horses in the ground beneath the mill," I said. "The smoke is the dust they kick up with their hooves as they gallop so fast, they spin the world."

Daffy made a turn and pedaled into the mill's lot. I followed her. We circled the building as she shouted for all to hear, "There are horses in the ground beneath the mill."

Men in the parking lot stood by their cars and watched.

"There are horses in the ground," she said louder. "Gallop, gallop, gallop." She leaned forward on her bike, her hair blowing back like a mane.

"And the smoke is the dust they kick up," I yelled, laughing with her.

We made one more circle, hollering as loud as we could as we headed out onto the road.

"Now everyone knows our daddy wasn't no asshole," she said, holding her feet off the pedals and letting her legs stick out as we rode down a hill. "They'll know he was smart enough to know about the horses."

We headed to the center of town, to the large houses where we imagined nice things. Pretty lamps, swept floors, yellow sunlight like a bright pattern on the walls. We believed that in the big, beautiful homes, everybody got what they wanted. That the mothers and fathers were spaced far enough away to be heroes and the children were never lost.

We had a particular house that was our favorite. A colonial brick that had pillars and shutters taller than either of us at the time. They said the house was built when the town first was. The house may have been old, but the swimming pool would be new. A backhoe had dug the hole for it in the backyard that very morning. Daffy and me parked our bikes across the street and sat on the ground, imagining the cool, crystal water that would one day fill the dirt hole.

"I'd love to have my very own swimming pool," Daffy said, pretending to swim her arms through the air. "Think we'll ever be that lucky, Arc?"

"We'll have a house that's twice as big as this one. Our pool will be as wide as the river."

"Gee, that'd be the life." Daffy pulled her knees up and wrapped her arms around them as we talked about what color the walls of our house would be painted.

"Pink and blue and all the shades of green on a lizard's back," I said.

"And we'll have lots of fancy things that collect dust," Daffy added. "But we won't mind, because fairies eat dust and they'll be our friends. I'll plant flower bulbs around the front porch. Special ones. They'll be called Daffocus. A flower that is part daffodil and part crocus. When they bloom, they'll whistle our favorite songs."

We talked about what other bulbs would grow in the ground at our imaginary house until the sun started to fall.

"Let's go home, Arc." Daffy shivered. "It's getting too cold."

"Just a little while longer." I wrapped my arm around her as she trembled against my side. "Just a little while longer," I said again.

"What we waiting for?" she asked. "It better not be ghosts or monsters or mud trolls."

"Nah. We're waiting to find treasures."

"Treasures?" She frowned. "Aunt Clover said Daddy wasn't no treasure. I think he was, Arc. Maybe you'll find him in the ground." She sat up taller. "Wouldn't that be nice."

Long after the sun was completely gone, I pulled Daffy up to her feet.

"C'mon," I said.

We ran across the street, staying out of the glare of any lights as we crawled the length of the manicured bushes by the side of the house. When we got to the backyard, we stood at the edge of the hole. The backhoe was still there, parked for the next day's work. I ran my hand across the big tires and the clumps of dirt. I broke off a chunk to hold and crumble, letting pieces drop between my fingers as I looked up at the dark windows of the house.

"They're in bed now," I said. "They won't see us."

"Won't see us doing what?" Daffy asked.

"Digging."

"Wait." Daffy grabbed my arm when I started to climb down into the deep hole. "I don't wanna go down there, Arc."

"You don't have to. You can stay up here and watch me. Let me know if you see something sparkling so bright, it's just gotta be a dinosaur bone."

"If I see something sparkling like that, you'll be the first to know." She sat down on the edge of the hole, her feet dangling off as she pushed her hands through her shirt to keep them warm.

I slid down the deep side and felt at home in the cool dirt. From the time I could remember, I'd look at the ground and feel a pull, as if to dig were to find the answer to who I was. Everything faded away when I was digging. The home I came from, the problems there, all those needles on the floor Daffy and me had to draw around, they didn't matter when I had my hands in the ground because all I could think about, all I could taste in the back of my throat, was the overwhelming excitement of what I could discover with my own two hands. There was power in that. I was someone with a purpose.

That night, in the back of that big colonial house, I dug harder than I ever had to that point in my life. Perhaps because the hole was already so deep, I felt certain there was going to be a big find in it.

As the hours passed, Daffy curled up on the ground and fell asleep while I had enough dirt beneath my fingernails, it would take days to clean out. Through the night, I'd found rocks and roots and things that make their home in the deep and in the dark. Then as the morning sun started to rise, my hand felt a hardened edge of something I knew was unlike anything I'd ever found before.

I thought at first it was the thing that had belonged to my mother. The thing she'd lost. It felt that special of a find, but when I dug it up and held it in my palm, I saw it was something much older than what my mother had lost. I held tight to it as I quickly climbed out of the hole, certain the people who lived inside the house would be getting up for their breakfast of homemade pancakes and pure maple syrup.

"Daffy." I shook her awake. "Look what I found."

She refused to come out of the tight ball she'd curled herself in. Finally, she opened an eye. "What is it?" she asked, sitting up.

"Indians made it," I said, laying it into her trembling hand. "It's an arrowhead." I whispered in case someone was listening who might want to take it from me. "It's very old."

"Older than us?" she asked.

"A million years older," I said. "Maybe even a billion years older."

"Wow." She smiled. "And you found it?"

"Yep."

"You must be special to find something like this, Arc."

I looked at my sister, straightening my shoulders and making myself a little taller.

"I suppose so," I said. "Yeah, I suppose I am pretty special."

She nodded as she wiped her running nose on her arm.

"I'm sorry I kept you out here all night," I said. I could feel the dew on her skin as I wrapped my arms around her.

"I'm glad we stayed," she said, her teeth chattering. "I feel like I got to find an arrowhead, too."

"We found it together. C'mon." I helped her stand. "I wanna show Momma."

We ran from the house and hopped onto our bikes. It took Daffy a little while to get her legs warmed up enough to pedal straight while I stared at my discovery the whole way home. When we got there, Aunt Clover was on the sofa watching the sands of the Sahara swirl across the TV screen.

"Look what I found, Aunt Clover." I held the arrowhead in front of her face.

"Spittle, spittle, spider, where you gonna hide her?" Aunt Clover spit on the tip of her finger and laid it on the point of the arrowhead. "Right there," she said, "and that's bad luck."

"No, it's not," I said, bringing the arrowhead back to me. "It's a special find. You're just trying to ruin it for me."

"It's killed things before," she said. "It's got the bloody, blood, blood from the past on it."

She put her nighttime scarf on top of her head and went on and on about what furious creatures ancient men were.

"You might think the past is the past and we're too far ahead of it for it to ever come again," she said, picking the coffee can up and holding it to her ear as if Mom were speaking in the other end. "But you'd be wrong, Arc. You'd be dead wrong."

Daffy walked past, picking a blanket up off the floor on her way into her bedroom. I gave Aunt Clover the middle finger as I raced into Mom's room. Despite what Aunt Clover might have thought, Mom wasn't at the other end of the can. It was lying against her leg on the floor, the can's open end pressed against the hole in the mattress that was like a growing abyss.

"Mom?" I asked. "You awake?"

She turned over, her eyes moving behind their closed lids. I held the arrowhead to her earlobe to be certain it wasn't hers. She didn't smile like she would have had the arrowhead been the thing she had once lost, so I took it into Daffy's room. She had already gotten in bed. I climbed in with her, curling our cold feet up together.

"An arrowhead," I whispered. "Daffy, can you believe it?"

She didn't answer, so I laid it between us on the pillow. Once I fell asleep, I dreamed of the plains, of blue and pink dust there, and me, churning it up toward the sky. I'm not sure how long I was asleep before the dust started to shake. My shoulders were shaking with it. When I opened my eyes, I saw Daffy.

"Wake up, Arc." Her voice was as tight as her grip on my shoulders. "They're fighting."

"Who?" I raised up.

"Momma and the man. I'm scared, Arc."

I heard the yelling for myself. His was a deep voice using the words we always heard men call our mother.

"Don't worry," I told Daffy. "It's just another fight. Same as always. Go back to sleep."

"I can't." She covered her ears and squeezed her eyes shut.

"I have an idea," I said. "Let's draw."

She slid out of bed with me, down to the floor, taking the blanket with her to wrap around her shoulders. But before we could even start our picture, Mom went running by the doorway toward the living room, the man chasing after her. He was saying she had stolen his lucky keychain and he wanted it back.

"It's all right," I whispered to Daffy. "Nothing is gonna happen."

Our mother screamed, followed by a loud crashing sound.

"Arc?" Daffy shot up to her feet. "You think he hurt Momma?"

"C'mon," I said, standing. "Let's go see."

With Daffy's hand tightly gripping the back of my shirt, I led the way out into the dark hall and saw that the one photo we had of Mamaw Milkweed was on the floor. The glass inside the frame was broken into slivers.

"Watch out for that," I said to Daffy. "Step where I step. Okay?"

Together we tiptoed around the shards scattered over the drawing on the floor we had done of ourselves walking with elephants.

"He's killing her." Daffy pointed to the living room where we saw the man and our mother on the sofa. He was on top of her, his hands tight around her neck. Daffy yelled for Aunt Clover, but she had already gone out. She then screamed for our father, but she forgot he was dead.

"I'm scared, Arc." She gripped my shirt tighter. "Don't let anything bad happen to Momma."

"I won't." I pried my sister's fingers off my shirt and darted back to her room, sidestepping the shards along the way. I grabbed the arrowhead from off the bed and ran as fast as I could back to the living room, forgetting about the pieces of glass. My blood tracked with me and left spots on the drawings that would stain. At the time, I didn't feel the wide gash on the arch of my foot. I was running to save my mother's life.

I screamed like I'd seen warrior women do on TV, then stabbed the arrowhead into the man's side. He stared down at the blood seeping through his white shirt as he slowly removed his hands from around Mom's neck. She gasped for air while he raised his shirt to look at the wound. He wouldn't die, this man who came for our mother in ways all the men did. But the wound was deep enough for him to know I was there and I was ready.

"You little shit." He set both feet down on the floor, his boots big and leathery.

"You stay away from my momma." I held the arrowhead up and growled like our neighbor's pit bull did at squirrels. I even barked for good measure. She was my mother and I wasn't yet ready to lose her to the wolves.

"I got this arrowhead from a big deep hole," I told him. "And if you don't get on outta here, I'm gonna lay you down in that hole, if it's the last thing I do. Now you leave our momma alone. I'll tell my daddy on you. And he'll help me put you in that big ol' hole."

"Stupid little cunt." He cursed on his way to the door, pointing at Mom and swearing he'd be back.

Mom curled up and rocked on the sofa, whimpering. Daffy and me sat on the floor beside her.

"Your blood is really red, Arc," Daffy said as she wrapped her blanket around my foot.

"I know."

"Is his blood on that?" She pointed to the arrowhead.

"Yes," I said. "It'll always be on it."

As Mom dropped off the sofa and crawled back into her room, Daffy said, "We're like the Trung sisters, huh? As brave as they were?"

I had told her the story about the Trung sisters after I'd read about them in a book at the library. Ever since then, it was a story she wanted to hear over and over again.

"Tell me about them, Arc," she said, picking up a marker and starting to draw on the floor.

"In a place far away from Ohio called Vietnam," I said, "when it was ancient and old, there were two sisters who shook their fists at bad men who tried to take everything away from them. Who tried to make them live like something they weren't. The sisters refused to give their freedom away and they got angry and formed a whole army of women. This army pushed the mean monsters back. The Trung sisters won, and everyone was happy, and they were made queens."

"Queens." Daffy smiled.

I watched her draw on the floor, the pain growing in my foot. When I started to cry, Daffy kissed me on the cheek and said everything was going to be all right. She got up and ran into the kitchen. When she came back, she was carrying one of Mom's vodka bottles.

"Drink this," she said. "Momma always goes to sleep after she has it. You'll go to sleep, and when you wake up, your foot won't hurt no more."

"I don't know if I should."

"Your foot hurts, don't it?" She handed me the bottle. It was already open. Our mother's lipstick around the rim of it.

When I took a drink, it burned.

"Yuck, it tastes like 'possum piss. It's bad." I tried to hand the bottle to her, but Daffy said, "Drink it until it ain't."

I filled up with a couple more sips, each one hard to keep down. Then I started to feel like the room was floating around me. I blinked and saw Daffy. I blinked again and saw Aunt Clover. Her barbed-wire eyeliner was smeared down to her cheek, and she was carrying her shoes.

"What is all over the floor?" she asked.

"Blood," Daffy told her.

"Blood? Let me see you, Arc." Aunt Clover held up my foot in ways my own mother should have. "My God, Addie, have you seen her foot?" Aunt Clover shouted down the hall to Mom's closed door. "What the hell happened?"

"Wasn't my fault" was all I said as Aunt Clover took the liquor bottle from me.

"Shit fire, it's a good thing you filled up on this gasoline," she said. "What you got coming, ain't gonna feel nice. Daffy? See if that old sewing needle is still in that drawer over there."

The last I saw was Aunt Clover hovering over me, the ceiling light catching on the sewing needle in her hand. Then the room spun so fast, I had to close my eyes so they wouldn't whirl out of my head. When I came to a little while later, Aunt Clover was sitting on the sofa watching a program on the Great Wall of China. My foot was propped up on her leg. Daffy was on the floor with a red marker, drawing a picture of my foot with the new stitches in it.

"You shouldn't have done what you did, Arc," Aunt Clover said as I sat up.

"What I did?" I looked at my sister.

"Sorry, Arc," she said. "I had to tell her what happened."

"You never goad 'em," Aunt Clover continued. "You let the men do what they're gonna do. They eventually stop on their own. But you risked making him madder. What if he'd been a dealer? He'd have cut ya far worse than the glass did."

I knew what she was going to say. She was going to say, *You don't fuck with a dealer.* When she said it, I said it, too. Her lips thinned as she made a face at me.

"You know why I wear this barbed wire?" She pointed to her eyeliner. "So I'm not the one who gets cut. They are."

"He was just a john," I said as if I were old enough to know what that meant.

As Daffy looked down at my foot, she asked Aunt Clover why she hadn't put any of my blood on her belt.

"Because only my blood goes on my belt," Aunt Clover said.

"I don't . . ." I hung my head off the edge of the sofa. "I don't feel so good."

"Well, I'd say not." Aunt Clover snickered. "You drank hard liquor, like a dumb little pig. You gotta sweat it out now."

As I lay back on the sofa, I began to think about my mother, whose door was still closed at the end of the hall. I began to think it was her fault after all.

Why didn't she look at my foot the way Aunt Clover did? I thought. *Why wasn't it my mother who picked me up in her arms?*

Mom never said anything to me that night, but she tucked me into bed. Something she hadn't done since before Dad died. As she kissed my forehead, I held on to the arrowhead so tight, I could feel its edges dig into my palm like something ignited.

"What's that?" she asked.

"It's an arrowhead I found. Momma? My foot hurts," I said, but she was already staggering toward the door. She was nearly knocked over by Daffy, who pushed past.

"I wanna sleep with you, Arc." She climbed into bed with me.

Our mother looked at us both. She seemed to smile as she turned out the light. We could hear her hoarse whisper from the hall.

"What'd she say?" my sister asked me.

"She said she loves us," I said.

Maybe that was only what I wanted to hear her say. Or maybe she really did say it as she softly padded down the hall to her mattress on the floor.

Daffy looked at me. I knew what she was going to ask next.

"Put the strings up into the square, Arc. Turn it to the beautiful side."

As she laid her head against my chest, I said, "There was a man here in the house. You came into my room frightened. I told you there was nothing to be scared of. To prove it, I took you down the hall where we saw the man with his hands around Momma's throat."

"Choking her," Daffy said.

"No," I said. "He wasn't choking her. He was giving her a pretty necklace. And the yelling wasn't yelling at all. It was laughing. Best of all is when the man stepped back to look at the necklace around Mom's neck, we saw it wasn't just any man. It was Daddy.

"'Don't she look beautiful,' he asked us as Mom spun with a big smile on her face, showing off her new necklace.

"'It shines like the stars,' you said to her.

"That's when I ran back down the hall to my room to get the arrowhead."

"To stab the man," Daffy whispered.

"That was what happened on the savage side," I said. "But on the beautiful side, I got the arrowhead to give to Dad. He held it in his palm and closed his fingers around it. When he opened his hand back up, the arrowhead had changed into a shiny locket that had our photos in it. He took the locket and hooked it to Mom's necklace, which made her even happier."

"What about the blood?" Daffy asked. "The blood from where you cut your foot?"

"It wasn't blood," I said, "because there was no glass, because there'd been no fight and Mamaw Milkweed's picture never got broken. What looked like blood was really just the red color shining from our drawings. They had come alive. It wasn't just me who had the red color on my foot, it was all of us. And it wasn't only red. It was blue and yellow and every color of marker we ever used. Dad took off his army boots, so he could be barefoot like us as we danced and danced around the house, spreading all the colors from room to room until it was a rainbow. We danced all night like bears wearing bells."

"I've always wanted to dance," Daffy said as she tucked her head under my arm.

"You're still shivering," I told her.

"Haven't ever gotten warm from last night," she said.

She blew her nose on the blanket and fell asleep, her snores raspy.

I gripped the arrowhead tightly as I said to it, "I must be special to have found you."

The next morning my hand would be empty, and the arrowhead would be gone.

DRIP, DROP. DRIP, DROP.

In the lower respiratory tract, there will be gifts from the river in the form of dirt and plants. The river gives these things because it is what she has to give.

In the woods around, a coyote cries. The woman's body moves. It jerks. It splashes. But not because it has come alive. It is because of the fish. They have entered the mouth, the wounds, the holes that no longer close. They have entered in search of a soul, finding instead something to eat.

CHAPTER 6

I will stay gone, unless you hold on.

—*Daffodil Poet*

IT WAS A FLU THAT WAS PARTICULARLY TERRIBLE THAT YEAR. DAFFY was under the blanket. She'd been in bed for a while, when she wasn't throwing up in the bucket.

"You should prepare yourself in case the girl don't make it," Aunt Clover spoke into the can to Mom. I was sitting on the sofa with my aunt because, as she said, "I couldn't be trusted not to be a fucking sneak and go into Daffy's room."

"Can't we watch something else?" I asked her, staring at the TV.

It was another documentary showing some place that wasn't Chillicothe.

"I don't know why you watch these shows," I said, scratching around the stitches in my foot. "You're never gonna go to any of those places, Aunt Clover."

"Hey." Aunt Clover grabbed my chin. "Don't you dare say that about me."

"Well, you're not."

She slapped my cheek.

"That hurt, Aunt Clover." I held my skin, the sting something I'd gotten used to.

"You ain't got no right to speak to me like that." She wrapped her nighttime scarf around her shoulders and straightened her faux fur leopard collar.

No one ever thought much of Aunt Clover. I suppose even I was guilty of that.

We sat in silence as images of Italy drifted across our TV. It was on PBS, one of Aunt Clover's favorite channels, and it was a series about art and the places it's created in. A full-color painting of a woman with a slight smile on her face appeared on the screen.

"Can we at least watch it with the volume on?" I asked.

"What you need that for?" She propped her leg, covered with new sores, up on the coffee table.

"I wanna know what I'm looking at," I said.

"You're looking at the *Mona Lisa*, ya little idiot. The *Mona Lisa*," she said again like a scholar. It surprised me that she knew the painting's name, let alone that it existed. I lowered my head for thinking of her as everyone else did, as nothing but some stupid addict and woman of little dreams and small mind. My aunt. A woman with a gap left from her rotted-out teeth that she'd spray water out at you through. Both she and my mother were women who could have been queens in a different parade, had they not been so at home in the hole they seemed to dig deeper with each passing day.

"I've always wanted to see that in person," she said, leaning toward the painting.

"Why don't you go to see it?" I asked. I thought if she had something like that to look forward to, it would give her a good reason to stop holding lighters beneath spoons. In my young mind, I thought it could be that simple.

"Don't be a stupid bitch," she said. Then, in the blue light of her own thoughts, her frown changed into the look of someone who was about to cry.

"I'll never see that." She spoke the words with a light chuckle at the end as if there was nothing to sadness but a change of face. "Except on the TV."

"You could see it," I said, "if you wanted to go to—"

"If I wanted to go to what?" She turned to me, leaning back against the sofa like she wanted to get a good look.

"If you wanted to go to one of those places," I said.

"One of what places?"

"Teacher at school says there's a place that takes the drugs away and makes you better."

"Rehab?" Aunt Clover laughed. "You wanna know what rehab is?"

I nodded.

"It's a place of mirrors," she said. "They force you to do nothing but look at your own reflection all day and all night. No fucking way am I going to the place of mirrors. I know what I am. I know what I ain't. There's no point in drinking from the wishing cup. An addict is an addict forever. You understanding me? There's nothing that'll change us of our ways. Nothing."

She picked up the can and spoke into it.

"Hey, Addie, listen to what your dumbass daughter just said."

I got up from the sofa and ran on my good foot down the hall.

"I'll tear the skin off your ass if you go in your sister's room," Aunt Clover's voice followed me. I paused at Daffy's closed door. It was shut tight. I leaned down and stuck my finger inside the keyhole, pushing it farther and farther—

"Arc, you better not be at that goddamn door."

I ran at the sound of Aunt Clover's voice and didn't stop until I was in Mom's room. I sat beside the hole in the mattress. It had gotten even bigger since I last saw it. I could see new things were stuffed inside.

"What you got in here, Momma?" I asked as she turned over, her face sweaty. She had a needle in her hand and was pressing on the skin up and down her bruised arm.

I reached my hand into the hole and pulled out a pair of men's sunglasses, a rabbit-foot keychain, and empty pill bottles. There were keys and belt buckles, even a bill cut off a baseball cap. There were other things I couldn't see, pushed deeper back into the mattress. Things that were too far out of my reach.

"Momma, why you putting all these things in your mattress?" I asked.

"It's your fault Daffy is sick, Arc," she said. "You shouldn't have kept her . . . kept her out all damn ni . . . night. You let her get co . . . cold. It's all your fault."

"Momma, you see my stitches?" I held my foot up to her, but she only pushed it away and picked up the telephone can instead. She tugged the string to make sure it was taut, then spoke Clover's name into it.

Aunt Clover came in a few seconds later. "I'm right here, Addie," she said. "What you need?"

"See if you . . . find a vein" was all Mom said, holding the needle out.

As Aunt Clover took Mom's arm in her hands and searched, I limped down the hall and stood at the closed door of my sister's bedroom. I quietly opened it. I thought the room would look different than it had when Daffy was well. Being a sick room, I thought everything would be changed. The colors faded, the light dimmed. The walls themselves peeling. I thought I would touch things in there, and they would be mushy like rotting fruit. But the hard things were still hard, and the solid things were still solid.

The room did smell like an onion. Aunt Clover had stolen one from the store. She cut it the way Mamaw Milkweed always said to. Until your eyes water. Then she put it on a plate and set it on Daffy's bedside table. I suppose Aunt Clover thought if she said the right words over the raw onion, it would be as magical as Mamaw Milkweed said, and it would take the illness out of the room right swift. All that happened was that an onion sat for a very long time on a plate in the room of a very sick little girl.

I stood against the side of Daffy's bed and looked down at her red-rimmed eyes. She was staring up at the ceiling, watching the fan go slowly around. She was wearing a sweatshirt Mamaw Milkweed had gotten for her. It was cream, with powder-blue sleeves. Holly Hobbie, a girl in a long raggedy dress and a bonnet on her head, was on the front of it. Under the sweatshirt, Daffy wore a pink slip. The lace on the bottom of it had roses and leaves. She had on chocolate-brown knee socks, but one of them had fallen down around her ankle.

When I gripped the blanket, she slowly turned her sweating face to me and said, "What you doing? You're not supposed to be near me. You'll get sick, too. Go away, Arc."

"In 1918," I said, "the Spanish flu killed more people in a single year than those who died in all four years of the First World War."

I had dog-eared the fact in one of my favorite history books.

"Am I gonna die, Arc?" she asked, too sick to feel the fear of her own question.

"You would if you didn't have me." I climbed into the bed and snuggled up against her, holding her tight. When I wrapped my good foot around hers, I could feel the cold sweat having soaked her socks. She breathed through her mouth. Her hot, stinky breath hitting my cool face. I closed my eyes and imagined her germs as centipedes that crawled from her skin to mine, where they burrowed deep inside me.

"We'll kill the monster together," I told her.

We fevered and vomited and filled buckets with the dark face of illness. I remember our mother in the room once. She was saying, "I told you to stay the fuck out of here, Arc."

Her figure retreated to stand in the doorway, her head turned toward the living room to tell her own sister, "Arc is in here. She's in bed with Daffy. You were supposed to watch her."

"Ain't no watching Arc," Aunt Clover yelled back. "She's too eager to be a bitch. Worst, she's stubborn as a bloodstain."

Aunt Clover appeared beside Mom.

"You don't tap death on the shoulder when he's looking in the other direction," my aunt said. "Arc's done tapped his shoulder now. Best put lipstick on them both so at least they'll be pretty when death comes."

I felt Mom's cold hand grab my chin and put lipstick on only my bottom lip. She reached over and put some on the top of Daffy's.

"You're half of the same mouth," Mom told us. "Don't you both look pretty now."

When I looked again, it wasn't Mom at all but Aunt Clover.

"Spittle, spittle, spider, where you gonna hide her?" Aunt Clover spit into her palm and smacked it against my forehead. "Right here in a fever."

"I think I'm getting sick, too," Mom was saying as she walked down the hall to her own room, unsure if the nausea she was feeling was because of the flu her daughters had given her or if she was riding the fumes of her high.

"Arc, I'm scared." Daffy gripped my arm. I still remember how quickly her fever had climbed and how, when she coughed, she spotted her sweatshirt with blood.

"Momma will be angry," she said as she stared down at the blood.

Later that night, no matter how much I shook her, my sister wouldn't do anything more with her eyes than roll them. I wiped the sweat from her face and told her everything was going to be all right. Then I fell asleep with my head on her rattling chest.

The next morning Daffy was sitting up against the headboard, smiling at me.

"It took you a long time to wake up," she said.

"You, too," I said, staring at the arrowheads she had drawn all over the headboard. "Why'd you draw so many?" I asked.

"I know you lost your arrowhead, Arc," she said. "But now we got all we'll ever need."

She grabbed me into a hug, and together we laughed. What had been lost felt like it was now found. For a moment, we were the happiest sisters in the world.

IT IS CALLED WASHERWOMAN HANDS. THE WAY THE SKIN WRINKLES when left in water for too long.

It is a cutaneous change of immersion, but the river knows it as just another layer of life being stripped away.

There will also be a marbling of the flesh, a staining of soft tissue. It will look as though there is a series of small streams beneath the surface of the skin. As if the river had birthed something of herself inside the dead.

Beyond the marbling, beyond the wrinkles, the skin will start to fall away. This begins with the hands and feet, the very things we hold and walk the world with.

Deep in her waters, the river will keep what pieces she can. As if someday, someone will come to take them home.

CHAPTER 7

Who? Who? Said the wind as it blew,
the words we already knew.

—*Daffodil Poet*

1983

ONE YEAR SURVIVED BY A FLU THAT WAS STRONG ENOUGH TO KILL more than a few members of our community, my sister and me celebrated our tenth birthday. There was no cake, no presents, no birthday card. Left alone, we would throw ourselves a party by drawing a cake on the floor and pretending that lime-green confetti was raining down on us.

We drew our cake in what we called the birthday corner, which was the far-right side of the floor in Daffy's bedroom. The cakes from our pasts overlapped there. There was a purple frosted cake drawn from the time we were five. A pink one from when we had been seven. We decided to draw a pretty blue cake for our tenth birthday. We would draw the whole cake, then a slice, then a bite, ending with drawn crumbs scattered around our forks. If we closed our eyes tight enough, we tasted the blue frosting with the little red roses.

We also drew presents we wished we'd gotten. A globe so we could see all the places in the world we were certain we would go when we were tall enough to not have to drag a stool over to see our reflection in the mirror on the wall. We drew a bracelet that had charms, like the one a girl at school had. We would watch the charms jingle as this girl, who always had the answer, raised her hand in class. Daffy and me decided that we would like our wrists to jingle, too. Lastly, we drew a pair of wings.

"Because you can't fly without them," Daffy said.

Wings were the one gift we kept giving ourselves. Each year we would draw them with more feathers, hoping they would be big enough to be real. No matter how hard we wished, or how large we drew the wings, we never got more than a foot off the ground, the highest we could jump on any given day.

"If we don't get wings this time," Daffy said, "we'll never get them."

"We'll have to wait and see what being ten is like," I told her.

It turned out that being ten wasn't much different. We painted our nails with imaginary nail polish and wore hair ties for bracelets. Though they did not have charms, they were things we pretended did. It was between the nail polish no one saw on our nails and the bracelets no one heard jingle that our mother brought more and more of her work home.

She had a long strand of gold-painted beads from the discount store that she hung on her doorknob. She overlapped the strand several times until it clumped. The beads were the sign to Daffy and me not to enter our mother's room. They seemed to always be there, their gold paint flaking off and revealing the white plastic beneath.

In the beginning, Daffy and me would lay our ears against Mom's cold door and listen to the sounds on the other side. Sounds that seemed knotted together like the beads. I began to think it was the reason Mom and the men would emerge from the bedroom with red necks, arms, and legs. When the door was closed, we would look through the keyhole and see movement that we didn't understand. Daffy would always stick her finger inside the keyhole and turn it, then look through the keyhole again, as if the scene on the other side would be different. It never was.

The moaning and the groaning caused Daffy and me to draw jungles and lions and big leaves that shadowy things hid behind on the floor. There were times when we listened at the door that we would hear nothing. These times would confuse us even more. For the silence we drew bright red mouths, tightly closed. These we didn't place on the floor, but rather on the dingy walls of the hallway leading down to Mom's room. Mom would sometimes stand before these bright red lips. She would lay her own over them, us watching in the shadows.

I had heard the words *whore, slut,* and *tramp* all my days growing up. It was what I was told my mother and my aunt were by those who believed they were better. All I really thought about my mom and my aunt when people called them whores was how my aunt could sing "The Star-Spangled Banner" in all the right notes and how my mom could draw a cathedral, or a covered bridge, or the Empire State Building in perfect lines. I think Mom might have been an architect. I could see her. The needle turning into a pencil in her hand as she put on an architect's jacket, which as a kid, I always thought would be golden with bright blue tassels on the elbows.

"See ya later," I imagined she'd say as she left the house with nothing more than drafting paper and a million buildings on her back. I don't think she called me Arc only because I dug in the dirt and pretended to be the best archaeologist in Ohio, if not the world. I think she called me Arc for the architect within her. Maybe she thought if she laid her dreams upon me, hid them in my name, she would, in some way, succeed if I were to. But no one ever saw her or my aunt as women who would flourish in anything more than spreading their legs.

Daffy and me didn't know what the word *john* meant when we were young enough to still believe in love. All we knew was that our mom and Aunt Clover had a top-notch collection of low-cut shirts and a series of boyfriends because of it. By the time my sister and me were as tall as we needed to be to ride the Ferris wheel at the county fair, we knew you could pay for sex and that our mother and our aunt set their own prices on it. I would come to be told the men were called johns. When I first heard that, I thought it odd they all had the same name.

"John is the name we give them," Aunt Clover explained to me, keeping her voice as steady as she could. "That is our power. That we name them."

Not long after that, I understood that sex is not like it is in the movies. It's not a nice man and a happy woman in a bed. He's not hovering over her smiling face. Sometimes sex is this. But not always. At least, it wasn't in our house.

Aunt Clover would take her johns to the Blue Hour motel. I suppose the original owners had a nice establishment in mind when they first built it in the 1960s, but somewhere along the way, the blue-painted brick of the Blue Hour darkened and became the hangout for drug users and prostitutes. All the rooms were accessible from the outside, as was the staircase, with its black iron railing that took you to the doors on the second level. On any given day, you could book a room and find bedbugs and a dirty needle with a spoon beneath the mattress. It had become a disgrace to the community as a whole, announced in the skyline by a large brick rectangle that served as its signage with BLUE written in cursive, to give it some class, and HOUR written in big block letters to appeal to the average workingman.

Before Aunt Clover would leave for the Blue Hour, she'd put on her mascara. She preferred it in the same color our mother did. Electric blue. She seemed to load her lashes with enough of it to tar the streets she walked on. She never left without drawing her eyeliner with its little *x*'s.

"My barbed wire," she would say as if to remind herself. Then she'd look into the mirror, take the clear tape, and find another part of herself that had cracked in the reflection of it.

Aunt Clover had begun to stink more and more. Mom did, too. Body sweat, the smell of hair gone a thousand mornings without wash. Then there was the smell of something moist that coated the nose. It made me think of puddles created by the melting of women too hot to realize they were burning alive.

"I can't stand the smell," Daffy would say, holding her nose.

We started a game where we listed all the things we thought our mother and our aunt smelled like.

"Like dog breath," Daffy said. "Like mud on the bottom of a shoe."

"Like dishwater," I said. "And wilted lettuce and blood on a knife blade."

"Worst of all," Daffy sighed, "they smell like the johns."

My sister and me had nicknames for the men who would come to the house for our mother. There was the one we named Fuck and Go, because of how quickly he came and went. Tight Ass was a man who wore jeans as if they were plastic wrap, and Assassin was a guy who always had his black hair slicked back. When our mother was with him, she screamed so loud she sounded like he was killing her. Then there was the Holy Ghost, who would float from room to room, his cross necklace swinging from his neck.

Over time, all of them came to look alike to Daffy and me, so we drew one man on the floor to represent them all. We gave him brown hair, brown eyes, and no smile. We put money in his hand and a broken heart in his chest. We drew him on the floor of the hallway so the johns would step on their own selves as they walked to our mother's room, closing the door behind them, the beads shaking against the knob.

Daffy and me did our best to avoid the men. They usually left the house angry, yelling at Mom for stealing this or that.

"Where's my fucking hat, Addie?"

"Where's my goddamn sunglasses?"

"You're nothing but a thieving whore."

Some of the johns looked at Daffy and me as they left and seemed embarrassed that we'd seen them. They would walk quickly from the house with their heads down and their car keys ready. Other johns would walk by us like they had all the right in the world to be doing what they were doing.

We're men, their walk seemed to say. *We're men and we fuck. So what if what we're fucking is your momma?*

Then there were those who would look at us with pity. We didn't see them often. Sometimes we'd never see them again. It was as if not even the lure of cheap sex could stop them from thinking of the two little girls watching cartoons in the living room just down the hall.

When we first saw him, we were unsure of what type he was. He had black hair, shaved on the sides, but long on the top and slicked back. His protruding brows were black and thick against his pale skin. I'd never seen such close-set eyes, dark and shiny, like crude oil was caught there. He was dressed in all black. A long-sleeved shirt and slim fitted pants. You might not have known he was there, if not for the tapping sound.

He took slow steps with elongated strides. Unlike his feet, his fingers moved quick and jerky, his yellowed fingernails making loud tapping noises while walking the walls with him.

By the time he sat down beside us, we knew he was unlike the others. Aunt Clover had left for the Blue Hour, so Daffy had the arm of the sofa all to herself. I was in the middle, sitting with my legs crossed beneath me. He didn't say anything for the longest time. He just played with the gold chain around his neck. When I looked at it, I saw it had strands of human hair, in various shades, wrapped around the chain as if caught there.

"Why you got hair around your necklace?" I asked him, but he only stared at the TV. Bugs Bunny was on. The man watched the rabbit hit the devil over the head with the hammer.

"You have weird eyes," he said, not looking at us.

"They're witches' marbles," Daffy told him. "The blue eye is for water. The green eye is for the earth."

"The TV's too loud" was all he said. "Turn it down."

Daffy grabbed the remote and lowered the volume.

"It's too quiet now," he said. "Turn it up."

I took the remote and made the show so loud, Daffy covered her ears.

"You do what you're told. Good girl." He smiled without looking at us.

"His breath smells like black flies," Daffy whispered into my ear.

He reached his arm behind my head. I moved closer to Daffy.

"Our aunt Clover is gonna be home soon," I said, then felt a pinch on top of my head. "Ow," I cried out and leaned away from him. "That hurt."

He held the long hair he'd taken from me in between his fingers.

"You didn't scream for your momma?" His words were as slow as his walk had been.

I rubbed my head as he wrapped the hair around the gold chain, adding it to the other strands of hair already there.

"I love this part," he said, his eyes on the TV.

No one ever says the demon will smile or that he'll laugh along with you as the rabbit takes the hunter's rifle and shoots him with it over and over again on a cartoon that always seems to be the only thing on when a man has his hand under the blanket and on top of a little girl's thigh.

I didn't say anything as the three of us kept watching the cartoon. By the time it ended, he removed his hand. He stood, buttoning his shirt, which had been open ever since he emerged from our mother's bedroom.

Later that night I couldn't sleep. I thought of his gold necklace and the hairs wrapped around it. I could hear the groans from down the hall in Mom's room. You can't escape the seconds in what seems to be an endless night. Men in a house, then suddenly, one in my room. His shadow like the shadow of the spider on the cartoon he watched with us.

I quickly got off the bed and started throwing the dirty laundry onto it. Then I got back in, trying to hide myself in the pile.

Still he found me.

"If you scream," he said, "I'll kill everyone in this house. They'll blame you."

As he unbuttoned his pants, I closed my eyes and thought about history, reciting all the facts I had in my head from the books I'd checked out from the library. When he pushed me back onto the mattress and held my thin wrists down above my head, I imagined being with Howard Carter the moment he unearthed the tomb of King Tutankhamen. Egyptian gold and a pharaoh's lands built into pyramids all around me while the man yanked my legs out to either side of him.

My bedside lamp was on. It cast our shadows on the wall. I watched as his two arms became eight legs. They moved the same way I'd once watched a spider in the backyard attack a moth in the web. When the pain started and I felt like I would be ripped in two, I thought about the ancient Romans and the brave gladiators in the arena with the lions. The crowd cheering them to their deaths, the lion roaring for the jungle it had been taken from.

"Good girl." The man tapped the side of my leg with all eight of his when he was through. "Good girl. Do what you're told."

Weeks would go by before I saw him again. Then suddenly there he'd be. I moved the only bedside table I had over to block the door. Still he came in. I pushed my bed over. Still he came in. I put a line of salt down in the doorway because it was what Mamaw Milkweed said would keep the evil spirits away. Still he came in.

One time he brought a Happy Meal with him. He set it on the floor but wouldn't let me have it until after. I thought of the food the entire time. I stared at the red box with its little yellow handles so hard, I thought it might lift off the floor and float over to me.

As soon as he was done, I quickly put my clothes back on and sat down far away from the box so I could admire it.

"It looks like the one from the TV commercial," I said, sliding in a circle around it.

"Ain't ya ever had one before?" he asked.

I shook my head. He pulled his pants up but didn't button them as he sat down on the edge of my bed. I watched him take a cigarette out and light it, then I asked, "Why?"

"Why what, ya little shit?" he asked.

"Why'd you bring me a Happy Meal?"

He didn't answer, so I turned back to the box. I wondered if to open it meant I would have to destroy the golden arches.

"Ain'tcha gonna eat any of it, crissakes." He picked up my one blanket and blew his nose with it.

I scooted across the floor, closer to the box, and opened it like I'd seen the kids do on the commercial. I expected the food to glow like it did for them but no light came. I slowly looked down and counted five nuggets. The man watched me as I ate two and saved three. There was a small pack of fries that had spilled out. They were greasy and cold, but I had to stop myself from eating them all. I couldn't remember if I'd eaten that day or the day before. I knew I'd had three crackers on Monday, but that felt forever ago.

I wanted to eat the whole meal and the box. Instead, I stiffened and ate only five of the fries, tucking the others neatly down in the wrapper.

"Why you keeping food back?" he asked, stretching his legs out and crossing them at the ankles. "Got a dog I ain't ever seen?"

"It's for my sister." I gently laid the remaining nuggets down by the fries.

"Her bedroom the one next door?"

I didn't say anything as I picked the toy up from the box. It was in a plastic bag. I had to bite the corner to open it and get to the princess. She was beautiful with her long black hair and purple eye shadow that matched the purple jewels in her crown. I smiled and cradled her in my hand.

"Why is it girls always like princesses so damn much?" He held the cigarette between his lips as he leaned back on my bed to zip his jeans.

"Because when you're the princess, you'll be queen one day," I said. "Then you get a crown that no one can take from you, and you get to rule the kingdom all by yourself."

I ran my fingers along the hard plastic of the princess's pink dress.

"You gonna save her for your sister, too?" he asked.

I kissed the princess as he blew the smoke from his cigarette out into the room.

"Don't smoke around her," I said, covering her face so she wouldn't have to breathe it in.

He stood and buckled his belt before leaving. I played with the princess awhile longer, walking her along the edge of my bed and pretending she was strolling the grounds of her kingdom. She wasn't any bigger than my ten-year-old hand, but she was the only doll I'd ever had that was brand-new. I once found a baby doll in the dirt with her plastic face caved in and there had been the pink teddy bear Mom and Dad had gotten me when they promised they would always be sober. But that bear had been sold, along with Daffy's and the baby doll, in a yard sale in which everything from our early years was tagged and discounted.

I knew I'd never get another doll as long as I lived. I would have to share her with Daffy, but not yet. I needed the princess to be only mine for just a little while. I stuck her between my mattress and the box spring. I told her I'd be back later as I carried the Happy Meal into Daffy's room.

I thought the pile of dirty clothes and the blanket in her bed was her, but when I pulled them back, there was nothing.

"Daffy?" I whispered. "Where you at?"

"Here," she whispered back.

"Where?" I turned on the light and stared at the twigs glued to the back wall of her room. Some of the twigs were held on by gum. Others by a paste made out of flour and water.

"What you think Aunt Clover's making in here?" Daffy stuck her head out from under the bed.

"Don't know." I shrugged.

Ever since we had the flu, Aunt Clover had been collecting twigs and sticks from outside, always carrying a plastic grocery bag with her to do so.

"Maybe it's a witch's spell," I said. "So we never get sick again."

I got down on all fours and peered into the darkness beneath the bed. "I brought you something, Daffy." I pushed the Happy Meal across the floor toward her.

"Give me." She reached out and grabbed it.

"Why are you under here?" I asked as I crawled beneath the bed to lie beside her.

She tore the box when she opened it, the arch handles something that'd never stand up again.

"There's only three nuggets left, Arc. And where's all the fries?"

"I had to eat, too, you know," I said.

With her mouth full, she asked where I'd gotten the Happy Meal.

"Aunt Clover." I lay back on the floor and stared up at the bottom of the box spring.

"Where's the toy?" she asked.

"What toy?" I shut my eyes.

"On the commercial they always get a toy," Daffy said. "Where is it?"

"You have to pay extra for that," I said. "You know Aunt Clover. She ain't gonna pay extra for a silly little toy."

Daffy licked the grease from her fingers as she laid her head back and scooted it over until it was touching mine.

"Why you under here?" I asked.

She wouldn't answer. For a while, all I focused on was the musty smell of pee coming down from the mattress through the box spring. I was going to ask her if she was wetting her bed again, but she was asleep by then.

I snuck out and returned to my room. I felt my hand under my mattress until I found the princess, then I climbed up into bed. I stared into her eyes and did a voice for her.

My name is Princess Moonriver. What's yours? she asked me.

"My name is Arcade," I told her. "But everyone calls me Arc."

Are you a princess, too? she asked.

"No. I'm just a girl. But my long-dead mamaw was a witch. They burned her at the stake. They burned Mamaw Milkweed, too. They'll probably burn me."

Who burned them? That man who was here? she asked, trembling in my hand.

"No, he's just a john."

What's a john?

"A man who takes things."

What has he taken?

"Everything," I said. "But he's gone now. He won't come back the rest of the night," I told her so she wouldn't be frightened anymore.

I spent a little more time stroking her hair and telling her how pretty her pink dress was.

Thank you, she said, because she was polite.

"And I like your crown," I told her.

Thank you.

"One day, I'll wear a crown, too."

I know you will, Arc.

"I better put you up. Someone could find you. You'll be my secret princess for a while."

Okay, she said. *I'll hide for you.*

I placed the princess back under the mattress.

"I miss you already," I told her as I lay back and stared up at the white and cracked ceiling.

"When we're taller, Daffy and me will reach the ceiling and draw on it, too," I said, wondering if the princess could hear me through the mattress. "We'll draw all kinds of things." I spoke louder. "Things that would be happy on a ceiling like birds and clouds and the blue sky. I'll draw you up there if you want me to."

I reached back into the mattress and grabbed her out.

"I only wanna hold you a little while longer," I told her. "I love you. Don't ever leave me. Please."

Night after night I'd speak to my secret princess and tell her one day we would both be queens. Night after night I'd put her back under the mattress. But each time I'd hold on to her a little while longer. The night I fell asleep, she'd felt so warm in my hand that I dreamed of castles and lands that were all our own. The sound of something cracking tore all that apart and woke me up to the pitch black of my bedroom.

"What the hell?" His voice was angry.

I quickly turned on the bedside lamp. The spider was back. When he lifted his foot, I saw the princess had been crushed on the floor beneath his big, ugly boot.

"You killed her." I got down on the floor by her broken body. "I hate you. You killed my friend. I wish you were dead."

I screamed until he slapped me in the mouth and told me to take my clothes off and get back up in the bed. I tried to concentrate on facts from history that night while his hot breath blew out on my face, but all I could think about was the princess, dead on the floor.

"Shut up your crying," he said.

No matter how much I tried, I couldn't. Instead, I got louder.

By the time Aunt Clover stumbled into the room, the man was still on top of me.

"What the hell is going on in here?" She turned on the ceiling light. "What the—get off her, you dirty motherfucker."

He just grinned and continued, his weight bearing down on me.

"Get out, you asshole," she screamed.

I could hear her fists landing on his bare back, making a smacking sound.

"Stop, stop it." Her voice was the loudest I'd ever heard it be. "Goddamn you. Get off her. Stop or I'll fucking kill you."

He reared back and slapped her across the face, causing her nose to bleed.

"Get out, bitch," he said, "or I'll slice you, ear from ear."

She backed against the wall, sliding across it on her way to the door. She started to walk a little too fast for him.

"Hey." He stood up. "Don't you think about going out there and calling no one. Y'hear?"

She nodded. Still he walked over to her and grabbed her head. He held it tightly between his palms as his fingers quickly tapped against her skin. I looked at the shadows cast on the wall. His eight arms were back.

"I could squash you like a bug," he told her as he pushed in so hard, her gaunt cheeks were shoved into her mouth.

"I'm not gonna do nothing." Her voice came out mangled. "I fucking swear."

Just when I thought her skull would be crushed, he dropped his hands. She fell to the floor, sobbing and crawling out into the hall in time to not get hit by the door he was slamming shut. I thought she might come back for me. *She's only going to get a knife out of the kitchen,* I thought. *Or a rock from the yard. Then she'll be back to save me.*

She never returned. I buried my face in the blanket as I heard the bed creak under his weight. I shut my eyes tight. When he finished he pulled up his pants and left.

I slid down to the floor and tried to put the princess together, but she broke right back apart.

"I'm sorry," I told her. "It's all my fault."

I waited for her to speak.

"Please," I said, "say something. Please don't leave me."

When she didn't speak, I threw her under the bed, scattering the pieces of her into the dark corners.

OUTSIDE THE ANGELS ARE ABSENT, FLYING AWAY AS THE BODY MATE-rializes into a brown matter known as corpse wax. If you be close enough, you will know its sickly, sweet scent. The river tries to wash it away, but it is difficult to interfere at this stage when death has its own promises to keep.

Creation ends the way it begins. With hunger.

By this time, it is hard to imagine the remains had ever been a person. Ever been someone who laughed at her father's jokes. Smiled at her mother's touch. Danced barefoot with her lover across the cold lino-leum of the kitchen floor. Her fingers had an identity that belonged to her. She was the rosemary, the red winter wheat, the houseleek, the pinkroot. Now she is not seen by the color of her eyes, the length of her grin, the flow of her hair. She is seen by the wax upon her. The rot in her mouth. The swell in her breasts. She is not heard by her song, her voice, her words. There is only the silence, when there is not the gentle chomping on what had once been a woman who walked the earth, unaware her death would overshadow her life.

CHAPTER 8

Hold on tight. With all your might.

—*Daffodil Poet*

THE NEXT MORNING, AS AN AERIAL VIEW OF THE GRAND CANYON LIT up the TV screen, Aunt Clover sat on the sofa with one arm out, her finger slowly tracing in the air the edges of the canyon.

"You'd love the Grand Canyon," she said as I sat on the sofa beside her, my braid fallen down over my shoulder and my shirt torn. "Did you know, Arc, there are layers of rock that are two hundred and fifty million years old, lying against rock that is over a billion years old. Where's all that record of time that was supposed to be in between? How can over a billion years of rock just be missing? No one knows what happened to all of it. It's called the Great Unconformity. Spittle, spittle, spider, where you gonna hide her?" Aunt Clover spit into her palm and got up to walk over to the TV, where she smacked her palm against the screen over the image of the canyon. "Right there."

When she returned to the sofa, she put her plastic grocery bag on her lap and started sorting the recent sticks and twigs she had collected.

"No one will ask me," she said, "but I know why that rock is gone. It's gone because the Grand Canyon is a woman who was once a little girl who was hurt. And she took the record of all that hurt and she buried it. Made it disappear. As if it never even happened in the first place."

I saw fresh blood added to her white belt as she turned to me.

"Don't tell your mom about the man," she said. "She wouldn't get over it. It would be too much for her to bear."

"Too much for *her* to bear?" I dug my fingernails into the sofa cushion.

Aunt Clover wiped the tear off my cheek.

"Things have changed for you now, Arc. You've got to be like the Grand Canyon. Make your hurt disappear. But not your heart. You've got to protect that from your own bitterness that will come for you now."

"What you mean?"

"You'll become angry, cruel even." She turned her eyes back to the TV as her hands searched on their own through the bag of twigs. "You have to keep a corner of yourself hidden from all that cruelty."

"How?" I asked.

She set the bag of twigs down on the floor by her feet as she reached for the empty paper box on the coffee table. The box was years old, dented in on the side, and had once held cookies but was now used as an ashtray. Aunt Clover examined the box, finding the cleanest flap, from which she tore a corner and handed it to me.

"Sometimes you gotta hold on to something to remember it exists," she said. "And when you remember it exists, you remember to protect it. Keep that corner safe, Arc. It's part of you."

She picked the bag of twigs back up and put it on her lap as I carried the corner into the kitchen. Daffy was sitting at the table, trying to find cereal in the bottom of an empty box.

"What's that?" she asked, pointing to my hand.

"Aunt Clover gave it to me." I slipped the corner into my pocket.

"Why?"

"I had a spider in my room. A big ugly one," I said. "The spider has crooked legs and thin lips that vanish when he smiles." I bent my arms up like spider legs. "He has black eyes. Oil is caught there. *Ooo, ooo.*" I came at her like a ghoul, but she didn't laugh.

She looked up at the spider's web in the corner of the kitchen. "The same spider has been in my room," she said in the hushed way all girls say the monster's name.

"What do you mean, Daffy?" I asked.

She dropped her eyes to mine. "You know what I mean," she said.

I searched my sister's face, seeing in her eyes the same eight-legged shadows on her walls.

"No, no, no." I grabbed her by the hand and yanked her to the sink. I threw the dirty dishes out and down to the floor, breaking the ones that were not plastic. Using the frayed rag, I held it under the warm water, then rubbed it up and down Daffy's arms.

When I started to scrub her face, she said, "You can't wash him off, Arc."

I threw the rag down and ran to Mom's room. The beads were on the knob, but I didn't care. I threw open the door. Mom was on the mattress with the john we called the Holy Ghost. She was putting a needle in his arm.

"Arc, get the fuck out of here," she shouted.

"Mom?" I ran in and tried to fall down on her lap. "You've gotta do something. There's a spider and he's hurting Daffy and me and—"

Mom got up and grabbed me by the arm, yanking me back to the door.

"Momma, you've gotta help us." I tried to slip out of her grip. "Momma, please. He's hurting us. The spider is hurting us."

She threw me out into the hall so hard, I fell down.

"I don't fucking care." She slammed the door.

"What are you doing, Arc?" Aunt Clover was standing at the end of the hall.

"I hate you." I got up and ran past her, grabbing Daffy by the hand along the way.

Together we escaped the house down the street as I tried to think of where to go.

At the stop sign by the corner, we saw the back of a policeman. He was removing the yellow tape from a house that a woman had died in a few days prior when she injected more than her veins could hold.

His black shirt was nicely ironed and was something I smiled at as we got closer and closer. I didn't care what telling the cops would mean for my mother or my aunt. I didn't care if they were taken away until time fell apart. All I knew was that I wanted to tell so I could save my sister, like the way little girls are saved from the monster on TV. I imagined the applause of an audience as we got the sitcom ending I was certain would come.

"Excuse me, policeman, sir." I rose on my toes and tapped him high on the back. "Sir?"

When he turned around, I realized spiders come out in the daylight and they wear official clothes to try to cover up who they are at night. But you can't cover up the eyes that look like black oil is caught there.

He looked at my sister and me, his badge gleaming in the sunlight in ways that made me want to capture it and set him ablaze.

"Go home," he said as Daffy huddled behind me, peeking around at the man who looked even taller in the daytime. "I'll see you tonight."

Who do you tell about the demons when the demons are the ones who you tell?

We could feel his eyes on us as we ran back down the empty street. The house seemed darker than we'd left it.

"Arc?" Aunt Clover's voice came from the sofa, but we ran past her, into my room, where we shut the door and stood against it as if he might come back then and there.

Daffy saw the princess's broken legs sticking out from the shadow under my mattress. She didn't say anything about it, except "Put the strings up into the square, Arc. Turn the savage side beautiful."

She went over and sat down, pulling the pieces of the princess out to lie on the floor.

"Once upon a time." I sat down beside her and picked up the red marker. "There was a spider who would come into the house at night." I began to draw scribbles around the body of the princess. "Mom would scream, 'Get that nasty spider out of the house.' But the spider couldn't be caught. We feared we would have to live forever with him. Then here came Dad, in his big army boots and his big army walk. He chased that spider down and squashed him beneath his boot heel.

"'No spiders allowed in my girls' rooms,' he said.

"Dad ground that spider's body until there was nothing left, not even one of his eight legs. The spider was destroyed, and Dad knew it would never, ever, come again for his little girls."

"But it's not true." Daffy watched me draw the scribbles. "No matter how much we try to turn the savage side beautiful, the spider is still alive. He'll still come for us, Arc."

"Then we won't be here." I threw the marker down and stood. "He can't get us if we're not here."

I went into Mom's room. This time it didn't matter, because her and the john were laying on the mattress with their eyes closed. I took

Dad's army bag she used as a blanket and carried it into my room. Daffy stayed on my heels, gripping the back of my shirt, as I packed the bag with a change of clothes along with a pillow and a blanket.

"Where are we going?" Daffy asked.

"Somewhere the spider will never find us," I said.

PREDATION, WEATHER, TIME. IT HAS ALL ALTERED THE BODY. IF NEVER found, the fish, crustaceans, and even turtles will remove the last of the flesh until there are only the bones.

They will sink to the mud at the bottom of the river, and she will keep them as the artifacts of the person they used to be.

P
A
R
T

II

OFFICE OF ROSS COUNTY MEDICAL EXAMINER
CHILLICOTHE, OHIO
REPORT OF INVESTIGATION BY COUNTY MEDICAL OFFICER

DECEDENT: Harlow Katie

OCCUPATION: Keeper of the birds

EYES: The color of her mother's

HAIR: A flame extinguished

DESCRIPTION OF BODY: Partly clothed, one wet sock, one baby shoe tied around wrist

GENDER: As female as the river

AGE: A flash of lightning

BODY TEMP: A blue chill

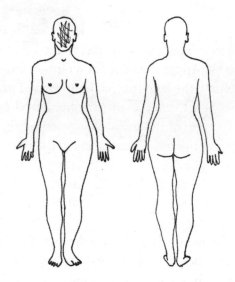

WOUNDS AND MARKS: Deep cuts on feet. She tried to run away. Moonchild. River mud in between the toes. River goddess. Fractured ankle. Faraway dancer. Multiple tattoos of birds in flight. Blue, yellow, pale green. Sweets found in stomach with still water. Blue, yellow, pale green, mud brown. Cigarette burns on left inner thigh. Traces of red lipstick in the cracks of lips and a constellation of bruises. Slits in ear lobes. Earrings are gone. The eyes are, too. Somewhere we'll never know. Her lungs are found to be overinflated, consistent with a woman lost to water. On top of her head, a crown of twigs and sticks. Moonchild. River goddess. Faraway dancer.

PROBABLE CAUSE OF DEATH:

Being a woman.

CHAPTER 9

I still burn. No matter how many flames I return.

—*Daffodil Poet*

1993

AS I STARED DOWN AT THE WOMAN FLOATING BEFORE ME, I THOUGHT of the trees. The old Appalachian chain wrapped around their rough bark, binding them to the land that has been cursed in smoke and rust and now dead women. I stared at the way her hair floated out around her head, and I thought of the trees. Their rings deep inside, recording history, all its lightning and thunder. Had the trees' rings recorded the dead woman? Was her body moving with the current in the heartwood as she had in the river's? Were her lungs full of the brown water in that infinite course? Or would she be allowed to finally breathe?

Her name? Her name?

I imagined the woman's mother, whether she had one or not, shouting as I swam her daughter's body across the river, my hands over the bruises on her arms. Around me, I heard the splashes and Mamaw Milkweed's voice.

"Swim now, girls. Kick your legs high. Keep your arms strong, but startled by any ripples. And in still water, float like a god-fearing leaf fallen down from the trees. There is water everywhere in this world, my darlings, but if you swim like you know all the secrets, you'll never drown."

The ghosts of Daffy and me as children swam by as I dug my heels into the mud and pulled the woman up onto the bank, the sunlight shattering against the shadows of the tree branches overhead. I fell down beside her. She who had floated like a feather, like a ripple, like a woman who wouldn't be home for dinner. And now she was like a stone, washed up on the bank, sinking down, little by little.

"I can't believe this is real," Sage Nell said. She was squeezing her fish magnet to her chest. "I just can't believe . . ."

We fell silent with the chill, studying the woman on the ground before us, trying to find her story. We weren't sure if that story was in the new cuts up and down her arms, or in the old ones, scarred over. Her ears were pierced, but no earrings were in them. It appeared they'd been ripped out, the skin torn into slits that divided each earlobe. Had the earrings she'd worn been jewels of brightly colored gems or just brown and green, like the farmlands? Maybe they would have been simple silver hoops that swung every time she laughed.

I imagined her as a woman who would hold her hand out when she'd walk by a chain-link fence to let her nails hit against the metal. Maybe she'd carved her name into a tree and picked her teeth when watched by the men with knives in their eyes. I couldn't stop imagining her life. In the winter, her pulling her coat tight against herself and pretending to smoke the cold air. I didn't know her enough to imagine the big moments of her life. I could only envision the small ones.

Her standing at the sink washing the milk out of her glass or keeping her eyes on the sky and the birds there. Maybe she'd even pinched her cheeks in the morning, to match the color of her lips. Her lips that had been eaten away as her eyes had. What was left were the leaves. Her mouth was full of them. The ones that had fallen early and turned brown. Caught in them was a thin piece of plastic off a hard candy or a cigarette pack or some other spiraling thing.

"Something is moving inside her mouth." Sage Nell pointed down. The leaves pushed out. A small black spider came crawling over her chin and down her neck, to the ground. Daffy and me watched until the spider disappeared into the tall grass. We turned back to the woman. Her bruises seemed lodged, as if someone had used a slingshot and fired rocks into her skin for all the time in the world. The cuts were as numerous. Some of them small, others deep. It was a wonder to me the wounds weren't like an arriving storm. Something that could split the trees and knock the electric out for days.

"Why the hell is she naked?" Thursday asked.

We looked from each other to the sock, tugged low on her left foot. It was the only thing she was wearing. A little more way down the river, she would have been found without it. What had she been dressed in before all her clothes were removed? I imagined her in a black shirt, tight, with a scooped-out neck and long sleeves that fell like bells over her wrists. The kind of shirt she'd wear tucked into jeans, loose on her hips. Maybe she would have entered some doors in high heels, but most of the time she wore sneakers, clothing herself for long walks, if not for something greater, like a migration. I could tell by the tattoos around her ankles. Tattoos of birds flying in circles. I imagined her heart, her mind, even her lungs opening like boxes and letting the life out of them as if it were all nothing more than those birds released from cages.

I got the feeling that her ghost was not so easily released and not even the insects who had eaten at her neck, nor the wild animals with their threatening hunger, could turn her ghost away, as if she would always be haunted by her own death, carrying the river on her back for eternity.

"We have to call the cops," Sage Nell said, her voice as unsteady as the rippling water behind her.

"No, thank you," Thursday said. "Are you fucking crazy? They'll bust us."

"We didn't kill her," Daffy said.

"We're not exactly angels." Thursday gestured to the needles on the ground. "Get the picture now, Chillicothe Queens? God." She sighed and threw her arms up. "I wish to fuck we'd never come down to the river today. Ain't nothing good can come out of stumbling around the riverbank. Why the hell did we even think there could be? I ain't ready for something we can't handle, and this here is something we cannot fucking handle. I gotta go home." She started picking up the needles and dropping them into her purse. "If I can even remember where the hell it is."

"We can't leave her." Sage Nell tried to stop Thursday. "She's—"

"She's already halfway to disappearing," Thursday shouted. "She ain't even got her eyes anymore. I done lost my own fucking eyes in this world. Ain't no way I can help her find hers."

"Arc?" Sage Nell turned to me. "Would you talk some sense into her?"

I laid my hand on the dead woman's hair. Stems and leaves were tangled in the strands. But at her crown, the twigs seemed to be tied. In certain places, even knotted.

"This is weird," I said, showing them a knot. "Don't you think?"

"Arc, stop touching her, for chrissake," Thursday said. "You've already left enough fingerprints on her already. They're gonna think you fucking killed her. You're gonna—"

Her eyes landed on the woman's arm.

"What is that?" Thursday asked, pointing down to a baby shoe tied to the woman's wrist by the shoelace. The shoe had once been white, but days of floating had discolored it to brown. The laces were frayed. The plastic tips at the end of them were already gone. The sole of the shoe was as filthy as if it had been walked from one end of the world to the other.

"I know that baby shoe," Thursday said, dropping to her knees by the woman. "She found it on the street. Said she was going to hold on to it until she found the foot it belonged to."

"You know her?" I asked.

"I didn't think at first. Looking as shitty as she is." Thursday moved the woman's hair off her chest, revealing a tattoo. It was swollen with the skin. The color had faded. Insects had eaten some of the ink away, but enough of it was visible to know it had been something with wings.

"A hummingbird." Thursday swallowed hard, keeping whatever was trying to come back up, down. "Yeah, I know her. Her name was Harlow. She was a new chick to the street. I wore crowns with her a couple of times. She was nice. I'd say fucking all right. I even thought she might one day like to come here with us to the Distant Mountain. I guess, in the end, she did."

"Where was she from?" Daffy asked.

"I asked her," Thursday said. "She told me she lived in the shadows or some shit like that. She never did say a whole hell of a lot about who she was, but I sure the fuck didn't think she was the type of woman to die when no one was looking."

I tried to tell if I had seen Harlow before. Tried to imagine her face without so much of it taken away.

"Last time I saw her," Thursday said, "she was sucking down a big blue slushy and showing me this tattoo." She laid her finger on the hummingbird. "She'd just got it. She said that when ducks leave for winter, hummingbirds hitch a ride on their backs, so they don't have to fly all that way themselves. She told me she was gonna be like the hummingbirds. Wait for a flock of ducks, then hitch a ride to warmer weather. When I ain't seen her for a while, I thought she ended up in Florida. Oh shit, Harlow." Thursday ran her finger gently across Harlow's face. "What the hell happened to you, girl?"

Thursday frowned as she stood up, wiping her hand on the side of her jeans.

"We gotta get back to my trailer and call the fucking pigs," she said.

"I thought you didn't want to?" Sage Nell asked.

"That was before I knew who she was," Thursday said. "All right? She had sat in my damn kitchen. I can't leave her out here for some starving animal to drag off. She deserves more than that. Right? We'll just tell the cops we came down to the river to celebrate a birthday. And that's all the fuck we were doing down here. And we happened to look out on the water and see something that shouldn't have been in it. Okay?"

Thursday slung her purse over her shoulder and looked one last time down at the woman we now knew as Harlow.

"All we have in this fucking life," Thursday said, "is what we can do the most of. The most of anything we can do now is to tell the world she's been found."

Who we told was the cop who came, his lights flashing, but his sirens off. He looked over at us and walked down to the river. He then came back up to smoke waiting for what he called the meat van to come pick up the body. Daffy and Thursday disappeared inside the trailer, leaving me and Sage Nell sitting on the porch steps, watching the flashing lights. I was looking down at a rock I'd picked up and was turning it over in my hand when I heard his voice.

"What's that you got there?"

I dropped the rock. A sudden sensation of nausea passed over me as I thought of the eight-legged shadows on my bedroom wall when I was a kid.

"I said what you got there?" he asked again. His words were slow. As slow as the steps I remembered him taking toward my bed at night. When I looked up, he was turned from me, but I saw his eyes.

As dark as oil. As lifeless as it, too. I quickly looked away before he saw my eyes.

"You all find the body?" he asked.

His suit was black, matching his shirt and tie. He chewed his gum, like most law enforcement, aggressively and in the corner of his mouth. He had stayed thin, his yellowed fingernails tapping against the black leather of his belt where his detective badge hung.

"What were you all doing that far down the riverbank?" he asked, looking at the trailer like he knew exactly the type of people who lived in it.

"We came to see the river," Sage Nell said as she nudged me.

"Yeah," I said, my voice shaking. "See the changing leaves. Shit like that."

"Today is her birthday," Sage Nell added. "We walked down to the water to celebrate."

"Mm-hmm." He switched his gum to the other side. "How old are you?"

"Twenty," I said, still keeping my eyes hidden.

"You were celebrating when you found the body?" he asked. "I bet I can guess what you were celebrating with." He smiled as he stuck his finger like a needle in his arm. When I looked up to watch him, he finally saw my eyes. He slowly dropped his hand and stared back at me as if staring at a ghost.

"Witches' marbles," he whispered under his breath.

I glanced down and said, "I found the dead woman in the water when I was walking out in it to see the Eye of God."

He slowed his chewing and tilted his head, his eyes fixed on me, studying everything he hadn't noticed at first glance.

"The Eye of God?" he asked.

"You know." Sage Nell wiped her nose on her sleeve, but kept her eyes down. "The way the leaves fall on the surface of the river. It looks like the Eye of God."

"If you stare into it, you can see your future," he said, nodding. "Ain't nothing but some hick horseshit. So?"

He stepped closer, his shadow falling over me. Somewhere in the distance, I could still hear the sound of the bed creaking under him and me burying my face in my tattered blanket.

"What?" I asked, standing up out of his shadow and leaning back against the wooden rail.

"Did you see your future?" he asked.

"I only saw the woman," I said.

"What do you think happened to her, sir?" Sage Nell whispered as she wrapped her arm around her stomach. "How do you think she was killed?"

"Overdose." He said it briskly, as if the case were already over.

"But she's naked," I said.

"And there's bruises and marks all over her body," Thursday said. She had appeared behind the screen door. "How the fuck do you explain that?"

He took a toothpick out of his pocket and started to clean his teeth with it.

"If you're a dead body," he said, "you don't want to end up in the river. It'll toss you this way and that way. And in this Ohio town, the currents are angry. Likely threw her into the rocks."

"The river didn't do all that to her," I said. "It couldn't have."

I glimpsed the top of the gold chain necklace he had tucked down beneath his collar. A blonde hair was sticking up from it and catching the sunlight.

"Well, it didn't do nothing more to her that she didn't do to her own damn self." He stared at only me for what felt like eternity, then turned to leave.

"Do you know him, Arc?" Sage Nell waited to ask until he was back in his black car.

"Yeah," I said.

"Who is the asshole?" Thursday asked.

"A spider." I looked up, watching the smoke from the paper mill float across the sky above us.

CHAPTER 10

In spite of the night, she will gather her eyes,
and burn bright.

—*Daffodil Poet*

1983

THE SMOKE FROM THE PAPER MILL FLOATED ABOVE DAFFY AND ME
the night we left home with our father's army bag dragging on the
pavement behind us.

"I already got a mean ache in my feet, Arc," Daffy said. "Where
we going?"

"The horses will tell us," I said, pointing up to the smoke. "Now,
stop acting like a dumb little bird."

"I'm not acting like no dumb little bird." She stood up straighter,
walking ahead.

Neither of us said the smoke from the paper was disappearing.
Had, in fact, already disappeared one block back. We merely kept on
until, a little while later, Daffy lowered her shoulders and said, "I'm
tired. Can't we sit for a bug's minute?"

She was already headed to the bench by the sidewalk.

"Daffy." I dragged my feet and the bag after her. "We have to keep
going."

"To where, Arc? We ain't got no rocket ship to take us to the stars.
We ain't got no submarine to take us to the whales. Heck, we ain't
even got your shovel to take us down to the center of the earth. This
bench here. This is the only place we have to go."

I looked up at the building the bench was in front of. It was large
and gray. Cinderblock, like our house. The sign in front listed all the
things the building had inside it. A gymnasium. A racquetball court,
and an indoor pool.

"We're at the recreation center," I said.

"Ugly place, ain't it?" Daffy turned around on the bench and sat on her knees. "A big gray nothing."

When she saw the words INDOOR POOL on the sign, she said, "Ain't never seen enough water inside a building to swim in it. Have you, Arc?"

"You know I ain't." I sighed. "We gotta keep moving. We haven't gone far enough."

"We've walked forever," she said.

"C'mon." I grabbed her arm and tried to yank her to her feet, but she wouldn't budge. "We got to keep going, Daffy. The smoke is leaving. If we wait any longer, it'll drift completely away."

"It already has, Arc. We don't have anywhere else to go. Besides, we don't have anything to survive with. We should have brought Daddy's hammer to have something to build with. Should have brought Momma's bottles to have something to drink. Should have brought Aunt Clover's nighttime scarf to have something to frighten the monsters back with. We didn't bring nothing but ourselves. And we ain't got enough magic to grow fruit out of the gutter."

"Fine." I threw the bag up onto the bench and sat down beside her, crossing my arms.

She laid her head on my shoulder and swung her feet.

"I'm sorry your plan didn't work, Arc. What we do now?"

The road was empty. The buildings on the other side were dark. Behind us, exterior lights shone on the recreation center. That seemed to be all there was. I used to believe if birds could soar, we could fly, too. But sitting there on that bench, I started thinking Aunt Clover must have been right when she said Daffy and me were just a couple of dumbasses, with nothing before us.

"Maybe we could live in the hills," I said.

"The wolves will eat us at night." Daffy growled.

"We could sleep up in the trees when it gets dark."

"The birds will peck out our hair and use it for their nests." She frowned.

"We could crochet ourselves hats so they can't get to our hair," I said.

"We'll end up like wild animals, drinking outta the river until it turns our teeth as brown as the water. We'll be so hideous, we'll have to live in the mist at the edge of the county. I don't want that, Arc. I don't wanna live in the mist. I definitely don't want brown teeth." She swung her feet higher. "Tell me about the Trung sisters, Arc."

I wrapped my arm around her and sighed. "They were sisters who lived a long, long, long time ago in Vietnam. They refused to be told what to do. Refused to be held down by the spiders around them. They rose up and fought and won. They ruled all on their own and became heroes. There's streets in Vietnam named after them even."

"I bet they're the prettiest streets," Daffy said. "You think we'll get a street named after us one day, Arc? If we ever find a place to go, that is?"

I looked around for some answer I could give her. When I stared back at the recreation center, I saw a figure standing in the light. The end of their cigarette glowed red.

"Daffy," I said, "there's a man back there."

"Who is it?" She scooted closer to me. "Is it Spider? Please say it's not him, Arc."

"It's not him," I said, looking back again to be sure.

"How you know?"

"He ain't tall enough. And his eyes reflect the light. He's wearing glasses. Spider never did wear any of those."

She turned and peeked at the man over the back of the bench.

"He's walking over here," she said. "Should we be scared? Because I am."

I gripped my sister's hand and our father's army bag, ready to run with both.

"Just ignore him," I told her. "He'll go away."

"He's not going away, Arc. He's coming over."

We listened to the fall of his footsteps.

"Are you lost?" His voice was gravelly like he hadn't used it in a while.

"Go away," I said, as both Daffy and me kept our eyes down. "Daddy will be here soon. He used to be in the army. He's got great big boots. If you hurt us, he'll hurt you."

Daffy buried her face in my shoulder as the man stood in front of us.

"I said leave—" When I looked up and saw his face, I nudged Daffy.

She raised her head from my shoulder. "Violin man?" Her eyes widened.

I stared down at his suede shoes. "Hey, you still got 'em," I said.

They were the same brown shoes he'd worn when he first showed up at our house after the accident. They were dirtier, with water stains that had set in. Gone was his white button-up shirt, khakis, and tie. They had been replaced with a dark green button-down and a pair of cotton work pants in the same color. They hung loose on his thin hips.

"He stinks," Daffy whispered into my ear as he reached into his shirt pocket. He pulled out a small blue bottle and took a large swig from it. His hair had not been brushed in some time. The hard gray aged him, as did the heavy beard. But we knew it was him. We would never forget his eyes. The color of the sky he had been looking at when he ran Mamaw Milkweed over.

"Do you still have the violin?" Daffy asked.

It took longer for him to recognize us. He leaned forward, looking about to turn over. As he found our eyes with his, he said, "One blue and one green." He held his mouth open for several seconds, then mumbled, "Amazing Grace."

He pointed over to the parking lot and the only car there.

"Violin," he said with a grunt. The word led into a coughing fit that only ended by the time the three of us got to the car.

"You never fixed it," Daffy said as she felt the edges of the dent that still carried the shape of Mamaw Milkweed. I set Dad's bag down on the ground and walked to the back, pressing my face against the window.

"What are you doing?" he asked.

"I'm looking for it," I said, cupping my hands around my eyes to see better. "If you still have the car and you still have the dent, maybe you still have the violin in the exact same place it was that day."

"Do you see it?" Daffy joined me at the window.

"It's too dark," I said. "Wait. I think I see something." I made out a shape on the back seat, but it appeared larger than any violin case. "There's something—"

"Why do you have this?" He held up Dad's old army bag. "Hey, I'm talking to ya. Get away from my car now."

I dropped my hands from the window and stepped back.

"What is this for?" he asked again of the bag.

"It's got a change of clothes—"

"For running away," Daffy interrupted me.

"Would you shut up." I elbowed her.

He frowned at me. "What are you up to?" His voice had grown harder than it was when we first met. He had lost the last bit of kindness he'd had, drowned it away with the bottle he kept drinking from.

"There's a spider in our house," I said while he tore open the bag and looked inside.

"Where you running away to?" His frown got harder.

"Don't know," I said. "Don't really have any place, I guess."

"Maybe to the pool here," Daffy said. "Maybe that'd be okay."

"You think you're gonna stay here?" He handed the bag back to me. "This isn't a motel."

"There's a spider in our house," I said again.

"Why don't you kill it?" He shrugged as he kicked a piece of gravel under his car.

"Like you killed our mamaw?" I asked.

He turned to me, a stiffness in his eyes. When he started to grind his teeth, I looked down.

"Look." He softened his tone. "You can't stay here, all right?"

"Why not?" Daffy asked.

"Who you live with now?" He took a drink out of the bottle.

"Aunt Clover and Mom," I said.

"Won't they wonder where you're at?" he asked, wiping his mouth on his sleeve.

"They won't check," I said. "They don't do things like that."

"I can't let you stay here." He started to pace. "I could get into trouble. I would lose my job. And right now, it's the only thing I have."

"Please." Daffy's voice was small. "The spider will be back, and he'll be angry. He might make his web so big, we'll never get out of it. Mamaw Milkweed would want you to help us."

He looked through Daffy to the dent and clenched his jaw. "You can't tell anyone you're staying here."

"You don't have to worry about that," I said. "No one cares what happens to a Doggs girl."

He turned and quickened his pace toward the side doors marked as the maintenance entrance as he said, "Always come in this door. Less chance of anyone seeing you."

"Boy, this place is bigger and grayer up close," Daffy said. "I'm gonna call it Big Gray."

Inside, the hallway was cold and empty. Daffy and me grabbed hands as we followed him under the flickering and harsh glare of the overhead lights.

"You can get food out of here." He stopped along the way at the chip and candy vending machines. "There's this one if you're thirsty." He tapped on one with several varieties of pop.

"Don't have no money." I eyed the candy bar in front of me as I licked my lips.

"Here." He sighed, reaching into his pocket.

He picked through cigarette butts and loose change to find a wadded-up dollar bill.

"Get what you want." He handed it to me.

"Thanks." I dropped Dad's army bag to iron out the wrinkles of the dollar against the edge of the machine. After I fed the money in, I had to wait for Daffy to make her decision.

"That one." She pointed to a candy bar that had peanuts and caramel on the wrapper.

"My cousin manages the building during the day," he said, leaning against the machine as the candy bar fell. "It's because of him I even got this job in the first place. I'm damn lucky to have it. Don't go ruining this for me."

I nodded as I broke the candy bar in half and gave the bigger one to Daffy as he took another swig out of the bottle.

"We all have our habits," he said when he saw us staring. "I'm on the mend, though. I'm in the empty bottles club. AA. You hear of it?"

We nodded.

"I haven't missed a meeting yet," he said. We watched him walk down the corridor to the rolling cart of cleaning supplies at the end of it. "My name is John, by the way." He stopped at the cart.

Daffy giggled.

"What's so funny?" he asked.

I realized I was giggling myself. "Nothing." I was quick to answer. "John."

While he took another drink, Daffy whispered in my ear, "He's a john. Can we trust him?"

"He's not a john," I whispered back. "He's just John. There's a difference."

"How?" She already had her candy eaten.

"Because," I said, "John was the name his parents gave him when he was still a baby, before he was even a man."

She took a bite out of my half as we watched him wipe his mouth in one long gesture across his sleeve. "Hey, you wanna see the pool?"

John didn't walk fast enough for Daffy. She stayed on his heels, following the smell of chlorine with her nose. It led us through a locker room and showers that opened to the large swimming area. The walls were painted peachy pink and hung with pool safety posters that had cherub-faced kids who looked to be leftovers from the 1960s. There was a small set of metal bleachers on the left side and a darkened office on the right with a large window. The door at the back had a sign leading to the sauna, and a black bathing suit had been left to dry on one of the two diving boards.

I looked up into the yellow and dim lights hanging from the ceiling where the wires and pipes were painted the same peachy pink as the walls. Daffy took off her shoes so she could slap her bare feet loudly against the beige tiles on the floor around the pool. It was larger than I imagined an indoor pool could be, the teal and white spiraling dividers creating several lanes.

"Do you remember when we used to go to the river with Mamaw Milkweed?" Daffy asked as she dipped her toe in and moved it around in large sweeping motions.

"Of course." I dipped my own toe in. "She taught us to swim."

"I miss going to the river with her, Arc."

If it was dirt that sang to me, it was water that sang to Daffy. We were sisters of the rocks and ripples. While I dreamed of the earth and the dust of time, she dreamed of rivers, lakes, and bodies of water that would carry her on the current. When she was on dry land, she was only half the girl she truly was. After Mamaw Milkweed died, Daffy had stopped swimming in the river, altogether. I would still catch her, though, sometimes lying on her bed on her back, her arms moving as if the air was water. She practiced her breath as she hung her head off the side of her bed, not breathing for as long as it took her to count the petals of the flowers we'd drawn on her bedroom wall.

"Is it okay to get in?" I asked John, who nodded as he took another drink, his eyes at times nothing but one drop of the liquor colliding with another.

"I'm gonna touch the bottom," Daffy said as we both dove into the water, our clothes still on and clinging to our skin.

Once Daffy came to the surface, she kept swimming down the lane to the other end, while I hung back on the edge, looking up at John, who stood over me.

"Don't go drowning on me now," he said. "That'll put me away for so long, there's no more time to come out to on the other side. I'll be left to lie in the dust. My face, a cup . . . a cup of bitter poison." He stared at the liquor sloshing in the bottle, then took a long drink.

"You don't have to worry," I said. "I'm a good swimmer. Not like my sister, though. She's the best."

"I sink." He looked down in the water. "When you're the son of a stone, you can't expect much else."

"You're the son of a stone?" I took a mouthful of water in, then spit it back out like a fountain.

"My momma drowned in the crick behind our house when I was a boy." He licked his lips, getting the last drops of the drink there. "I was the one who found her, floating facedown."

He got closer to the edge of the pool.

"Floating facedown," he said again.

He let himself fall forward, landing with a splash. His body bobbed until he floated across the surface, his face down, the blue bottle drifting out from him and filling with water until it sank as Daffy's thin legs kicked off the wall, making a turn into a new lap.

CHAPTER 11

The girl cries, the spiders spinning. She'll run.
Them all just a grinning.

—*Daffodil Poet*

1993

THE DAY OF HARLOW'S SHOWING, I WORE THE SAME BLACK DRESS MY mother had worn the day my father was buried, and I thought of the patch of tilled ground in front of Mamaw Milkweed's farmhouse. A patch of ground she kept unplanted and always wore her boots for, so she could weather the disturbed edges. It was what she called the uneven and crooked ground that made the line between the grass of the yard and the dirt of the patch. She told Daffy and me that the disturbed edges had taken the women in our family generations to braid.

"What do you mean by 'braid,' Mamaw Milkweed?" I had asked, thinking of how she braided our hair.

"I mean breathing," she said, "then after a long while, not breathing and taking those lost inhales and exhales, braiding them with mud until the earth makes a deep bowl of memories that are so powerful, the edges push through the layer of soil and rock, disturbing the generosity of level ground. Do not be frightened of disturbed edges, girls. Instead, let them remind you that you inherit the power to braid your life with the earth."

I thought of Harlow. Her body first braided into the river, soon to be woven with the ground, casting up the disturbed edges of her story. The story that led to her mouth being full of leaves.

"A part of me doesn't want to know what happened to her," Daffy said as we walked to the funeral home. "A part of me wants to think she caught a breeze in her hand and held on to it long enough for it to become a wind that blew her into the river. Nothing worse than that."

"Wasn't the wind that blew her into the river," I said. "It was the breath of a man."

"You don't believe what the spider said at Thursday's trailer?" she asked. "That it was only an overdose and nothing more?"

"When I looked at Harlow," I said, "I felt like something had reached out and grabbed her, laid her down on that water, and kicked her out into it."

"I suppose that's why we're going to her showing?" Daffy asked.

"Naw. We're going because it's what needs to be done."

I'd asked Sage Nell and Thursday to come with us. They said they didn't want anything more to do with it. They wanted to forget Harlow, all raw-boned and pale. And the river, with its ripples and deep dark depths.

"It's bad luck," Sage Nell said, "hanging around death. It's like walking in tall grass. There're things in it you don't want to know about. But if you go out far enough, you'll wish you weren't so distant from home, Arc. Funerals, no matter how close, always make you feel miles away from a safe place. Take it from this Sage and let the rest of the world walk in that tall grass."

The showing was held at the kind of funeral home that still had orange-toned wood paneling from the 1970s. The carpet smelled of dust and decades of perfume, while the funeral director solemnly nodded with his hands clasped behind his back.

"We don't have to stay long, do we?" Daffy asked as we stepped inside, wiping the mud off our shoes on the mat. "I don't like being in this place. Body after body coming through here from everywhere and nowhere. It's a place of large hands, Arc. Large enough to gather a person's whole life and put it in a coffin like there ain't nothing to it, but moving a pile of sticks from one place to another."

"Yeah." I lowered my voice. "I bet there's a mad dog that lives under the back porch and a door in here that always closes on its own."

"Don't say things like that, Arc."

"Don't worry, Daffy. We won't stay long," I said. "At least not long enough to see that door close on its own."

The room was not overly full. Those in attendance seemed to be the extended family who were growing old. Often their whispers to one another were followed by a cough or an uncle putting an unlit cigarette to and from his lips, deciding whether to go outside to light it.

We looked around for familiar faces but only saw one. Violet. Hers was a face most everyone on the street knew. She had what Mamaw Milkweed would call a rippling life. Someone who was never still. In Violet's case, her movement boiled down to her either being an addict or being sober. At the moment, she was the latter.

Violet always reminded me of images on stone tablets. The ones dug up with the old sand, their carved edges of women with long necks and arms and a look in their eyes that was at once both near and far. She had a strong face. The angles of the jaw, the broad dome of her forehead. A hieroglyphic of an entire civilization, dressed in shimmering lights.

We called her Butterfly Eyes at times, because of the way she mixed blue, yellow, and orange eyeshadow below her brow, like the wing of a butterfly. She often bit her lip as if she was running a to-do list in her mind. In another life, I imagined she'd put her energies into keeping a stocked root cellar for her family, expending calories stirring boiling jams and jellies.

When Violet was sober, she dyed her hair a color that in the box was called Purple Wind. It came out the shade of the flowers she was named after. A hue that remembered a long-ago season of spring and the blossoms that push through the ground. She would part her hair down the middle, revealing the tattoo on her scalp that read I AM IMPORTANT. When she was back to the needle, her hair would be brushed over, the tattoo and its words lost to her until she found them again.

"I'm glad you're here." Violet hugged Daffy and me at the same time.

"You smell like vanilla," I told her.

The small silver spoon earrings she wore dangled down to her shoulders.

"I put some on my neck after I baked the cookies," she said, gesturing to a long table against the wall that had some refreshments, among which was a platter of sugar cookies cut in the shapes of birds and frosted in a rainbow of color. She picked up one.

"It's a bird that hums," she said. "I figured Harlow would have liked that."

Violet was a cloud of flour. A pile of sugar on the kitchen counter. Her oven always seemed to be on in her trailer, her mitts thin from years of use. She'd drive around the worst streets of Chillicothe, where the dogs walked with their heads down and the women often had a day's worth of a black eye. She'd hand food out to those she knew could do with something in their stomachs other than the motion of hustling.

"Thank you, Mother Violet," those on the street would say. Maybe she did it all so she could hear someone call her "Mother" every day. She had an eight-year-old daughter, but she lived with Violet's ex-husband. The first thing Violet did upon meeting someone new was to pull out a wallet that had an accordion of photos of her daughter.

"I named her Grassy," she'd tell you, "because when I was carrying her, she moved inside me like a field of grass."

She had photos from her daughter's current age of eight, dating back to her infancy. She would linger on these photos the longest as she spoke about how quickly time goes by.

"As fast as something we don't understand," she'd say.

Daffy and me weren't surprised to find Violet at the showing. She attended every one for those who had walked the streets of Chillicothe with holes in their arms.

"To remind myself," she'd say, "of how easy it is to love something that'll never love you back."

Daffy took the cookie from Violet's hand, broke it in half, and kept the bigger one for herself. I didn't mind. I wasn't hungry, not in that small room with the walls closing in.

Violet pointed out Harlow's parents, who sat in chairs up by the pale pink casket. The mother kept getting up and walking, cringing with each step, as if she had rocks in her shoes. The dad kept excusing himself to the bathroom and would come back minutes later with redder eyes than before and a fresh tissue in his fist.

"I'll catch up with you later," Violet said, giving Daffy and me another hug on her way to greet someone else she knew.

"You gonna eat that?" Daffy asked about my half of the cookie still in my hand.

"Naw." I laid it down on the table. I thought she would pick it up, but instead she nudged my side.

"Isn't that the guy from the Blue Hour?" She pointed to the man standing slumped against the wall. "What's his name again?"

"Welt," I said.

He'd started working at the Blue Hour a few weeks prior. He did janitorial duties. There were some who called him the motel's maid. It went with his moplike haircut and his dishwater blonde hair falling into his eyes. He reminded me of a hawk. Not because of the profile of his nose, but because his eyes darted about the room as if always studying the slightest movement around him.

He was dressed as he always was at the Blue Hour. Thick slouchy socks pushed down over tan ankle boots. Long denim shorts. A tie-dyed shirt and a mauve knitted vest. Only the colors of the shirts and shorts seemed to change. The boots, the socks, the vest were all linchpins, as was the red leather glove, slim fitted on his right hand. Though I'd always thought the leather glove had something to do with cleaning, there were rumors as to why he wore it, and everyone seemed to have a theory.

"His hand might be twisted with scars," Sage Nell had said. "From a fire he thought would be just a flame. He looks like the type of man to play with matches."

Thursday said the glove hid the absence of a hand. "He leaned against the wrong fucking dog." She clamped her teeth on her fingers and snarled.

I knew a missing hand wasn't the case, and so did she. We'd seen all ten of his fingers moving in sign language. He was the only deaf man we'd ever known, and as he signed, we would all stare at the gloved hand, waiting to see if its secrets would be revealed, but the glove stayed tucked tightly in his sleeve.

"Why is he here at Harlow's showing?" Daffy asked.

"To pay his respects?" I shrugged.

"He's only been working at the Blue Hour a few weeks," she said. "I'd never seen him hanging around with anybody but his cleaning cart. Harlow wouldn't have been friends with him."

"You don't know that, Daffy. Besides, we didn't know Harlow either, but we're here."

"Yeah, but we're the ones who found her. If you find someone in the river, you got a hell of a good reason to be at their burying."

Welt slowly turned his head to us, staring out behind his long hair.

"Oh, he sees us." Daffy tried to hide behind me.

He clenched and unclenched his gloved hand as he slipped out the front door, his knitted vest blowing to the sides.

"He reminds me of the monsters in Mamaw Milkweed's old stories." Daffy stayed hidden behind me. "The ones who set the fires and steal the dreams." Her body shook in a chill. "I'd ask if we can leave, but he's probably out there now, creeping around, leaving black smudges from things he's already burnt."

"I'm sure he's harmless, Daffy. You coming with me?" I nodded toward the casket. "To see Harlow?"

"Naw." Daffy shook her head. "I seen enough of her back at the river to last a lifetime."

I slowly walked down the aisle. A part of me expected to get up there and find Harlow as I first had. Floating facedown in water, the coffin holding the leaves and twigs floating with her. I was almost surprised to find her faceup, her light red hair brushed and her long-sleeved white dress neatly ironed until it was but a smooth surface. Perhaps the funeral director had suggested a closed casket would be best. Instead, they let her lie there, with nothing more than a lacy veil covering her face in the same pale pink as the casket itself. The lace did little to take away the reality of what had already been eaten away or decomposed in the river. But I suppose her parents were the type of folks who delayed closing that lid for as long as they could.

I slipped my hand into my pocket, wrapping my fingers around the small rock I'd gotten that morning.

"I have something for you," I told Harlow. "A little jewel."

I took the red lipstick out of my purse and used it to color the rock. I placed it under her hand as I said, "I won't forget you, Harlow."

When I met up with Daffy by the door, her foot was tapping. "Can we leave now?"

I nodded.

Once we were outside, she let out a great exhale. "Felt like if I stayed in there any longer, they'd try to put me in a coffin."

As we walked, I didn't raise my eyes from the sidewalk in front of us.

"What'd you put in there with her, Arc?" she asked.

"A rock."

"Why'd you color it with lipstick?"

"To turn it into a red jewel," I said. "So that if her grave is ever dug up by a new civilization in the future, they will see it and know she was a queen."

We walked silently against the roar of the passing cars. It wasn't until we were stopped at a red light on the next block that Daffy said, "I wonder."

"You wonder what?" I asked.

"Who will do the same thing for us when it's time."

We walked with traffic down to an intersection that came out of several stores. People's cars full of freshly bought groceries, clothes, or something from the hardware store.

"Wish me luck," she said, reaching into her purse and pulling out a folded piece of cardboard. On it she had written, PLEASE HELP— NEED MONEY FOR HEART SURGERY FOR MY BABY in black marker.

She had cut the photo of a baby out from a diaper ad in a magazine and taped it to the cardboard, just below the words.

I headed to the opposite side of the intersection to catch the traffic going the other way. Tied around my waist was my father's old army jacket that I'd taken down from the window in the bathroom. I slipped it on and pulled his dog tags out from under my collar. I'd folded my own sign up in my wide purse. I grabbed it out and held it up: HOMELESS AND WOUNDED VETERAN.

Some days people dropped money into my can, it seemed, with relative frequency. But those days were few and far between. The black dress wasn't helping. It didn't quite go with the camouflage and sign.

I looked over the tops of cars speeding by and stared at Daffy. She was crying and shaking her fists in the air. It was part of her hustle. She was weeping for her baby and its weak heart that she needed money for.

She reminded me of something scattered. Like the empty nut shells Mamaw Milkweed would gather from the bowl in the kitchen and toss out into the yard. The pieces landing separate from one another, never to be whole again. If you would have told me this would be Daffy's future, I wouldn't have believed you. The future I had seen for her was as a great swimmer. The kind history remembers in world records and gold medals. The kind of life she herself dove into the water and held her breath for.

CHAPTER 12

In the past there is a song.
The one who sings it, can't always be wrong.

—*Daffodil Poet*

1984

DAFFY STOOD, HER TOES GRIPPING THE EDGE OF THE POOL, HER BODY bent forward, arched toward the still surface of the water. She had her arms out in front of her, her hands together, her fingers pointed in the direction she was heading.

"Say Daddy's in the bleachers watching me, Arc." She narrowed her eyes on the water, her braid pinned to the top of her head. "Say Mamaw Milkweed is standing at the other end of the pool, waiting for me. But most importantly, say ready, set, go."

"Daddy's in the bleachers watching you," I said behind her. "Mamaw Milkweed is standing at the other end of the pool, waiting for you. But most importantly, ready, set, go."

I shouted as she dove into the water, the splash exploding toward the ceiling lights. Nearly the entire night, Daffy swam laps at the recreation center we called Big Gray.

"I'm swimming all the way to your Nile River, Arc," she said. "I'll bring you back the best piece of the pyramids."

After school, we would go home to make an appearance and remind Aunt Clover and Mom that we still existed. Neither of them asked where we went at night, nor where we spent most afternoons, which was at Big Gray's pool. We snuck in so Daffy could race the other swimmers. She had to do so in her clothes because she didn't have a swimsuit. The kids made fun of her, but she still beat them in the water even if she had to do it in shorts and a T-shirt.

Walking the pool was a woman who had the broad shoulders of someone who had been familiar with chlorine most of her life. Her name was Tam. She was the coach for Big Gray's swim team. She had been watching Daffy each day, carefully studying her. When she blew her whistle and told Daffy to get out, Daffy stood there, wide eyed, dripping in her clothes.

"What's your name?" Tam asked.

"Daffy."

"Like Daffy the Duck?" Tam grinned.

"Not like some duck." My sister stood taller. "My full name is Daffodil Poet, but everyone calls me Daffy. Am I in trouble or something? Whatever I did, I'm sorry. I won't do it again. Don't kick me outta the pool. Okay?"

"You're not in trouble," Tam said. "I wanted to tell you that you swim fast. You ever try it in a bathing suit?"

"Don't have one." Daffy lowered her head.

"But you like swimming?" Tam asked.

Daffy raised her eyes. "It's everything. I wanna swim until the end of time. And then I wanna know where the river goes after that. Wherever she goes, I'll go with her. I have to, you know. See my blue eye." She pointed to it. "I'll always be part of the water."

"You've got a fish's heart," Tam said. "Would you like to be on the swim team?"

"Am I allowed?"

"Of course." Tam laughed. "But you'll need some things. A swimsuit for one. And a pair of goggles and a cap. Have your parents come see me. They can get those things when they sign the permission slip."

"Permission slip?" Daffy bit her lip.

Tam blew her whistle at two kids in the pool who were playing rough. "Cut that out," she told them.

After the kids separated, Tam turned back to Daffy. "You'll need a permission slip signed by one parent, or your legal guardian. You can't be on the team without it."

"Do they have to sign the slip in person?" Daffy asked.

"No." Tam moved her eyes across Daffy's face. "But usually the parents like to meet me."

"My mom is very busy. She's a"—Daffy looked at me—"an arc. An architect. She's very busy making tall buildings that birds make their nests at the top of. I could take the slip home to her. Bring it back to you, signed."

"You could do that," Tam said. "But I would like to meet your mother at some point."

"Oh, sure." Daffy nodded. "Of course. She'd love to meet you."

Daffy followed Tam into the glass-enclosed cubby by the pool. Taped to the window were various newspaper articles about swim meets. Daffy read them standing up on her toes while Tam searched through her drawers.

"Here's a slip." Tam handed it to Daffy. "You bring this back, and you'll be set for this year. You'll be behind the other girls, but our first meet isn't for a while, so you'll have time to practice."

"It says there's a thirty-five-dollar fee." Daffy pointed out the bold lettering on the bottom of the paper. "What if I can't pay that?"

"It's the same fee for everybody. You're a wonderful swimmer, Daffy, but I can't hold you to different standards." Tam ran out of the office to once again blow her whistle at kids splashing one another.

"Mom will never give us the money," Daffy said on our way home. "Neither will Aunt Clover."

"We'll worry about the money later." I wrapped my arm around her wet shoulders. "We can go ahead and get the slip signed."

When we got home, we went into Mom's bedroom and placed a pen into her limp hand.

"Momma, you gotta sign this." Daffy tried to tighten Mom's grip on the pen. "C'mon, stop being a lazy cat."

"Go away. Momma's sleeping," our mother moaned. The hole in her mattress was larger. She'd started to take the coils and foam out, so she had more room to shove in all the things she stole from the johns. It was making the mattress lumpy and lopsided.

I climbed up onto the lumps and slapped Mom in the face. "Wake up." I held a scream for five seconds as Daffy counted them on her fingers.

"Goddamn it. Shut up, Arc." Mom screamed louder than me. "What the fuck do you want?"

"You gotta sign."

"Right here." Daffy laid the paper on her flat palm to give Mom a surface.

Mom grabbed the pen. With a great sigh, her signature veered into a downward spiral until half of it was off the edge of the paper.

"Happy?" she asked, letting the pen roll out of her hand as she turned over and closed her eyes.

"Yes," Daffy said. "Yes, I'm very happy."

Mom sat up again, the paranoia growing in her eyes. "What the fuck did I sign, Arc?" she asked. "You're always up to something. You're like sharp glass on the floor at night. Just waiting to cut my feet to pieces." She moved her fingers quickly through the air like she was picking at it. "You won't be happy until I have a scar like you."

She grabbed my foot and made me fall down as she dragged her finger across the scar I'd gotten that night the john choked her and I stabbed him with the arrowhead.

"Momma, stop," I said. "You're hurting me."

"You want me to be marked like you, you little demon." She pushed my foot back. "Now what did you have me sign away?" She slammed her fists into the mattress over and over again.

"Something that gives me the chance to swim," Daffy said. "That's all."

"Swim? Splash, splash, huh?" She laughed, and it was cruel. "You're half of the same dead fish."

She mumbled and lay back down as Daffy and me ran out.

"I'm on the swim team now, Arc." Daffy waved the paper in my face.

"We still need the fee," I reminded her.

"Oh, that's right." She quickly lost her smile. "Thirty-five dollars. Where will we get that kind of money?"

"I think there's someone who might help."

When we got to Big Gray that night, I carried Dad's army bag, freshly packed, to our sleeping spot in the arts and crafts room while Daffy ran to find John. As soon as she found him, she started talking about swimming this and swimming that. By the time she got to "thirty-five-dollars," he didn't know what she was saying.

"Calm down now, Arc." He held his head and said it was pounding.

"I'm Daffy." She threw her hands on her hips.

"I'm sorry," he said. "What are you asking me?"

"I'm going to be on the swim team."

"You are? Well." He reached into his pocket and took out the small blue bottle, taking a drink. "Congratulations, I guess."

"I can't be on the team unless I pay the fee," she said, her voice rising to its highest pitch. "It's thirty-five dollars. I was wondering . . ." She looked down at the floor. "Maybe you might give me the money? I could pay it back."

"You want *me* to give you the money?"

"Only thirty-five dollars," she said. "It's not everything."

He used the wall to steady himself as he reached into his wallet, sighing when he went through its contents. "I only have five bucks, kid."

"That's not enough." She cried into her hands.

"Calm down now." It took him several tries to get the wallet back into his pocket. "I got a buddy down the block who owes me. I'll be back in a few minutes."

"John, wait." I ran up after him. "Give me your car keys."

"I gotta go. I gotta . . ." He pulled the keys out of his pocket.

"You can walk there," I said. "You don't wanna hit another mamaw, do you?"

He gripped the keys so tightly, I thought he wouldn't hand them over. Then his eyes looked off, and he dropped the keys not into my hand but to the floor with a loud rattle that echoed off the walls.

After he left, Daffy got into the pool to do her laps. I started cleaning the toilets in the locker room. I imagined I was washing the stones of Machu Picchu with the water of their river and the soil of their land, readying the empire for the ruler of the Inca to stroll through and claim her place. The basketball courts disappeared and became mountains, the floor became rock and dirt, and the ceiling broke away to the fog of Peru.

By the time the fog started to disappear, I was yawning and putting away the mop and broom, having done John's entire shift that night. When I finally got the chance to lie down beside Daffy and get some sleep, I heard John. He had returned and was singing "Amazing Grace" through the corridor downstairs.

"He's back." Daffy woke up. "Finally."

She couldn't get to her feet fast enough. I lay there a second more, my hands still smelling of the soap from the bucket and my eyes so very tired.

"Wait up, Daffy." I ran after my sister.

I found her and John downstairs by the vending machines.

"You get the money?" she asked. "Hey." She tugged his sleeve. "You get the money?"

"Sure, kid." He rained several bills down over her head. As she picked them up off the floor and counted them, I asked him where he'd been.

"I stopped to pet a little doggie along the way," he said, adjusting his shirt as if he were wearing a tie.

"You've been gone all night." I stomped my foot. "I had to do your whole stinking job, all by myself."

I reached out and caught him, saving him from falling on his face. My arms shook as I tried to bear his weight. I managed to hold him up against the wall, where he slid down and laid his head on the floor.

"You can't lay here," I told him. "They'll find you in the morning. You'll lose your job. Daffy and me won't have anywhere to go at night. Don't you understand that?" I shook him. "We need you, or the spider will get us again."

He looked up at us, wiping his mouth. "I'm so . . . I'm sorry," he said.

He got on all fours, using the wall to stand up by himself.

"I'm sorry. I wasn't thinking." He started slapping his own face. "Stupid, stupid, stupid—"

"Stop it." I pushed him.

"I just—" He suddenly turned and vomited on the money in Daffy's hands.

"You ruined it," she screamed. "You stupid man, you ruin everything." She ran toward the bathroom, the money dripping in her hand and leaving a trail of vomit.

"I ain't no good for no one." He slid back down the wall.

While he fell asleep on the floor, I mopped the vomit up.

Then Daffy and me were able to get John to his car before any workers came.

"Thanks," he said as we helped him into the back seat to sleep the rest of it off. I threw the keys in the front.

"I hate him," Daffy said as she slammed the car door shut. She had cleaned the vomit off the money best she could and dried it with the hand dryer in the locker room. Later that day, after school, she proudly presented it, along with the permission slip, to Tam.

"It's official then," Tam said, handing Daffy a dark green bathing suit, a pair of white goggles, and an orange swim cap. "Welcome to the team, Daffy."

She jumped up and down, squealing loud enough that everyone in the pool stopped swimming, believing it was the high-pitched shrill of Tam's whistle.

Later that night Daffy modeled her bathing suit and goggles. It had taken her some time to learn how to put the rubber cap on over the flame on top of her head.

"Well done." John clapped when he saw her. "You'll be the best fish in the pool."

He was as sober as we'd ever seen him.

"I'm sorry about last night," he said. "I won't drink again. I promise. This time it's gonna stick. I'm gonna get sober. You believe me, Arc, don't you?"

"Sure," I said, aware of how many promises one person can break. "Sure, John."

I watched him all that night, pushing the cart around the building. I watched him reach into his jacket for the bottle, the blue glass picking up the glare of the overhead lights as he touched it to his lying lips.

CHAPTER 13

I will choke on my needs, for even evil has its seeds.

—*Daffodil Poet*

1993

IN THE WEEKS THAT FOLLOWED HARLOW'S BURIAL, I WOULD WAKE UP with the taste of dirt in my mouth, the feeling of little rocks on my tongue. I got the sensation of larger rocks embedded in my gums, the presence of long, slender twigs collecting in the back of my throat. Mamaw Milkweed used to call it wild mouth. She would whinny as a horse when she said it.

"It always comes when a girl or woman gets a taste of death," she'd told Daffy and me. "Wild mouth. A name as naked as the grief."

Her whinny would be so high-pitched, we'd have to cover our ears.

"How do we get rid of it, Mamaw Milkweed?" I had asked.

"Well, you never get rid of it, honey. You just pretend you do."

Daffy reminded me that I got wild mouth after Dad died, too.

"You're strange with death, Arc," she said. "You rake it inside you, like a pile of leaves in the autumn. You rake it all up into this giant heap. Make it something you can carry. I didn't think you'd do it for Harlow, but I guess if you find someone in the river, you're bound to carry it with you."

"It's because I can't stop thinking about her," I said. "Floating in that cold water."

"Even colder now," Daffy said.

It was no longer October. The branches were bare, and we could see our breath when we exhaled.

"It's the type of cold that I know you'd wanna wear a red plaid coat for," Daffy said to me, "and go off to chop wood. I swear, Arc, I'd think you were from another time. I'd say from a time when women didn't float down the river."

"I don't think such a time has ever existed, Daffy."

I had to try hard not to let my thoughts turn back to Harlow. Instead, I'd let the mist from the hills into my mind and push the images back into the shadows best I could, but there would come those moments when her bruised ribs would be everything I thought about, the twigs collecting more and more like a crown on her head while the sock left on her foot gave me nightmares of it slowly filling with the brown water of the river.

When I told Sage Nell I was seeing Harlow in my dreams, she said, "You should stop doing that," as if I had a choice.

We were walking down a street off Main. Daffy was with us. Sage Nell had a large drink she'd gotten from a fast-food place and a clear plastic grocery bag, the handle knotted so the snake squirming inside couldn't get out.

"I catch 'em by Thursday's trailer," she said. "She gets a million snakes in her yard. They come up from the river, I suppose. Don't tell Thursday I took one of her creatures."

"Can the snake breathe in there?" I asked, watching the plastic bag swing back and forth.

"I left a hole by the knot." She looked at the bag herself.

"But why do you even have a snake?" Daffy asked.

"If you take one to Highway Man," Sage Nell said, "he'll give you a tattoo for free. A small tattoo, but it still doesn't cost a dime or a piece of yourself."

I reached for the bag, but Sage Nell pulled it back and said, "I know what you're thinking, Arc. But I'm not going to let you set the snake free. If you were Thursday, you'd call me a cold bitch right now. But I know you. You'll do much worse. You're going to hate me from here on out."

"I just don't think you should have a snake in a plastic bag. I mean, c'mon, Sage Nell. You're delivering a live creature to a guy who doesn't have a heart." I crossed my arms and walked ahead. "Why does he even want a snake?"

"I've never asked him." She shrugged. "I think it would hurt to know."

The tattoo shop, its mud-colored door and dark brown brick that ran vertical, was coming into view. It had a large plate-glass window in front, bordered in rust-colored trim. Highway Man had covered the glass from the inside with newspaper so you couldn't see in. The articles he chose were about natural disasters. Floods, blizzards, droughts. Then there were the obituaries. Strangers' faces staring out, as you tried to stare in.

"You think you'll ever get a tattoo?" Sage Nell asked Daffy and me.

"Not from Highway Man," I said, looking up at the shop's sign. It was wooden, cut in the shape of a flaming skull and hanging from red chains.

"They say he's killed hundreds of people," Sage Nell said. "Do you know how he got his name?"

I had heard several variations of several different stories, but I still shook my head, curious which one she would repeat from the streets.

"He took a man who owed him money," she said, "and dressed him from head to toe in black. He laid him on a highway at night. Nailed him down or chained him down or did something so he couldn't get up. No one could see this man in the black clothes. The cars and semis kept going, even though they felt his body beneath their tires."

She threw her hands up and gripped the air like she was holding on to a steering wheel, making the sounds of acceleration, the snake in the bag thrown back and forth in her movements.

"Vroom, vroom," she said. "The drivers thought they were just running over a speed bump and they kept going." She dropped her hands. "Come morning light, everyone saw what was left of a man who had been crushed by the vehicles that had driven over him."

She took a big sip from her cup while Daffy and me stared at her.

"But," I said, "how was Highway Man able to put a man on the highway with enough time between cars speeding by to not get ran over himself?"

Sage Nell sucked on the straw until the drink ran out and all you heard was the gurgling of air.

"It was at night," she finally said. "Less traffic. Besides, even if it's not completely true, he had to have gotten his name from some sick deed. It's the type of name you say three times into a mirror and expect to get a knife in the gut."

"Aren't you scared to hang around him as much as you do?" I asked.

She set her cup down on the sidewalk and reached into her purse. I knew what she was going to pull out. Her pocketknife, which she called her bra wire. Sage Nell was known for wearing not only the same sweatshirt but also the same lacy black bra that had become something of a good luck charm. It had started after an aggressive john cornered her in a room at the Blue Hour. Naked, facedown, and seeing her ratty bra on the floor, Sage Nell grabbed it. She stabbed the john with the exposed underwire. Afterward she choked him with the bra straps until he passed out and she could escape, not before emptying his wallet for the hassle.

Ever since then, she continued to wear the bra. It was her shield and sword. But just in case the lacy fabric ever failed her, she swapped the bra wire for a pocketknife she carried with her at all times. And though it was a steel blade, to her it was that same cheap bra wire that had once saved her life. She said it had the blood of a man on it to prove it.

"I can take care of myself." She flipped the blade of the knife open. "You need to get you one of these." She moved it through the air in front of Daffy and me. "We don't walk down dancing roads in this town. We walk down the ones that smell like gasoline in the morning and piss in the evening. It's too easy to lean into the devil on these streets. What are you going to do when he starts leaning back if you haven't got anything to protect yourself?"

She folded the knife and slipped it into her pocket. As soon as she opened the door of the tattoo shop, the smell of cigarette smoke floated out into the street. Inside, the brick walls were exposed and graffitied in the type of images you'd expect to find on a highway in hell. A red sky cracked with orange fire. Devil eyes and devil horns. Explosions of yellow dust and silhouettes of hands reaching up from the nether regions. More images were on the columns running throughout the room, the long vertical faces stretched until they didn't look human.

Highway Man was at the tattoo chair, leaning over a customer reclined back and moaning.

"What have you done to him, Highway Man?" Sage Nell got close enough to see the tissue, soaked with red, that Highway Man was holding in the guy's mouth. "You bust his teeth out?"

"Ain't blood, you stupid bitch." He threw the tissue in the wastebasket with the others. "It's ink."

"I don't know if I can finish, man," the guy said, a tear rolling down his cheek already tattooed with a dragon. "It feels like you're stabbing my mouth to death, dude."

"Shut the fuck up, you pussy." Highway Man pressed the needle into the guy's gums, the red ink spilling over his teeth and filling his mouth. Though Daffy and me knew Highway Man, we'd always tried to keep our distance and had never been inside his tattoo shop.

He was a drug king at the time, who filtered from Columbus through Chillicothe and all the way down to Kentucky on Route 23, which came to be called Waste Away Highway. I always thought most of the rumors were things he made up to keep us in line and in fear of the man who was said to have once cut another drug dealer up into tiny pieces, then fed those pieces to the dealer's own dog.

"How many people you think he's really killed?" Sage Nell whispered into my ear as the three of us stood back against the wall, the snake in the plastic bag squirming and hissing. "He's probably going to kill that guy, whining the way he is."

The pockmarks in Highway Man's cheeks were deep and pitted like a honeycomb. Scars that proved he had once been an adolescent. Yet it was difficult to believe he hadn't been born hard and ugly. He was in his forties by then. His hair graying at the temples, but only if you looked close enough. If you were close enough, it was likely because he was about to hit you or worse. The way the skin stretched taut from the corners of his mouth reminded me of a photo I'd seen in a library book once. The photo of a figure unearthed in Mesopotamia. It was carved to be a hybrid between an alligator and a man. The human features rested in a skull elongated enough to be reptilian.

As Highway Man flipped the guy's lips up, the guy said, "Shit, I don't know if I can take much more of this, man. You said the gums wouldn't hurt."

I'm not sure if Highway Man was ever in the service, or if he bought them from the hunting aisle in the store, but he always wore camo pants. Though he was currently barefoot, he usually tucked his pants into high-laced boots that were said to have kicked in more skulls than any mortal ever should. He paired them with V-neck shirts, cut enough to expose the words tattooed on his chest: DIPPED IN EVIL.

He was lean, with pale hair and skin. His flat whitish eyes were like medieval coins I'd seen in encyclopedias as a kid, their carvings rubbed out by time.

"You should get this one, Arc." Sage Nell pointed to a butterfly in the book open on the table. It was full of tattoos. "Thursday would love it. She'd say you were inspired by her Butterfly Corner."

I turned back to Highway Man. Aside from DIPPED IN EVIL, the only other tattooing he had was a solid block of color on his hands, arms, legs, and feet. The ink was the color of blood, and on his right arm, it extended up to a wavy line beneath his tight bicep. On his left arm, the color ended below his elbow. His feet and legs matched this look, up to his calf on his right leg and to his ankle on his left.

"Why would he want his gums tattooed?" Sage Nell nudged me as the man started moaning louder and louder, his feet curling.

The three of us cringed with him, until Highway Man finally said, "Finished, dumbass."

The guy wiped the ink out of his mouth and rubbed his jaw as he paid. Before he left, he stopped in front of us and said, "Don't make this mistake."

He pulled up his top lip and showed us that the tattoo read TEETH.

"Why the hell would ya get that?" I asked.

"Seemed like a good idea at the time," he said, walking out with his head down.

"How's my Nell from Hell?" Highway Man came walking toward us.

His bare feet, and their solid blocks of color, were bright against the white tiled floor. I almost expected to see red footprints left in his path.

"You got something for me?" he asked Sage Nell.

She handed him the bag with the snake. She also gave him a wad of money from out of her purse.

"It all here?" he asked.

"Yes," she made sure to say quickly.

"Good girl."

She sold for him on occasion. "I only do it when I need a little extra," she told me once. "I don't like to think that other people get lost because of me. What if the something I sell to them ends up being the hit they don't come back from? The last high of their lives. But you know what they say. You can't go up without going down. Heraclitus said that. But what does a man know?"

Highway Man walked the cash over to the upright piano against the wall. He lifted its lid and placed the cash inside. Then he held up the bag and hissed back at the snake, whose tongue vibrated the plastic.

"What're you looking at, bitch?" Highway Man looked past the snake at me.

"Arc's cool, Highway." Sage Nell stood in between us. "You know that."

"Her eyes freak me the fuck out." He studied me up and down. "You got something to say, cunt?"

"She doesn't have—"

"What you gonna do with that snake?" I asked.

Highway Man laughed, a deep noise that growled. "You got some balls," he said. "You know how many have brought me snakes, but ain't one among 'em ask me just what the hell I do with 'em. You wanna see, little girl?"

I nodded.

"Follow me." He turned and led the way.

"Arc." Sage Nell grabbed my arm. "Don't go back there. You don't want to know what's in the abyss."

I looked over at Daffy. She was standing against the wall, biting her nails.

"I'm just gonna see." I shook out of Sage Nell's grip and quickly followed him to the back. I had to duck down from the low-hanging animal skulls in the doorway. It led to a narrow hallway, the exposed brick hung with framed photographs of the backs of people's heads.

I stopped in front of one that was of a woman's gray hair blowing out to the side and giving a glimpse of the pale skin on the nape of her neck.

"Why are they all facing away?" I asked.

"In the hourglass," he said, standing behind me, "the sand is not worthy to stare into the eyes of God. They must look away as the fools they are."

He kept walking to the open door at the end of the hall through which was his personal apartment. The brown plaid sofa, the wood paneling, the lamps with shades fifty years older, all reminded me of a place his grandfather might have had. Old books mixed with new ones on the shelf. The seasons there as vintage as an old spool of thread. It was hard to imagine he lived there. Hard to imagine he sat on that plaid sofa as a king of Chillicothe with white powder on his nostrils and a woman with smeared mascara at his feet.

There was a small kitchenette. The pine cabinets knotty and stained. The refrigerator was harvest yellow with wooden handles. Highway Man stood by it as he reached into the plastic bag and let the snake coil around his hand.

"You're a pretty thing," he told her. "Did you know, Arc, that snakes come out in storms? They eat the lightning. It lives inside them. Flashes out in the strikes of their tongues. Snakes are full of power from the heavens, and yet, they'll never be more powerful than a big man."

He chomped his teeth toward her face. She was only a harmless garden garter. Like one from Mamaw Milkweed's yard. She said such snakes were nothing more than women who were as ancient as the color green.

"These snakes make sure there are four-leaf clovers," she had said, "and beautiful things to grow in the fields for all to make their wishes over."

As Highway Man opened the freezer door, he said, "Have a look inside, Arc Doggs."

There were no boxes of TV dinners. No cans of juice. No cartons of ice cream. It was empty except for the frozen bodies of snakes. They were laid out in a contraption he had made out of a plastic tray, on the ends of which were clamps that forced the snakes to freeze in straight lines. He hissed at them in the flickering glow of the freezer's light. I felt as cold as the air hitting my face.

"Why?" I turned to him, my eyes searching the evil in his. "Why would you do something this horrible and cruel?"

"Why not?" He laughed, lifting up the clamp in the free space of the tray.

"Don't." I tried to take the snake from him, but Highway Man shoved my face against the freezer door, slamming my nose against the frost buildup and spotting it with a spray of my blood.

"Fucking bitch." He shook his head as I fell back on the floor, holding my face.

The snake squirmed in his hand, but he held tight, holding her head down with the clamp on one end. With the clamp on the other side, he pinned her tail, then he reached into the tray and removed one of the snakes already frozen. The garter trapped in the tray hissed and banged her body from side to side. I stared at her for as long as I could as he closed the freezer's door.

He grabbed me by the hair and dragged me out the door at the back of the kitchen, which exited into a small yard. Cutting through the grass was a cracked sidewalk. Scattered across it were numerous pieces of dark material being tended by the flies. I realized they were pieces of other snakes when I saw a head with the eyes opened to the sky.

"Stop, let me go." I shouted and cursed as he pulled me out on the sidewalk.

"Behold my power." He let me go and used both hands to wrap around the tail of the frozen snake. "Break a snake and know the devil's awake." He brought his arms up over his head, then slammed the snake forward, shattering her against the concrete.

He danced around the broken pieces, kicking some so they clacked against the concrete and scattered the flies from their feeding. I grabbed my mouth, the vomit shooting out into the grass while he laughed.

"You're disgusting," I said. I waited for his fist, but he only knelt by my head and tucked my hair behind my ear.

"I am the eater of heartbeats." He gently wiped the tears off my face. "I decide which ones go on and which will fall silent. You are alive because I allow it. No matter what direction you turn, it's my highway you travel on. Don't forget that." He forced my face to look down at the sidewalk. "You see how many pieces she broke into? When I break you, there will be so many pieces, no one will be able to believe you ever had a name. I own you and every breath you take."

He stood up over me, his shadow falling heavy.

"I've seen you digging in the ground around town," he said. "You're not innocent. What are you burying?"

"I'm not burying anything." I rubbed the vomit off my chin.

"Yeah. And I'm not breaking snakes." He looked down at the pieces. "You're within earshot of the spirits, girl. Tell 'em what you wish for, and they might make it come true."

Highway Man walked back inside. I sat up, watching the frozen pieces thaw in the sun and wiping my tears on the backs of my hands.

Daffy appeared at the screen door. "What you doing out there?" she asked.

"Where's Highway Man?"

"He's doing the illustration for Sage Nell's ink," she said. "I was scared when you didn't come back with him. He told us you had to get some air. That you got sick. What happened?"

"He's busy then?" I asked.

"Yeah, he's up front with Sage Nell. Why?"

"Keep an eye out for me." I stood and quickly stepped past her and back inside.

She followed. "What are you doing?"

"Just go out in the hall and tell me if you hear him coming."

She leaned her head out through the doorway while I opened the freezer and reached inside. After I lifted up the clamps, the snake slowly wrapped her tail around my hand. Her body was so cold, I shivered.

"You hear anything?" I asked Daffy as I closed the freezer door.

"Just his tattoo gun," she said. "What you gonna do?"

I ran back outside. Standing amid the pieces of snake on the sidewalk, I looked around.

"Arc?" Daffy asked. "What's going on?"

I went over to the fence at the back of the property that led through the overgrown grass of an abandoned grain elevator.

"You're free now," I told the snake as I helped her steer her head through the crack in the fence. "Go back home. Stay away from this place. Tell your sisters."

She slithered away, disappearing into the tall grass.

"Arc, hurry up." Daffy was standing by the screen door. "Before he comes."

I looked one last time at the grass to make sure the snake was not returning. Then I walked back to the door. Daffy took her sleeve and wiped the blood from my busted nose.

"Highway Man would like to see it," she said, "so he can feel like he did something to you. But you just keep your head up, and he won't get an ounce of satisfaction. We know that by now, don't we?"

We quickly walked back inside. Along the way Daffy whispered into my ear, "Maybe we should just go."

"No," I said. "We can't leave Sage Nell alone with him."

We stood against the wall, watching Highway Man tattoo Sage Nell. He looked at me once, chuckling and licking his lips as he used black ink to shade her arm. After he was finished, she came over and showed us her tattoo. It was a small circle within a circle on her right forearm.

"You okay, Arc?" She looked up from the tattoo. "He said you got sick?"

"I'm fine." I tried to smile. "What's your tattoo mean?"

"It's the symbol of Taoism. The philosophy dates to three hundred B.C.," she said as Highway Man sat back in the chair, watching us. "You'll appreciate that history, Arc." She looked back down at the tattoo. Bordering the large circle were lines, some of them broken. The small circle in the middle was both black and white.

"What does Taoism mean?" Daffy asked.

"It means way," Sage Nell said. "It's everything that makes the universe and all the things in it. The black and the white represent the two forces the philosophy believes drives the universe. The white is the yang. See how these lines are solid?" She pointed at the unbroken lines. "Those are male."

I looked over at Highway Man. He was now staring at Daffy.

"The black side is the yin," Sage Nell continued. She moved her finger across the broken lines. "They represent the female force in the universe."

"Why are the male lines solid?" Daffy asked. "But the female lines broken?"

"A man is a piece of iron," Highway Man said, standing. "A woman is a frozen snake. Guess which one breaks."

I wanted to tell him they weren't broken lines. They were a collection of all the things a woman is and can be. That the spaces were not something coming apart but something coming together, but then he stepped closer to Daffy, and I felt as though they were broken lines after all.

When he got close enough for his breath to blow the hair around her face, she kept her eyes on the red blocks of color tattooed on his hands and arms.

"Why you tattooed like that?" she asked. "Like you got blood all up and down your arms and legs."

"Why?" He ran his tongue over his teeth. "Because I was dipped in evil."

He stuck his chest out, holding his shirt open to show the words written there as if we hadn't already seen them.

"You know how you get dipped in evil?" he asked her. "The devil lifts you up."

He put his hands under Daffy's armpits and lifted her.

"He lays you down in the air," he said, "your arms and legs just a-dangling." He shook her until her arms flung out and her feet kicked. "He floats you up over evil, which ain't nothing but a river. The type that bugs and birds get their wings caught on until they die. The devil lowered me down toward that river."

He set Daffy back on the floor.

"What happened then?" she asked.

"I reached my arms in the blood-red waters," he said, "just enough to be the devil's son."

He moved his arms like he was submerging them in a river at our feet.

"It hurts," he said, "to be dipped in evil. It boiled my skin away and left its mark."

I just then noticed what the initials of DIPPED IN EVIL tattooed on his chest spelled.

"Die," I whispered the word as Highway Man grabbed Daffy's arm so quickly, Sage Nell screamed.

"You ever fuck a man dipped in evil?" He pulled Daffy into him as she took a deep breath and held it like she was diving into water and it would be quite a while before she found her way back to the surface.

CHAPTER 14

Her is a blur. She is who we were.

—Daffodil Poet

1985

DAFFY BECAME THE BEST SWIMMER ON BIG GRAY'S TEAM. SHE HAD the blue ribbons to prove it. She taped them to her bedroom wall, their long strips of fabric flowing down to her headboard, close enough, she could reach up and touch the ends with her fingertips. There was even talk of a swim scholarship.

"Now don't laugh at that, Daffy," Tam said. "I'm serious."

"You really think so, Coach?"

"If you work hard enough, then why the hell not? All Olympic swimmers start somewhere, Daffy. You have the same opportunity."

"What do you think, Arc?" Daffy later asked me in the locker room, when I was sitting up by the sink, watching her braid her hair. "You think I could make it to the Olympics?"

"You're the best swimmer I've ever seen."

I smiled at the strength in my sister's body. She had been lifting weights in Big Gray's gym. It showed in the way her biceps flexed and in the way her calf muscles became exposed when she raised up on her toes to get the towels off the top shelf.

"Why do you always have to have people tell you you're an amazing swimmer?" I asked.

"It's not for me to hear it," she said. "It's for the universe to." She smiled and grabbed her swim cap, heading out to the pool.

I hopped down and went out into the lobby to find John. I had just gotten a stack of books from the library on the study of pharaonic

Egypt, but I always had to check on John first to make sure he was doing his job. If not, I would have to pick up the mop.

"Where you at?" I called for him through the empty corridors.

I found his cleaning cart, but didn't see him.

"John?"

When I turned to go back the way I'd come, I saw him hidden by the side of the pop machines, nursing the blue bottle. His shirt had fresh red stains on it.

"Is that blood?" I asked, but he only took the bottle to his lips.

His eyes were watery and his nose was runny as he slouched against the machine.

"John?" I asked. "Are you bleeding?"

"It's not my blood," he said.

"Then whose is it?"

"You ever feel doomed, Arc?" He lowered the bottle. "I think I am. I think I'm doomed." He rubbed his thumb over the glass. "This here glass is the color of the shirt she was wearing that day. I never drank a single drop before then." He held the bottle out in the air in front of him. "Not a single drop."

He put his hands up as if on a steering wheel, driving straight. All of a sudden he made a sharp turn, his foot shooting out as if on the brake. The squealing sound he made with his mouth echoed off the walls.

"I just looked away for a second," he said. "Why did she have to be there in the road?"

"She was looking at a catalog of flower bulbs," I said as I sat down on the floor across from him. "A catalog Daffy and me made for her."

He frowned as he stared back into the glass of the bottle. "I never smoked," he said. "I never drank." The alcohol in the bottle sloshed against its sides. "I shaved every day. I was happy." He showed all his teeth and laughed. "I was a violinist. I was pretty good. You heard me play." He pointed the bottle toward me. "Wasn't I pretty good?"

"You were really good." I smiled for him.

"I was going to play in an orchestra," he said.

I waited for him to finish a long drink, then asked, "Why don't you start playing again?"

"There's no violin." His voice was low.

"It's in the back seat of your car, John."

"Yeah." His head swayed back and forth. "Yeah, it's in my back seat. Why don't you go get it for me?"

He reached into his pocket and grabbed his car keys. He meant to pass them to me, but he dropped them to the floor.

"Go get my violin for me, Arc Doggs."

I went out to his car but stopped to stare at the dent.

"Hey, Mamaw," I said. "How you been? I've missed you." I touched the edges of the distorted metal, then opened the door and got the case off the back seat.

When I returned inside, I found John where I'd left him, a few more drinks in.

"Go ahead. Get it out." He pointed at the case.

When I opened the brass locks and lifted the lid, the gold velvet lining fell, just as it had that day we first met him. As I held it up, I saw there was no violin inside, only a tiny piece of paper, crookedly cut into the shape of one.

"Where is it?" I asked. "Where's your violin?"

"I got thirty-five dollars for it," he said. "I got to keep the case. If I don't open it, I can imagine the violin is still inside."

"Thirty-five dollars?" I asked.

"For you to swim."

"For Daffy to swim," I said. "We didn't mean for you to sell your violin."

"Too late." He took another drink. "It don't matter anyways. I hadn't touched it since that day you asked me to play 'Amazing Grace.' It felt like a sin to pick it up again."

I closed the case and stared down at it a moment, then opened it back up.

"What are you doing?" he asked.

"I'm getting your violin out." I went through the motions of holding the fallen lining back.

"It's not there." He cursed and rambled as I reached into the case and grabbed the violin by its neck. "There's nothing there."

He threw and smashed the bottle against the wall behind me. Still, I pretended to pick up the bow.

"Play it for me, John," I said, standing with the violin in one hand and the bow in the other, offering them to him.

He looked at the emptiness.

"There's nothing there." His voice, fading away.

"For our birthdays," I said, "Daffy and me ate cake that wasn't there. For all the noise in our house, we would lay our ears against the floor and hear music that wasn't there."

I threw the dream of the violin into the wall.

"Don't tell me what is and is not here." I bent down and picked up the imaginary pieces, putting them back together again. "I create things out of nothing every damn day. You can, too."

He looked again at my hands as I offered them.

"Take your violin," I said.

He turned away.

I screamed, "Take your fucking violin, John, because I don't want it anymore."

He looked up at me a moment, then leaned against the wall to help him stand. He laid his hands in mine, our palms connecting and passing over one another as his fingers began to curl around the neck of a violin that did not exist. In his other hand, he took the bow from me.

As he positioned his feet in ways he had not done in years, he stood as tall and as strong as I'd seen him that day he played for my sister and me. He placed his chin on the rest and began. Shutting his eyes, his arm moved the imaginary bow across strings that did not exist, and yet music started to fill the quiet around us.

I laid my cheek against the cold wall and closed my eyes, too.

The music stopped just long enough for him to whisper, "I hate you."

Maybe he said it once more, but I only listened to the music in my head, hearing "Amazing Grace" to its very last note. When I opened my eyes, there was nothing but the case on the floor. John was gone. I slid down against the wall, sitting alone in the silence.

P A R T   III

CHAPTER 15

Bliss is easy to miss.

—*Daffodil Poet*

1993

THURSDAY HELD A DULL YELLOW APPLE IN HER HAND. IT WAS THE first day of winter, and a john had given it to her.

"Did you guys know," she said, "if you grab hold of an apple's stem and say the alphabet as you twist it, whatever letter you land on when the stem breaks will be the first letter of your true love?"

She twisted the stem of the apple. When it broke, she threw the stem down and said, "No fucking way I'd fall in love with a guy whose first name starts with a *J.*"

We were sitting on the curb just outside the Blue Hour. Sage Nell and Daffy were with us. So was a new girl. She had a head full of curls. Her eyebrows were plucked into thin lines above her wide eyes. She had a small silver stud over her lip that at times looked like a mole, and she wore purple gloves that could be turned into mittens anytime she unbuttoned the flap. It was her first time working the street. Thursday always liked for the new girls to know how much to charge so they wouldn't get screwed twice.

"Let me tell you, little girl, what everything is worth here on the street." Thursday dumped the contents of her tote onto the snow-covered sidewalk. Out spilled the plastic trinkets from the craft store, but to her they were real jewels. Tiny ones in the silhouettes of diamonds, others circular or cut into the shapes of hearts, stars, and tears.

"These ones," she said, pointing at the little green beads, "are emeralds. And these ones are sapphires." She ran her fingers over the blue stars. She went on to explain how the small clear plastic ones were diamonds and the red heart-shaped ones were rubies.

"For a blow job, take two of these." She picked up a couple of green beads. "Two emeralds. That's the price a john must pay. For going halfway, it'll cost them four sapphires. For all the way, it's all of these."

She picked up a handful of the clear plastic ones.

"For all the things beyond a fuck, it will cost this much," she said, pointing to the scattering of yellow beads. "These are the ones that are the most valuable. It's what they'll have to pay you for everything."

"What is there beyond a fuck?" the girl asked, then blew a bubble with her gum.

"Honey." Thursday *tsked-tsked*. "There are many things."

Thursday looked down at the yellow beads and said more softly, "There are many things."

"The yellow ones are my favorite," the girl said.

"They're like pieces of the sun, ain't they?" Thursday smiled. "I can see with them in the dark. They're that powerful."

"But." The girl bit her lip and dragged her teeth over the lipstick there. "I still don't know what to charge."

Sage Nell wrapped her arm around the girl's narrow shoulders. "I'll tell you what the real prices are."

She had done the same thing to Daffy and me after Thursday showed us her plastic beads for the first time. It wasn't too long ago that Daffy and me were like the new girl. Educated by those who sold their bodies on the street that was a paved swerve into the Blue Hour, where we could get a room for a good price. Or if the john preferred, we would do it right there in his vehicle parked in the discount store parking lot, or just down the street where we could watch the smoke from the stacks of the paper mill float up the sky.

This was rural prostitution. We didn't dress like the street workers in the movies. No spandex miniskirts or fishnet stockings. We weren't Julia Roberts meeting Richard Gere. Our hair was greasy, we smelled of sweat, and there was little to do with our faces other than frown. We bit our nails until they bled and stared down the street while we wore thin coats and dirty sneakers in the winter. In the summer, it was old jeans and torn tanks, like what Daffy and me wore that first time. It must have been pretty obvious how nervous I was then, because after Thursday showed Daffy and me her beads, Sage Nell pulled me aside and asked, "Are you a virgin, Arc?"

I shook my head, glancing over at Daffy, who was still with Thursday, looking at all the diamonds on the ground.

"When I was a kid," I said, "a spider would come into my room at night."

"Yours was a spider?" Sage Nell asked. "Mine was a big ugly cockroach."

I looked up into her eyes.

"Most of the girls out here," she said, "have their own spiders and wolfs and rabid dogs. If only we could begin again. Start over with our virginity and make a rule on how it's devoured." She took her arm off my shoulder to pass her fish magnet from hand to hand. "But that's beyond everything now. What you really have to know on these streets isn't the price. It's about the johns. They all have restless dicks, and they're going to treat you like trash. Like you don't have a soul. Strangers will look at you like you're guilty of something. All you can do is say you're not guilty, even though everyone in the world knows you are. But guilty of what? They'll tell you, but it never seems quite like the thing you're guilty of. I don't want to scare you, Arc, but I also don't want you to be ignorant on what it is that you're about to do."

We both looked up at the sound of rattling. Coming down the walk was an old woman pushing a shopping cart. Her skirt would have been long on a taller woman. On her it dragged the pavement, its hem torn and filthy. The closer she got, I saw that the sole of her right shoe was loose. It was brown leather, but her left shoe was an old, dirty canvas one, the laces gone.

"Who is that?" I whispered to Sage Nell.

"She's the owl," she whispered back.

"The owl?" I asked.

"The wise old one."

She wore several scarves. Some blue, some pink, but others faded to gray. They trailed out from her like smoke. The way she cocked her head, made her throat seem crooked, but her smile was level across her face. She walked with her eyes closed, her fingers wrapped with fabric knotted over her knuckles. Some time ago she had painted her bitten nails. Remnants of the frosty pink color could be seen around the edges.

"She can climb like a cat, like an animal, like a woman who gets chased." Sage Nell kept her lips close to my ear. "But she flies like an owl. She keeps her wings folded under the shawl."

The old woman's wrinkles were severe like the edges of metal. Her hair was steely gray, but with bright white strands around her oval face, which was covered in dirt that made the skin of her eyes look paler than it was.

"Where does she come from?" I asked.

"No one knows," Sage Nell said. "She was here before any of us. She'll be here long after. She, too, is shiny and rides among the stars."

Old cans tied to the sides of the cart rattled as she pushed by. More cans were threaded by string to the hem of her skirt, and they dragged on the ground behind her. The cart was empty, except for a dirty blanket wrapped around an old battered teddy bear, one eye and one ear less. A patch of blue fabric was sewn over a hole in the top of the bear's head, next to traces of lipstick still visible from a good-night kiss.

"Isn't she a fantastic dream?" Sage Nell asked.

As the woman passed, I could smell the scent of the street, of skin not bathed, and of the dust that comes with living in boxes and against concrete. Sage Nell watched the woman until she disappeared around the corner, then turned to me and picked up where she'd left off.

"Avoid the men with fingers dipped in poison, like Highway Man," she said. "I say that like you can, but really, it's something you can only hope to do. Eventually, you'll get repeat johns. Then you don't have to worry so much about if they're cops or not because you've serviced them before. There's familiarity in that. But it never gets easier. The longer you're out here, the more you start to do things like Thursday."

"What you mean?" I asked.

"Thursday didn't always cut holes in her clothes and I didn't always use to wear this sweatshirt all the time." Sage Nell looked down at it. "It's the last thing I have to hang on to."

We turned toward the sound of a horn and saw it was coming from a man in a truck.

"That's our name out here," Sage Nell said. "The one they call us by."

"What is?" I asked.

"Honk." She chuckled. "Honk is our name out here."

As she headed toward the man still honking his horn at her, I returned to grab Daffy by the arm, and we ran until the Blue Hour was behind us.

"What's the matter with you?" Daffy asked, pulling out of my grip.

"We'll find another way to make money," I said.

"What if we don't, Arc? I don't wanna go through the keyhole." Daffy looked up at the car slowing to a stop by the curb, the guy inside looking at her. "Besides, at least it won't be like it was with the spider. This time we get paid."

"You pretty young thing want a ride?" the guy hollered out his open window.

"Yeah, thanks," Daffy called back to him.

"No, Daffy, don't."

She ran off toward the car, me racing after. When she got inside, I tried to get in with her.

"No, Arc, I'll do this for the both of us, so you don't have to. Wait here for me." She pushed me back and closed the door. I grabbed the handle, but the car was speeding off. I chased it for as long as I could. When I lost my breath, I fell onto the curb. I tried not to think about my sister and what she was doing, but all I saw was the shadow of the spider on the wall, eating us both alive.

Needless to say, sex for us was not something made out of love. I looked back on history, trying to find the elusive bed of roses. All I saw were women under the heel. They say prostitution is the oldest profession, recorded as long as history has been. In the Second World War, they called prostitutes "comfort women." Those paid by the Japanese military to service upward of a hundred men a day. Some of these "women" were not women at all. They were little girls.

After I'd heard the word *prostitute* for the first time as a kid when someone had called Mom and Aunt Clover that very word, I decided

I would be like the Greeks, the Aztecs, the civilizations before me, who had believed in gods possessing powers we humans crave.

Prostitute.

She would be a god with nine arms. An odd number that she swung back and forth with the pendulum of time.

Prostitute.

She would have nine hands, but only eight thumbs.

Prostitute.

Her hair blowing in the wind as she outruns all those who chase her.

Prostitute.

No matter the power of my mythical female god, I knew, sitting there on that cold pavement, that there was little power women had on the street. Still I had to try. So I imagined my nine-armed god floating in the sky, her arms outstretched to me, bathing me in her warm blue light. Her long dress skimming the top of the sidewalk, and a pair of wings opening against the sky.

When my sister returned a while later, she held the payment for services rendered. "It wasn't so bad," she said.

We both looked away, up at the smoke piling in the sky from the paper mill.

"Can you tell anything different about me?" she asked.

"Yes," I said. "Your right breast is gone."

She looked down. "It is not."

"It is," I said. "Like the women warriors from the Amazon who cut off their right breast so they could draw their bows better."

"Yeah," she said as she sat down beside me. She moved the gravel beneath her foot. "It wasn't so bad," she said again, quieter this time. "And just look how much he paid."

I stared at the five bucks. She was gripping it so tight, all I could do was tell her it was enough for what she'd done. It had to be, because if not, the sky would have cracked open and the goddess would have fallen to the cold, hard ground.

CHAPTER 16

What is not found, cannot be crowned.

—*Daffodil Poet*

SOMEWHERE IN THE HILLSIDE, I KNEEL ON SOMETHING. SOMETHING barely there. I look up at the trees on top of the hill. They are covered in snow and ice. The air here is blue. *Blue, blue, blue.* But maybe it is only late. I am in a white dress made from my own ribs. They are not made of bone but of spools of *lace, lace, lace.*

There is water around me. It comes in a rush down the hillside. The winter at the top of the hill has thawed. The snow and ice melting down, causing a flood that I flow with to the bottom of the hill where the land flattens out but is not flooded. It is only wet, and it is where Daffy stands, in her own white dress.

"I have been waiting for you," she says.

We gather apples from the trees above us. We gather apples until it is late. She is blindfolded, with a hand on one of my ribs. By my rib, I lead her.

I lead her until I realize we are merely walking a circle around the same tree. I look up at the single apple hanging from the branch above my head. Its shape reminds me of my mother's as I reach for it, my hand closing in on its yellowed flesh. As I touch it, the fruit bursts apart into water, and I don't have the chance to twist its stem off and look for love.

"I believe the time for rain has come," I tell Daffy, my hair damp.

She walks away, taking my rib with her and unraveling me from that point on.

This is the dream I had after that first night we got in the cars of men. The john I had was a man I wish I hadn't.

"Your legs are sweet as candy," he said to me as he ate me out of ankle and knee.

I was paid five bucks. It felt wrong to take more than Daffy had for that first trick.

My sister and me never spoke about what we did with the men. We never told each other about the boundaries we crossed, the punches we took, the sex that often turned violent. We ignored each other's bruises and silently held our faces in the freezer because Aunt Clover told us it helps chase away the sore ache.

After that first time, when the johns would be somewhere inside me, I would think about their wallet, the money they'd give me out of it. But thinking about a wallet made me think about my father's. When he was working, it'd be in his pocket. When he was jobless, it'd be on the table. There'd be no money in it then, no matter how many times Mom checked.

She would leave it open, and I'd peek inside it myself, not in the pocket for money, but at the accordion of photos. There was one of Mom and him, young. He was lifting her up off the ground like a muscleman, and she was laughing. There was a photo of Daffy and me as infants. Over our heads, he'd written our names in marker on the photo, like a first-time father who couldn't tell his twin daughters apart.

And then there were the little notes on scraps of paper, written in our handwriting to him.

Love you, Daddy.

Ride the horses, Daddy. And come home.

I would think then, not of the wallets but of the brown horses my father once told me lived beneath the paper mill and ran so fast, their gallops kicked up the dust of the earth. As the men breathed heavier and heavier on top of me, I could hear the panting of the horses just behind me. I could feel the graze of their manes across my face. And if I closed my eyes tight enough, I could find myself riding on their backs across the field to freedom, and then it wasn't so bad to be a young woman in Chillicothe, Ohio, beneath a man she did not know.

Later, I would ask Daffy if she thought of the horses, but she would say that as the men were pushing into her so hard she had to grit her teeth from the pain, she imagined herself lying on Mamaw Milkweed's sofa, the granny square afghan covering her as if the john weren't even there.

"If they only knew what we were thinking about." She laughed until it broke on the edges. I came to think it was a good thing that we were our mother's daughters, because in our line of work, we had to be women who knew how to fuck without love and how to squeeze our eyes tight enough we could see beyond the men, who always seemed to be there, no matter what.

Sage Nell had been right about johns having restless dicks. She'd also been right about getting all kinds. Some liked to choke and spank. Those ones we called Rubber Mouth and Stinky Pants. "Creep" johns would pull out just so they could smear their semen on our face. What I've learned is that perverts leave stains. Piss, blood, shit. It's not having sex. It's being attacked. The thing of it is, you get more perverts than you do just men. The best johns are the old-school boys who want only a blow job or a little hometown prodding. Many of the johns have wedding rings. Plenty of them have good upstanding jobs, and not one of them will ask you what your real name is. They'll simply ask how much.

So while Thursday cut holes in her clothes, and Sage Nell held tight to an old magnet, I reached in under my mattress and found the corner my aunt had once given me off an old box.

"The corner of yourself," she had said. "Keep it safe."

I opened it up and wrote my name down, so I wouldn't forget I had one, while Daffy got a rock.

"Rocks can be flower bulbs," she said. "If we believe hard enough."

She planted a rock in every place she had been with a john.

"So something good will grow," she said, packing the earth down tight.

We clung to rituals like this because without them, we feared losing ourselves completely.

That winter after Harlow was found in the river, when the first of the icicles clung to the roofline, Daffy and me stood on the front porch with our hands up, clinging to what had been one of Mamaw Milkweed's biggest rituals. Catching the breeze. A ceremony we had promised our old grandmother we would always do. But we hadn't done it in years. As I thought about Harlow in the water, I knew it was time. Time to hold our hands up and catch something before it became too late.

"You have to hold your hand up higher, Daffy, to get the best breeze," I told her.

"You sound like Mamaw Milkweed," she said, raising her hand as high as mine.

When Mamaw had us practice the ritual, she first showed us the five pebbles.

"See these," she said of the five small rocks that lay in the dirt at the edge of her front door. "These are the fingernails of old women. It is why the birds hold their council here. Because they seek wisdom from those who caught a breeze in their hands and held it long enough for it to become a wind."

"But why, Mamaw Milkweed?" Daffy had asked.

"Because a breeze is a whisper and a wind is a scream," Mamaw said. "And after you catch a scream, you have to drown it in the river."

"Who does the whisper and scream belong to?" I asked.

"Men with the witch fever," Mamaw Milkweed had said. "Those who hunt the land for women who cry out against them, calling them witches. This fever spreads on the wind, but if you catch it in your hand and hold tight, you can stop it by drowning it in the river."

"Mamaw Milkweed would be proud of us," Daffy said as she stood at the edge of the porch. "Don't you think, Arc? Proud of us at least for this."

She closed her fingers and said, "I've caught the breeze. Quick, Arc. Catch it, too."

Feeling the air hit my palm, I swiftly shut my hand. Together we held our fists beneath our mouths and whispered the things Mamaw Milkweed had taught us.

"Headless crow," I said. "A cradle of eagles."

"Red horse." Daffy smiled. "Little orange dogs."

"Big dogs. Tree bark. Grandmother, grand water."

"Granddaughter," Daffy said. "Beyond great water. Dark blue."

"Blue light." I held my lips nearer to my closed hand. "Beyond blue."

"It's wind now," Daffy said.

Keeping our hands closed, we walked inside the house, passing

Aunt Clover on the sofa and going down the hall into the bathroom, where we filled the sink with cold water and held our hands in.

"Momma would be upset."

We looked up at the sound of our mother's voice and found her leaning against the doorway.

"You're supposed to drown the wind in the river," she said, "not in a fucking sink."

She kept her half-closed eyes on the water as she left. We let the water out of the sink and wiped our hands on our shirts as we followed her.

She was already in her room and on the mattress.

"I'm not going in." Daffy crossed her arms in the doorway. "It stinks in there. The smell will smear my mascara."

I walked over the trash and dirty laundry on the floor. Mom had been removing more of the stuffing and foam from inside the mattress. It was littered about the room, along with dirty camisoles, empty lighters, and crumpled-up foil. I looked back at Daffy as I sat down on the floor beside the mattress as I asked, "Momma, what's that smell?"

She only stared up at the ceiling.

"It smells rotten." I batted gnats and small flies away.

I rolled her over, looking beneath her. Even though she smelled like sweat and piss, the rotting odor wasn't coming from her. I followed the scent across the edge of the mattress to the hole in its side. Reaching in, I pulled out some of the new things she had collected from the johns. An empty cigarette pack, a blue button, a gray one, and several in shades of brown. There were boot and shoe laces tied into knotted balls that rolled out of my hand as I reached back into the hole. Feeling something soft and wet, I wrapped my fingers around it.

In the light, I opened my hand and found a partially eaten apple. The flesh, long since turned brown.

"Mom, you can't put things like this in the mattress." I held it up in front of her face.

"Don't you know," she said, "an apple will tell you who your true love is." Her voice at times sounded like something being overturned. "Yes, it'll tell you, little Arc. You just have to twist the stem off. Then you'll know. Where's my . . . where's my blue-eyed girl?"

She mumbled as she used her fingers to rake the items I'd gotten out, back toward the hole.

"Come on, Arc," Daffy called from the doorway. "She's nothing but a lifetime of bad luck. Best get out while you still can."

"Don't put food in the mattress anymore, okay?" I told Mom as I stood.

She only paid attention to the items she was putting back inside the hole, checking each by holding it up into the light as if to make sure it had not been altered or changed.

When I got out in the hall, Daffy looked at the apple and asked, "Ain'tcha gonna throw that away?"

"It's got seeds in it," I said. "You shouldn't throw seeds away. Let's take it outside."

Aunt Clover was still on the sofa with a plastic bag full of twigs on her lap. "You drown your wind?" She laughed as we pushed the screen door open.

I carried the apple down into the yard, putting it in the ground at the base of a tree stump.

"That way it'll grow into an apple tree," I said. "And we'll come out here and have fresh fruit every day."

"Nothing's going to grow here, Arc." Daffy reached into my back pocket for the deodorant stick. "Nothing but more crosses to bear."

As she rolled the deodorant under her arms, she said, "If I ever get to smelling as bad as Momma, just bury me the best you can."

She counted the layers of deodorant. "Remember how nice she used to smell when she first brought us home from Mamaw Milkweed's?"

"Like perfume," I said.

"And pancakes."

"And the candy she gave us from her pockets."

"Now she smells like old grass," Daffy said.

"Old apples," I added.

"Like something that will never be a mother again." Daffy sighed. "I'm gonna go make sure her door is shut, so the stink don't travel to my room."

She handed me the deodorant and went back inside. I put some on myself, then slipped it into my pocket.

"Arc? Hey, Arc."

I looked up and saw Sage Nell. She was walking quickly down the road with her arms wrapped around her stomach.

"Hey," I said. "What you doing out here?"

"I thought I'd stop by and see you for a while." She looked back over her shoulder. Aside from the sweatshirt, she wasn't dressed for winter. She had on a pair of thin cotton pajama pants and flip-flops.

"Everything okay?" I asked.

"I just don't feel like being alone." She wiped her nose, and some blood came out.

"We can hang out here," I said.

When we got inside the house, Aunt Clover was no longer on the sofa. She was kneeling in front of the TV and a documentary on South America. She had several of the twigs out of the bag and was measuring them against the lines of Machu Picchu.

"What is she doing?" Sage Nell asked, still trembling from the cold, or something more.

"Measuring her twigs," I said, "to make sure she's got the right length."

"Right length for what?" Sage Nell watched the way Aunt Clover carefully laid a twig against the TV screen and over the image of the edge of a crumbling ruin.

I took Sage Nell into Daffy's room and showed her the wall. "The right length for this," I said.

"Some kind of art piece?" she asked.

"That or some kind of madness," I said.

"Sometimes they're the same thing, Arc." Sage Nell's eyes looked like she'd been staring at fire all day.

"Are you okay?" I asked.

"A john tried to drink me this morning," she said. "Maybe he did drink me. I feel like a third of who I was." She rubbed her eyes, smearing the mascara even more.

Stepping closer to the wall, she was silent for a few seconds, running her fingers over the twigs. "You know, it's one of the deepest mysteries on earth."

"What is?" I asked.

"Time," she said. "There's plenty of theories, but there's not one person who can say what it really is. The world would be in chaos without it. I mean have you ever imagined what it would be like to not have time? It would be like hitting a pause button. All the things that drift would stop drifting. All the things that float would stop floating." She turned to me. "Thing about time is, you never feel like you have enough of it."

She went over and sat on Daffy's bed, crossing her legs beneath her. When she saw the photo of Daffy and me as little girls on the side table, she picked up the frame. "This you?"

"Yeah," I said, "when Daffy and me were just a couple of little bugs, as Mamaw Milkweed would say."

"Which one is you?"

"That one's Daffy." I pointed to the girl on the right. "And that's me." I pointed to myself on the left.

"God, you're identical," Sage Nell said. "Is that a good thing? Or a bad one?"

"It's nice having a sister." I took the frame from her and set it back on the table.

She watched me. "I guess it is, Arc." I thought she would say something else about the photo, but she asked, "Would you braid my hair? Like yours?"

She took her headband off. When she removed the scrunchie and pulled out the bun, her hair fell down to her mid-back. I hadn't realized it was that long.

I sat down behind her as she said, "I've never had my hair braided before. I suppose that's what I get for growing up without sisters."

She leaned her head back as I combed my fingers through the curls, breaking them up.

As I divided her hair, I said, "When I was a kid, Mamaw Milkweed would cut paper into thin strips and write things on them that she'd braid up with the hair."

"Like what things?" she asked.

"Like I was as brave as a lizard or thirsty as a sycamore. I never knew what that last one meant." We both laughed. When we grew quiet again, I said, "I suppose they were her way of making me feel special."

"That's nice." She sighed, her hands trembling in her lap. "What would you say about me, Arc?"

"Oh, I'd say you were a world of drifting secrets." I crossed the top sections of her hair. "That you're as primal as the sun. A daughter of knots. A cat on the linoleum washing her tooth."

She laughed louder. "What else, Arc?"

"Oh, a sip of warm tea." I finished the last of the braid, saving the final strand as I said, "And a great friend, but not to garter snakes."

"Maybe that's why I'm being punished," she said. "I've turned against the creatures of the earth and answered the call of evil men."

I used her scrunchie to tie the braid off, then laid my hands on her shoulders. "Why are you so nervous today, Nell?"

"Nell? I don't think anyone has called me that in a while. I've been Sage Nell for so long. Truth is, I'm not wise at all." She got up and looked down at her sweatshirt. "I thought I'd only wear this at school. Then after I graduated it'd be put in a box in the attic."

"Like an artifact?" I asked.

"Yeah." She started to smile but decided not to. "I wish I had my bra wire."

"Where is it?"

"I forgot it at Thursday's." She frowned. "Let's go to the Distant Mountain, Arc. We'll be so far away, no one will be able to find us."

"Is someone trying to find you?" I asked.

She looked down and softly said, "Hurry, get your truck keys. You can drive and I'll hold my arm out the open window and pretend to fly."

Before we left, I searched for Daffy, but when I saw the back door open, I knew she must have left.

Sage Nell was waiting for me in the truck. When I got in, she asked why there was writing all over everything. I looked down at the rhymes written in black marker on the leather of the seats, the dashboard, even on the steering wheel.

"Daffodil Poet" was all I said.

Sage Nell repeated the words as she leaned toward the photo taped to the dash. It was a photo of her, me, and the rest of our group standing in front of our Distant Mountain, smiling with our arms in the air like we were free.

"Chillicothe Queens," she muttered. "Yeah right."

I drove the winding turns while Sage Nell stuck her hand out the open window into the cold air and read the poetry written on her truck door, sometimes aloud.

" 'The power of a flower is that she can tower.' " She looked at me. "What a thing to say, huh, Arc?"

Evening had already set in, and the dark was chased away only where the headlights hit. That deep into the hills, I kept my eyes open for the deer that was sure to cross. When we got close to the Distant Mountain, Sage Nell said, "Don't go as far as Thursday's trailer."

"Don't you wanna go and get your bra wire?" I asked.

"I don't feel like going back there tonight. Besides, in this world of monsters, Thursday may need it more than me."

I pulled in the space between a couple of trees in the woods and parked. Sage Nell was out of the car and running before I cut the engine. I chased her through the trees and down the riverbank to our spot. She stopped just before her feet hit the water.

"What do you think Harlow thought about as she floated down the river?" she asked.

"She was dead," I said. "I don't know if she thought about anything more than that."

"Do you believe in an afterlife, Arc?"

"Sometimes I only believe in hell. But I suppose if it exists, there has to be a heaven, too."

"Tell me what it'll be like," she said.

"Your philosophers have already described it in a million sparkling ways, haven't they?"

"I want to know what you think it'll be, Arc."

"I don't know." I sighed. "I guess it'll be drifting clouds and bright wonders and the moment like a wheel, turning and turning until we know what it was all for. Or maybe it'll just be horses galloping by so fast, they make us dizzy."

She looked out on the water and asked, "Where would we be if no one had ever said the word *God*? Had never said the word *heaven*? Hell? All those things which deepen the shade of the ripe fruit. Where would we be without a creation story? Without the say of sin? Where would we be if we could just live without the fear that the life we've had has not been good enough to spend eternity with the harps? No sense of shame or guilt or of doing the wrong thing.

Who was the first idiot to say, 'We are more than evolution. We are morals and ethics and creation. We are the feel, the made, the what that has come from the hip bones of a God above.' Truth is, we're all just pieces of shit the universe has born out of its ass. Now, that's a philosophy I stand by."

She sat down on the ground, her hands cold enough that she pulled her sleeves down over them.

"Sit with me, Arc," she said, looking up at me. "Be my sister by the river."

I nudged against her side, and she curled her toes up in the flip-flops as we watched our breath exhale.

"I keep thinking I might find a clear night and be free." She sighed, looking up at the sky. When she lowered her eyes, she looked at my lips. "Why you only wear lipstick on half of your mouth, Arc?"

"Growing up, Mom would tell Daffy and me that we were half of the same," I said.

"Half of the same what?"

"Anything. Half of the same keyhole, the same storm, the same body of water. It feels like I'm taking over Daffy's half if I cover my whole mouth."

"But if you don't," Sage Nell said, "doesn't it feel like you're only half of your own self?"

"I've never really thought of me without her," I said.

"You should, Arc. I mean, I think you have to, or you'll never get to be you."

She exhaled, leaning her head against my shoulder.

"How did we end up here?" she asked.

"At the river?" I looked out upon it and its cold water.

"No," she said. "In our lives. How did we end up here? We make believe that we ride among the stars wearing crowns. But the only things resting on top of our heads is the hand of a john whose sweat we taste just before he pays us to swallow him. I wanna know how it all started. How we got to this."

I looked out at the water. Something had made a splash. The ripples were coursing toward the other side.

"It started with a flower," I said.

"Tell me about it, Arc." She kept her head on my shoulder.

"A flower that the ancients named the flower of joy," I said. "The poppy. A seemingly innocent arrangement of soft petals upon tall green stems. The type of flower a child would give their mother knowing she would say, 'My, what a pretty little thing.'

"Did you know the poppy is worn as remembrance for fallen soldiers? That is when it's not a symbol of dreams. In the oldest of the old stories, it is the flower used as gifts for the dead. In Persian literature it's been called the flower of the heart. Somewhere along the way, in between the joy and the heart, someone figured out if you injure this flower, make her bleed, then you will have something more than a dead plant. You will have opium."

"Our crowns." Sage Nell's voice was faint.

"The cultivation of opium dates back to 3400 B.C.," I said. "Ancient civilizations grew the flowers for pain relief. This quest for the end of suffering would bring us through many periods. First there was morphine, a wonder drug that dulled everything that kept us up at night. A little mixing by a chemist in 1874 brought the first synthesized version of heroin. It wasn't called this yet, though. It wouldn't be until years later that Bayer, the folks who make our aspirin, coined the name *heroin* taken from a German word meaning 'heroic' because of the feeling the drug gave those who took it. They advertised it as a miracle. The *perfect* painkiller. It was the medicine of choice used to treat everything from bronchitis to tuberculosis. Mothers gave their children a small dose of heroin at night to help them sleep."

"I don't believe it." She started to laugh, but it disappeared in a sigh.

"You could pick it up in cough syrup," I said. "T drops, and menstrual tablets, prescribed to women for their fits."

"Our fits," she whispered.

"In the First World War, wives and mothers would send their husbands and sons kits that included a needle and vials of heroin. They thought they were mailing them medicine. Something to make them feel good while they were away from home. They couldn't have known their tender gesture would change the face of those they loved, for the men they'd sent away came back full-blown addicts. The chemists, these medicine men, who had so calmly bestowed this gift upon the world, said it was nonaddictive, but by 1911 the use of heroin and prostitution were linked. By 1913 heroin addicts were part of the general population.

"Bayer began to limit the heroin they were producing before it became altogether illegal to manufacture. By then, it was too late. The feeling, the euphoria, it had been released upon the world. There's no going back from that."

"No," Sage Nell said. "I don't suppose there is."

"Best feeling of your life, man." I laid my head against hers.

"Makes you warm all over." She shut her eyes.

"The greatest thing I've ever taken."

"The greatest high I've ever had," she said.

"I fucking hate it," I yelled as loud as I could. As she cried, I said more softly, "Wound a flower, make her bleed. In the pain, the flower cries and you risk becoming something else."

"And we've all become that, haven't we, Arc?"

She reached into her pocket and pulled out the kitchen magnet. More paint had chipped off the fish, revealing large spaces of white plastic beneath.

"Magnets have souls, did you know that?" She looked at it as she ran it across the bruises on her legs. "At least that's what Thales believed. He was the earliest known philosopher from Greece. He thought that since magnets can move iron, it meant they had souls. Too bad they can't move bruises."

She gently slid the magnet across her skin.

"I figured since I lost myself a long time ago," she said, "I'd keep a magnet close so I could remember what it felt like to have a soul. How stupid, huh? I'll never get my soul back." She squeezed the magnet in her hand, then pitched it into the river. I waited to hear the splash, but it never came.

"Thales was the first philosopher who tried to discover the source of everything," she said. "The origin of all things. He believed it was water. This river, Arc. This river is the beginning of everything."

She opened her hand, revealing the magnet still there.

"Truth is, I carry it because it was my mother's," she said. "It was always on our green refrigerator. She'd use it to hold her to-do lists, sometimes her grocery lists. Other times, my report card. Hard to believe I got all those A's. When did I get so stupid?"

She leaned her head back and released a heavy breath.

"We're carrying too many secrets, Arc."

"Are we?" I asked.

She looked at me. "I know your secret, Arc. I know—"

"*Shh.*" I held my finger against her lips. "Let's not say. Someone might be listening."

I held my hand up over our heads.

"What are you doing?" she asked.

"Catching the breeze until it becomes a wind," I said.

"And then what?"

"And then we drown it in the river."

CHAPTER 17

I am not home if I continue to roam.

—*Daffodil Poet*

IT WAS NIGHT WHEN DAFFY SHOWED UP ON THE FRONT PORCH WITH blood all over her face. It took me a moment to focus and realize it was my sister I was staring at. The whites of her eyes were large and bright. Her lips trembled. I asked her to say something, but she was so quiet, I had to insist she speak just so I knew it was her.

"It's me," she said.

"What happened?" I asked. "Come inside the house and tell me."

"No." She shook her head, stepping back. "I don't wanna go in. Don't want Aunt Clover to see the blood. She'll laugh, or worse, try to tell me I need my own white belt."

She stepped to the side of the porch. Neither of us in coats. We huddled together against the wall of the house.

"Tell me what happened, Daffy."

At first, she wouldn't say. She just said she'd stared at a small rock too long. "It hit me in the eyes," she said. Then she said she walked in front of an old man exhaling. "His breath pushed me down." Both her hands were clenched tight, blood dried between her knuckles.

I begged her to tell me what really happened.

Finally, she sat on the porch steps and asked, "Do you remember how warm Mamaw Milkweed's hands were?"

"Yes," I said.

She wiped the blood off her chin. As she stared down at it, she asked, "Do you remember her grape jelly?"

"Yes." I remembered the dark purple jam inside the crystal-clear jars.

She looked up at the night sky. The light pollution from town meant we never saw any stars from our house, but still Daffy pointed up and said, "There's Mamaw Milkweed's work," and I knew she was talking about all the stars we couldn't see. "That's her work. But not this." Daffy stared back down at the blood. "Mamaw Milkweed didn't make this. Highway Man did."

As she told the story, she moved closer to me.

"He picked me up in front of the Blue Hour." She sighed. "I'd just come from a john. The room was cold. Outside was colder. I saw a snake slithering by on the ground. I got a handful of dirt from her path and put it in my pocket because Mamaw Milkweed always said to. Remember?"

I nodded. "Tell me what happened with Highway Man."

"He was looking for Sage Nell," Daffy said. "I told him I didn't know where she was. He told me to get in his fucking car anyway."

"Never go anywhere with Highway Man, Daffy. You know that."

"I had the dirt from the snake in my pocket for protection. I thought it'd be fine. We drove out to Thursday's trailer, but Sage Nell wasn't there. Neither was Thursday. He drove down the road to where the neighbors keep those cows. You know the ones with the white faces? He pulled over by the barbed-wire fence and said Sage Nell had stolen from him and that when he caught her, she'd never steal again. Then he just stared at the fence for so long, I thought we'd run outta gas. Finally, he got back on the road, drove us to his tattoo shop. He left the closed sign on the door after we went in. I didn't wanna go with him, but he told me to. Said he wasn't finished with me yet and that if I didn't go in, he'd take my eyes and put them in his freezer so he could break them on the sidewalk.

"He sat down at his work table and took a piece of paper and started drawing. I thought he was sketching a new tattoo, but it took up the whole paper. Before I knew it, he'd drawn a face. Sage Nell's face. He made me hold it up in front of me. Then he wrapped tape all the way around my head until there was no more tape on the roll and Sage Nell's face was stuck over mine."

I looked and found pieces of tape still in Daffy's hair. As I carefully pulled them out, she winced.

"He told me that since he couldn't find Sage Nell, I'd do just fine. 'A bitch for a bitch,' he said. The paper was so tight against my nose and mouth, it was hard to breathe."

She described the way he had punched through the drawn face to her own. He hit her in the nose, then busted her mouth.

"The blood was pooling against the paper," she said. "He'd taped it so tight around my chin, it held the blood like a bowl. I tried to get it off, but he grabbed my head and yelled, 'Keep the face on, bitch.' I thought he was gonna hit me again, but then he used a pair of scissors to cut the eye holes. When he cut a hole at the mouth, the blood spilled out. I could finally breathe. He yanked me to the mirror so I could see the bitch I was, he said."

Daffy opened her hand, revealing a crumpled piece of paper, soaked in blood. When she flattened it, I could make out the remnants of the ink drawing.

"I finally managed to tear Sage Nell's face off on the way here," she said.

"I can't believe Highway Man let you go." I hugged her to me.

"He wouldn't have if I hadn't thrown the snake dirt in his eyes."

She showed her knees and the way the jeans were dirty there.

"I kept falling down when I got outside," she said. "I couldn't see so good until I got the face off. When I did, I found this with the blood on my chin."

She opened her other hand, revealing a bloody tooth.

"I tried to put it back in." She cried as she tried again, pushing the tooth up into her bleeding gum. "It won't go back in, Arc. You've got to drive me to the river, so I can wash it in the water. It's what Mamaw Milkweed would do. She always said the river sang to women and her daughters and that she blew her trumpet to the sky, blowing all the sorrow with it. Maybe then, I can get the tooth to go back in my mouth."

"Where's Highway Man at now?" I asked.

"He stopped chasing me when I got across the street," she said. "He'll kill me when he finds me, Arc."

I stepped inside the house and got the truck keys along with a black marker.

"Where you think you're going with that?" Aunt Clover asked

from the sofa. "You need to stop writing all over that truck. Just like a damn child growing both ways."

Outside, I lifted Daffy up from the porch steps to her feet. While I drove, she uncapped the marker and wrote a rhyme on the last free space on the tan leather of the steering wheel.

I am not home if I continue to roam.

I headed in the direction of Mamaw Milkweed's old farmhouse, but turned off before we got there, taking the back road that led to the part of the river closest to her place. We left the truck and walked across the cold ground. Daffy looked up at the sky and said it was starting to snow. The light flakes fell softly on top of our heads as we got closer to the river. It was cold enough for the water to start freezing. The currents that were still free flowed over the ice sheets.

"This spot is good," I said, kneeling and using a rock to break the hard ground to make a small, shallow grave.

"Did you know," I said, "in Greek mythology, the Grey Sisters shared one eye and one tooth. Some say the sisters were monsters. Others say they were swans. More say they were merely the white foam of crashing waves."

"What'd they do with the one eye they shared?" Daffy asked, getting down on her knees.

"They saw the world with it."

"What'd they do with their one tooth?" she asked.

"They wished upon it," I said.

"Wished?" Daffy held the tooth up between us. "Let's wish on it, Arc."

We closed our eyes. We never told each other what we'd wished for, but we had a good idea that we were asking for the very same thing.

When we opened our eyes, she looked down at my sweatshirt, then at her own.

"They're gray." She giggled. "We're wearing gray sweatshirts. We're the Grey Sisters after all. Do you think we look like monsters? Like swans? Or like the white foam of crashing waves? I think we're like swans," she said before I had the chance to answer. "Or maybe crashing waves. Then we're water, and we're the largest bodies of anything on earth. We could drown all the monsters like Highway Man before they dare take anything from us."

Satisfied, she placed the tooth into the shallow hole and covered it, knowing how to bury something so well.

"Years from now," she said, "an archaeologist like you, Arc, will dig my tooth up and I'll matter because I'll be from the past. They'll wonder who I was and they'll give me a better story than my truth."

She smiled, wrapping her arms into mine. And though we grew colder, we stayed by the river, giggling as we talked about what would grow from her bloody tooth. We imagined trees of magical fruit better than ordinary apples and pears.

"Something special," she said. "A fruit that will never rot. That will always keep." She fell silent, then said my name. "Arc?"

"Yeah?"

"There's something in the water." She loosened her arms from mine and stood, her finger pointing out. "There's something out there floating."

I stood up beside her.

As I saw the body float with the current and slide across a patch of ice, I said, "It's not something, Daffy. It's *someone.*"

CHAPTER 18

Even death settles in the fresh flower petals.

—*Daffodil Poet*

1990

OUR LAST YEAR IN HIGH SCHOOL, DAFFY GOT DOWN ON HER KNEES and stared through all the keyholes in our house. The one that opened to my bedroom. The one that opened into hers. She even looked through the small keyhole of the small closet in the kitchen. Then she walked down the hall and looked through the one that entered our mother's room.

"Do you remember when we would put our fingers through here?" she asked, trying to fit hers through the hole once more. "Did we think our fingers were keys? Were we hoping to unlock the doors? Or lock them? I still don't know."

She removed her finger and held her eye to the open hole, the light shining through and cutting out the shape on her face.

"I keep hoping I'll look through these keyholes," she said, "and see a future that goes for all the miles it takes to get outta this stinking town. But all I see is a woman on a mattress in a room. Do you think that's our future? I don't wanna call that my life, Arc. But I'm scared I've made certain it will be now."

We had both been on the honor roll that year. She would be going to college to swim. I would be going to learn how to make a living out of digging in the dirt. Those were our plans. The ones we talked about that whole year. No one knew that was also the year Daffy began using. She swam too good to think that.

"I couldn't tell you, Arc," she later said. "I'm such a loser. I didn't want you to know. I thought I could kick it before you even found out."

She started missing her swim meets. The ones she did attend, she no longer won. The scholarship talk faded, as did any conversation of anything more, like the Olympics.

"Yeah, I guess it was silly to think," Tam said as she watched Daffy place last, barely able to keep up with the girls who just the previous season, she'd beaten in an easy sweep.

Her bathing suit got a tear in it and was not replaced. John was gone anyway, so there was no money for fees or suits or caps, especially for a girl who was no longer worth the expense. In the chlorinated circles, no one remembered her name, except to say she was the girl who threw up in the water during the hundred-meter freestyle last time she was in a pool.

"She nearly drowned," one girl would say to another as they waited their turn to dive into the same water. "They had to pull her out and give her mouth-to-mouth. Can you imagine? All that vomit. How gross."

When Daffy was finally kicked off the team, she cut her bathing suit up and threw it into the trash. Both her big toenails were dead by then. That was how she had been injecting, so no one would see the track marks on her swimming arms.

"How could you, Daffy?" I shouted at her. "How could you fuck up this badly? How could you do this to me?"

"I was just trying to put the strings up into the square, Arc. Like Mamaw Milkweed did."

Daffy held up the needle full of enough to get the high she'd become addicted to.

"Mamaw used a crochet needle, Daffy," I said. "Not a dirty one."

"A needle is a needle." She looked at it. "And you know what? When it's inside you, it does turn the savage side beautiful. Nothing feels bad here, Arc. All the sadness goes away. The warmth washes over you. It's the most magnificent thing. It makes me feel like glass. The way it breaks me into pieces. But I love being broken by it. Because the next time I use it, it makes me whole again and it holds me so tight. It loves me. It's a friend for a thousand years. It's a father who's still alive. A mother who hugs me. It's Mamaw Milkweed coming back with the flower bulbs. Your stories weren't turning anything into the beautiful side, Arc. This stuff does."

"You sound like Mom and Aunt Clover," I said.

"I know now why they do it."

"You could have made it out of this hellhole, Daffy. To college. The Olympics."

"You know why that sounds so dumb when you say it?" she shouted back. "Because it is dumb."

I watched her find a vein, the needle filling with her blood.

"I swear I'll quit, Arc," she said as she removed the rubber band of her goggles and tied it around her arm. "This is only for a moment, just to clear my head. Then I'll stop, and it'll be like it never happened. And we can be like the Trung sisters. Queens with our own army. Tell me about them, Arc. Tell me about them."

I was watching my sister change, and there seemed to be nothing I could do to stop it. I thought back to the time she had gotten the flu, then I thought about the spider. Just as then, this was a new monster she couldn't fight without me.

For some reason I never thought about getting addicted myself, so while she was passed out in her childhood bed, I picked up her needle and did just as I'd watched Mom and Aunt Clover do a million times over. I emptied the little baggie into the spoon, added the water, and held a lighter beneath it. My hand shook as I tied the rubber band from her goggles around my arm.

I was young and stupid. I believed we could be strong enough to beat it together. That it wouldn't hold me the way it held the other women in my family. I thought it'd be different for me. That I could make one wrong decision and be okay the next day. But I didn't prepare myself for the feeling. The overwhelming sense of peace, the warm wash of euphoria that took every single drop of my pain away. I never knew such a feeling could exist. It spoke to me. Told me it would protect me, keep me safe, and close the doors on all the things that had once hurt me. Sweet lies that glistened, and I believed them.

It was a single moment that made the idea of returning to life unbearable. That was when I knew why some people did it. Why my mother did it. Why my aunt did it. Why my father, long ago, tied the army belt around his arm. And then of course, there was Daffy.

A girl who merely wanted to forget it all. How could I blame her, or any of them, for that? That urge to be free from the truths that hurt too much to know.

We humans have always been in pain. History tells us that in the artifacts civilizations have left behind. Pain is there in the broken vases, the fractured poetry, the overwhelming music we have played for centuries. We belong to grief until the engine goes out. Then we belong to the dirt, our bodies identical to other fallen things.

As it coursed through my veins, I felt removed from this pain. This is the unattainable feeling it gives you. This is the trick it plays.

What it doesn't say is what it takes in return.

When I opened my eyes, my sister was on her knees at my feet. She rubbed the spot on my arm where I'd injected and asked, "Why'd you do it, Arc?"

"So we can kill the monster together, Daffy."

She smiled. I have never forgotten that.

P
A
R
T

IV

CHAPTER 19

You can only soar so much and no more.

—*Daffodil Poet*

1993

THE CLOUDS DRAPED DOWN FROM THE NIGHT SKY AS IF THERE WERE no place for them left in all the world, as Daffy and me pulled Sage Nell from the river. Her long, curly hair tangled around her face. Her skin had been changed in color and texture by the icy-cold water that had enveloped her as she floated until found. Rain-washed and brutally moved, her bruises were those of someone who had been dragged. Her gray eyes had clouded over. Her lips had turned blue. She had a look on her face that said she just wanted to go home.

I wanna go home, go home, go home . . .

"Her jaw." Daffy stared at it.

"Broken," I said.

Daffy studied it as if she could make it right again.

"The one who broke it must not have known," I said.

"Known what?" Daffy asked.

"That a woman with a broken jaw can still speak."

We looked at the words Sage Nell spoke to us in every cut and wound. They told us she had been more than drowned. More than a woman washing her overdose off in the river. Like there had been with Harlow, there were twigs, leaves, and insects wrapped in Sage Nell's hair, piled on top of her head in ways that didn't seem natural. She was naked. Not a single sock.

"She wasn't supposed to end up like this," Daffy said. "Not our Nell. I always thought she'd get out of Chillicothe. Take a drum and beat it for the jaguars and the cheetahs."

Daffy took her hairbrush out of my purse and tried to run it through the tangles of Sage Nell's hair.

"You might be brushing evidence away," I told her.

"She would wanna look nice, Arc," Daffy said. "You know how much she loved her hair. All those headbands and barrettes. I wanna be the one who brushes it. The cops ain't gonna care. They'll pull her hair too hard. They'll hurt her."

"No one can hurt her anymore, Daffy."

"I hope she wasn't scared." Daffy cradled Sage Nell's cut cheek in her hand. "When it happened, I hope she wasn't too scared."

I took Nell's hands and searched them. "It's gone."

"What is?" Daffy asked.

"The magnet." I looked out at the river. "It's gone."

We used the phone of the first neighbor to open their door to us. When the spider showed up, he asked, "Mighty odd you being the one to find another dead woman in the river, don't you think?"

"Just hanging around by the water," I said.

"In this cold?" he asked. "Why is there blood on your face?"

"An angry boyfriend." I looked away. "The cold is good for things like that."

Three days later Sage Nell's sweatshirt was located, half-buried in debris at the side of the river she'd been found in.

"Was she in college?" someone new to the street asked.

"Yeah, but she fell out like a rock," another woman said. *"She'd been a philosophy major."*

"What's a philosophy major?"

"Someone who thinks a lot about things."

"Oh. I wonder what she would think about this."

I'd only heard Sage Nell talk about her family once, when she said, "They told me I wasn't their daughter no more. But that's okay." She had wrapped her arms around Daffy, me, and Thursday. "Because you're my family now."

Her parents had her cremated. When Violet called them to find out when the service was, the dad told her there wasn't going to be one. Not for a girl who was no longer worth the expense. They allowed the funeral home to release the ashes to Violet. I held them on my lap in a small brown box as she drove. We were headed to the Distant Mountain, where Thursday and Daffy were waiting.

When Violet took a different turn, I asked, "Where we going?"

"I just wanna stop by and see my little girl," she said.

I looked out the window at the playground as she parked by the sidewalk in front of the redbrick school.

"They should be getting out for recess any minute now," Violet said. "You mind, Arc?"

"No." I watched the doors. "I don't mind."

It wasn't more than five minutes later that they opened, and a throng of children came running out. They fired off in every direction. Some to the swings. Others to the slide. More to the monkey bars, their knitted caps falling off their heads.

Violet got out of the car and crossed the walk to the chain-link fence surrounding the playground. It was windy. I made sure to keep a tight grip on the box as I got out.

"There she is." Violet pointed to a girl with a low ponytail and brown eyes. "That's my Grassy. Look at how long she can hang from the monkey bars. She's strong. A lot stronger than I ever was. Well done, baby." Violet clapped.

As she hollered her daughter's name and clapped louder, Grassy looked over.

"Mommy." She squealed and dropped to the ground. She ran so fast, she bounced against the fence, the chains springing back with her as she squealed again. "Mommy. Where you been? When you coming to get me?"

"Soon, baby, soon. Hey." Violet knelt so she could be eye level, the fence between them. "You remember how I told you I was gonna be buying my own place to bake?"

The little girl nodded so quickly, the fuzzy ball on her cap bounced up and down.

"Well." Violet smiled. "I've found a building. I think I can buy it."

"I can help you make cupcakes there?" Grassy asked as she reached through the chain-link fence and rubbed off some of Violet's eye shadow.

"All of 'em," Violet said, laughing at the way Grassy tried to add the eye shadow above her own eyes. "And the cookies and the pies and the doughnuts and whatever else you wanna make. I'll put you in charge of the sugar."

"Okay, Mommy. And then you'll come get me? I don't like living with Daddy."

"How come?" Violet asked, her bare fingers turning red on the cold chain-link.

"Because you're not there," Grassy said, "and he can never seem to find you, no matter how many doors he looks behind. He always bakes cookies from a roll of dough from the store. They always end up burned. He's not as good as you, Mommy."

The teacher blew the whistle.

"I gotta go," Grassy said. "Recess is over. I'll get in trouble if I'm late."

"Wait." Violet ran to her car and reached into the back seat for the box of doughnuts she had been handing out on the street earlier.

"Chocolate glazed." She tried to pass Grassy one, but it was too big to fit through the fence.

"I gotta go, Mommy." Grassy was stepping back, the teacher's whistle shrill in the air.

"Wait, wait." Violet pushed the doughnut through, smashing it out to the ground on the other side. Grassy was already on her way across the playground, the swings still flying on their own.

"You go on, baby," Violet hollered after her. "We'll see each other real soon. I promise."

When we were back in the car, I asked, "What building are you talking about buying?"

"Oh," she said. "I'll show you. It's not far from here."

Violet drove to a vacant commercial space on one of the streets off Main. The building was nestled in between a coffee shop and a thrift store.

"I've been saving up," she said, looking out her window at the FOR SALE sign. "I'm gonna call it Grassy and Violet's. She'll come here every day after school."

She kept her eyes on the sign as she slowly pulled away. She talked about the bakery some more, about the colors on the walls.

"It's gonna be blue and pink," she said, "like the cotton candy I once had at a fair when I was a kid. The counters will be pistachio. The color of my father's favorite pudding. And there's gonna be mason jars lined up, full of red carnations. Those were my mother's favorite. They'll sit by the stand mixer, but Grassy won't be able to use the mixer until she's older. Sometimes she's got the habit of reaching toward something that swirls and whirls, thinking there ain't no danger in it. She's gotta get a little older to know that sometimes there is."

By the time she was pulling into Thursday's driveway, Violet had informed me about the color of the doilies on the trays and even what stickers she'd put on the sides of the cash register.

"Rainbows and unicorns," she said, "because they're Grassy's favorites. And come night, when me and her are sweeping the powdered sugar up off the floor, we'll call it snow, and she'll laugh." Violet wiped her cheeks.

"It sounds great," I said.

Her smile faded. "I just hope I don't fuck it up."

She reached into the back seat to get Sage Nell's sweatshirt. We got out of the car and walked across the road through the frozen cornfield. The old stems had been broken by a tractor, leaving a few cobs behind. Though they had no kernels on them, the crows scratched them up and tossed them into the air as we walked down through the trees.

"The woods will miss Sage Nell," I said.

"Because," Violet added, "she lives alone."

We headed down the wooded slope, the winter having killed the tall grass that would have softly touched our legs in the summertime. Once at the river, bare branches of the trees fanned against the sky, while Daffy stood by the water's edge, her eyes on its currents. Thursday was standing beside her.

"You two took forever," Thursday said. She looked at the box in my hands. "Is that her? Is that our Sage Nell?"

"Yes," I said. "What's left of her at least."

Violet took the sweatshirt over to the tree that Sage Nell used to climb up on when she wrote her sins on the leaves.

"Who's gonna get it up there?" Violet asked.

"I'll do it." I handed the box of ashes to Thursday.

I had climbed only a couple of trees in my lifetime. The things I wanted to explore were beneath my feet in the ground, not above my head. I held on to the sweatshirt and used the rock Sage Nell had always stood on. The wind knocked me off-balance, and it took me more than one try. Finally, I had enough strength to pull myself up. Straddling the low branch, I tied the sweatshirt by its sleeves to it. Violet pulled a rubber band out of her back pocket and wrapped it around the hem of the sweatshirt hanging down, closing it up like a bag.

"Hand me Nell," I said.

Thursday stood on the rock, reaching the box up to me. I wrapped my fingers around it tightly, not allowing the lid to come open as I put it down inside the sweatshirt's collar. I slowly dumped the ashes in, not losing any to the wind just yet. After I dropped the box, the wind carried it across the river, as I climbed down the tree.

We stared up at the blowing sweatshirt, the ashes contained inside by the rubber band. Several moments of silence went by, the four of us watching the sweatshirt.

"I remember the time me and Nell made chocolate cake together at my house," Violet said. "She wanted to leave it in the oven longer than it needed. I told her it was gonna burn. She said that was okay. That she wanted the kitchen to smell like her mom's."

"I remember," Thursday said with a chuckle, "when she crammed her mouth full of hard candy because I told her she couldn't fit more than ten pieces. She proved me wrong. She almost fucking choked to death, but she proved me wrong."

Thursday's laughter filled the silence, then she, too, went quiet.

"One time," I said, "I'd been sitting on the curb. Just come out of the Blue Hour. It was raining, but I still sat there. The mascara burned my eyes. I still sat there. When I didn't feel the rain on top of my head anymore, I looked up. Sage Nell was standing over me with her arms out. 'I'll be your umbrella,' she said."

Thursday laid her chin on my shoulder. "She is shiny and rides among the goddamn stars."

"She is shiny and rides among the stars," we all said, the chorus of our voices echoing off the water. We hooted and howled and said it three times more.

Daffy fell into a sigh. "I hope she knows how much she was loved."

Violet stepped over to the sweatshirt. When she placed her hand on the rubber band, Thursday held her arms up so her bracelets rattled as she started to sing "Bette Davis Eyes."

"What?" She shrugged when we looked at her. "It was Sage Nell's favorite song. She thought the lyrics were written about her. And who's to say they weren't?"

Against the sounds of her bracelets and her voice, the wind picked up, and Violet removed the rubber band from the sweatshirt. It flapped open as the ashes flew out. I chased them into the river. The water was cold as I dove into it.

When I surfaced, I heard Violet shouting from the riverbank, "Arc, come back."

"Are you trying to kill yourself?" Thursday's voice echoed.

"I've got to find it," I yelled back to them. When I dove under again, I tried to reach the river's bottom. I held my breath as long as I could before returning to the surface.

"Arc, get out of there." I heard Violet's shrill cry.

"I'm not leaving until I find it." Back under, I swam the deepest I had. I couldn't see in the brown water. As I reached my fingers out, I could only believe I was close. Close enough to run my hand in the mud, hoping to find it. The artifact of her.

Refusing to go back to the surface, I ran out of air and inhaled. The cold water flooded my nostrils and spilled down my throat. Turned around in the murky water, I could no longer find the surface. It was nothing but darkness before a pair of arms wrapped around my stomach and yanked me upward.

At the surface, I coughed, the water shooting out.

"You're crazy, Arc Doggs." Violet's voice swam me to the bank, where she dropped me.

Daffy knelt over me as I spit more water out. Shivering, I lay against her side as she held me into her.

"You'll probably get pneumonia now, ya dumbass," Thursday said, yanking Sage Nell's sweatshirt down from the branch and wrapping it around me along with her warm arms. "Going into that icy water like that. What the fuck were you doing, girl?"

"Trying to find it," I said.

"Find what?" Violet wrapped her arms around Thursday's until I was cocooned by the both of them.

"Sage Nell's magnet," I said, my words trembling with my body.

"That ugly old fish magnet?" Thursday asked.

I nodded and said, "The one from her mother's kitchen. I thought she would want it. It's out there somewhere in the water. I just thought she'd want it back."

I cried, and it felt like something I'd been holding in for a long time.

"*Shhh.*" Violet's warm breath felt good on my face. "It's okay, Arc. Wherever she is, she has everything she needs."

"Yeah, that's right," Thursday said. "There ain't nothing lost to her now. And that fish magnet, well, it's in the river. It's turned into a real fish now. I don't know if there's anything that'd make ol' Nell happier."

As we stared out at the water, Sage Nell's ashes had already disappeared. Daffy slipped her hand in mine. For a moment, I felt we had everything we would ever need.

OFFICE OF ROSS COUNTY MEDICAL EXAMINER
CHILLICOTHE, OHIO
REPORT OF INVESTIGATION BY COUNTY MEDICAL OFFICER

DECEDENT: Sage Nell

GENDER: A reflection of herself

OCCUPATION: Rides among the stars

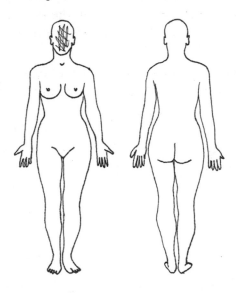

WOUNDS AND MARKS: Shiny. Body is cool to the touch. Rigor present in the limbs, head, and neck region. Shiny. Vertical wound extending from collarbone to suprapubic region. A crown has been made out of leaves and twigs. Evidence of brutal assault after expiration. Kick prints. Size eleven boots. Shiny. Dragged before put in river. Rope burns. Severe fractures, sustained over time. Evidence of someone having lifted her from under the arms, shaking her until she was no more a keeper of dreams.

PROBABLE CAUSE OF DEATH:

Letting the devil know her name.

CHAPTER 20

If you take her bones,
carve her name, so she's not alone.

—*Daffodil Poet*

THE WEEKS THAT FOLLOWED SAGE NELL'S DEATH WERE COLD. THE
January of 1994 was Daffy blowing her breath onto her fingers while
she wrote rhymes on the leather seat of the truck. It was an old coat,
thin as a scrap of paper, wrapped around tight. Cigarette after cigarette on the sidewalk in front of the Blue Hour. It was the heaviness
of Sage Nell's name in the backs of our throats. The absence of her
laugh. The realization that when we called her name, no one would
come.

During this time, the sun was difficult. It was difficult to feel. Difficult to know. Difficult to find. Daffy would talk of meadows. I would
speak of dandelions, the yellow color something we tried to birth
in that gray world. Violet sought her colors in the sprinkles on her
cupcakes, while Thursday found hers in the bracelets, necklaces, and
rings she made. When she didn't have money for beads, Thursday
would make jewelry out of dried corn and things she found on the
street like bottle caps and small tin cans.

"Garbage jewels," she'd say, but still wore them as if she had just
escaped from a diamond mine, its largest gems on her wrists.

It was a good day when her parents brought her groceries, because
she always saved back some of the pizza money they gave her. Toward
the end of that month, she called and asked if I wanted to go to the
craft store with her.

"I need more lapis lazuli, pearls, and sunstones," she said.

Daffy and me waited on the front porch for her to pull up. We hopped into her car, the heater sputtering and alternating between cool and warm air.

"I swear if I can get one fucking dream to come true," Thursday said as she banged her fist on the heater vents, "it'll be that there's at least one damn winter I ain't shivering myself to pieces."

She drove hurriedly over the salted streets while she sang. Her voice sounded like the field behind her trailer at night in July. Part hoot of the owl, part chirp of the cricket, part horn of the bullfrog, verses not of words, but of sounds. When she stopped singing, the silence fell heavy.

"When I was a kid," she said, "and my mom would drive my older brother and me to the craft store, my brother would tell me this story about Chillicothe, how the town was a fugitive on the run. Like the whole town. Like Chillicothe itself was a living entity. He said never yell out the words, 'Caught you,' because being a fugitive meant the town thought you were saying that you had caught it. Anyone who said this phrase while in Chillicothe, fucking disappeared, never to be seen or heard from again. He said the town was the one who made them disappear. God, it freaked me out so much.

"And what do you know, but when we got to the store, my son-of-a-bitch brother got out of the car and yelled 'caught you' at the top of his lungs. I was scared to death he was going to disappear, I cried until he slept with a rock tied around his fucking foot that night." She laughed to herself, remembering.

"I didn't know you had a brother," I said.

"No." She stopped laughing as she turned into the parking lot. "I don't anymore. He overdosed when I was still a kid. I suppose the town made him disappear after all, huh?"

Daffy stayed close as we walked against the gust of wind on the way inside. A pop can blew across Thursday's feet. She quickly picked it up and put it in her purse. I knew she would poke a hole through the end of it later. She'd find glass bottles, tin cans, anything she could look through one end to see through to the other side. As she would say, "You'd be surprised how many telescopes one can find on the streets."

Inside the store, she grabbed a basket to shop with. The bead aisle was at the back. As she walked by the bolts of fabric, she unraveled a sheer purple one and draped it around Daffy and me until we laughed. The worker passing by said, "Stop that," as she yanked the fabric off us and wrapped it back around the bolt.

Thursday rolled her eyes and headed on, past the paint by numbers that she glanced at with a grin. Daffy and me stopped at the aisle of yarn, while Thursday walked on ahead. We held our hands out and ran them over the skeins.

"The same dye lot," Daffy said as she picked up a roll of blue yarn. I picked up one myself and compared it to hers.

"Half of the same blue," I said.

"Half of the same honey in the hive," Daffy spun by the yellow yarn.

"Half of the same plum," I said by the purple.

We held on to the skeins for the length it took us to walk the aisle. Our eyes slowly moved over each color, until we laid down the skeins and didn't look back as we walked away.

Thursday was a few aisles over. She was holding a pack of bright orange beads.

"These are carnelians," she said. "Do you like them? Or do you prefer amethyst?" She grabbed a bag of bright purple beads in the shapes of ovals.

"I like both," I said.

"And those." Daffy pointed to the small heart-shaped pack.

"Those are garnets." Thursday picked them up and dropped them into the basket.

She stopped in front of the green beads and said, "My guy would have eyes like these emeralds. Well dressed, with sapphires for buttons." She ran her fingers across the bags of blue beads, leaving them swinging. "He can name every planet in our solar system in alphabetical order. Best of all, he'd say he's looked through all the telescopes in the world but has never found a more beautiful star than me. You think such a guy exists?" She turned to us.

"Crazier things have been found," I said.

She laughed, grabbing a pack of multicolored beads that she said was the whole damn treasure chest.

When we got back to her trailer, she pulled up alongside her mailbox. She emptied it out and tossed the mail onto my lap. It consisted of envelope after envelope from various wildlife charities and animal rights groups. There was one asking her to help rescue donkeys, another for bees, one for whales. The image of each animal or insect was printed on the exterior in bright detail.

After we got inside, she dumped her beads out on the table. She took the mail from me, pulling out the free address labels and small notepads. One even had a bumper sticker inside.

"'Help end factory farming,'" she read aloud.

She peeled the sticker off but didn't take it outside to the car. Instead, she carried it to the Butterfly Corner, the part of her trailer where the living room and kitchen met. There she would hang the various gifts and pamphlets she got in the mail from the charities.

"They put all that money into address labels and stickers and cards," she said as she stuck the bumper sticker on the wall in between bookmarks that had PLEASE SAVE THE FROGS on them and notecards with the faces of gorillas and elephants. "I don't know why they don't put the money into taking care of the animals."

When I first saw the Butterfly Corner, I had asked why charities mailed her so much free stuff to begin with.

"I once gave to this shelter for dancing bears," she had told me. "It was only about ten bucks. I ain't gave any more since, but they must have put me on a list. Now I get mailings for everything from pigs to horses to animals I ain't never even heard of."

"What's a dancing bear?" I had asked her.

"Where they kidnap a bear from the wild, chain her up, and make her dance for money."

She had a photograph of a bear on the wall with glazed eyes, a muzzle over her mouth, and chains around her neck and legs.

"I wonder if she saw any of that ten bucks," Sage Nell had said as she ran her hand gently over the bear. "I like to think I made her life a little easier."

The focal point of the Butterfly Corner, and the reason for the name, was a large poster of a Monarch. On the back, the Monarch's migration was explained, and so was the threat to it. But you didn't see that. You only saw the butterfly's body running down the shared line of the walls with each side of the poster stretched out like open wings, showcasing the vibrant orange with black stripes. The poster was about three feet wide and still had the crease lines from the time it had been folded up in the envelope.

After Thursday smoothed out the bumper sticker, she stood back and stared at the butterfly.

"One day," she said, "we'll live in a world where no one will receive this mail because all these species you see here will have gone extinct waiting for us to save them from our own fucking selves."

The pounding knock made the three of us jump.

"Who the hell is that?" Daffy asked.

The moment Thursday opened the door, he was like a tall, hard, solid object, blocking the light and casting a heavy shadow.

"Good to see you're home." He moved inside, pushing her back. He was wearing sunglasses with mirrored lenses, reflecting our images in them.

"Hey, Highway Man." Thursday swallowed hard. "How you fucking doing?"

"Hey, Thursday. How's my favorite day of the week?" He took his sunglasses off, hanging them over his open collar. He was wearing a bulky coat, the hood lined in the fur of an animal I thought was likely pictured on Thursday's wall.

"You want anything to drink?" Her voice was trembling nearly as much as her hands.

"Yeah, sure, baby."

He only called us bitch this and bitch that. To hear him call her baby sounded like the worst name coming out of his mouth.

"Got some cold beer," she said, turning toward the kitchen. "How many you want?"

"I don't want nothing cold," he said.

He walked around the room, looking at the framed photos on the shelf, including one of the group of us. We'd taken it at the Distant Mountain, the hills rising behind.

"I want something hot," he said, leaning toward the photo.

"Hot?" She stopped in her tracks.

"I want it scalding." His voice was deep and low. "Hot enough to burn the skin off."

"Hot enough to burn skin off?" she asked.

"If it ain't boiling, it ain't gonna be mine." He smiled, and his large teeth looked like flaming snakes.

"I'll see what I got." She backed up and stepped into the kitchen.

He twisted his head around to look at Daffy and me. I nudged her to keep her eyes down. He kept his on us as we heard the microwave hum.

"Here ya go." Thursday came in holding the mug by its handle. "Some instant coffee."

He peered into the cup and dipped his finger in. "Ain't hot enough to even bother a fly," he said.

She looked from the coffee to him. "I'll be right back." She turned and was in the kitchen again.

Perhaps while she was in there, she thought of running out the back, her eyes on the distance she could make between him and her. *How far can I get?* she must have wondered. I don't know why she ultimately decided not to push open the back screen door and run like hell across the two acres to the woodline. I can't say for sure why she came back in with a mug of liquid hot enough to burn the skin off, the steam rising up into her face.

"Sit it down." He nodded at the table.

Before she did, she blew on it.

He waited until the mug was out of her hand, then smacked her. "I tell you to blow on it, bitch?"

She shook her head and kept it down as she sat in the chair.

"Do something, Arc," Daffy whispered in my ear.

"I can't," I said.

Highway Man turned to me. "That's right, you can't. You can't leave. You can't speak. You can't do nothing but keep quiet right there." He pointed to the sofa.

Daffy and me quickly sat on it.

He turned back to Thursday and ran his tongue over his teeth. "The delivery didn't arrive," he said calmly, as he picked the mug up by its handle, the steam still rising.

"I don't know who you've been talking to," she said, "but I delivered that cash."

He stood by the chair, holding the mug above her head. She hunched forward as if she were already feeling it pour down on her.

"Whoever told you this shit is lying." She started to cry. "I swear. Please, don't fucking do this. I didn't steal from you. I wouldn't do that, baby."

He started to tip the mug.

"Cut it out," I said, rising up.

"You stay put." He pointed his finger at me. "Or you're next."

Daffy tugged my arm until I sat back down.

Highway Man smiled as the hot coffee got closer and closer to the lip of the mug he tilted even more in his hand. Thursday whimpered and tried to get up, but he grabbed her shoulder and held her down.

"C'mon, man," she screamed. "Stop, I ain't fucking done nothing."

"I told you what would happen if you ever stole from me," he said.

Daffy buried her face into my shoulder, and I shut my eyes just as Thursday covered her head with her hands. I waited for her scream, but only his laughter came.

I opened my eyes to see him setting the cup down.

"Stupid bitches," he said. When he kept laughing, Thursday joined in.

"Man." She sighed. "For a minute there, I thought you were gonna—"

He grabbed the necklaces around her neck, breaking them, the small plastic gems scattering to the carpet.

"Shut the fuck up." He slapped her across the face.

Staring into her eyes, he reached into his coat pocket and pulled out the type of brush I'd seen Welt use at the Blue Hour when washing the brick. The wooden handle was the full length of Highway Man's hand. I could tell the bristles were stiff, because they reflected the ceiling light like copper wires.

"It's a scraping brush," he said, holding it in front of Thursday's eyes. "Here, feel these."

He picked up her hand and put it on top of the bristles.

"What do they feel like?" he asked.

"Like something that hurts," she said, pulling her hand back.

He smiled, touching the bristles himself as he said, "A brush like this scrapes off paint. Daddy used it around the doors and windows in the summer when he repainted the house. It scraped the old paint off like it was butter."

He wiped his nose on his fingers, the bright red tattoo covering them, seeming even brighter.

"Take your shoes off," he said.

"C'mon baby." Thursday held her hands together under her chin. "Please, I'm begging ya. I wouldn't steal from you." She tried to reach up and take his face, but he smacked her.

"I said get your goddamn shoes off." He removed his coat and draped it across the coffee table. His shirt was cut low, showing the words DIPPED IN EVIL.

Thursday cried louder as she bent over to untie her laces and slip her shoes off.

I grabbed Daffy's hand and tried to slowly get up.

"What did I tell you?" He pulled the handgun out from the back of his waistband and pointed it at me. "You move, and I'll shoot you." He leaned in, his voice calm and steady. "All you'll be is a little iron butterfly, unable to fly away. You understand?"

I nodded, falling to a seat on the sofa with Daffy.

"Now give me one of those feet," he said to Thursday as he laid the gun on the coffee table.

"No, please." She tried to sit on her feet and hide them.

He grabbed her by the hair. "If you don't give me one," he said, "I'm gonna use this on your fucking face." He pressed the wire bristles into her cheek.

She let loose a piercing scream.

"Shut up." He pressed harder until she was but a whimper. "That's a good pussy cat." He meowed and yowled like a tomcat in heat.

When he pulled the brush back, her skin was marked with deep imprints by the bristles. "Now, let's see that foot."

"Don't," I said. "Whatever you're gonna do, Highway Man, don't. We can get the money back to you."

"You could pay me a million dollars right now," he said, "and I'd still fucking do it. You know why? Because a bitch gotta learn her lesson."

He sat on the edge of the coffee table in front of the chair, yanking Thursday's foot out and laying it across his lap.

As Thursday whined and cried, he said, "Let's see. I think old Daddy did it back and forth like this and the paint just peeled right off."

He moved the brush in the air less than an inch from the sole of her foot. She cried louder, trying to pull back.

He kept a tight hold and laughed. "Yeah, I think he did it just like this." He smiled as he stabbed the bristles into the bottom of her foot. Each time he pushed the brush up and down, her skin shredded.

She screamed and pushed her hands against his shoulders. When that didn't work, she slapped the side of his head and pulled his hair, but nothing could get him to stop. Not able to stand the pain, Thursday threw herself back, grotesquely twisting her body to bite the back of the chair in agony.

I stared at the gun on the coffee table.

"Arc, don't," Daffy whispered into my ear. She tried to hold me back, but I made a lunge toward it.

Highway Man let the brush fall to the floor as he got up, grabbing the gun before I could.

"Stupid bitch," he shouted. "You wanna bleed for me, too?"

Before I knew it, he was standing over me. My head was snapped back to the sofa cushion as his fist knocked me in the middle of the face. At first, I felt each blow that followed. But the more he punched, the less I started to feel, until I was certain I had no face left at all. All I saw and tasted was blood.

"That should keep ya down." I could hear his voice but no longer saw anything more than a scattering of light. "Where you think you're going?"

I didn't know who he was talking to or who he was chasing. Only when I heard Daffy whisper into my ear, "I'm here," did I understand it must be Thursday screaming. I wiped my eyes until the flashes of light finally started to dim, and I could see he was dragging Thursday across the floor, back to the chair.

"Bloody bitches think they can get away," he said, forcing her down. "Ain't no getting away from me."

"Thursday?" I screamed for her but didn't make it farther than the coffee table before I collapsed. The room was spinning. My head felt like it'd been cracked open. I laid my face down against the carpet. I couldn't feel its scratchy fibers against my skin.

"Stop hurting her," I think I said as I raised my limp arm, the blood spilling down my throat until I heaved and threw it back up.

Highway Man laughed as he held the brush once more to Thursday's foot. Its wooden handle was soaked in blood. I could see pieces of her skin hanging off the bristles.

"Stop. Stop." I dug my fingers into the carpet and pulled myself across the floor, while Daffy tried, but failed, to lift me to my feet.

"You ass . . . you asshole. Stop." I couldn't lift my head any longer. I laid it back down.

When Thursday finally stopped screaming, I rolled my eyes and saw her, motionless, in the chair.

Highway Man reached into his coat pocket and pulled out a bottle. My vision was blurred, but I could see enough of the label to read the words on it.

"Don't," I screamed.

Once he squirted the rubbing alcohol over her foot, she shot up and cried the loudest she had.

"I want you to hear me good, you Chillicothe queen." He grabbed her face in his hands, covered in her blood and mine. "Next time you try to walk off with my dope and money, you remember how much it hurts to steal from the king."

The last thing I saw before blacking out was him taking her other foot in his hand. He moved the brush back and forth until the blood seemed endless.

CHAPTER 21

The beast has had his feast.

—*Daffodil Poet*

I REMEMBER SMELLING DISTANT CLOVER, THE AMBROSIA OF MAMAW Milkweed's house in the spring. I remember feeling like someone was gently pulling my hair back, putting pins in it, to keep it out of my face. I remember my hair felt wet. My tender skin like it was humming, the vibrations alternating with a feeling of stillness.

But most of all, I remember hearing Thursday's voice. "Mom? Dad? Please come. I need you."

Then I heard Daffy. "Arc? Get up. We gotta get outta here."

There was the feeling of grass on my bare feet. The sounds of sirens. The red lights whirling as they became the red scarves around Mamaw Milkweed's neck.

"It's my birthday," she was saying. *"Find me a treasure, Arc."*

As the red lights got closer and one of the scarves blew over my eyes, Daffy said, "Get down, Arc."

We lay with our faces against the ground. I inhaled the smell of the moist earth, cutting through the smell of blood, as the ambulance sped past, the sirens fading in the distance and the lights going with them.

I felt an arm around me. "C'mon, Arc," Daffy said. "Keep going. You've got to do this."

Barely able to keep my eyes open, I dug my fingers into the ground and dragged myself until my head went heavy. I closed my eyes and entered the dark again. Mamaw's sheer red and blue scarves whipped about, as if caught in a wind. Things became blurred after that. I opened my eyes barely able to see Daffy. I leaned on her as we walked.

"That's it, Arc," she said. "We'll get you home."

I saw Dad. He was standing at the end of the road, waving us on. He was wearing his old army uniform. He'd decided to carry his boots. I wasn't sure if he was holding them out to me or just swinging them by his side.

"Daddy?" I tried to run to him, but he was just a bone on the ground.

"Daffy?" I reached for her. "I don't know where I am."

Mamaw Milkweed's scarves rained down from the sky and covered my face until I heard Aunt Clover's voice. "You're a bloody, bloody thing, Arc."

I found the sofa cushion with my hand. I slid across it so far, I ran into her arm.

"I'm not surprised, Arc," Aunt Clover said. "I always knew a girl like you was born to bleed. This will make ya feel better."

She took my arm in her hand. I felt the belt tightening against my skin. I didn't feel the prick of the needle she was pushing into me, but I did feel the warmth it carried through.

"Spittle, spittle, spider, where you gonna hide her?" Aunt Clover's voice floated to me as I laid my head back. It vibrated with the motor of the truck, loudly sputtering its noise as she drove us back home.

"I thought we were home." My voice climbed out of my stomach.

"Don't ever give the name of who done this to ya," Aunt Clover said as she helped Daffy lead me into my bedroom. "If we got rid of every man who wanted to kill us, there'd be no men left in Chillicothe."

She wrapped my head with the sheet until she said I looked like a mummy.

"Sweet dreams, little mummy. Spittle, spittle, spider . . ."

I closed my eyes on her and Daffy standing side by side.

Mamaw Milkweed was just behind them. It was her who followed me, not into a dream, but into the memory of the time she turned her bedroom in her old farmhouse into an Egyptian tomb.

"It's my birthday today," Mamaw Milkweed said.

The three of us were standing in the hall outside her bedroom.

Daffy and me were just a couple of six-year-old girls, waiting for our mamaw to open the door. When she did, we saw she had replaced her floral pink curtains with new ones she had sewn with shiny gold fabric.

"On discount in the Halloween bin at the craft store," she said with a big wink.

She had used the fabric to make a new bedspread and shams, complementing the sheer bright blue scarves she draped over the lamps and tacked up onto the ceiling to stream down.

She'd taken foil, colored it with marker, then crumpled the foil up into balls. The red ones were rubies. The blue were lapis lazuli.

She'd also bought a stained-glass window panel. A small one, with pears, grapes, and apples in the glass, meant to be hung in a kitchen. She placed it in the tall window behind her bed. As the sun shone through the glass, it cast a kaleidoscope of colors that danced across the gold and blue of the room.

"Did you see the hieroglyphics?" She pointed out the figures she'd drawn in chalk on the wood paneling of the walls. There were figures of baskets and hills, of lions and owls. She'd drawn horns and crocodiles and a house with the rising sun.

"That one's an ostrich." She pointed to the bird with the long neck. "And that one's the waning moon." She used her fingers to outline the image as she said, "The Greeks called hieroglyphics holy carvings."

Mamaw Milkweed drew the animals with the same crude lines as the cursive on her recipe cards, but I couldn't have been more thrilled. As we stepped farther into the room, I saw a bulge on the bed beneath the coverlet. I could make out the shape of what appeared to be a head and feet with their toes pointed up.

"Is someone in the bed, Mamaw Milkweed?" Daffy asked, making a sprint toward it.

Mamaw grabbed her before she could make it. "You can't just barge into an Egyptian tomb," she told her. "You've got to be an explorer along the way, Daffy."

Mamaw set Daffy down and grabbed the purple hat with the sheer veil that was on the right bedpost. She put it on top of Daffy's head. Then she grabbed the red hat with the long sash from the other post and put it on mine.

"These don't look like Indiana Jones's hats," Daffy said.

"They're better," I told her, spinning around until my sash flew like wings after me.

We explored the room, all its hieroglyphics and foil jewels. There were even little pyramids Mamaw Milkweed had made out of paper, spritzed with her perfume.

"The aroma of Cleopatra," she said.

When it got dark, she kept the lamps and ceiling lights turned off. Then she handed us a flashlight. We stepped on the rug lightly as if we were stepping across centuries of dust and sand. As we shined our light on the balls of foil, the edges reflected brightly. We threw the light up into the blue streamers as Mamaw Milkweed blew them with her breath as if caught in a wind.

When we got closer to the bed, I said, "I can't believe it. A genuine scars of kiss."

"A *sarcophagus*." Mamaw Milkweed corrected me. "Well what are you waiting for? Make a discovery."

I pulled the blanket back. Mamaw had piled pillows up underneath and wrapped strips she'd cut out of a white cotton sheet around them.

"A real mummy," I said.

For the head, she put one of her hatboxes there. When I threw back the lid, I found a jar of honey inside. Holding it up in the light from Daffy's flashlight, we *ooed* and *aahed* at the way the amber color shone.

"You found the treasure of Egypt," Mamaw Milkweed said.

As I ran my fingers over the strips of cotton, I asked, "Who is the mummy?"

"A powerful woman," Mamaw Milkweed said. "A queen of her people. Her perfume is the musky earth. Her eyes are pools of dandelions. And if you allow it, she'll sing you back your name."

She took the jar of honey from me and held it up to Daffy's ear first. "Do you hear it, Daffy? Do you hear your name?"

Daffy listened, her mouth parted.

"Daffy?" Mamaw whispered on the other side of the jar. "Daffy. You're wonderful. Daffy, you're powerful. Daffy, you are the keeper of the butterflies."

"I hear it." Daffy smiled. "I hear the mummy singing my name."

"Me next," I said, bouncing up and down.

Mamaw took the jar and laid it against my ear.

"Arc?" she sang out. "Arc, do you hear me? You're amazing. Arc, you're powerful. Arc, you are the one who will protect the women from the wolves."

"What?" I looked up at her.

"Protect the women from the wolves, Arc."

Mamaw Milkweed faded as the echoes of Thursday's screams cracked the glass of the jar, causing the honey to spill out over my ears like blood.

As the blue scarves fell down from the ceiling around us, I screamed with Thursday, until Daffy shook me by the shoulders.

I opened my eyes and saw I was sitting up in my bed.

"Stop screaming, Arc," my sister said. "Everything's okay. You're home."

PART

V

CHAPTER 22

A woman who is hard to tame
is a woman who is easy to blame.

—*Daffodil Poet*

"NEVER TRUST A MAN WHO'S NAMED AFTER A HIGHWAY, ARC." MOM'S voice seemed the clearest it had been in years. "He'll go too fast and take you with him. Before you know it, there's no exits. You're stuck there. Ain't no sense in hitchhiking either. Ain't nothing but decomposing flowers behind the wheels."

I never told my mother the one who had attacked me and Thursday was Highway Man. And yet she had lived enough life to know there are some men whose clothes you hang on the windows of your house and some men who tender nothing but the violence they give you.

As the winter turned its cold, barren page to spring, I thought of Highway Man's brush with its wire bristles. Sharp. Restless. Beating with the pulse of hell. I thought of the way Thursday's skin hung off them. Bloody. Raw. Naked. The pieces of her dropped to the floor in ways that would dry and shrivel, as if their humanness had been erased and now carried a sense of otherness, like something shaken from a branch, blown in from the woods, or scattered like sawdust at the paper mill.

Though I dreamed of Thursday, of her wearing a crown of fog and sweat, I had not seen her since our blood pooled together in the fibers of her pale blue carpet. I couldn't bear to see her. I knew her parents were there, taking care of her from the unkind hours to midnight. I hoped it was enough in the absence of a friend.

Only after it rained three days and the old abandoned bowl in the backyard spilled over did I finally gather my courage, along with a box. I carried it out to the front seat of the truck as Daffy followed.

"You want me to come with you?" she asked, raising her leg and slamming her foot down against the ground. She twisted her heel in and caused the wet mud to ride up the sides of her foot and push up between her toes. I had seen her do the same thing twice already that day. Once in the kitchen. Later in her bedroom.

"Why do you keep doing that, Daffy?" I asked.

"I'm squashing the bugs," she said, digging her heel in deeper like she was grinding a body and all of its many legs.

"What bugs?" I asked.

"The creepy crawly ones eating on me."

She smacked her forearm, then flicked the imaginary creature off her skin.

"So, you want me to come?" she asked again.

"I don't think Thursday would want you bringing all them bugs with you," I said.

She ran her finger on the back of her hand in swirling lines. "You hardly ever wanna take me anywhere with you anymore. If you're not careful, Arc, I'll fold up my poetry."

"Don't fold up your poetry, Daffy. You'll just put creases in it."

"I'm serious, Arc." She stared not at me but at the sky above us. "I worry that time is rippling us apart. One day I'll open my eyes, and you'll be on the riverbank, while I'm still in the water, left alone with my reflection in the currents."

Before I could tell her that not even a ripple could keep us apart, Aunt Clover yelled for me from the porch, "Someone's on the phone for you."

As Daffy peeked inside the box on the truck seat, I stepped back into the house. When I picked up the phone, I heard a woman's voice on the other end. "We have an opening," she said. "Are you still interested?"

I looked out the window at Daffy squashing more of her imaginary bugs as I twisted the phone cord around my finger. "Yes," I said. "When can I come?"

"Tomorrow morning. If you miss check-in, the spot will go to someone else."

"I understand."

I listened to the woman give instructions on what to expect, then say, "See you tomorrow."

I slowly hung up the phone and counted my steps out to Daffy.

"Who was on the phone?" she asked.

"We'll talk about it when I get back."

I thought she might ask again to go with me, but she only wrote another rhyme on the truck's glove compartment. After she closed the door, she stood out in the yard, watching me leave.

When I got to Thursday's trailer, I could hear her and her parents' voices coming from inside. "If you don't tell us who did this to you, we can't help you," her dad was saying as I carried the small box up to the front door.

"You've got to say who it is," her mom said. "The police will lock them up."

"You don't understand, Mom." Thursday's voice was hoarse. "If I snitch on him, he'll do more than take the skin off my feet. Okay?"

I knocked on the screen door. The voices inside went quiet.

"It's just me," I hollered in. "Arc."

"Arc." Thursday squealed. "Mom, let her in."

Her mother appeared behind the screen, her dark blue dress swirling around her calves. "Arc, how are you doing?" She held the door open for me.

When I stepped inside, she stared down at the mud on my bare feet.

"Sorry." I stepped back outside and wiped them on the doormat. "Our yard was flooded from the rain earlier."

"Don't worry about it, Arc," Thursday said. She was sitting in the same reclining chair and waving me in.

I stared at her feet, they were propped up on the coffee table and wrapped in bandages.

"I'm sorry I didn't stop him from hurting you," I said.

"Would you tell us who did this?" Her mom placed her hands on my shoulders. "Please."

"Mom, stop. Arc ain't gonna say a thing." Thursday made a face at me. "Are ya, Arc?"

I tried to find something else to stare at besides her mother's pleading face. "I don't remember much." I looked down at the blood-stain in the carpet in front of the chair. "I got hit in the head pretty bad. All my memories are kind of scattered now."

"See, Mom, I told ya." Thursday reached for me and grabbed my arm, pulling me to her close enough to whisper, "Don't say a fucking word, Arc."

I didn't have to hear it from Thursday. I knew what happened to women who told.

"Hey, Mom? Dad?" Thursday sat up. "Why don't you go in the kitchen and make that chocolate cake you talked about baking earlier?"

Her mom looked at both of us. "All right, sweetie," she finally said, rubbing Thursday's chin as she passed by. "Chocolate cake it is."

"Good to see you, Arc." Her dad cleared his throat as he followed his wife.

Thursday craned her neck toward the kitchen, waiting for the sounds of dishes before turning back to me with a smile.

"Is it very painful?" I asked, pointing to her feet.

"I'd be the loudest scream in Chillicothe if I didn't have my crowns," she said. "What about you? You been getting by? I've missed you, you know. Feels like you've been gone a whole century and a half."

"You *wanted* to see me?" I asked.

"Hell, yeah. Why'd you stop hanging around? Scared he might come back?"

"I was scared you'd blame me."

"Blame you? Hell, Arc, you did more than I would have. And you got your face caved in in the process."

"I thought you'd hate me."

"C'mere." She pulled me into her and wrapped me in a tight hug. "I don't hate you. It's him I hate. I thought he'd killed you at first. You didn't move for so long. I think he thought he'd killed you, too."

"What'd he do?" I asked.

"He stepped over your body and left out the fucking door." She looked at the box in my hands. "What's in that?"

"Oh. I was trying to think about what I could bring you to make ya feel better."

"A gift?" She grabbed the box and threw open the flaps. Grinning, she reached inside and lifted the small jar of honey out.

"I didn't have a hatbox for it," I told her. "That's what it should have come in."

"Honey?" she asked.

"The treasures of Egypt."

I laid my hand on the back of hers, pushing the jar up toward the ceiling light so it could cast through the liquid.

"It's the color of the Nile River," I said. "The color of the glow in the tombs. The color of their jewels."

"Yeah." She smiled. "Hey, I see it. It's put carvings in the ceiling of pyramids and sphinxes."

"If you listen closely," I said, "you can hear it sing your name back." I took the jar and laid it against her ear.

"I don't hear nothing," she said.

"Thursday?" I whispered her name. "Do you hear me? Thursday, you are amazing. You are powerful. You are the ruler of turquoise jewels."

She giggled and I did, too.

"I know it's silly," I said.

"I fucking love it." She took the jar back into her hands. "Thanks, Arc. You gonna stay and get a piece of cake? Mom makes the best. It's really Dad's recipe, but don't ever tell."

"Naw, I gotta get home," I said. "I just wanted to come by and see how you were."

"I'm better now." She held up the jar. "I got a little piece of Egypt in my lap." She looked down at her bandaged feet. "Hey, I'm halfway to being a mummy, huh?"

I gave her one last hug, then stepped over the stains of blood leading to the door and slowly closed it behind me.

I drove around until it got dark. Once home, I found Daffy in her room, sitting on the edge of her bed. She was looking at the growing collection of twigs Aunt Clover had been gluing to her wall.

"Highway Man gave you a scar over your eye," she said. "Am I gonna have to get one there, too?"

"Daffy, I have to talk to you about the phone call I got earlier."

"Don't you feel trapped, Arc?" she asked. "Trapped in this room, in this house? Sometimes I feel like I'll never leave this savage side. That I'll always be here with no escape. Caught in the center of the spider's web."

"Daffy—"

She shot up and ran out the door. I chased behind her, down the hall, and out onto the porch.

"Daffy, wait up."

Her feet hit the steps first, as I tried to catch up to her. Not knowing where we were going and not trying to stop her, I hoped maybe she was running to a better place for both of us. We ran past the paper mill, past the bearded men gathered outside on their smoke break. We ran over glass broken on the sidewalk, and by the shacks in their various shades of faded greens, blues, and browns.

"Daffy? Daffy!"

When she stopped, I stopped, too, and looked around at the swings and the merry-go-round. I realized we were at the playground we used to play at as kids. It had been old then and was even older now. The merry-go-round half tilted on its side. The seesaws broken off and left discarded on the ground.

We didn't say anything as we got on the swings and swung as high as we could, the chains leaving little flecks of rust in our palms as they squeaked beneath our weight. It started to rain, the small drops coming down onto our faces upturned to the sky.

"I think of Dad when it rains," she said. "The puddles on the ground, the flooding in the gutter . . ."

"It's our father," I finished the thought for her.

She swung so high she nearly went over the top rail.

"Daffy," I said, "I wanna talk to you about the phone call."

She pointed to the ground by the merry-go-round. "There's something there," she said. "Go see what it is, Arc."

I got off the swing and walked over to the jump rope lying on the ground. I stared at it, for a moment thinking it might not be a jump rope at all, but a coiled snake. I nudged it with my muddy toe. When the rope didn't hiss, when it didn't slither, I picked it up and carried it back to Daffy.

"My ankles were always too weak for jump rope," she said, slowing her swings.

"No, they're not." I wiped the rain out of my eyes. "Listen, the call today was from the Evergreen Daughters, Daffy. They have spots open for us."

"The Evergreen Daughters?" She dragged her feet on the ground, causing the swing to come to a stop. "The place of mirrors?"

"I signed up a while ago to get on the list," I said. "Will you come with me?"

She jumped up off the swing and grabbed the jump rope out of my hands. "You think I could do ten jumps, Arc?" she asked.

"Sure ya can."

She smiled as she held tight to the wooden handles. I stood back and watched her swing the cord around, the rain flicking off each time it swung, once, twice, three times.

"C'mon." I clapped my hands. "You can do it."

By the time she got to ten she was out of breath.

"That was hard, Arc. I don't know if I can do any more."

"Do you remember," I asked, "the hieroglyphics Mamaw Milkweed wrote across her bedroom walls that year on her birthday?"

"Yeah. But I didn't know what any of them said."

I used my finger and wrote through the rain on the metal frame of the swingset, drawing the hieroglyphics that Mamaw Milkweed had put over her headboard.

"What do they say?" Daffy asked.

" 'Be as fearless as women wearing scarves and riding the backs of trains.' " I turned to her. "Come with me to the Evergreen Daughters, Daffy."

She looked down at the jump rope. "You think I could do ten more?"

"You can do it, Daffy."

She swung the rope over her head. "One, two, three." She counted, smiling wider and wider as she got to ten, her feet splashing in the rain.

Not stopping, she continued until she counted to twenty. Struggling for breath, she dropped the jump rope and grabbed her knees, bending over.

"You see how many I did?" She looked up at me.

"I knew you could do it."

She grabbed my hand. Together we walked back home, the rain left to puddle around the jump rope.

CHAPTER 23

Light the dark in an ark.

—*Daffodil Poet*

THE NEXT MORNING I SHARPENED THE BLUE EYELINER WITH A KNIFE in the kitchen, the way the women in my family always have. Then I applied it to Daffy's eyes. I extended the blue line out to her temples, and put little *x*'s on to make barbed wire. The way Aunt Clover did.

"You know the ancient Egyptians made eyeliner by grinding malachite and galena with animal fat?" I said. "They believed eyeliner stopped evil spirits from getting into the eye and corrupting the soul."

"I bet blue eyeliner is best for things like that," Daffy said. "Why blue, Arc?"

I smiled, remembering Aunt Clover's words. "Because when our skin drops off, blue is the color we'll be beneath."

I closed my eyes so she could draw the lines out to my temples and put the *x*'s as carefully as I had for her.

"Half of the same," I said.

"Half of the same dance." She smiled. "Half of the same house."

"The same broken wing. The same firefly."

"The same fire," she said.

"The same power." I squeezed her hand. "It's time to go, Daffy."

She laid the eyeliner down and picked up Dad's old army bag we had packed. We locked hands and walked to the front door. Aunt Clover was sitting on the sofa, fanning herself with the lid off an old candy box while watching TV.

As I held open the screen door, Daffy paused long enough to ask, "Where you at in the world this time, Aunt Clover?"

The three of us watched the TV screen light up with an aerial shot of a white dome.

"The Taj Mahal," Aunt Clover said. "It's a tomb built for a woman."

She picked up the dented can with the faded creamed corn label and held it to her mouth.

"White marble, red sandstone," she spoke into it. "Addie? Can you hear me? The tomb reflects a woman in water. Spittle, spittle, spider, where you gonna hide her?" Aunt Clover spit inside the can. "In the water."

She laid the can back down on her lap but did not stop fanning herself with the candy box lid as she looked up at Daffy and me. "A lot of eyeliner," she said, licking her chapped lips. "You going somewhere fancy, fancy, fancy?"

She slowly drifted her eyes across the room, back to the TV screen.

"While you're out," she said, "remember to take your blood and feed it to the wolves to buy us our crowns." Her voice was so low, her words were like a growl. "Make sure they're of white marble, red sandstone."

"We won't be back for a while," I said.

She looked up at us again, her face tightening.

"I could never trust you." She coughed, not covering her mouth but letting it flop wide open. "Where you slithering off?"

"To stare into mirrors," I said.

"Stare into mirr ... mir ... mirrors?" Aunt Clover's eyes rolled side to side. "I know ... I know that place ..." She slowly stretched her lips, the cracks in them bleeding. "Ha-ah." She slapped the side of her thin bruised leg with the candy lid, then grabbed the can and spoke into it once more. "Addie, listen to this. She thinks she's gonna get—"

I slammed the door on Aunt Clover's voice.

"I hate her laugh," Daffy said. "It sounds like it's tangled up in mud."

"It's because she's never happy," I said, holding my hand out into the light rain falling. "When a woman like Aunt Clover laughs, it's bound to sound like she's tangled up in something."

We turned at the sound of a horn. Violet's bright orange car was taking the turn sharply, as if she'd been speeding the whole way.

"Thanks for the ride," I said, as Daffy slid across the leather seat to squeeze between Violet and me.

I locked the car door, suddenly afraid I couldn't trust myself not to open it and run as fast and as far as my feet would take me to the nearest needle.

"You're gonna love this place," Violet said, turning her wipers on higher as we pulled away from the house. "I ain't gonna say you won't be restless or angry or sick as a dog in the beginning. But that's just a scratch of the claw. Once you get over that, you'll wonder why you took so long to get clean in the first place. I'm telling you, I ain't ever lived in a house with a chandelier. But I figure being sober is the same feeling. Something nice and bright."

"How'd you know when you were ready?" I asked, the rain sliding down over the glass of the window Daffy was looking out of. "Ready to quit the shit?"

"I was driving," Violet said, "wearing my crown. I ran over something. I stopped the car and got out. The air was hot. The sky was gray. The snapping turtle I'd hit was still moving. I was on a road by the river. She'd come up to lay her eggs. Her shell was crushed. The eggs were falling out all over the place. Turtles, even when they get their shells destroyed so badly you think they gotta be dead, they usually ain't. They can live for a long time after, just suffering. They're queens of the earth, turtles."

"What'd you do with her?" I asked in the silence Violet had fallen into.

She cleared her throat. "I picked her up. Her head and arms just dangled, but her eyes kept darting from side to side. It's terrible to be in pain. It's even worse to be in pain and be scared. I told her everything was gonna be fine, then I put her in the back seat there."

Both Daffy and me turned around and saw the blood still staining the light leather on the seat.

"I never cleaned it off," Violet said. "I wanted to leave it as a reminder."

"Where'd you take her?" I asked.

"I was so out of it, I couldn't find the animal doctor. I ended up driving her to the paper mill. One of the guys took her and put her out of her misery. I didn't see it. I only heard the sound of the gun as I was driving away."

The rain had stopped. The wipers were squeaking across the dry glass.

"When I was looking back," Violet said, I saw an egg on the seat. It must have fallen out of her when they got her out. It wasn't crushed like the others. Not even a tiny crack in it. I drove back to the river and dug a shallow hole to lay it in. I figured it was the least I could do for her. That was the moment I decided I wouldn't live that life no more."

She wiped her cheeks before turning to us.

"You're gonna love this place," she said again.

We smiled like we believed her.

The Evergreen Daughters was located a few miles out of town. Far enough to be in the woods on several acres, heavily shaded with pines, but close enough to smell the awful stench of the paper mill with each blast.

"There it is," Violet said, her hands sliding over the steering wheel as she made the turn.

The main building was covered in wooden shingles, dark brown like a mountain retreat. It was triangular shaped, the slanted roof edged in moss.

"This place was built in the 1950s," Violet said. "It used to be a summer camp. But it's been a rehab since the eighties."

I opened the car door slowly with Daffy gripping my arm.

"I wish someone would have told me it was going to be windy today," she said as we got out. "I might have waited to come. I don't like my hair blowing in my eyes when I'm walking to a place I've never been before."

I knew if we had waited for the perfect moment, we would either be dead, our obituaries written by the street, or we'd be old women with dirt on our feet, living in the back bedroom with our mother and the other ghosts.

We stepped toward the building, wondering if Aunt Clover had been right about all those mirrors.

Don't go in. Come back to me. I'll make you feel good. I'll take away all the pain. Come, I'll be your crown. You can't survive without me. I live inside you.

"Something is chasing us, Arc," Daffy said. She wiped the back of her neck the way our mother did her own, like she was trying to keep her head from falling off.

"Whatever you think is after us," I said, "will get caught in the barbed wire of our eyes."

Daffy made me promise that everything would be okay, but she had been right. Something was chasing us, and it caught us that first day at rehab.

You can't ever leave me. You need me. You need me to live. You will feel everything without me. I can take away your pain.

Detox was a different monster than the flu we had when we were kids. Sure, there was nausea, diarrhea, chills, and fevers, but it all had gasoline poured on top and lit. Left to the flames, I gave the fire my hands. It took them and asked for more. I gave my feet, my legs, my arms. It took them and asked for more. I gave my eyes, my breasts, my ribs, one by one. The pain took them all and asked for more. That was when I realized that a woman holds most things in the back of her throat. And that these things come out in vomit and screams and cries.

You belong to me.

Tartarus. The name the ancient Greeks gave to the darkness below the earth. It's said a dropping stone would take nine days to reach Tartarus. It took me less than one. There it waited for me.

You will never be free.

And yet as the flames started to recede, I opened my eyes and thought I could be.

CHAPTER 24

The air is clean, and I feel even more like a queen.

—Daffodil Poet

THE SPRING WAS HEAVY AND HOT, BUT BEING OUT AMONG THE TREES was nice. Daffy and me started to go on long walks every day. We cut the legs off our pants. We had brought shorts with us, but turning old jeans into something new gave us the chance to imagine the shorts hadn't been worn on the sidewalk in front of the Blue Hour, or slid across the leather seats of some john's car.

Violet had given us pen and paper, and we wrote. We wrote to Mom and Aunt Clover, wondering if they read our letters or threw them down, unopened, with the bills. We wrote to our dead Mamaw Milkweed, too. Told her we were wearing her scarves like women riding the backs of trains. And we told her we blew our hot breath on the window glass at night and drew circles around the stars we thought were her.

"You know, Arc," Violet said to me one day, "there's a shovel in the groundkeeper's shed. They won't mind you borrowing it."

I put my makeup brush in my back pocket and headed outside to the shed.

"You can watch me, Daffy," I told her as I grabbed the shovel.

I chose a place under the pines. There I dug into the hard soil, flipping over the grass and telling Daffy I was digging in the sands of Egypt.

"You're not going to find anything in this land here, Arc." Daffy lay back on the ground, staring up at the blue sky. "The trees have sinned, and the soil is hot. It's boiled everything to dust."

"Oh yeah? Then what's this?" I picked up a flat rock with jagged edges.

I used the makeup brush to dust it off, like I'd seen archaeologists on TV do.

"This is an effigy pipe of the Adena," I told her.

Daffy flipped over onto her stomach, propping her face up in her hands. "Is it now?" She smiled, tapping her fingers across her cheek.

"And this," I said, picking up the discarded cigarette butt, "this is the evidence of people before us. Their civilization must have been made of women who ate red plums and raised white rabbits and painted their barns blue."

"Well." She sighed. "I sure hope those women survived better than we are."

She got up, dusting the back of her shorts off.

"Where you going?" I asked.

"Just for a walk," she said. "You keep digging, Arc Doggs. Find Momma's horse and set us all free."

She slid her hands into her front pockets, leaving her thumbs out, which she twirled as she disappeared into the pines. I stabbed the shovel's blade in deeper.

I stayed out there awhile longer, finding a frayed shoelace, a door handle broken off from a car, and even a glove with the thumb missing. It had been lying on top of a rusty license plate. I wondered why they were there in the dirt at Evergreen Daughters, but sometimes it's easier to just fill a hole back in.

After I did, I headed to the shed to replace the shovel. I looked for Daffy but couldn't find her outside. Back at the main building, I stared up at its triangular roof.

"Unusual shape for a building, don't ya think?" A voice came from behind me. The type of voice that made me think of something earthy and warm.

When I turned around, I saw a woman wearing a mismatch of florals. A tiny calico print of purple flowers in her top, paired with a white denim skirt colored with the type of roses you'd find on wallpaper. Short bangs arched across her forehead, while the rest of her hair fell to her shoulders, the long strands held with bobby pins behind her bare ears. The only makeup she was wearing was blush. A pink shade that matched the roses in her skirt.

"Yeah," I said. "I haven't seen many triangle-shaped buildings."

"A squalene to be exact." She smiled. "Notice each side is unequal." She pointed with her finger and used it to trace the sides in the air. "Such triangles are called squalenes. Now if it had at least two equal sides." She made the number with her fingers. "It would be called an isosceles. And if all three sides were equal, it would be an equilateral triangle. I'm Indigo." She held her hand up and fluttered her fingers. Her press-on nails were filed into square ends.

"I'm Arc," I said.

When I fluttered my fingers against hers, we both laughed.

"Arc?" Her smile grew larger. "I know that name. The joining of two points by a curve."

"I'm sorry?"

"I used to proofread math books," she said as we dropped our hands. "I read more than one paragraph on arcs and their applications in mathematics, believe me."

She was wearing a wide-brimmed hat that looked orangey red to me, but she said it was the color of an unraveling fire.

"An unraveling fire?" I asked.

"It's when flames remember how to be free," she said. "And remember that they used to be women."

On the bright blue ribbon of the hat, she had a collection of things.

"These are roots," she said of the thin fans that still had dried dirt on them in places. "I wear them so I don't forget I was born from the earth. And this is my flapping feather." She flicked the long gray feather that stuck out taller than even the dried seedpods. "It belonged to a purple bird. I'm responsible for that bird flying too high. I figured at the very least, I should keep the feather safe."

"But if it belonged to a purple bird, shouldn't the feather be purple?" I asked.

"I know," she said. "That's what makes it such a mystery." She laughed some more. "Most people think I'm a little weird. But I have a feeling you might be a little weird, too."

She reached toward my bottom lip, the tips of her fingers lightly touching it.

"You always wear lipstick on only half of your mouth?" she asked.

"I'm half of the same," I said.

"The same what?"

"It's different things at different times. Sometimes I'm half of the same ghost, of the same ruin, the same wild dog."

"You're cool," she said. "Like a lost language. I speak three of them." She held her three fingers up, counting down to one. "First time in rehab?"

I nodded and asked, "Is it yours?"

She shook her head. "But Momma used to say I was like our old truck. I needed a few starts to get going. I'm gonna do it this time. I feel it in my bones."

"What's it feel like?"

"Like a butterfly tapping against the glass of a jar." She tilted her head and stared longer at my eyes. "I guess you hear this all the time," she said, "but your eyes are pretty damn awesome."

"They're witches' marbles," I said.

We turned to the sound of a weed eater. The guy using it had his back to us while he chopped down the new dandelion growth around the foundation of the building.

"That's Theresa," Indigo said over the sound as she hooked her arm through mine. "He takes care of the grounds."

Following the growth of the dandelions, the man turned around. He was bald on top, his hair worn in a low ponytail. He had gotten new eyeglasses since the last time I saw him. Silver aviators that had the tendency to slide down his nose that had the same crook in it.

"Hey." Indigo steadied my arm. "You're shaking. Everything okay?"

The man still had his eyes down on the ground, surveying it to make sure it was neatly trimmed. When he finally looked up, he saw Indigo first.

"Hi, Indigo." He cut the motor of the weed eater. "Warm day for spring."

He took a handkerchief out of his pocket and ran it across his forehead in one large motion. Only then did he notice me. He furrowed his brow and adjusted his glasses.

"I'd recognize those eyes anywhere," he said. "Arc Doggs."

"You two old friends?" Indigo asked.

"He . . ." I paused, watching him lower his eyes, perhaps afraid I would bring up why he had a dent in his car. "He used to work at the place my sister and me would swim as kids."

"It's been a long time," he said.

I looked down at his shoes. The suede was gone, replaced by white canvas with red shoelaces, double knotted.

"It's good to see you again." He started to hold his arms out for a hug but thought better of it. He shook my hand instead. "So, Arc, you're checked in here at the Evergreen Daughters?"

"Yeah," I said.

"So that means . . ."

"Yeah," I said more softly.

"Well." He cleared his throat. "I'm sorry to know your life led you here."

Indigo looked at him, then back at me.

"Why don't you two catch up?" She unhooked her arm from mine. "I've got to get back to my study of the wind."

She pulled a thin paperback from her back pocket and turned to leave.

"I'll see you later, Arc." She looked back at me with a smile over her shoulder. "The joining of two points by a curve."

When she was out of sight, he pointed to a picnic table beneath the pines. "We can sit over there."

On the way, he took off his glasses to wipe the sweat from his eyes.

"It's really nice to see you," he said again. "How's Daffy?"

"Fine," I said, dusting the dirt off the seat, then sat down beside him. "We both thought after you left Big Gray, we'd never see you again."

"I was close to disappearing." He put his glasses back on.

"Where'd you go after you left that night?" I asked.

"I stayed drunk for a while. Blacking out and waking up in places I couldn't remember how I got there. Then I got arrested and served time for a while. That was the start of turning my life around."

"What were you arrested for?" I asked.

He pushed his glasses back with his middle finger and squinted up toward the sun.

"Something I wish hadn't happened. But enough about that." He cleared his throat. "I never thought I'd see you in a place like this."

He brought his eyes back down from the sun to mine.

"I never thought you'd need a place like this," he said. "I thought you'd be working in a museum somewhere. Digging up blue-colored pottery and broken crosses for 'em."

"Yeah, well, life took a different turn." I bit my nails and tasted the dirt beneath them. "Indigo said your name was Theresa now?"

"After I buried the bottle," he said, "I decided to go by my middle name. It's my mother's. But you can call me John Theresa if you'd like. Since we're old friends."

On his palm, he had the tattoo of a butterfly.

"I got it a few years ago," he said, seeing me stare.

"Why'd you get it on your palm?"

"I like knowing I can have something so fragile in my hand and not crush it to death." He closed his hand into a fist. "No matter how hard I squeeze." He did so until the veins on the back of his hand popped out. "The butterfly is not harmed." He opened his hand, his palm flat, and the butterfly still safe.

I saw that instead of two antennae, the butterfly had five.

"Why so many?" I asked.

"Oh." He covered his hand quickly with the other. "Just keeping track of something. Hey, wanna see what I have?"

We both slid out from the bench and walked across the field to a small cabin tucked away. There were potted plants out on the porch and some sheets drying on a clothesline.

"Welcome to my home," he said, opening the screen door and holding it back with a rock. "It used to be the old counselor bunk from when it was a camp. It's the groundskeeper's cabin now."

It was all one room, with none of the living spaces divided. The kitchen ran into the living room, the living room into the bedroom. I imagined the one closed door I saw was to the bathroom. For all the ways he kept the grounds neat and tidy, his place was a mess. There were piles of clothes on the floor and the bed was covered with books, newspapers, and unfolded maps. It looked like he spent most nights on the sofa, the TV pulled up within inches of its cushions. When he had moved in, he likely planned to paint. The yellow and pale blue swatches still smeared across the exposed timber walls. The only tidy space on the table was dedicated to jars full of muddy water.

"What are those for?" I leaned in closer. There were things both sunken and floating in the jars, but before I could see what they were, he picked up one of the shirts off the floor and draped it over the jars.

"That's nothing," he said. "What I wanted to show you was this."

He reached for a violin case on top of the refrigerator. While he did, I noticed the rain boots by the back door, their soles covered in sand and mud, not yet crusted over. He saw me staring at the boots and pushed them back as he carried the cheap plastic case to the kitchen table. He had to shove some dirty dishes over to make space. It wasn't like the case he'd had before, with the velvet lining. Nor was the violin inside as expensive.

"I'm playing again." He tucked the violin beneath his chin. "What would you like to hear?"

I started to open my mouth, but he said, "Wait, I know what you'd like."

While the notes of "Amazing Grace" filled the cabin, I looked back over at the muddy boots by the door, wondering how often it was that he went down to the river.

CHAPTER 25

Find rest in this nest.

—*Daffodil Poet*

THE WALLS WERE BEIGE AND THE FOLDOUT CHAIRS WERE METAL with flattened padded seats. While we dragged them into a circle, Daffy complained about how dry her elbows were. It wasn't just her elbows that she was complaining about. Like most of the women, we hated the group meetings. All of us sitting slumped in the chairs, arms folded, expected to feel comfortable enough to travel the miles of our lives out loud and in enough detail to give the counselors the answers to their questions.

The day Thursday came in singing "Girls Just Want to Have Fun," one of the women was in the middle of talking about a room painted blue. She never got to the point of that room or why she hated it so much. Thursday had everyone's attention. I thought the next time I saw her walk, it would be with a limp. But the bandages were off, and she moved no worse than a woman who had once sunburnt the soles of her feet.

Thursday had yet to notice Daffy and me. She was checking out the rest of the room like a cat who'd just come in from outside. Usually her clothes were fitted, her shirts often left to ride up. This time the loose blouse she wore fell long over baggy jeans with holes in the knees. Around the holes, she had taken a black marker and written, *I made these, bitches.*

"Please take a seat," the counselor said. "And welcome."

Daffy waved both her arms at Thursday, finally getting her attention. Thursday grabbed an empty chair from against the wall and dragged it across the floor to us, the screeching sound echoing.

"You're gonna have to move over, Buffalo Butt," she said to the woman beside me, who rolled her eyes but picked up her chair and carried it to a space in the circle on the other side.

"I'm so fucking glad to see you," Thursday said to Daffy and me after she flopped down in the chair. "I just got outta detox." She stuck her tongue out and crossed her eyes.

"Well, maybe you'd like to talk about that with the whole group?"

We turned to the counselor's voice and saw everyone's eyes on us.

"Sure." Thursday kicked out her legs. "What you wanna know? The beginning of my story?"

"Everyone's got one," the counselor said.

"Not this bitch." Thursday shook her head. "Mine washed away a long time ago. I put it out to dry. The wind caught it. The river flooded. Ain't seen my goddamn beginning since."

As Thursday started to sing again, the counselor tapped her pen against her pad of paper. A few of the women cracked a smile. Some frowned and clenched their jaws harder than before. Others looked out the window, unaware anything else was happening. But Daffy laughed, and when the session was finally over, Thursday grabbed us by the hand and pulled us over to the doughnuts on the table.

"I didn't think you'd come to this place," I said as she chose a powdered-sugar long john to bite into.

"Me neither." She coughed the sugar out. "But something came up and gave me a great big shove. Mmm." She took another bite of the doughnut.

"Delicious, ain't they?" I asked. "Violet made 'em. It's been nice to have her around."

Thursday shoved the rest of the doughnut into her mouth and led the charge down the hall to the back where the kitchen was. We spotted Violet at the counter, opening a can of peaches. Thursday yelled out her name as she skipped over to her.

"You seem happy." Violet laughed as Thursday hugged her and wiped the powdered sugar onto Violet's sleeve.

"If I don't pretend to be, then I can't be, right, Butterfly Eyes?" Thursday dipped her finger into the bowl of icing on the counter. "You busy right now? We could go down to the river like old times. Well, you know." She rolled her eyes. "Like old times, minus the crowns. How about we pack some of this icing and get the hell out of here?"

Violet got a sack from the kitchen and collected some goodies with cold cartons of milk from the cafeteria. Passing the empty rooms out in the hall, Thursday rested her hand on her stomach as we walked outside into the light.

Once we got to the picnic tables under the trees, I saw Indigo reading a book. Her legs were on the bench, and her hat propped up on her knee.

"Hey," I called to her. "Wanna come with us? We're gonna hang out at the river."

She looked at the bag Thursday was wagging back and forth.

"We got sugar and all kinds of fattening stuff to eat." Thursday smiled.

Indigo plopped the hat onto her head. "Will there be rocks at the river to skip on the water?"

"Of course," I said.

"And will there be any wild animals along the way?" she asked.

"You can see one right here." Thursday grabbed my braid and held it up above my head as she growled and panted. Daffy laughed while I rolled my eyes at her.

"In that case, count me in." Indigo closed her book and tucked it under her arm as she came over.

As we found a path through the trees, Thursday filled us in on what we'd missed from the street.

"This one girl," she said, "disappeared, and everyone freaked out. Thought she'd be the next body floating down the river or whatever. But after a few days, she showed back up. She'd been in Columbus, getting high up there. It's like a bad cough, these rumors. Someone disappears, and she's gone, until she isn't. Hell, there's probably rumors about us. Those who don't know we're here. Here at old Evergreen Daughters." She kicked the dirt in front of her. "Hey, Violet? Why they call this place the Evergreen Daughters anyways?"

"I guess because there's so many evergreens planted around here," Violet said.

"A better reason than that." Thursday held her arms up toward the sky. "Please, somebody."

"Did you guys know," Indigo said, "that built into the leaves and needles of an evergreen is a ratio combination of nitrogen and carbon? A bond of organic chemistry that makes it harder for ordinary trees to grow around them, because when an evergreen's needles or leaves drop and fertilize the soil, the ground is being prepared with an evergreen in mind. Out of all the trees in the world—the mighty oak, the strong sycamore, the valued walnut—it is the evergreen that grows the tallest and the strongest, towering in the skyline like a giant from another time."

"They're not really giants," I said. "They're women. At least, that's what Mamaw Milkweed would say. She said if you ever look at a pine tree, you'll notice it looks like a woman in a dress. She said the trees uproot themselves at night and dance in the moonlight, twirling their branches and dropping off their pine needles. In the morning, the needles would be gathered for medicine. It could be used for coughs or sore throats or aches and pains." I picked up one of the fallen pine needles and touched its sharp point. "She called them God's needles."

"Well that's . . . fascinating." Thursday jumped onto Violet's back. As Violet told Thursday she was too heavy to carry, I dropped the needle and whispered to Indigo, "I don't really call this place the Evergreen Daughters."

"You don't?" she asked as Daffy listened in. "What do you call it?"

"The Mirrors," I said.

Daffy looked back at me as she walked ahead to join Thursday and Violet.

"Why do you call it that?" Indigo asked.

"Because it shows our reflections. Who we've been, who we are, who we could someday be. Most of all, it shows your reflection of how you look when you run away from home." I looked down and kicked at the gravel. "I haven't ever seen you around Chillicothe before."

"That's because I'm not from here," she said. "I was up in Columbus and got on a list at a few rehabs. Evergreen Daughters was the first to have a spot available. I'm glad it did, though." She smiled. "Or I wouldn't have heard about the echoes of storytellers. What else do you know, Arc? The curve between two points."

I pointed at the small pebbles scattered at the base of one of the trees.

"What is it?" she whispered as the others walked out of sight.

"My mamaw always said five rocks together are the fingernails of old women," I said. "This is where the birds hold their council."

"Is that so?" Indigo squatted, running her fingers over the rocks. "Where they talk about flying? And feathers? And the way worms come out in the rain?"

"That's right."

"I'll always be looking out for the fingernails of old women," she said, standing.

Locking arms, we ran ahead, the sunlight casting down through the branches onto our faces. We looked for a spot by the river on the sandy bank, finding one by a large piece of sandstone overhanging the water.

Thursday dropped the sack of doughnuts and stretched in a yawn. When she noticed the book in the crook of Indigo's arm, she reached out and snatched it.

"'Analytic geometry relative to algebra.'" Thursday read the back cover. "'Makes one able to write equations—'"

A dried flower dropped out to the ground.

"A secret?" Thursday smiled as she picked it up.

"Not really," Indigo said. "I like to press flowers before they fall off the corner."

"The corner of what?" I asked.

"The corner of the world," she said. "That's milkweed." She watched as Thursday spun the flatted stem between her fingers.

"Milkweed?" Thursday looked up at her.

"Monarchs lay their eggs on it," I said, remembering the moles on Mamaw's neck.

Daffy was staring at me, so I left Indigo and sat down beside my sister.

"It's a very important flower," Indigo said as Thursday held the book and milkweed out to her, but Indigo took only the book back.

"Keep the milkweed," she told Thursday. "A gift from me. Besides, I got plenty of other wild things pressed and tucked away." She flipped through the pages, showing us all a collection of butter weeds, ferns, dandelions, and the bright things that grow at all our feet.

"Thanks." Thursday saluted Indigo with the milkweed and sat down beside her.

"I like your bracelets," Indigo said, looking at the layers of jewelry on Thursday's wrist.

"I make 'em myself," Thursday said. "Which one you like the most?"

Indigo inspected each bracelet, quickly looking over the red and orange ones, to the blue one dangling with flower-shaped beads.

"That one," she said.

"Then you shall have it." Thursday took it off her wrist and put it on Indigo's. "A bracelet in exchange for a milkweed."

The beads clacked as Indigo turned her hand over so Thursday could close the clasp.

"It was made for you," Thursday said as Indigo held her arm up, the sun catching on the clear sides of the beads. "Those are star sapphires and blue topaz."

"They're beautiful," Indigo said as Thursday lay back on the riverbank, placing the dried milkweed on her stomach.

We listened to the birds in the woods around us, the soft rippling of the river over the rocks. When I started to dig into the mud, Indigo laughed softly and said, "You're a mudlark."

"A what?" I asked.

"A mudlark," she said. "You search for treasures in river mud."

"Arc's always searching for something in the ground." Thursday sighed. "Especially at the river."

"It looks so wide, don't it?" Violet said, as she looked out at the water.

"You can measure it with trigonometry." Indigo sat up straighter.

"Trigonometry?" Daffy asked.

"It's how you measure a river too big to cross. A mountain too tall to climb."

"So, measure the shit out of it," Thursday said, propping herself up on her elbows.

But when Indigo started to talk in numbers and equations, Thursday moaned, "I didn't think I'd end up back in math class."

"You didn't let me finish." Indigo shook her bracelet. "The real equation is one drop of water plus nine rocks divided by a hundred grains of sand minus—"

"A footprint," I said, "divided by a swimmer."

"Multiplied by the hours in a day." Indigo sat on her heels to face me.

"Equal to the width of the surface of the earth." I faced her.

"Equal to the surface of the earth?" Indigo blew a raspberry. "Then we're already drowned."

"It's a beautiful spot to be drowned in," Violet said, bringing her knees up and closing her arms around them. "I'll have to bring Grassy here sometime. She'd love it."

While Violet talked about Grassy playing T-ball over the summer, Thursday looked off, across the river. She bit her lip the way she always did when there was something heavy on her mind.

"What's wrong, Thursday?" I asked.

"Nothing." She shrugged.

We each looked at her until she rolled her eyes and said, "Fine. I do have to tell you guys something. Someone's gonna be calling me Mom, if you can believe that shit." She laid her hand over her stomach, the dried milkweed flattened between her palm and shirt. "It's why I decided to get clean."

"You're pregnant?" Violet jerked around to her.

"I thought about not letting her be born into this world," Thursday said. "Not with everything nailed to darkness the way it is. But then I couldn't stop wondering what color her eyes would be. I got to feeling that I couldn't wait to find out."

"Her?" Violet asked.

"Well, no one's told me yet," Thursday said, "but I figure I've got a good idea."

Violet got up and sat down beside Thursday, wrapping her arm around her shoulders. "Don't be like me, Thurs. Don't let her grow up without you."

"You have a name picked out yet?" Indigo asked.

Thursday brushed the milkweed across her stomach. "I was thinking Eagle."

"Eagle?" Indigo smiled. "Why that name?"

"Because," Thursday said, "eagles are protected from hunters and poachers. She has less of a chance ending up on the endangered list that way."

"That's beautiful," Violet said.

"Yeah." Thursday squeezed her eyes closed.

"What's wrong?" Daffy asked.

"I don't know who the fuck he is." Thursday's voice was quiet.

"Who?" Violet nudged against her.

"The father." Thursday turned her face and buried it into Violet's shoulder. "It could have been any one of them. I mean what the hell am I gonna tell her when she's old enough to ask? 'Oh, Mommy was a whore, and your father was a wallet of money and dirty jeans and bad breath'?"

Thursday's soft cries were muffled by the pats Violet gave her on the back. Daffy, meanwhile, looked at her feet, digging her toes into the ground. Indigo stared at her bracelet, her lips moving silently as if repeating Thursday's question.

"I know who he is," I said.

Daffy turned to me, but before she could ask, I said, "It's that guy. You know him, Thursday."

She wiped her nose and asked, "Who?"

"He has brown hair," I said. "He's got green eyes like emeralds. Well dressed, with sapphires for buttons. He smells like the dust from the moon, and he's so tall you can always find him in a crowd. It's probably why he can count every planet in our solar system, in alphabetical order. And he's looked through all the telescopes in the world but has never found anything more beautiful than you."

"I know that guy," Violet said. "He has a heart as sweet as sugar."

"I bet Thursday is his favorite day of the week," Indigo added.

Thursday covered her mouth, smiling behind her hand, the rings on her fingers sparkling with their plastic stones.

"I fucking love you guys." She pulled us all in, and we rolled across the riverbank until we landed on the bag, flattening the cookies and doughnuts inside.

"It's okay," Violet said, standing. "The fish will be glad to get our crumbs."

She grabbed the bag and hummed as she reached inside.

"When I was a little girl," she said, tearing the doughnuts into pieces and throwing them out onto the water, "the preacher would march by our house with his flock of followers on their way to the river. I ran after them one time and saw him dunk their heads under the water. I thought he was attacking them at first and I screamed for him to stop. To stop drowning them. But then someone in the crowd told me it was okay. It was just a baptism." Violet laid the bag down and stood, staring out at the water. "Why don't we do that?"

"Do what now?" Thursday asked.

"Baptize each other." Violet turned around to us.

"I'm not a Baptist," Indigo said

"You don't have to be." Violet was already taking off her shoes. "We wouldn't be doing it for religion or for a preacher or anyone else. We'd be doing it for ourselves."

Violet stepped out into the water and splashed us until we laughed. "What do you say?" she asked.

"I don't know," Thursday said. "I mean, is it really worth getting our hair wet? What do you think, Arc?"

"Well, my mamaw would say it is definitely worth it." I smiled. "She used to say that water was full of endless angels. She'd tell Daffy and me that whenever we stepped into the water, the angels would return us."

"Return us to where?" Thursday asked.

"To wherever we needed to be," I said.

Thursday stood, using her foot to slip her shoes off. We all thought she might crack a joke. At the very least, hold her hand up to her mouth like a microphone and belt out a ballad. But instead, she removed her shirt and jeans. Left in only her bra and panties, she walked out into the river, her growing stomach now visible. The brown water splashed up her thin calves and on the stars tattooed there until they were submerged.

Violet followed behind her, her jeans rolled up.

"What the hell do I do?" Thursday asked as Violet put her hand on her lower back.

"You trust me," Violet said.

Thursday took a deep breath, allowing Violet to gently lay her down into the water until her head disappeared beneath it. When she came back up, she coughed and said, "Water went in my nose."

Violet laughed as Thursday grabbed her into a hug.

"Thanks, you old bear." Thursday pulled Violet into the water with her until they were both laughing and flapping their arms, creating ripples around them.

Indigo stood up next. "Why not give it a go," she said. "Endless angels, here I come."

She ran out into the water, splashing it up like a whole herd of animals.

"I'm trying to scare the fish away," she said, "so they don't swim inside my ears and turn me into an ocean."

She held her nose tightly as Violet put her down in the water. When she came up, she shook her head like a dog.

"You can go next," I told Daffy as Indigo and Thursday stood on either side of Violet and dipped her back.

"Naw." Daffy shook her head and scooted farther back up the bank. "I don't wanna, Arc. I'm scared if I go in with my back first into the water, I might not come back up."

"You sure?" I asked.

"Yeah." She nodded. "You go on. Do it for the both of us."

I stood, letting my bare feet sink into the mud with each step out into the water just as Indigo and Thursday raised Violet back up.

"It's cold," I said, shivering as the water got higher and higher up to my hips.

"Well, my momma always said to wash blood out with cold water," Thursday said. "I reckon sins are probably the same."

Indigo was the one who came over and put her arm behind my back.

"Ready," she asked, "the joining of a curve between two straight lines?"

I looked at Daffy one last time on the bank, then raised my eyes to the bird flying above as Indigo let me go gently back into the water. I kept my eyes open, until the bird disappeared, and the river washed over my pupils. For a moment, the world was nothing more than a rippling surface and a woman's hand on my back.

I became submerged in the thoughts shared with water. I summoned bright colors. Yellow. Like the curtains. Blue like a scarf. Cosmic like a goddess hovering. It takes strength to hold your breath. To let yourself drift into the elemental. To allow yourself to say nothing. I put on the water, like I would put on an old shirt. Something that took me back to being a child at the table with my mother and father. To know his belt was around his pants, and that it'd stay there. To know her eyes were open and would always be. That nothing would come for Daffy and me in our rooms at night. That all our veins were fresh with blood and nothing else.

I touched the water with my bare hands, and the river touched me back with hers. I wanted to leave my old life behind as easy as leaving a cup on the counter and walking off. I asked the river if this was possible. And she said everything but the word *yes* and the word *no*. Instead, she was a friend, a sister, an other who then became myself. I knew then that the migration of us was tied to the migration of the ripples.

When I rose, the bird was gone, but my friends were still there. We walked back to the bank, wringing our hair out in turns. I wrung mine out on top of Daffy's head until she laughed. Then we sat silently, drying in the sun, as the surface of the water rippled in the breeze and carried the bracelet that had slipped off Indigo's wrist and was floating off into the distance, taking the long way home.

CHAPTER 26

What always seems to last are the miseries of the past.

—*Daffodil Poet*

THE FIVE OF US OFTEN WENT BACK TO THAT SPOT BY THE RIVER, talking about the spring beetles or the rash on the inside of Indigo's wrist.

"Poison ivy." She sighed. "Either that or it's red jewels, eh, Thursday?"

Indigo had helped John Theresa pull brush up from one of the flower beds at the Evergreen Daughters. He always seemed to be around us. If not pulling or cutting weeds, he was often just a few feet away, hedge trimmers or shovel in hand, even if there wasn't always a hedge to trim or a hole to dig.

"Have you noticed how much he smokes now?" Daffy asked me.

"You lose one habit," I said, "you pick up another. At least he's not drinking."

"But sometimes he only pretends to trim bushes," she whispered.

"What do you mean?"

"I mean sometimes he's just listening to us. Other times he's just staring into our eyes, Arc. Like he's looking for something hidden there."

I could have told Daffy she was imagining things, but I had seen John Theresa myself, standing at the bushes, his trimmers snapping the air just above the leaves, watching Thursday make a new telescope out of a toilet paper roll or Indigo put lipstick on her teeth to make us laugh.

"Maybe he's studying us to draw us," Indigo said when I told her.

"He doesn't draw," I said.

"Then what does he do?" she asked.

"I don't really know him now," I said. "But I know what he used to do."

"And what was that?"

"Drink," I said.

I waited to see his hand slip into his pocket and pull out a flask or maybe another blue bottle to replace the one he'd broken all those years ago. But if he had alcohol, it wasn't in his pocket.

"Maybe he's got it in his cabin," Daffy said. "Hiding his secrets in there."

I waited until Wednesday afternoon. That's when he always went into town to shop. While Daffy laid out on a blanket in the sun, I headed down the path to John Theresa's cabin. The screen door was closed but not latched. I opened it, unable to escape the loud creak of its hinges.

There was the smell of cigarette smoke and of something having burnt.

"What are you doing here, Arc?"

At first, I didn't see him sitting at his kitchen table behind the pile of dishes. He had one spot cleared for a single glass to sit in front of him.

"I'm glad I caught you," I said, keeping my voice steady. "I thought you might have left for town already."

He looked down at the glass. Inside it were small pieces of paper.

"I decided not to go today," he said. "What'd you need me for?"

"Oh, um, just to ask if I could cut some of the, uh, flowers . . . the peonies, for my room."

"I don't mind." He kept his eyes on the glass. He picked it up and poured out the pieces of paper, scattering them across the table. He handed one to me.

I read the writing aloud. " 'The hills go black.' "

He handed me another slip.

" 'Monsters are born,' " I read.

The third paper he handed me said, "The end of everything."

I stared down at the remaining slips of paper on the table. "What are they?"

"Whenever I get the urge for the bottle," he said, "I get this glass down from the cupboard and fill it with all the things that happen when I drink. If I drink these slips of paper, reading each one, by the end, I ain't got no more thirst."

He smiled on one side of his mouth and put the papers back into the glass.

"Have you had lunch yet?" he asked, getting up. "I've made a habit out of grabbing a bite to eat in town, but I could make us something."

"All right."

He grabbed a box of macaroni and cheese off a shelf. As he filled a pot with water, I stood over the jars of muddy water on the counter. When I picked one up, the things in the bottom slid across the glass.

"What are these jars for?" I asked as he set the pot down on the stove.

"They're killing jars." He lit the burner. "You run across a lot of pests when you're the keeper of the grounds. At first, I'd just smash 'em. But that way seemed more of a torment. Then I remembered my great-uncle. He was a collector of butterflies. He used to catch them and put them in sealed jars with a cotton ball soaked in ether. Afterward he would fill the jars up with water because he said the butterfly's souls clung to the glass and he had to wash them free.

"That gave me an idea one day when I was down at the river. I just finished off a jar of lemonade I'd made. There was a beetle walking across a rock. I filled the jar up in the river and put the beetle in. It treaded the water for a long time, nearly got enough traction on the side to crawl out, but it always slid back in. Wasn't coming out alive after that. That's when I decided water would fill my killing jars. Water from the river feels more natural than the tap."

I set the jar back down.

"You think it's cruel?" he asked. "You're looking at me like I just stuck a shotgun in your mouth."

"Yes, I think it's cruel," I said. "I think the insects deserve their time on earth. They certainly don't deserve to be drowned and you watching them die."

"I don't do it to watch their death," he said. "I do it to set them free. Did you know a soul can only be free if it sees its own reflection? Water is nature's mirror. It gives their souls the chance the bottom of my boot doesn't. I don't watch them drown. I only make sure they die facedown, so their soul can see its reflection."

He went over to the refrigerator where he got his violin case off the top of it.

"Do you find Evergreen Daughters is a useful place?" he asked.

I wiped my eyes on my sleeves and nodded.

"I found the therapy sessions to be most helpful on my own path to being free from the bottle," he said, setting the case on the counter. "You don't do much talking in the sessions here, though."

I watched him open the case and lift the violin out as I asked, "How do you know?"

"There's always been something you keep turning the screw tight on. Even at Big Gray. Even as drunk as I was, I knew that much at least."

"I just don't like talking in front of groups, is all," I said.

"If you don't talk about it, you won't get better." He positioned the violin beneath his chin.

"They want to talk about the past so much."

"Talking about the past is good," he said as he started to glide the bow over the strings, the sound filling the cabin.

"They ask me about my mom and dad." I stepped over to the stove and turned the flame up higher.

"You don't want to talk about them?" he asked.

"It makes me think about when they came to Mamaw Milkweed's to get Daffy and me." I watched the water boil. "We had been living with her for a while. We'd been happy, but on our fourth birthday, Mom and Dad showed up. They swore to Mamaw that they weren't using anymore.

" 'We'll be better this time,' Dad said.

"It was true Mom and Dad looked all shiny and fresh. The gel in Dad's hair. The eyeshadow across Mom's eyes. They were showered and dressed in spotless clothes. They'd both gained enough weight to not look like the skeletons they'd been before. Mamaw Milkweed even said she couldn't recognize them. Not Dad with his clean cut and charming smile. Not Mom with her soft hands, smelling like perfume. Mom said she wanted Daffy and me back. That they'd fixed up rooms at the house for us. I still remember how Dad knelt in front of Daffy and me and told us we'd feel like princesses.

" 'They are princesses,' Mamaw said as we hid behind her legs.

"She told them she'd have to see the house and make sure it was clean. So, they took her there and showed her the canopy beds in each room and the flower printed sheets and the pink stuffed bears they had gotten. I imagine, as Mom told Mamaw that Daffy and me would each have our own beds, that she held her arm out like a game show girl, revealing the prize, 'A canopy bed in each.'

"Mamaw didn't let us go at first, but Mom just kept calling and begging. 'Please, give me my daughters back. If I don't have them, what do I have to stay clean for?'

"Mamaw prayed and prayed and by the end of it, Daffy and me were crying as our things were packed, and we were moved out of the room we had come to think of as our own at Mamaw Milkweed's farmhouse. Daffy grabbed the stair rail. Dad had to pry her fingers off. Mamaw watched from the front porch as they loaded us into the car. We pressed our faces against the back window where we looked out at her as she waved with one hand and cried in the other."

"Then what happened?" John Theresa asked, still playing the violin.

I closed my eyes to the steam rising from the boiling water.

"For the next ten months," I said, "Mom laughed a lot and brushed our hair while Dad stayed faithful to the hours of his new job at the paper mill. When Mom relapsed, she did so while still being a mother. She would flip our pancakes in between crushing pills with the bottom of our cereal bowls. She would give us our baths, then dry her hands and use a hollowed-out pen to snort off the rim of the pink sink. At night, she would read us our bedtime story and have the vodka finished off by the end of it. She would tuck us in tight in the same bed, only to vomit on the quilt she had just covered us with. We'd have to climb out and sleep on the floor, while she passed out on what was supposed to be our pillow. But she always washed the vomit out of the quilt the next morning when she said, 'Everything's gonna be better today, kiddos. I promise.'"

"Did you hate her?" he asked.

I turned from the water, nearly boiled out.

"I never held her broken promises against her," I said, "because I figured she cared enough about us to make the promise in the first place. My father never did that much for us. If anyone would have asked me, who is your father? I would have frowned and said he's a junkie, because he was never a father in between the drugs. After he relapsed, he was only ever the drugs. Just some dirty, sweaty man who would peek out at me and my sister through the strands of his long greasy hair."

"And yet, he is the only father you've ever had and ever will have," John Theresa said.

I pushed the pan off the burner. The pan was dry anyways.

"That night you left us," I said, "you had blood all over your shirt. You said it wasn't your blood. Whose was it?"

He stopped playing the violin on a high, screeching note.

"I was so fucked up at that time." He shrugged. "I don't remember. Why are you asking me about it now?"

"I thought we were talking about the past," I said.

"Well, some things should stay there."

He laid the violin back down in its case.

CHAPTER 27

They walk the hills in the mist.
It is what the women insist.

—*Daffodil Poet*

ON MANY A SUMMER DAY, MAMAW MILKWEED WOULD WALK US DOWN to the part in the river that ran close to her house. Her pants rolled up to her strong calves, a wide-brimmed hat on her head to protect her from the glare of the sun. She would wear a sleeveless top and complain about her arms the whole way.

"Look at how they wiggle." She'd wave, the aged skin flapping. "I shouldn't wear sleeveless shirts no more. I'm too old and floppy now. But it's just so hot, I can't help it. I shouldn't wear them. I know that. But hell, can't an old woman wear what she likes going to the river?"

"I like your old arms, Mamaw Milkweed," Daffy would say. "I like how they jiggle like grape jelly."

"You're the only one." Mamaw would put a bounce in her step to keep up with me and Daffy. "Do all your big waving while you're young, girls. Don't save any of it back. Waving is a young woman's sport."

We would wave our arms the rest of the way to the river, running around Mamaw Milkweed, who would give in and laugh as she waved her arms, too.

Once we were at the river, she would sit on the bank and let her feet get wet while Daffy and me splashed and swam in the river. "Why's the water so brown?" we would ask.

"Well, you got mud on the bottom of a river, you got mud on the sides, you gonna have mud-colored water," Mamaw Milkweed said. "Just the way it is, girls. The earth is dirty. But it's a nice kind of dirty. I tell you what, I'd rather swim in muddy water than in a sparkling swimming pool. Just don't dream of muddy water, girls. If you do, it means someone is gonna go to ghost."

"Go to ghost, Mamaw Milkweed?" Daffy and me asked at the same time.

"Die, my sweethearts. Someone is gonna die."

"Mamaw Milkweed?" Daffy swam closer to the bank. "I dreamed of muddy water the night before Daddy died."

"You did not." I splashed her.

"I did, too." She splashed me back. "You're just angry because you didn't dream it."

"I dreamed of something." I gathered water in my mouth and spit it out at her.

"What did you dream of, Arc?" Mamaw Milkweed asked.

"I dreamed a chicken got her claw caught in the screen of our front door." I lowered my head at the thought. "She died there, waiting to be freed."

"Oh, dear child." Mamaw Milkweed fanned herself with her longest scarf. "You did dream of your daddy's death then."

"But it wasn't muddy water," I said.

"Muddy water is not always muddy water," Mamaw Milkweed said. "Sometimes it's a chicken with her claw caught."

It was the latter that I dreamed as our time at the Evergreen Daughters came to an end.

"Arc?" Daffy sat beside me and laid her head on my arm. "After we leave here, will we be okay?"

"We'll be okay, Daffy." I flipped her braid so it stuck up from the top of her head. "We'll burn all the monsters back with our fire."

"I'm serious, Arc. Sometimes I think the earth has a slant for us, and we're all headed downhill. We're like the women before us, Arc. We carry great terrors on our backs. We take them to bed with us and get up with the same demons."

"We aren't on the savage side no more, Daffy," I said. "We're on the beautiful side. Where you are the captain of daffodils and rhyme, and I, well, I'm the one who's going to find the horse Mom lost in the dirt a long time ago."

Daffy wasn't the only one worried about the outside. The closer we got to release, Thursday kept her hand on her belly, and Indigo highlighted line after line in her math books, as if she could find an equation that would solve everything. Ever encouraging, Violet turned our attention to the things we looked forward to. The things we hoped we could do in a life after heroin.

"I watched this documentary once," Indigo said as we all sat at one of the picnic tables, "about this old guy whose one job is to climb this tower out in the middle of the wilderness. He stays up there with his binoculars, keeping an eye out for any signs of wildfires. I thought, man, I'd love to have that job, be out in the middle of nowhere, climbing step after step to get to the top of a tower to look out for fire. After I get outta here, that's where I'm headed. To the wilderness."

"The wilderness?" Thursday asked. "Shit, I guess it's no wilder than Chillicothe."

"What are you gonna do, Thursday?" Violet asked, perching her face in both hands.

Thursday was no longer cutting holes in her clothes. She seemed older with all the fabric in place. As if she was able to embrace her wholeness, without losing any of it to a pair of scissors.

"I'd like to go back to school," she said. "Use a real telescope."

She was currently making one out of an old baking powder can Violet had given her. She had gotten construction paper from the craft room to wrap it. She was using a glue stick to add some glitter.

"This telescope will see Mars better than any," she said, holding the can up and staring at all of us through its end.

Indigo turned to Daffy and me. "What will you do?"

"Try to survive," I said as Daffy looked down.

"You will all do fine," Violet said. "We should do something to celebrate the start of your new lives."

"Like what?" Daffy shrugged.

Indigo draped her arm around my shoulder, "Well, Arc's always talking about witches. We could dance naked in the woods until the townsfolk try to burn us at the stake."

"I do have a great pair of dancing shoes," Thursday said.

I looked down at Violet's watch on her wrist. I thought of Sage Nell's words when she spoke about time and there being so little of it.

"What about a time capsule?" I asked.

"A time capsule?" Violet's eyes widened. "Now that's an idea."

"We could bury it here somewhere," I said. "Years from now, we can come back and dig it up and remember who we were at this very moment."

"I love it." Indigo smiled.

"What do we put in it?" Thursday asked.

"Anything we want," I said.

We searched for the perfect container and found it in an old metal tackle box that was next to the shovel in the groundskeeper shed. We dumped out the lures and hooks and even took a wet rag to wipe the dust off the dark green metal. Then we headed to the river.

"We shouldn't bury it too close to the water," I said, "in case it floods in the future. Might bring the box up from the ground."

Taking turns, we pushed the shovel into the earth. Then we sat down and laid out the items we'd brought. When Violet laid down the yellowed recipe card, with batter on the old cursive, she said, "This is my favorite recipe. Baking powder biscuits. It was my mother's. The first one we made together."

The other item she had was a violet made out of construction paper. You could tell the paper was old by the way the sun had bleached its edges. Years of tape had been needed to keep the small tears in the petals and the stem from becoming something more.

"Grassy gave this violet to me on my birthday a few years back," Violet said. "She told me it had grown out of my head in this spot right here." Violet touched the words tattooed on her scalp. "Grassy said she picked the violet while I slept."

"You're the only woman in the world who can grow violets outta your head," Thursday said. "My turn now."

We weren't surprised when Thursday showed us her items, the first being a handful of plastic beads. "Emeralds," she said of the green ones. "And rubies and sapphires and plenty of diamonds." She had a whole handful. "Enough to make a beautiful necklace when we dig this back up."

She next put in the baking powder can she had turned into a telescope earlier that day.

"A telescope, so I can remember that even on the streets, there were stars," she said.

Indigo turned to me. "You can go next, Arc."

"No, you go," I told her.

"All right." She unfolded a sheet of paper and pressed it down on the ground. On it was her ink drawing of a triangle in a circle. We all tried to figure out what it was.

"Remember how I told you trigonometry measures the unknown?" she asked. "Well, this triangle and circle are the measurement of me. The distance across to the other side. Maybe in the future, I will have finally got there."

She pulled a pair of scissors out of her pocket and cut a piece out of the rim of her hat.

"Unraveling fire," she said, dropping it in.

They turned to Daffy and me next. I set a rock down.

"That's it?" Thursday asked.

"There are three things inside this rock," I said. "It is a carved goddess. See her eyes?"

I pointed out the indentations in the rock. They all agreed with oohs and aahs.

"It's not just a figurine, though," I said. "It's also a flower bulb."

Daffy smiled.

"What's the third thing, Arc?" Violet asked.

"An afghan," I said. "Without a savage side."

"I like it." Indigo nudged me.

After all our items were safely inside the tackle box, we closed the lid and placed it in the hole. We grabbed the dirt in our hands until the box was covered. Then we danced on the top layer of earth to pack it down.

"Can't forget this," I said, picking up a stick and poking holes in the dirt. "So rumors will be that we danced naked like witches in high heels that stabbed the earth."

Indigo was the first to grab another stick. Then we all poked the dirt as Violet asked, "When we come back to dig it up, how will we be able to know which tree? They all look alike."

"You know what's great about a catchy song?" Thursday grinned.

She dropped to her hands and knees, pressing her lips into the ground and singing Foreigner's "I Want to Know What Love Is." She sang, "Through the clouds, I see love shine," louder than any of the lyrics.

"Now," she said, standing, "the ground won't be able to get that song outta its head and it'll still be singing it years from now. We'll only have to listen."

"Just in case," I said, "we'll carve something into the tree."

"My fingernails are sharp, Arc." Indigo held hers up. "But they won't cut through bark."

"I got what we need." Thursday reached into her pocket and pulled out Sage Nell's pocketknife. "So what should we carve?" She clicked open the blade.

I took the knife and, as Daffy looked over my shoulder, pressed the blade into the bark.

"'Chillicothe,'" Thursday read the first word aloud.

"'Queens,'" we all spoke the second.

"We have to promise each other we won't dig up the capsule until we're all here to see it," I said.

"I hope no one cuts the tree down first," Violet said.

"If someone does," I said, running my hands over the freshly carved words, "the sound of the tree falling will echo, and all our dresses will suddenly catch fire."

Indigo made ghostly noises and threw her arms up in our faces until we laughed.

"The flames will lead us back to the stump because we are Chillicothe Queens," I said.

"Chillicothe Queens," we all chanted, our echoes disappearing into the darkness around.

~

CHAPTER 28

Looking for new gods, we run with the old dogs.

—*Daffodil Poet*

ADDICTION IS A THIEF. IT STEALS THE MINUTES FROM THE DAY. THE color of the sky. It steals the hero from the story, the leaves on the trees, the answer to the question, *Who am I?* The thief doesn't go completely away because you've stopped holding the needle to your arm. Sobriety is just a better hiding spot for the minutes of the day, the color of the sky, the answer to the question, *Who am I?*

Trying to figure that out, Daffy and me brushed our teeth morning and night. We shampooed and showered and felt success in being squeaky clean. Daffy kept her head wet by holding a comb under the faucet. Sometimes I thought it might have been so she could feel like she did when she was swimming. Maybe it was only because she felt she looked cleaner. We worried about how we looked. It was something we worked on, feeling that by wearing clothes in sizes too large, we were able to hide what we wanted to conceal about ourselves while still looking like a couple of fresh-faced women coming home from the Evergreen Daughters.

"Why you leaving me?" Mom stood against the wall and pressed her forehead into it, watching Daffy and me pack what things we wanted to take with us. "Don't leave." She moaned. "If you do, the man will come."

"What man, Momma?" Daffy asked.

"The man who eats last fingerprints." Her words were one long slur. "He'll sense you're gone and his belly will growl with his hunger and he'll come to eat everything you last touched in this house. He'll eat the doorknobs and the kitchen counters and the toilet seat and the walls in the hallway. Then he'll smell and sniff." She took heavy inhales, her nose scrunched up like a snout. "And it'll lead to me." She started to rub up and down her body. "You touched me here and here and here, and he'll know it. He'll smell it. He'll devour me to get your fingerprints, and it'll be all your fault."

Tired by the stream of words, she leaned her whole body against the wall as she hollered to Aunt Clover on the sofa.

"Hey," she yelled louder when Clover didn't answer.

"What?" Aunt Clover appeared in the doorway.

"Don't leave me alone, okay?" Mom swayed from foot to foot. "Don't ever leave me."

"My blood is full of whispers now," Aunt Clover said. "And whispers only have one ending in mind. I couldn't leave now even if I wanted."

Aunt Clover returned to the sofa while Mom walked against the wall as she headed to her room. At her door, she briefly touched the beads still wrapped around the knob, their gold paint completely chipped off.

"'Bye, Mom," I whispered on our way to the front door.

"You'll be back," Aunt Clover said from the sofa. "You ain't got the courage to make it. I wouldn't even trust you to walk me to the end of the street. You have the blood of unknown women inside ya. Unknown because they were never brave enough to be named."

Her legs were on the coffee table, spaced so far apart, the small electric fan could blow between them. She had a pile of sticks in her lap that she was sorting while watching a show on TV about the history of Spain and its stained-glass cathedrals.

"See ya another day, Aunt Clover," Daffy said. "Maybe a better day."

"Turn the fan on high. It's hot enough to boil blood around here" was all she said.

Daffy did her the favor, pausing to stare at the needles on the coffee table. I had to pull her away.

We were headed to an efficiency apartment that was part of the sober living program. It was a small place. The bed pulled out from the sofa. There was a bright white bathroom and a yellow kitchenette that had enough counter space for the few things we bought and cooked. It had a tiny table that folded down from the wall to a cubby with exposed shelves and two pint-size glass doors. We didn't mind the smallness of the apartment. It was clean. It was ours. We pulled the bed out from the sofa and jumped on it that first night.

"We've got to gather flowers and bones," Daffy said. "The two best things to decorate a house of women."

We bought a disposable camera and took photos of ourselves, remembering to smile. We got the film developed and put the photos in cheap frames we got from a yard sale the old woman down the street had the week before. Remembering Mamaw Milkweed's hands, we picked up yarn at the store and spent our nights after work crocheting a black granny square afghan with multicolored squares. We finished it in a month and draped it over the back of the sofa. We even bought two potted violets in dark green plastic containers because they were two for a dollar at the grocery store. We set them in the one window. It overlooked the kitchen sink.

"In the old legends," I said to Daffy, "they called violets the most beautiful thieves around because it was said they would steal your ability to smell with one inhale."

"Is that true?" she asked.

"Yes," I said. "There's a chemical in the flower. When you first smell a violet, you can't smell it a second time. But it doesn't steal anything for very long. A violet is the type of thief who gives what she takes back."

Daffy smelled the flower, then said, "There's someone following us, Arc."

"What do you mean?" I asked. "Who?"

"I don't know yet."

"Then how do you know—"

"The same reason you do," she said.

We locked the front door and checked it twice on our way to bed.

The next day Daffy went on what was supposed to have been a quick run to the gas station to get the truck filled up so we wouldn't have to leave earlier in the morning before work. Evergreen Daughters had lined up jobs for us waiting tables at the local restaurant that had been the cheeseburger capital of Chillicothe since 1953.

I heard the front door open and close. I was in the kitchenette washing the dishes.

"Daffy, that you?"

When she didn't come into the room, I called again, reaching for the knife in the bottom of the sink just as she slowly stepped in.

"You scared me." I dropped the knife and added another squirt of soap into the water.

She had her arms wrapped around a bulge in the upper portion of her shirt.

"What are you up to?" I asked as I scrubbed the already-clean cereal bowl even harder.

The bulge started to move.

"Daffy, what do you have?"

A meow answered. Daffy looked down at the bulge, which moved higher up her shirt. A kitten's black head suddenly popped up behind her collar.

"Daffy. No. Take that cat back to where you got her." I threw the sponge down into the sink, the soapy water splashing back on me.

"Someone dumped them at the gas station in a cardboard box." She pulled the kitten out. She was black with four white paws and a white bib. "Five babies. Can you imagine, Arc? Someone doing that to them like they could never be loved?"

"You didn't get all five, did you, Daffy?"

"I wanted to," she said, "but I knew you'd be a grumpy old bear about it. There was a little girl there with her mom. They said they'd take them. They have a farm. It sounded as nice as sunflowers in a field. They said I could have one of the babies, if I wanted. I chose her. I thought she looked like she knows a thing or two about poetry."

"We can't take care of a kitten." I frowned.

"Who says?" She held tight to the creature. "We're doing okay, ain't we? I mean, we're doing pretty goddamn okay if you ask me. But you walk around here, tiptoeing, like you don't deserve even an inch of the day to do anything nice with. You're always just cleaning. You're a shadow mopping the floor or washing the walls. At night, you're just the shape of you sleeping in the chair because you don't even think you deserve the bed. It's like your face still hurts where Mom smacked it and called you worthless when we were six years old. I don't wanna live with the window only half open, Arc. Only half of the sun. Only half of the moonlight. Only half of the breeze. I want the whole thing. I want a whole life." She hugged the kitten and nuzzled faces. "Please, Arc. Let's keep her. She's part bird, I know it.

Once a year she'll let us watch her fly. We won't break her. We'll take care of her. She'll be a good reason for us to not stay out late. She'll keep us away from the needle."

"That was the old promise Mom gave us, remember?"

"Please, Arc. I'll scoop her litter box. I'll feed her. You won't have to do any of the work. You'll just get to pet her and listen to her purr. Listen, she's purring now." Daffy held the kitten out.

I could hear the slight rumble sounding from her tiny body.

"Someone just left her there like she was a piece of trash. Nothing more," Daffy said. "She's one of us, Arc."

I looked from my sister's pleading face to that of the kitten, her yellow eyes so bright, they reflected my image in them.

I picked the sponge up out of the sink. As I started to wipe down the counter, I said, "We'll have to get a litter box and food."

"I already got everything." Daffy stepped into the living room to grab the bag of supplies and run it back in to me.

"I see you got the litter box." I glanced into the bag. "But did you get the litter?"

"Oh." She looked down. "No, I forgot that."

She set the bag on the floor and started to hand the kitten to me.

"Daffy, my hands are wet."

She shoved the kitten against my shirt. I had no choice but to take hold of her.

"Watch her while I go back to the store," Daffy said.

I sighed as I picked up the kitchen towel and wrapped it around the kitten to dry her wet fur.

"Don't be gone long," I hollered to Daffy as she headed toward the front door. "And don't come back with anything but litter this time."

"Not a puppy?" she asked. "With floppy ears, brown as tree bark?"

"Daffy, I'm serious."

I could hear her giggle as she left. I carried the kitten into the living room and saw the front door open.

"Daffy?" I stepped out into the hall, but it was empty. I held the kitten tighter as we went back inside the apartment.

"Everything's going to be okay," I spoke to the kitten as I closed the door. "Daffy will be back soon." I sat down on the sofa with her. "Well." I rubbed the towel on the wet spot on top of her head. "I will admit, you are a cute little thing. I bet your mamaw was a tiger and the one before her a blue lioness. Who would drop you off? Hmm? Who could let a sweet creature like you go?"

I held her little body up to my ear and listened to the purring.

Do you hear the violin? I imagined Daffy asking.

"Yes," I would have said to her. "Yes, I hear it."

By the time Daffy got back from the store, me and the kitten were curled up together on the sofa, the afghan draped over the both of us.

"I thought you didn't want her," Daffy said as she closed the front door quietly and set the litter down. She knelt by the sofa and laid her head against the afghan, staring at the kitten's sleeping eyes.

"I've named her," I whispered as I petted my finger down her soft little nose.

"What'd you name her?" Daffy looked up at me.

"Petticoat."

"Petticoat?" Daffy tilted her head. "Like the ruffled skirt thingy women used to wear under dresses? I bet you have a whole history on it in that little head of yours, don't you?"

"Back in 1916," I said, "women in a small Oregon town became tired of the place being in ruin and run by the politics of men who didn't care to better the town or its inhabitants. The women got together and decided they would use their right to vote granted to women in Oregon in 1912."

"You're an old ancient book, Arc." Daffy put her face in both hands and propped her elbows on the sofa's edge.

"It was a secret ballot," I said. "The women, in their grand plan, wrote in their own names. When they counted the votes, the women had won all four council seats. They voted themselves into the offices of the treasurer, secretary, and recorder. A woman by the name of Laura J. Starcher became mayor, defeating E. E. Starcher, the man confident he would be voted mayor again. A man who happened to be Laura's husband."

"I bet she danced in the forest that night." Daffy seemed to purr with the kitten.

"Instead of electing men," I said, "the women took the power into their own hands. Together these wives, mothers, and now politicians repaired the cracks of the town. They invested in a sewage system, restored sidewalks, and met the issues the men hadn't. They named what those women did the Petticoat Revolution. Whenever a woman governed or rose to power within the political ranks, they called it, and still do in some circles, Petticoat government. Maybe some men thought they were diminishing the women and their power by calling it the thing they wore beneath their skirts. But in the end, it was a power no one could take away from them. That's why I named her Petticoat. She's a vote for ourselves."

"I told you she'd bring us music." Daffy smiled.

"Yes." I smiled, too. "Music and magic. They can never take her away from us."

"You know what else she's got, Arc?" Daffy smiled wider. "Enough fur to keep us warm."

She got up on the sofa with the kitten and me. For the rest of that night, the three of us slept in one another's arms.

CHAPTER 29

In the water, we drown like daughters.

—*Daffodil Poet*

WE SHOWERED THE KITTEN WITH TOY BALLS AND TREATS AS THE DAYS and weeks passed. We played peek-a-boo with her in blankets and took her photo by the potted violets. We watched old movies together, all cuddled up, and laughed as she purred. We also studied for our GED and even looked into courses from colleges we thought might accept us. Through it all, Petticoat grew, sleeping between us on the foldout sofa or unraveling our balls of yarn for the next thing we planned to crochet. It was nice to have something more on our minds than the Blue Hour, the crowns, or the johns.

"Speaking of johns," Daffy said, "did you remember to make Petticoat's appointment to get spayed?"

We were at the grocery store, buying things sober people eat.

"They couldn't get her in until next month," I said, putting the sugary cereal in the cart along with some oatmeal.

We passed by the housewares aisle and saw the blue-and-white-dinnerware setup in the same display the store had had since we could remember. The design on the dishes was of pagodas and something farther east than Chillicothe.

"Mom got a few of these plates when we were little. Remember?" Daffy picked up a plate and turned it over to the stamp of a crown. "I think we should collect them," she said. "Finish what Mom started."

We decided to buy the dishes with extra tip money we made at the restaurant. We got the plate first, then the gravy boat, the sugar and creamer, followed by the big platter you'd serve a feast on come Christmas. We even got the teapot and pretended to pour tea into the cups on the little saucers, while Petticoat watched from our laps. Aside from pretending, we never used any of the dishes. We set them on display in the little built-in cubby over the fold-down table. I would pass by this cubby and smile at the dishes filling the shelves.

Daffy started stealing the small pieces first. A saucer from the stack, then the teacups and mugs, the salt and pepper shakers that were shaped like women. Then she moved on to the bigger pieces because the small ones were all gone. The platter. The covered casserole. The plates, one at a time, until all there was left was the very first one we'd bought. I held it against my chest the night she came in at three in the morning. I was sitting at the fold-down table.

"We almost had the whole collection," I said quietly. "We almost had enough to set the table with. We almost made it. Didn't we, Daffy?"

She didn't try to stop me as I rolled her shirt sleeve up. I stared at the fresh track marks.

"I thought I could just do a little," she said. "And still stay out of the deep water, you know? I don't know why I thought that. It's never been an act of love."

"You sold all our dishes, when we almost made it." I stared down at the plate.

"I just took a piece here and there," she said. "Before I knew it, I'd taken them all."

"Except for this one." I held the plate up.

"Don't hate me. Please, Arc."

I handed her the plate. She quickly left, maybe thinking if she didn't, I'd change my mind. I picked up Petticoat who had been lying on my feet. I held her as I sat there, staring into the emptiness of the cubby.

When Daffy returned home, she pulled her chair up to the table while I set Petticoat down on the floor. She meowed loud and long, butting her head into our bare ankles while I rolled up our sleeves.

PART VI

CHAPTER 30

I am near to my fear.

—*Daffodil Poet*

MY DREAMS CAME IN LAYERS. LIKE I WAS PUTTING ON CLOTHES. THE fabric thin enough that the light could pass through. Some dreams were of people I knew, carved up by the words already said. In others, I did nothing but collect hinges off doors, windows, boxes, while women bent over on the streets. Then I dreamed of Daffy going to get her hair done. The women in the chairs around her wore beehive hairdos and cat eyeglasses from a decade we never knew. The hairdresser started to brush Daffy's hair. Dead insects got caught in the bristles.

The hairdresser dropped the brush so she could use her fingers to pull out the leaves and twigs that had gotten tangled. No matter how hard she pulled, the debris wouldn't come out. Daffy screamed until her throat bled. The hairdresser used the blood to dye Daffy's hair.

Daffy and me had grown up listening to Mamaw Milkweed feed us stories of how we'd come from women who were closer to the stars than they were to the earth. Women who would dream of muddy water just before someone died. Mamaw Milkweed told us these things in a grandiose but hushed tone as if our power were an immovable tradition.

"The witch hides in you," she would say while clutching the cross around her neck as if she wanted to cover the ears of God. "She gives you the power to dream the truth. You must believe that whatever nightly visions you see will come to pass as real as water falling through your fingers. You must feed the witch for what she gives you."

"Feed her with what?" I had asked.

"Your thoughts," Mamaw Milkweed said.

"Like of cauldrons and bats and spells?"

"No, honey. With thoughts of your elbows and your collarbone and the way you open your eyes in the morning."

I then fed the witch with thoughts of my own self, and as the dreams came, I knew they were trying to tell me something.

"Are you sure it's me?" Daffy asked after I told her about the hairdresser and the way her fingers tried to pull out the twigs and bugs. "It could be you, Arc."

"I'm the one watching."

"Are you sure?" She laughed over the sink as she cleaned her hands to try to wash the dream down the drain, just as Mamaw Milkweed had taught us.

The closest we got to speaking about the dream again was the time we talked about Mamaw Milkweed and how she would put us to bed with a flower bulb beneath our pillow.

"So it will take root in your dreams," she had told us. "When you need to leave the dream, you merely find the flower, pluck her of her petals, and you will waken."

"An old woman's wisdom," Daffy would say in a whisper.

After we slid back into the mud, we seemed to talk more and more about Mamaw Milkweed. We were both glad she had died before she had lived long enough to see us standing on the side of the street, holding up signs, asking for money.

"Remember the way her angel food cake would crack on the top?" Daffy asked.

"Remember her old yella cat and her single fang?" I asked.

We thought only of Petticoat then. She had come to live with us after we were kicked out of the efficiency apartment and had to move back in with Mom and Aunt Clover.

"A little kitty cat." Mom scooped Petticoat up, who hissed and growled and scratched Mom until she dropped her. "Damn lion whore," Mom said as she stumbled to her bedroom.

Petticoat jumped at every sound, and the fur on her back stood up as she sniffed her way from room to room. The smells, noises, and filth were different from the small but clean apartment she'd come from, with its violets in the windowsill and the afghan on the back of the sofa and the framed photos of smiling girls. While the violets died, we sold the frames and tore the photos up. We got whatever money we could for anything else, including our afghans.

We stopped buying cat litter first. Petticoat went to the bathroom on the floor or just outside the back door we opened for her when we were aware enough to do so. Next to go was her cat food. She was forced to eat the things that were left on plates until she stopped coming back into the house. I pulled three hairs from her tail and put them under the back porch steps.

"To keep her home," I told Daffy when she asked why.

Still Petticoat stayed longer and longer outside, finding that some of the kinder neighbors put out dry kibble for strays. Her fur got dull and stiff. She lost the baby fat she'd once had. She grew up quick, and not long afterward she got a bad eye. It ran with pus, half-closed, as she screamed and howled while a tomcat, some mangy creature himself, bit the back of her neck and forced himself inside her in ways that would change her from the curious and gentle kitten she had been to the dirty and mean cat she would now be expected to be.

"I wish we would have made it long enough to get her spayed," I told Daffy.

"Yeah," Daffy said. "I bet she wishes that, too."

Petticoat became just another frightened creature of the street, sometimes staring into my eyes until I looked away, burying my face in my hands. Daffy never said Petticoat's name, as if to say her name would be reminded of something more than the cat we had abandoned. She would ask, "Have you seen the stray?" as if the cat had never been our responsibility and was instead a nameless creature who lived separate from us. Nothing but a stray. Certainly not someone we had loved for the time we had been sober.

"I knew you'd be back," Aunt Clover said that first night we were home.

"Oh yeah?" I sat down beside her on the sofa. The old awful smells of a woman cracking and a house falling filled my nose.

"Of course," she said. "You're your father's daughter."

She had temporarily put aside the bag of twigs to brush the faux leopard fur collar as she told me about the time my father and mother met.

"He was the first boy your momma ever danced with," she said.

"Your momma was only fifteen at the time. He was all the way old to us at twenty-two. She didn't tell nobody about him. He was a divine secret. She knew Momma would make her leave him in the trees like the animal he was." Aunt Clover sighed. "She went to his place and went to bed with him that first night they met, not even learning his name until the next morning when he wore nothing but jeans in the kitchen and had a bowl of pancake batter in the crook of his arm. Maybe she thought she'd never see him again by the time she licked all that syrup off her plate, but they ended up fucking for the rest of that year. Somewhere the jungle was applauding.

"When he got her pregnant with you and your sister, I sure as shit wasn't surprised. He was a good boy about it. Signed up for Uncle Sam. Said he'd make an honorable family. He served well in the beginning. Got some badges. I think they call 'em medals in the army. You like history, Arc, so you'll like hearing this." She pointed her finger at me. "What they don't tell ya in the history books is that war is fought with sober intention but not always with sober minds."

Aunt Clover wasn't wrong. I had learned this going to the library as a teenager to read about the history of war. As long as there've been soldiers, there's been a way to make them better killing machines. Going back to when the land was forested more than it was indus-trialized, tribesmen would take hallucinogens. It gave them courage to run toward the spears and not away from them. Battles have been fought with soldiers high on mushrooms, and certainly alcohol has always been present. Whether wine, vodka, or whiskey, they would drink in order to survive war itself. Hitler had his own pill that he would send out to his Nazi troops. It was called Pervitin. A pill to make them better fighters. Little did the Nazi soldiers know, they were taking crystal meth.

Speed, cocaine, heroin. Our wars have been fought not with the sobriety that tradition so admires, but with the use and the aid of enough narcotics to super our heroes.

"It was while your daddy was in service that he got addicted," Aunt Clover said. "He was on uppers first to keep him awake. Then he moved on to cocaine, which opened the door. When he punched his superior, he was just another cry in the night. After they dishon-orably discharged him, he dragged himself home. The great Flood

Doggs flooded our lives. We ain't been outta the high water since. That son of a bitch. It was left to me to save your drowning momma."

She picked up the old creamed corn can and held it to her ear.

"I don't hear Addie breathing," she said. "I best go check on her."

"I'll go." I stood up before she could. "You take care of your leopard."

She looked down at the collar. It was so old and filthy, you couldn't tell its spots were anything more than shadows.

"Looking good, don't you think?" she asked. "Meow, meow." Her cat sounds were deep and guttural, more like hisses and growls.

I walked down the hall, stopping at Daffy's room. She had laid down with her back to the growing collection of twigs and sticks on her wall.

"Aunt Clover's been busy," she said. "She must have brought in ants on some of the sticks. They're in my bed, eating on me."

When I didn't step into the room, she asked, "Where are you going?"

"To check on Mom."

"Don't, Arc. She'll eat your fingers off and call it love. I hate being back in this hellhole of a house. The same dog barking outside. The same light flickering out in the bathroom. The same smell of shit. The earth blurs here, Arc. We can close our eyes, having never slept."

She flipped over, facing the wall and knocking the ants off her skin. I turned toward the darkness of the hallway. When I passed by the bathroom, I glanced in at the mirror. Aunt Clover had put so much tape on the glass, in some places it was layered. The reflection was now skewed and altered, a blur of everything around.

I kept my hand on the wall, dragging it along as I stepped over the mess of our house. Mom's door was partly open. I pushed it the rest of the way. It was dark inside the room, but I could make out her form on the mattress.

"You need light in here, Mom." I stepped in and parted Dad's clothes on the windows, tying them back so the day could come in.

She grunted and squeezed her eyes shut as if the light burned them. When I sat down on the floor by the mattress, I saw the hole in the side of it was now much larger. The newest additions to her collection of stolen items from the johns was an old movie ticket stub, a crumpled-up pop can, and a book of matches.

"Mom, take this junk out." I started to reach inside the hole, but she said no.

"Leave it be." Snot was running from her nose and her eyes were red.

"I don't know how you can stand to lay on all that junk," I said.

"Arc? Arc?" She suddenly sat up like she was unsure who was in the room with her.

"I'm here, Momma."

"Don't go into Daffy's room." Mom tried to find me with her eyes. "She's got the flu. You'll get it, too. Double the vomit. Double the cleaning. I can't do it. I'll have to fall out the nearest window just to be free."

She wrung her hands. It was like bones sliding over one another.

"Momma," I said, "that was a long time ago."

"No, it was just this morning." She violently shook her head and stared down at her hands.

"Momma?" I asked.

"Yeah, baby?"

"Do you wish you had never met Daddy?"

"Daddy?" Her eyes rolled as she held her finger up like she was trying to point to something. "I don't recall anyone by that name."

The tears slipped down her cheeks in crooked lines.

"I'm as cold as all the winters, in all the years," she said.

"Why don't you get some rest, Momma?"

I stood, picking up Dad's old army bag and shaking it off.

"That sounds nice," she said, curling up in a tight ball.

She no longer cut or bleached the ends of her hair. It had grown out, long and stringy. The once-vibrant red shade of her youth had faded, and the coarse white hairs colored the crown of her head the same shade Mamaw Milkweed's had been. Mom's skin had thinned, becoming translucent. For a moment, I thought there was nothing left that was hers.

"This will make you warm, Momma," I said.

She nodded as I draped the army bag on top of her.

"Don't go into Daffy's room, Arc." She grabbed my arm. "She's got the flu."

"I won't, Momma." I tucked the bag around her as her hand slid off my arm.

When I was reaching under the mattress to get the other side, I felt something with my fingers. I grabbed hold and pulled.

"Diary." I whispered the word inscribed in gold on the blue satin cover, dirtied and tattered. I recognized my mother's handwriting as soon as I opened it.

"Don't go into Daffy's room." Mom's voice was strained. "You'll get sick, too, Arc."

"I won't, Mom."

"That's good. Where's my blue-eyed girl?"

I shut my green eye for her.

"Where's my green-eyed girl?" she asked.

I closed my blue one.

"It's not the same." She laid her cheek on the back of her hand. "Without Daffy, you're just half of something that don't exist no more."

"Sleep now, Momma."

I hugged her diary to my chest so hard, it nearly stole my breath as I walked out of the room, closing the door just as she closed her eyes. I knew she would soon open them, having never slept.

CHAPTER 31

Dry dirt turns to mud in a flood.

—*Daffodil Poet*

1979

IF YOU WERE TO ASK ME AS A KID IF I'D EVER DO DRUGS, I WOULD have said, "Hell, no," then eyeballed you like you were stupid for asking in the first place. I didn't account for all the life in between being a child and being an adult. I was so certain I knew who I was. I suppose at some point in their lives, my mother and father thought the same thing about themselves.

I try to think of my father sober, but in what few memories I have of him, he is always the addicted one. The memories are being devoured. The day he died, he came into the kitchen and handed me a spoon for my cereal. Thinking back on it, I don't know if he was truly handing me the spoon, or if he was merely getting it for himself and I took it out of his hand as he was passing by. Either way, he surrendered to the spoon being gone and sat at the table to watch me eat. I still remember how big his dirty T-shirt was on his thin frame. There was a large piss stain on the front of his pants I try to forget. In his army photo, his eyes looked blue. By then, the color was that of the pieces of gum I often found in the dirt. Colorless, chomped things that had at one time been bright before all that color was chewed away.

I tried to reconcile the man in the army photo with the person in front of me. But sitting there at the kitchen table, he was a man who had an overwhelming gauntness not had in the photo. His cheeks hollower, as if his bones were buoyant things on top of deep water. His nose looked sharper and longer. His lips pale. His hair grown out to his shoulders as just another mess within a mess. In the photo, his hair was barely long enough for me to see it was the color of the brown waters that first flooded around him.

In the photo, the man stood tall, as if he would one day be king. But the one before me, who watched me eat cereal, sat slumped, as if the only kingdom promised to him was that of the vomit he so often fell asleep and woke up in.

"What'd you find in the dirt today, shovel hand?" he asked.

I stopped eating to dig into my pocket and pull out the bloody and used bandage.

"I found this, Daddy." I held it toward him.

"Don't pick up things like this, Arc." He yanked the bandage away from me. "Dirty, dirty. Don't you understand?"

That moment was the only time I remember my father raising his voice. For all the chaos around, he never seemed to be one of the yelling monsters. It startled me so much, I cried.

"I'm sorry, kiddo." He threw the bandage down as he stood and lifted me up in a hug.

He stunk. A combination of sweat, piss, vomit, and something I could not name. I wanted to get far away from him, out into the clean, fresh air. But I didn't, because I couldn't remember a hug prior to that one. I knew I could have lived another million years with my father and never gotten another, so I let him hug me, and I hugged him back because it seemed to be my one and only chance to know how it felt to be in his arms.

"I didn't mean to yell at you," he said. "I'll tell ya what. Today, when you get home from school, we'll go digging. I'll take you to a spot I've heard there are dinosaur bones."

"Dinosaur bones?" I hugged him tighter. "Really?"

"Yes." He grinned. It's the last smile I have from him. "Better than a dirty bandage, huh, Arc?"

I nodded until I thought I'd nod my head off. Later that day I couldn't get out of school fast enough. The whole bus ride home, I sat by the window and bounced, waiting for our street to come into view.

"What are you so excited about?" Daffy asked.

"Dinosaur bones" was all I said.

When the bus stopped at the end of our street, I pushed past my sister and got out into the aisle first.

"Wait up, Arc," she yelled as I darted down the bus steps and took off, full speed ahead, toward the house.

When I heard the sirens, I came to a dead stop across the street.

"What do you think happened?" Daffy asked, once she caught up to me.

I started running again, nearly getting hit by a car as I crossed the street. I told the cops in front of the house that I needed to get inside because my daddy and me were going digging for dinosaur bones.

"He promised me," I said to them as they tried to hold me back.

I didn't realize at the time that my father was under the white sheet on the stretcher they were loading. If I had looked, I would have seen his dirty, track-marked arm dangling from under the sheet. All I saw was the house and the front door that I wanted to get through so I could find my daddy and together we could find something more.

I imagined him on the sofa, waiting for me to come into the house. I was determined not to disappoint him by being late.

"He's waiting for me," I screamed, but I couldn't get past the officers. One of them picked me up and held me. I punched his chest with my little fists and tried to break free.

"It's gonna be all right, honey." He tightened his arms around me. He had a scar on his left cheek that looked like two fishhooks tangled together. The rippling skin rose and almost boiled up. "Everything is going to be all right."

"Poor kid." I heard one of the other officers say. "Breaks my heart to see shit like this. Damn parents. Don't care nothing about what they do to their own."

"Give it a few years," the one holding me said. "We'll be arresting this kid for the very same thing. Just a cycle for 'em."

"I've got to see my daddy," I yelled until I was hoarse.

When Mamaw Milkweed showed up, they released me into her open arms. I immediately told her they wouldn't let me into the house to get Daddy so we could go hunting for dinosaur bones. She held me so tight, I thought she was going to squeeze me to death.

"I tried to tell Arc." I could hear Daffy's voice in the background. "I tried to tell her Daddy is dead, but she won't stop talking about dinosaur bones."

I was six years old. The only death I had to compare to my father's was the death of a minnow I'd had for three days. I was more disappointed in the fact that we would not be finding dinosaur bones than I was in the fact that I would never see my father again.

My sister cried, Mamaw Milkweed cried, my mother cried. Hell, even Aunt Clover cried at Dad's funeral.

Daffy cut a purple heart out of construction paper and laid it on top of his body. "Army men get a purple heart," she said when I asked her why she did it. "I saw it on TV. I thought he should get a purple heart, too."

Fatherless, my sister and me looked toward our mother, but in the rooms of our house, there was only the silence of a woman left alone after her husband overdosed.

I tried to find another mother. The one in the photos. Adelyn Milkweed was her name, this woman who was young, sober, and pretty. I thought if you smiled in a photograph, you smiled forever, and anything else that came after that smile didn't matter because the moment that was captured on film was the moment that mattered for eternity. I guess it was just another myth for the heart to believe.

P
A
R
T

VII

CHAPTER 32

I am near to my fear.

—*Daffodil Poet*

1994

THE BLACK CRIB SAT OUTSIDE ON THE DRY BROWN GRASS. ONE OF THE rails was cracked, but not broken. In some ways, it looked too heavy to move. As if it would have roots, as black as it, stretching deep into the ground, pushing past sharp pebbles and restless worms.

Violet had picked the crib up from her ex-husband. When Thursday saw it, she said, "There's something very *Rosemary's Baby* about black cribs."

Her dad bought a can of paint in the color of blue that he felt best represented Thursday's description to him.

"Something like the color of the sky," she had told him. "But also the color of the mountain mist. A shade that is both young and old. One that remembers. One that discovers."

The color he came back with was a blue she smiled at.

"I'll paint it for you if you want," her dad told her.

But she said, "Us women have to paint the crib, Dad. So that we can leave our secrets like lullabies. Now get the hell outta here. We've got work to do."

Thursday handed Violet and me each a brush. For a few moments, Violet stayed, but then she laid the brush down and disappeared inside Thursday's trailer.

"I almost don't wanna say it," Thursday said, dipping her brush into the can, "but you notice anything different about Violet?"

"Yeah," I said, focusing only on the way the paint left my brush. "Yeah, I notice something different."

Thursday exhaled. "Let's talk about anything else then." She ran the bristles of her brush across the top rail of the crib. "I've decided, Arc, I'm not going to marry a man at all. I would like to marry a whip-poor-will. I heard someone say the name once. I suppose it's a bird, but I ain't never seen one. Have you?"

"I imagine a whip-poor-will is part man," I said, "with bird feathers on his face. Standing erect out of the thicket. His tongue sparkles. He'll eat beetles and nuts."

"I won't mind," she said. "We'll have a child who is born silent." She rubbed her stomach. "She'll betray us by speaking a single word."

No one had to ask Thursday if she was using again. The holes in her clothes had started to reappear. In the shoulder of her shirt, in the hem of her shorts. Even the socks had holes, cut to the same measurement as the ones she imagined in the celestial skies.

"I think this will be beautiful once we've finished." She stepped back to look at the progress. Though there was still more black than blue, she smiled. "Yeah, it's gonna be fucking beautiful."

I knew if Daffy had been there, she would have groaned about the work, but likely would have painted her fingernails with a laugh. I had left her at the house to lie down. She said she felt like her hands were vanishing. I told her she was imagining things, but still she asked me to say her name. I did until she closed her eyes and said she could feel her fingers again.

"Why the hell you think Violet got a black crib?" Thursday asked.

"Why don't you ask her?" I used my brush to point toward Violet. She had reappeared, only to sit on the bottom step of the trailer, her arms around her stomach, rocking back and forth.

"Hey, Violet, how come your crib ain't purple?" Thursday asked.

Violet looked up, her eyes slowly blinking. "You have anything you could give me?" She dragged out her words.

Me and Thursday kept painting. She gripped her brush so tightly, her knuckles bleached.

"Do you have anything you could give me?" Violet asked again louder. "I just need a little something to get by."

"You better be talking about aspirin or some shit like that, Violet," Thursday said, clenching her jaw.

"I thought you were my friends?" Violet tightened her arms around her stomach. "I just need a little bit. I'll pay ya back."

"Is that what you think it's about?" Thursday turned around to face Violet. "Fuck you." She threw her brush down. "You said you'd never use again. You fucking promised, you bitch. You fucking addict whore." Thursday rattled off every name she'd ever heard someone call her. She kicked the crib, then turned and sat down hard on the ground, her arms crossed against her chest.

"How'd you get back on it?" I asked Violet.

"That stinking fucker," she said, wiping her face like she was washing it. "He gave me some shit to hold. I knew I shouldn't have, but he said it showed trust. He said if he trusted me, he could get Grassy back to me for sole custody."

"Who told you this?" I asked.

"No one." She quickly stood, wiping her nose on her arm. "Forget it. Forget I said anything."

"Forget it?" Thursday shouted. "Forget you."

Violet walked toward her car with her head down, but stopped at the crib. Before I could tell her that the paint was still wet, she reached out and gripped one of the rails. When she removed her hand, she stared down at the paint on her palm.

"I'm sorry," she said. We weren't sure if she was apologizing to us or to herself.

She ran the rest of the way to her car. It took her a couple of tries to start it. When it finally did, she backed up fast enough to squeal her tires.

"You shouldn't have been so mean to her, Thursday," I said, dipping my brush back into the can and picking up where I'd left off on the crib.

Thursday frowned at me but uncrossed her arms as she stood.

"We couldn't stay sober either," I said, "if you remember."

"Yeah, well, fuck you, Arc." She picked up her brush and swung it around with each word. "We're screwups, me, you, but Violet was the one who was supposed to make it so we'd know we could, too, one day. I mean, what the hell does she think she's doing, using again? She ain't never gonna get her kid back now. She fucked everything up."

Thursday dipped the brush into the can but didn't wipe the bristles. The excess dripped across the grass and onto a cricket.

"Oh, shit." Thursday dropped the brush and cupped her hands around the cricket. "Get the door for me, Arc. I'll wash her off."

At the kitchen sink, she held her fingers like a cage around the cricket. As the cool water washed over, the blue paint circled down the drain.

"You'll be okay, little cricket," she said. "I'll take care of you."

The insect made a sudden attempt to escape. Thursday's hands, slippery with water, tried but were too late to catch the cricket mid-air. She landed in the bottom of the sink, the flowing water picking her up.

"No, no." Thursday cried out and tried again to get the cricket. Last we saw was a kicking leg just before she went down the drain.

"Fuck." Thursday slid down the cabinets to the floor, holding her head in her hands. "I'm a mess. I can't do anything right." She stomped her foot against the floor. "I try to save a goddamn cricket, and I kill the poor thing. What the hell am I gonna do with a kid? Huh?"

"You're gonna be a great mother," I said.

"Oh, yeah, right. I mean, if Violet can't do it, what the hell kind of shot do I have?"

She looked up at the Butterfly Corner.

"All this shit." She yelled, throwing herself up on her feet. "Fuck it." She ripped the postcards, calendars, and stickers off the wall. "*Help the elephants. Donate for big cats. Stop the extinction of the rhinos.* Why they sending these pleas to me? I ain't gonna do anything."

When she got to the large Monarch butterfly poster, she tore it off the wall by the wings. She threw it to the floor and dropped down beside it.

"I'd like to be the type of woman who can open her mail," she said, "and have a few dollars to send back in the white envelope. To know I was part of something bigger, you know? That I was helping to save the ivory tusks from poachers. That in the future, I could tell my kid I did something more than love the drug." She put her two fists on either side of her mouth as she said, "I'm scared, Arc. I'm scared my destiny is to be some wingless creature."

"That's not your destiny, Thursday." I sat down beside her.

She laid her head on my shoulder.

"*The flower man came to say,*" she started to sing slowly, "*I am no more after this long day. His hands like roses wilted down. His arms as lilies turning brown. The disappearing has begun, her face no longer in the sun.*"

"What's that song from?" I asked.

"My life," she said as she rested her hand on her stomach. "It's not my first, you know."

"Not your first what?"

"Pregnancy." She fell silent, then said, "It was a few years back. I lost it. Ugh, that makes it sound like I lost a receipt or a sock in the dryer."

She wiped her face on her sleeve and blew her nose into it, her thumb pushing through the hole in the fabric.

"They say they buried my baby in the ground," she said, "but I buried her in the sky. Come night, I just lay on my back and held the shovel up, digging into the sky and tossing the night over my shoulder until I had a hole six feet deep in the galaxies. After she was in, I covered her with the stars and erected a gravestone as big as the Milky Way." She held her arms open to either side. "Did you know our telescopes are strong enough to see sorrow from space, Arc?"

She looked down at the Monarch poster on the floor. Its left wing had gotten torn.

"It's ruined," she said.

"Only on the savage side," I said. "But we can change it into the beautiful side."

I grabbed the tape from her shelf and picked up the Monarch, taping it once again to the wall.

"On the beautiful side," I said, "the butterflies are safe." I laid down the tape and knelt beside her. "And these aren't holes in your clothes." I grabbed her sleeve and held it up toward the ceiling, framing the light. "They're telescopes to other worlds."

As she stared through to the light, I picked up one of the envelopes she had torn off the wall. Inside it was the donation form to save orangutans. I took my last dollar out of my back pocket and placed it inside, writing Thursday's name on the outside of it.

As I sealed it up, she said, "I don't have any stamps, Arc."

"You don't need any on the beautiful side." I showed her the pre-paid postage mark on the envelope.

She leaned back against the wall, and I sat down, leaning back with her.

"You will be a good mother," I said, putting the envelope in her hands.

She stared down at it for a couple of minutes, then said, "In 1987 giant arcs were seen by astronomers. Three of them. Some half a million light-years long."

"Arcs in the universe?" I asked.

"It's what they call the arches of light in the vastness of space," she said. "It's said the arcs shone as bright as if they were powered by a hundred thousand billion suns. I just realized, they had the fucking telescope on you." She laughed and I laughed with her before the high-pitched shrill of the ringing phone sounded. She kept hold of the envelope as she reached up to the counter, grabbing the phone down by its long cord. When she said hello, no one answered.

"Who is it?" I whispered. She held the receiver to my ear. I heard breathing and a sound moving on the other side. It lasted a few seconds before whoever it was hung up.

"I keep getting them," she said. "They don't ever say anything. You hear the breathing? I don't know who it is. I had a weird john the other day. I mean really weird. Maybe it's him. I don't know. Maybe it's no one. Hell, maybe it's a wrong number. Just breathing and static."

"That wasn't static, Thursday."

"Then what was it?" she asked.

"It was the sound of the river."

CHAPTER 33

I once ran from a man. It was grand.

—Daffodil Poet

HE WANTED TO GO TO THE BLUE HOUR. I THOUGHT HE'D BE AN EASY john. Then I saw the cross necklace he was wearing and knew he'd want to spank me or worse. It was the latter. After it was over, I stepped into the sunlight, feeling as if I'd been inside the dark room for days.

I found Daffy standing on the walk and putting more deodorant on.

"We stink, Arc," she said. "We stink like Mom and Aunt Clover and the house and the Blue Hour. I could choke on the stench. It smells like all the promises we've broken."

She rubbed her wrist like it hurt. The makeup she'd applied heavily was smeared. The eyeliner and mascara now on her cheeks. The lipstick on her top lip left faint red lines out to either side of her mouth. Her hair was so flat and greasy, one might think she had just walked in from the rain if there'd been any. And there, beneath her eyes, the circles were darkened as if the nights had smashed into her.

"Arc." She exhaled my name. "Tell me something nice."

"I don't have anything nice to say." I grabbed my sore neck.

"Tell me about the Trung sisters," she said.

"Daffy." I sighed. "I'm tired."

"Please, Arc." As the shadows hit her face, the lines of makeup appeared to be cracks.

"In ancient Vietnam," I said, the words feeling so distant, "there were two sisters who revolted against the power that tried to change the Vietnamese culture into Chinese. The sisters, witnessing the cruel regime, formed an army of women. This army pushed the Chinese forces back. The Trung sisters were declared queens."

"Queens," Daffy echoed.

"For three years, they ruled in their independence. To this day, the sisters are heroes in Vietnam. There are streets named after them. There are schools. There is even a national holiday." I sighed with no energy to do anything more. "Why you like that story so much, Daffy?"

"If they could fight back a whole army, maybe we can fight back a whole town."

She slipped the deodorant into my pocket as we stepped out of the way of Welt's cleaning cart. He kept his head down, his long hair swinging into his eyes. Sometimes I could swear his eyes were blue. Other times green. That day they were as brown as his T-shirt.

He stopped the cart in front of us. His knitted mauve vest draped down as he got a fresh washcloth off the bottom rack. As we stared at the red leather glove, I saw the gold tip of what appeared to be a charm dangling out.

He grunted as he held the washcloth up to my face and dabbed the blood off my busted lip.

"Thank you." I made sure to say the words slowly so he could read my lips.

He left the washcloth with me as he pushed the cart away.

Daffy looked at me. "How many rivers you think that man took to get to Chillicothe, Ohio, Arc?"

"He's not so bad," I said.

"Because he gave you a washcloth to wipe your blood? The devil is in men like that, too, Arc. I think he's hid cameras in the rooms, so he can watch us with the johns."

"Don't be weird, Daffy."

"I'm serious," she said, watching him stop outside one of the open rooms. He left the cart, taking in a bottle of bleach and a scrub brush. "I've heard from some of the other women that once upon a time, he lost his mind so completely, they put him away for it. His eyes hold the edge of something, Arc. I think it's his sanity."

"You only say that because of the glove."

"Don't you ever wonder what he hides with that thing?"

"Maybe it's not something he hides," I said. "Maybe it's something he protects."

Before she could say anything more, a horn honked. A small yellow car pulled up beside us. I leaned down and looked into the open passenger window. Indigo smiled at me over the boxes of clothes in her front seat. She was wearing her hat, the long gray feather sticking up above the fan of plant roots around the brim.

"I thought I could find you here," she said as she got out of the car. I saw that her back seat was full of more boxes.

Daffy stepped over and leaned against the wall of the Blue Hour, watching us.

"Going to work in that fire tower?" I asked Indigo as she hugged me.

"Not yet." She smiled. "I'm headed to my brother's. He lives in Iowa. He's got a job lined up for me proofreading textbooks. Then I'm off to the wilderness. Why didn't you call me back, Arc? I left a million messages on your answering machine."

"I didn't wanna hear you say you were leaving," I said. "I wish you would stay."

"If I stay," she said, "Chillicothe plus me multiplied by the Blue Hour, minus good sense divided by the devil, times a million and one needles, equals just another addict. Why don't you come with me, Arc? It's hard to start over in a place you've already finished last in. You know?"

I looked back at Daffy. She was laying her head against the brick, closing her tired eyes.

"I'm tethered to this place," I said.

"I worried you might say something like that." Indigo reached into her car and got a large hardcover book out.

"C'mere." She sat on the edge of the curb. "Sit beside me."

As I did, I read the cover aloud.

"The Most Important Archaeological Discoveries of Our Time."

She rested the book on her knees and ran her hands over the photograph of the Great Pyramid of Giza on the cover.

"I got this for you." She smiled as she opened the book. Inside were more full-color photographs of finds from places like South America, Mesopotamia, and Egypt. When she turned the page after the photograph of Petra, there was a small amount of dirt spread out on top of the paper.

"Why is there dirt?" I asked.

"Because you have to dig and see what you discover." Indigo's smile grew larger. "Go on. Excavate the page, Arc."

She nudged me until I used my finger like a tiny shovel, revealing a piece of paper beneath the dirt.

"Read it aloud," she said.

I hesitated, until she nudged me harder.

"'I am incredible,'" I read the note in a shaky voice.

"That you are," she said.

When she turned the page again, there was more dirt.

"Dig, Arc, dig."

I pushed the dirt off the page, discovering another note that read, "I am amazing."

"You're that, too," she said.

On the next page, the dirt gave way to a photograph of King Tut's sarcophagus.

"Look what you found," Indigo said. "The discovery of a century."

"I didn't find it."

"But you could, Arc. You could find it and so much more. Men might think they're the big dog archaeologists. But only women know how to dig because we make sure to go deep enough. Problem with that is, we risk the sides falling in on us and burying who we thought we'd be. You're more than this life, Arc. Come with me and we'll start over."

"I told you." I closed the book. "I'm tethered to this place."

"You know all you have to do when you're tethered?" She made her two fingers into scissors and cut the air. "We could work in the wilderness together. Two women plus the mountains minus concrete."

"Divided by the leaves on the trees," I said. "Multiplied by the stars in the sky."

"Equals a life of our own."

I looked over my shoulder at Daffy. She was no longer leaning against the brick wall with her eyes closed. She was staring at the way Indigo laid her hand on top of mine.

"I can't." I pulled back, turning away.

"What about all the dreams you have for yourself?" Indigo asked.

"I said goodbye to my future a long time ago," I said.

"In another time," she said, taking my cheek in her hand, "we would have been the hunters, Arc Doggs."

We stood up together as she placed the book in my hands.

"I want to give you something else." She reached up to the plant roots around the brim of her hat and broke off a tiny piece. "Here." She slipped the root in between my lips. "To keep you grounded so you remember you're a powerful goddess and no one can take that away from you."

I carried the small root across my tongue to the back of my throat as I looked down at the book, running my hands over its cover.

"If you change your mind," she said, "I'll be making a stop at the Evergreen Daughters before I leave. John Theresa said he wanted to tell me something before I left."

She looked past me at Welt. The cart in front of him was now full of ballooning garbage bags. He had stopped and was watching the two of us.

"Can I help you?" Indigo asked, putting her hand on her hip.

"He's deaf," I told her.

"Oh. My cousin was hearing impaired." She started to speak sign language to Welt.

He gripped the cart's handle so tight, the knuckles of his bare hand went white.

"He signs, right?" she asked me.

"I guess. I mean, I've seen him doing it."

She tried again, moving her hands slower this time.

"What are you saying to him?" I asked.

"Just hello," she said, "and asking if he was born deaf."

He finally raised his hands in a series of swift movements. Then he quickly pushed the cart away.

"That was weird." Indigo watched him until he stopped in the middle of the sidewalk.

"What's weird?" I asked. "What'd he say?"

"He didn't say anything," she said. "That's what's weird."

"What do you mean?" I asked. "I saw his hands moving."

"Yeah, they were moving," she said. "But that's all they were doing. He wasn't speaking sign."

Welt slowly turned back to stare at her. The look on his face reminded me of a dream I'd once had, the one in which a large object was dropped into the river. He reminded me of the water washed ashore on the riverbank after the last ripple had broken.

CHAPTER 34

Gone is my soul, lost through the hole.

—*Daffodil Poet*

WHILE THE STRAY DOG BARKED WITH HUNGER FROM HER LITTLE piece of the earth, I found the gray feather caught in a breeze and flapping against the brick of the Blue Hour. At first, I tried to tell myself it had fallen from a bird flying high above. But when I picked it up, it had the smell of a woman I knew on it.

"It must have blown out of Indigo's hat when she was here last," Daffy said when I showed it to her. She was in her room, staring at the new twigs Aunt Clover had added to the wall. There were so many, they reached floor to ceiling. The stool Aunt Clover used to stand on was now a constant fixture in the corner.

"Will you go fishing with it?" Daffy asked of the feather as she slipped it out of my hand and sat down on her bed with it. "Will you?"

"Yes," I said, remembering how Mamaw Milkweed once told us if you fished with a feather, you'd catch an angel.

"A river angel," she had said. "Because if you have a river angel, you're never alone in the wilderness."

"Won't Indigo be mad, though?" Daffy asked. "If you get her feather all wet?"

"Not if I catch something amazing to show her." I looked down. "If I ever see her again."

"You will," Daffy said. "You just have to get rid of me first, then you can get rid of Chillicothe, and be free." She looked off and lightly giggled. "You found a feather. Wanna see what I found?"

She got up and went to her closet. She stood on her toes to reach the top shelf and pull something down.

"One of my old bulb catalogs," she said, knocking dust off the cover. "I thought I'd thrown them all out after Mamaw Milkweed died."

She carried the catalog over to her bed. Sitting cross-legged, she opened it.

"Did you know we still had this?" she asked as I sat down behind her. I ran my fingers through her loose hair.

"I saved it back," I said. "I knew you'd want to hold on to at least one catalog. I read your poems from time to time."

"I was a poet, huh?" She chuckled as she read aloud some of the lines. "'You can only soar so much and no more. The power of a flower is that she can tower.'"

I braided her hair while she pointed out the illustrations she had made for her make-believe bulbs.

"'An Irislip.'" She read the description she'd written. "'A flower that has a tulip's colors and a tulip's laugh, but an Iris's patience for tall grass.' Oh, look at this one, Arc." She laid her finger on her marker drawing of a flower with a bright yellow center and long thin petals in shades of blue. "'The spring bell is kind. Loves to be touched, but hates to be missed. Best watered with the river.'"

"That one was Mamaw Milkweed's favorite flower," I said, working my way down her braid. "Your hair is thinning, Daffy."

"I know."

"It's where you're not eating anything. You're not getting any nutrition."

"I can't find any more veins in my arms either," she said. "You think an apple a day will help me with that, Arc? I don't have the teeth for such fruit."

She opened her mouth. I stared inside at the rot.

"It's why I have a fear of my own reflection," she said. She scratched her cheek, opening up the sores there. "Tell me, Arc. Do I have all ten of my fingers still?"

I counted them for her as she echoed the numbers.

"Someday I might ask you for a favor," she said. "To hold me, while I vanish. You know what sound I keep hearing? The sound of the dry beans Mamaw Milkweed shucked into the metal bowl. The *click-clack*. Then I think it's not that sound at all, but the sound of rain hitting the rocks on the riverbank."

"You need to get out of this house for a bit," I told her. "Come to the river with me. We can fish with the feather together."

"The hills are as steep as a hundred billion breaths today," she said. "I can't climb something that tall." Keeping the catalog pressed against her chest, she lay down. "Oh, Arc, I envy the woman who is not tired. If such a woman exists."

Before I left, I covered her with a blanket.

"Click-clack, click-clack," she whispered, closing her eyes.

I grabbed the feather and stepped out into the hall. I followed the old dirty string to the can in Aunt Clover's hand on the sofa. The TV was on. This time the wild lions and wildebeests of the Serengeti were running across the screen.

"Don't go into Daffy's room with more of your twigs right now," I told Aunt Clover. "You'll disturb her. She's trying to rest."

Aunt Clover looked up at me briefly, but turned back to the flame she was holding beneath a spoon.

"Where are you going?" she asked.

"The river."

Her eyes shot back up at me. "Stop going down there," she said, her tone settled into her frown. "The river ain't no place for a woman with haunted blood like yours. Just opening your mouth, you risk letting the ghosts out. And I know how much you love to see things float."

I slammed the front door behind me as I stepped out onto the porch. As I slipped the feather into my back pocket, I saw him leaning against his car. He was facing the house. His arms were folded, and his eyes were hidden behind sunglasses. I wondered how long he'd been there. As I walked down the porch steps, he came across the road, meeting me at the edge of the yard.

When he removed his sunglasses, I turned away from the eyes that looked like black oil was caught there.

"I think you're gonna remember today," he said, grabbing my arm and yanking me across the road to his car. He shoved me in, hitting my head on the top of the door. He reached down to the cinderblock on the floor mat. I didn't see the fishing line tied around it, nor the fishhook, until he pushed it through my thumb.

"What the hell?" I screamed, but he wasn't afraid of anyone hearing. Not on that street.

"Guess I caught me a fish, huh?" He laughed, pulling on the line.

He slammed the door and walked around to the driver's side. I tried to remove the hook, but the barb was too deep.

"I hate you, I hate you, I hate you. Why won't you just leave me alone?" I punched his side with my free hand as he got in behind the steering wheel. "You ruined my fucking life."

Grabbing me by the hair, he said, "If you don't behave yourself, I'll put that fishhook in an even worst place. You hear me, whore?"

I jerked back from him as he started the engine.

"Don't get all that blood on my seat," he said. "I have a feeling you got a county's worth of wrong in ya."

"Where the fuck are you taking me?" I tried to work the fish hook out as he drove past the paper mill.

He turned and glanced at the back seat, then smiled at me. I saw a white duffel bag on the seat. I could tell something large was inside it.

"My dog," Spider said. "He died today. I had him all the way back when you were still a little girl. He would howl and howl. I was gonna bury him in my yard, but you always seem to be scratching here and there at the ground so much, I figure you might know of some good places to dig. How about we bury him at the place you found the first woman? Her name escapes me."

"Harlow," I said, watching the blood stream down the back of my wrist. "Her name was Harlow, you son of a bitch."

"Sometimes I don't think they ever really have names at all."

"Harlow. Her eyes were the color of her mother's." I turned to face him, my breathing matching my racing heart. "Harlow. She loved birds. Was going to fly with them to someplace warm. Harlow. She was found naked, only wearing one wet sock. Harlow. There were bruises all over her body and cuts and slashes that *you* claimed were from the river. Leaves stuffed down her throat. Her earrings ripped out of her fucking ears. Harlow. Harlow. Harlow! Maybe that will help you remember her name."

"Nah," he said, "I doubt it. The day ain't decent enough for me to remember nothing of the sort."

I looked once more into the back seat, seeing the blade of the shovel just behind the bag. As he tapped his fingers against the steering wheel, I gritted my teeth against the pain in my thumb and watched the rabbit foot swing back and forth from his keychain.

When he saw me looking, he said, "When you cut a woman's foot off, it turns into a rabbit's. All women start their lives as rabbits. Small, frightened things who run stupidly toward the cage. That's some Chillicothe, Ohio, wisdom for you. The type of wisdom that sticks to the bottom of your shoe like mud."

He took a sharp turn off the road and parked among the trees, so far back in them, the tips of the branches dragged against the roof.

"We walk from here," he said.

He took the pair of pliers from his pocket and snapped the fish-hook so it could be removed from my thumb, but not before he tugged on the fishing line until I cried out.

"You fucking bastard." As I held my thumb against my chest, the blood soaked my shirt, and I wondered how fast he could run. How fast I could.

"Not fast enough," he read my thoughts as he grabbed the bag out of the back seat, along with the shovel, which he forced me to carry. He made me walk in front of him, the bag dragging the ground behind us.

"You think I'm a monster, don't you?" he asked.

"I know what you are," I said.

"What am I?"

"A spider," I said. "You crawl up walls and wait in the corner for something to catch. Mirrors hang cracked around you."

"Do they now?"

The silence that followed was filled by the sounds of our steps crunching over the sticks and rocks on the ground.

"When I was a kid," he said, "I got a splinter from a rotten piece of board my daddy was using to nail the dog chain down to the side of the barn, so the dog would stop roaming. I tried all that night to get the splinter out while the dog howled."

He himself howled.

"Tried all the next day, to get that damn splinter out," he said. "But my skin had done swallowed the thing whole. All my life, the splinter has been making its way back to the surface. That's all it is. Just something rotten, coming back to the surface. There ain't nothing more natural than that."

He dropped the bag to the ground and wiped sweat off his forehead.

"This place," he said, stepping through the bushes and digging his shoes into the sand of the riverbank. "This is where we'll bury it." He looked from the ground to me. "Start digging, bitch."

I stabbed the shovel's blade in. The ground was full of tree roots and was hard to break.

"The police department got an anonymous letter," he said, removing his suit jacket and draping it across one of the low branches. "It was about me. The details in the letter were broad, to say the least."

I didn't look up from digging, though my hands grew tighter on the handle.

"The letter said that the police department should investigate me and my past behavior. That I had committed crimes of depravity." He stepped closer. "You know who might have written that letter?"

"No," I said. "I don't."

He opened the bag, dumping the dog's body out. He was tan, with long hair and floppy ears.

"I thought you said your dog died of old age?" I asked, seeing the blood on his mouth.

"Well, he was old when he died, that's the damn truth." He used his boot to kick the dog over into the hole. "Bury it."

I started to use the shovel, but he yanked it out of my hands.

"You bury him like the whore you are," he said. "On your knees."

I lowered down to the edge of the hole, using my hands to push the dirt over on top of the dog's fur.

"The tender turns of burial." He paced behind me. "You know what that is, Arc? You pick up the dirt, make a circle with it, then let it fall back into the grave." He picked up a handful of dirt, spinning with the shovel until it nearly struck my head. He threw the dirt not into the hole but on me.

"I liked this dog," he said. "But you should know something, Arc Doggs." He dropped the shovel to the ground. "The damn thing just kept howling and howling, making all kinds of noise."

When the shadow crossed my face, I stopped pushing the dirt over and stared up into the barrel of his handgun pointed at me.

"A man rises with each moment," he said. "A child lives in his palm, and a woman takes his fingers to her lips, begging for her life. Beg for your life now, Arc Doggs."

As he laid his finger on the trigger, I closed my eyes. When the gun fired, my whole body froze, and I wondered why it didn't hurt to be shot in the face.

"Open your eyes, you dumb bitch," he said.

When I did, the world was not red with my blood. It was not fading away around me. The sun was as bright as it had been before the bullet. I looked at my shirt, expecting to see pieces of myself splattered and dripping down to it. But I was not the one who had been shot. It had been the dog lying in the grave, the fur ripped open by the bullet. No blood came out of the wound. Only white, fluffy stuffing.

Ruff, ruff," he said with a loud howl.

"The dog's not real?" I asked, just before the spider grabbed me.

He pushed me down onto the ground, pinning my arms beneath his knees. He took a handful of the loose dirt from around the grave. With his other, he held my mouth, forcing it open.

"Say what I did to you," he said. "Say it."

"You came into my room at night," I shouted.

He exhaled, his lips curling up as his eyes rolled back beneath his closing lids.

"Say it again."

"You got into my bed, you bastard. And you—"

With my mouth open wide, he dumped the dirt in on my words.

"Bury it, you fucking bitch."

I spit the dirt out and yelled, "I won't."

He grabbed another handful. This time, after he forced the dirt into my mouth, he held his hand over my nose.

I spit what I could out between his fingers. Struggling for air, I could feel tiny rocks at the back of my throat. They spilled down it as I inhaled.

"You bury it, bitch." His yell was deep and loud.

I tried to shake my face free of his hands, but he was pressing so hard, I thought my head was going to pop between him and the earth.

"You raped—"

"Bury it," he shouted.

I swallowed more of the dirt he shoved in. It filled my throat until

I started to gag. Only then did he let me go. Gasping, I crawled to the edge of the river and scooped water up into my mouth.

As I coughed it back out, he knelt behind me and whispered, "Have you buried it, Arc Doggs?"

He held his hand in front of my face, a large pile of dirt spilling out between his fingers.

"Yes," I said.

"I can't hear you." He sang out. "Have you buried it?"

"Yes." My voice echoed off the water. "I fucking buried it."

He looked down at me as I fell to my stomach. I could feel his hand reaching into my back pocket.

"What's this for?" he asked, holding up the feather.

"To fish for an angel." I dropped my face to the ground.

"The angels are absent, Arc Doggs." He threw the feather out onto the water. "Too bad it don't skip like a stone. Just floats, like a woman facedown."

CHAPTER 35

If I leave too soon, find me in the moon.

—*Daffodil Poet*

"NEVER PRAY ON YOUR KNEES, CHILD," MAMAW MILKWEED WOULD say. "You get to where you can't get back up again if you do."

When Daffy started praying, she first went to the craft store with a pair of scissors in her purse to cut off a strand of red yarn. In her bedroom, she held it between her hands, the end left to dangle to her wrists, the way Mamaw Milkweed had taught us.

"Why do we have to pray this way, Mamaw Milkweed?" we had asked her.

"Because most of the time, God is a bird," Mamaw said. "What do birds love best?" She wiggled a piece of yarn in the air above us until it appeared to be squirming. "Worms. If you hold one between your palms, God will see you as she flies over. She'll come down, perch on your fingertips, and take the worm while you speak."

When I asked Daffy what she was praying for, she said, "That you will find what you're looking for in the dirt, Arc. That Thursday will have twin daughters. That the horses running beneath the ground at the paper mill will be free. That Violet will bring us doughnuts again and smell like vanilla as she did before. Most of all, I pray my lips will stop being so dry."

She ran her tongue over the bleeding cracks.

I took our lipstick out of my purse and started to put it on her.

"Only on my top lip now, Arc," she said. "We're half of the same, remember? I can't take your half. You can't take mine, or one of us won't exist no more." She looked out the window over my shoulder and said, "It's the stray."

She held Dad's pants back so we could see Petticoat walking in the side yard. She hissed at the single cinderblock she passed, even swatted it to be sure it was nothing more than a piece of concrete.

"She'll never forgive us," Daffy said. "We made her life shit."

Petticoat had already borne a litter by then. I could tell from the way her once-taut stomach had gone bald and hung lower. Where her kittens were, what fate had befallen them, we did not know. All we knew was that she had nursed and mothered as best she could in the world given to her. Through it all, she had turned feral, clinging to the chain-link fence that was fallen down on its side in the backyard. We had done that to her.

Daffy turned away and took the few short steps to her bed that she fell onto. "I'm tired of this world, Arc. I keep thinking about Dad."

"That's why you're so tired," I said. "Thinking about a dead man is exhausting."

"I keep thinking about what he left us the day he died," she said. "A bottle of warm pop on the kitchen table. A candy bar he had started but didn't finish. I still don't know if that was nothing at all, or if it was an entire treasure."

She curled into a tight ball. She had gotten leaner in the face, her cheeks sinking and causing her red-rimmed eyes to bulge. She'd also been picking at her skin more. The new sores like wild wounds against the old scars. I didn't tell her, but she had started to smell, no matter how much deodorant she put on. Similar to the way the earth smelled beneath my fingernails after digging it up.

"Lay with me for a while, Arc." She reached her arms out, and it reminded me too much of Mom.

"I can't. I'm going to Violet's to check on her," I said, taking a step back.

She raised her head from the pillow. "Arc, why have you stepped away from me?"

"I haven't." I looked down.

"You better start praying, too, Arc. Praying to be forgiven for your lies." She turned over, the twigs on the wall casting shadows on her face.

Out in the hall, I passed Aunt Clover walking to Mom's room. She was taking her a piece of bread smeared with peanut butter.

"Here you go, Addie," she said, pushing open Mom's door. "It's a nice bowl of potato soup, lots of dinner rolls, a scoop of green bean casserole . . ."

While Aunt Clover rattled off every food the sandwich wasn't, I left the house.

Petticoat had made her way from the side yard to the front.

"Hey there, girl." I held my hand out. She scratched the back of it and hissed.

She watched me get into the truck, but once I started its loud engine, she scurried to the back of the house. I knew she would go to hide beneath the fallen chain-link fence, her eyes darting around her until she became exhausted enough to close them.

I quickly pulled out of the drive. The leaves on the trees still had the light green shade of spring, but they were darkening in the places summer was taking over. The season of lizards and serpents, where the bottomlands were of stripped soil, and the hilltops were for the fog. Soon goldenrod would line the back-country roads, while the river flowed idly by beneath the branches as hard as the folks who called Chillicothe home.

Sometimes being in the truck, I would think about what it would be like to keep driving, past the familiar places, to a land unfamiliar. One where I would not see stacks in the skyline, nor the rising smoke of them. If I held tight enough to the steering wheel, I could dare myself to press the pedal down, but then I'd think of Daffy. My foot would rise, and I would make the turn back onto the roads I'd always known.

Violet's trailer was on six acres at the base of two hills. It was white metal with a red stripe. She rented it off some guy who had several run-down properties in the area. Hers was on a dirt road, the type where sofas sat in the front yard, while neglected chickens ventured and dogs were chained to houses they could never run from.

After I parked the truck, I stood outside it a moment, inhaling deeply. Each time I'd been there before, the smell of vanilla or cinnamon had come from her trailer. All I smelled now was the smoke from the neighbors burning their mattress.

Violet had once kept her property neat and tidy, even putting a doormat at the door. But ever since she'd started brushing her hair back again, her yard reminded me of an old field, left to grow its grasses tall enough to hide all the things that said a mother used to live there.

His black car was parked in the gravel beside hers. I quietly walked to her front door. It was open, but the screen was closed. I laid my ear against it and heard only silence before he said, "Arc Doggs, why is it I feel like every time I turn around, I see you?"

I stepped back as the spider came out. He looked down at my muddy sneakers.

"Little girl with dirt on her shoes. Where you been walking? The river? Have you brought it with you?" He narrowed his eyes at me. "Are you here to drown the place?"

"What are you doing here?" I stared at the blue latex glove he was wearing.

The back of his shirt was slightly pulled out of his pants, and his gold chain necklace was flat against his collar. In some places, there was so much hair wrapped around the necklace that the chain couldn't be seen.

"I'm just making a visit." He took the glove off and pushed it down into his pants pocket. "How have you been since we buried my dog? Find any more bodies in the river?"

"Violet, you okay in there?" I started to step inside, but he blocked the door.

"You look like a pretty little butterfly." He ran his long finger across my cheek. It made me think about those nights when I was a child in bed and he'd come into my room and say the same thing.

"Don't touch me." I jerked back and yelled Violet's name over his shoulder.

"She's fine." He smiled. "I don't know how fine she'll be after seeing you. Maybe she'll end up in the river like your other two friends. What you say, Arc? You gonna put her in the river, too? It's odd, don't you think?" He rolled his chewing gum across his tongue as he stepped closer. "You finding both bodies. Can you honestly tell me you've never put anyone in the river?"

He forced me back until I was against the rail, his long arms coming around me. I looked away and saw that the shadow cast on the ground wasn't that of a man with two arms, but of the familiar spider with eight legs.

"Get away." I pushed him back. When he started to reach for me again, I slipped my hand into my purse.

"What do you have in there?" he asked.

"A gun."

"I don't believe you," he said.

"Do you really wanna find out?" I asked. "Seems like a lot of trouble."

He ran his fingers through his hair. Then leaned in and whispered, "I get to visit you every night when I close my eyes. The small little thing you were. I get to fuck you over and over again. There's nothing you can do to stop me."

He laughed as he walked out to his car. My hand was shaking so badly, my purse was shaking with it. I waited until he drove away before I dropped the lipstick tube I'd been holding back into the purse.

"Violet?" I wiped my eyes and threw open her door. The trailer was littered with trash. It looked as though an animal had come in and run its claws down the beige and pale pink wallpaper, ripping it to shreds. Dishes were left out on all available surfaces, while empty fast-food cups were lined up in the windowsills.

"Where are you, Violet?"

As I followed the beer dripping out of an overturned can on the counter, I found her. She was sitting slumped against the bottom cabinets. Her clothes hadn't been changed in days, and it looked like she had started to apply her vibrant colors of eyeshadow, but decided to smear it in long lines down the sides of her face. Her greasy hair was brushed back, the tattoo on her scalp no longer visible.

"Hey, Arc," she said as I pushed the needle and belt over with my foot. "You bring any crowns for us to wear, Arcky, Arc, Arc?"

"Why was that detective here?" I asked.

"We were just talking." She used the cabinet to help her stand.

"He's a predator, Violet. He wears the scent of hell for a reason."

"Once the rain stops, I'll stop talking to him." She held her arms limp as she walked to the sofa.

"What have you been telling him?"

"Nothing." She pushed me back. "He just wanted to know some things. Who this is and who that is. What they're doing. Things like that."

"Violet, you know what happens to snitches. If Highway Man or any of 'em find out—"

"He said he could help me get Grassy back if I did some things for him." She fell down on the sofa.

"He's just kicking you around," I said. "He's not gonna help you."

"He says I should watch out for you, Arc. That you killed Harlow and Sage Nell."

"He's trying to make me sound crazy, is all," I said. "You don't believe him, do you?"

"I bet you got some shit in your purse, huh?" Her eyes rolled up at me. "Let's do some."

I turned away from her and kicked the trash on my way back into the kitchen. The cookbooks that had been on the shelf were now thrown on the floor, their recipes torn into tiny pieces.

"Why do you have everything on the floor?" I asked.

"A silent creature is walking around my house at night," she said. "I put things down so I can hear him moving about."

"Where's your mixer?" The spot where it used to sit was full of empty cigarette packs.

"I sold it," she said.

I saw some of her muffin tins were missing as well. Her oven, where her delicious pies and cakes were once pulled out, was now full of empty milk jugs and smashed boxes.

"Why would you get rid of all your stuff?" I asked. "You're gonna need it."

"What I needed was the money." She slapped her knees, reminding me of Mom. "Sometimes the only thing left to do is to be a beautiful girl, nice enough not to scream when they break you over their knee. I mean our whole lives, we get ready, Arc. We do our hair, we get dressed up. For what? To live a hundred devastating years? No, thank you."

Her refrigerator door was open. The little bit of food inside was warm and spoiled. I closed it, just to be rid of the stench. A photo of Violet with Grassy was held up by a magnet on the door.

"Do you have anything to give me, Arc?" Violet's voice floated in. "Give me a little something? That detective didn't bring enough."

"Was it him who first gave you the drugs to hold?" I stepped back over the trash into the living room.

"It don't matter," she said, moving side to side on the sofa. "None of that matters."

"Look, Violet." I knelt in front of her. "This is just you forgetting to lock the door. You've been here before, okay? And you always get out of it. Right, Butterfly Eyes?"

"Not this time, Arc. But you know something? I'm less scared now than I was when I was sober. Because every day I feared fucking things up. I was so terrified I would get Grassy back, and everything would be fine and we'd be happy, but one day I would just fuck it up again and she'd be here to see it. Now, I've already fucked up. I ain't scared of doing it no more. So, I'm gonna stay right here and just keep fucking up, because I was bound to anyway."

"No," I said. "You were gonna buy that place. Open your own bakery. It'd be blue and pink, remember? The color of the cotton candy you once had at a fair. The counters would be the color of the pistachio pudding your dad would eat. There'd be carnations in jars on the counter."

"The flowers my mother would keep." She held her eyes back behind her closed lids.

"That's right," I said. "And the kids will come in and dangle their legs from the high stools, and you'll put a pinch of light brown sugar in all the hidden corners to feed the gods who watch over women who refuse to fail. Like you, Violet." I squeezed her hand until she opened her eyes. "Don't throw all that away."

She hung her head as I sat down on the sofa beside her and wrapped my arm around her.

"Sometimes joy hides," I said. "You just have to find it. That's all it's doing now. It's hiding, and we'll find it."

"I'm not sure, Arc. I'm not sure I can ever find it again." She rubbed her face. "I thought drugs was something you did in high school, you know? Not something you did after you're a mother. Grassy was a painful birth. I ever tell you? A difficult one. The doctor said he had something that could help. I didn't think if a doctor gave you it, that it was bad. Pill after pill, I thought each one would make me better like the doctor said they would, but they just became something I couldn't stop, not even when he stopped writing the prescription.

"When I first heard someone offer me heroin, I thought they'd said 'heron,' and I thought of the white birds on my mother's apron."

Violet held her arms up and slowly flapped them like wings, only to lower them to her lap. "Momma's apron was bright blue. Any flour or powdered sugar that got on it, she would just pat it into the fabric and say she was feeding the herons. I thought something that sounded like that couldn't be bad."

She wiped her nose on the back of her hand.

"When I was in high school," she said, "she was in a car wreck. My mother died with windshield glass in her face. After that, I'd turn the oven on just to feel the warmth coming out. Make it feel like her kitchen again. Whenever she baked, she would open a bag of flour and start singing. I thought there was song in the flour itself. After she was gone, I opened the flour in her pantry, but no song came out. I tried to find it. I'd take money I got from babysitting and buy bag after bag of flour, but I could never find her song again. I figured I best not let all the flour go to waste. That's why I started baking. All these years, it's just been me trying to find my mother. Making muffins and cookies, but the silence is always there. I never did find her song or my own."

As Violet laid her head back on the sofa and stared up at the ceiling, I returned to the kitchen. Searching through the debris, I found chocolate chips spilled out and leading to the pantry. The flour was dumped onto the floor. I picked the bag up and took the photo of Violet with Grassy off the refrigerator and placed it inside the bag. I set it on her lap and stood behind her, raking her dirty hair with my fingers.

"My mother has been an addict for most of my life," I said. "I used to believe she would wake up one day and not be one. I tried to help her the only way I knew how as a kid. I'd take little objects. A spoon, a clothespin, a bottle cap. I'd put them on the edge of the table and push them off, pretending they were the bad things in her life, and if only they were to fall away from her, everything would be okay and she would stop unraveling. When that didn't happen, I started to think it was because she didn't love me enough. I started to hate her. But the more I hated my mother, the more I hated myself. Those things are connected, you know. And even when I'm in a room full of people, I am always astonished at how lonely I can be, because the one person I need isn't there. A daughter is a woman lost at sea. A mother is the one who saves her. But if she's not there, the daughter will always be lost."

I parted Violet's hair and ran my finger down the tattooed words.

"If you don't wanna do it for yourself, Violet, at least get clean for Grassy."

She looked down at the flour bag in her lap.

"Is my song in this?" she asked.

"Yes," I said as I came around and sat beside her. I took my purse off my shoulder and put it down on the coffee table. She looked at it a moment, then opened the flour bag. She reached in and pulled out the photo of her and Grassy. She stared at it as if she were having trouble recognizing the woman in it.

"My mamaw Milkweed used to say that in life there is a savage side." I took the photo from Violet and turned it over to the blank side. "But she also said you could turn the savage side beautiful." I flipped it once more to her and Grassy's smiling faces.

"It's a nice thought, Arc," Violet said. "But a thought is all it is."

She pushed the flour bag off her lap and reached for my purse. She dug through it until she found what she was looking for.

"This is my song." She held up the baggie of dope. "This is what sings for me."

CHAPTER 36

⁓

I sing for the king.

—*Daffodil Poet*

THE JOHN WAS DRIVING US BOTH TO THE BLUE HOUR. HIS VAN WAS old. My jean shorts were sticking to my skin from sweat. His air conditioner, he said, didn't work, and the summer was only getting hotter.

"It's my first time paying for sex." He had a lopsided grin. "The girls on the street, they always look dirty, you know? But you." He glanced over at me. "You look okay. Finders, keepers." He grabbed my nose, pinching it.

When I'd first got in the van, he'd said the same thing. Instead of taking my nose, he'd squeezed the inside of my thigh.

"That's funny." I gritted my teeth, pulling away.

His skin texture reminded me of cooked fruit, colorless and boiled. His hair was dark brown. A temporary dye. I knew because as his sweat rolled down his face, the color rolled with it. I assumed his natural shade was as light as his eyelashes.

"Hey." He looked over at me. "Your eyes are kind of funky looking. Never seen two different colors like that. They ain't one of them sexually transmitted diseases, right? I mean, like a symptom of any? I sure the shit don't want one of those."

"No," I said. "I didn't get these eyes on the street. I was born with them."

He was chewing gum and kept the tip of it out between his lips. When I asked why, he said, "Rat's tail," then laughed. "It's a dumb thing my granddaddy long legs said once. He said, 'Whippersnapper, why you always stickin' that gum out? Looks like you're chewin' on a rat's tail.'"

He did a voice that I suppose he thought sounded like his wheezing grandfather's. To me, it sounded like a rope had been dropped down his throat and he was gasping for air.

When he noticed me staring at the red birthmark on his neck, he pulled up his collar. "This mark got me a lot of teasing in school," he said. "They made a mockery of me. I made the mistake of lettin' 'em, but never again."

It was hard to imagine him as a child. He looked to be in his fifties, with deep crow's feet around his eyes. He had what Daffy called the cigarette squint. Those johns who constantly squinted like smoke was blowing into their faces. His boots had the earth on them. Clumps of mud rode the sides and back heel. Leaves and twigs were tangled in the laces as if the boots had been lying in the woods and he'd tied them so quickly, he'd taken handfuls of whatever was around him.

"Finders, keepers." He grabbed my hand and took it to his mouth, pretending to chomp my fingers.

"Just keeps getting funnier," I said, pulling my hand out of his. He had a red naked woman tattooed on the back of his middle finger.

"I ain't seen ya around these parts before," I said. "You from here?"

"I'm from a real small town. Just passing through up this way, is all. I'm a widow now. Guess I'm celebrating a little. Momma always said if I married a whore, I'd get left. And I was."

I watched the silver eagle, hanging on a chain from the rearview mirror, swing back and forth, knocking against the small American flag also hanging there. In the back of the van I spotted a bloody apron.

"I work in a slaughterhouse," he said. "I call it the trailing-out place."

"Why?" I asked.

"Because everything's always trailing out in a slaughterhouse. Guts trailing out of bodies. Brains trailing out of heads. It's a terrific show, if you got the stomach for it. You know, sometimes I feel sorry for all them animals. I mean they got hooves and shit, but that don't protect 'em none from fear. Sometimes, right before I drive the knife in, I tell 'em I'm their mother."

I carefully studied the grin on his face and tried to keep my voice steady. "Why would you tell them you're their mother?"

"To give 'em comfort." He licked his teeth. "Wouldn't hearing your momma is right there with you make you feel less afraid?"

"Not when someone is holding a knife to my gut," I said.

"You know what I can tell about you?" he asked. "You wouldn't have the stomach for it. You'd see all them insides trailin' from them bodies, and you'd up and cry. I don't blame ya. It's the woman in ya. Finders, keepers." He grabbed my left breast, squeezing it as he pulled into the Blue Hour's parking lot.

On our way to the room, we passed Welt coming out of it. Just before the john closed the door, Welt put his foot in the way, holding up a Bible in his gloved hand. He carried it over to the table by the bed. He glanced at me as he left.

"That fella gives me the shivery shoes," the john said, closing the door. He had brought a small canvas bag with him. He set it on the bed. Before he reached inside, he grabbed me between the legs.

"Finders, keepers," he said.

He clicked his tongue as he got a measuring tape out of the bag.

"One time," he said as he started measuring the walls, "I made the mistake of stayin' in a room I didn't measure."

"What happened?" I asked.

"I found somethin' I didn't wanna keep."

He'd left the canvas bag open wide enough for me to see the torso of a blonde doll wearing a bright red bathing suit top. Her bottom half had been severed. In its place was the long blade of a knife.

"Don't go gettin' no ideas now." He picked up the doll by her head, pointing the blade of the knife at me. "This ain't gonna be for you if you're good." He took a wad of money out from his back pocket and held it up as he said, "This will be for you if you are good."

I looked from the knife to the money. "Can you just tell me what you wanna do, man?"

"All right, all right, don't pinch your pussy." He dropped the knife and the money into the bag. He dug down to the bottom of it, pulling out a roll of tape and two small pieces of paper. I saw they were eyes he'd cut out from a black-and-white photo. The brows arched. The eyelashes coated in mascara. He taped them to his forehead.

"I've got to be able to see," he said.

I'd been with johns before who made me feel like the room was smaller than it was. Made me feel like I was about to have a bottle broken over my head and all I wanted to do was to hide under the bed from them, but he was the first who made me feel like he'd slice my face off and tack it to the wall just for the fun of it.

"I should go," I said, backing up toward the door. "I'm sorry I couldn't help you out."

He grabbed my arm. "Finders, keepers."

He yanked me into the bathroom, closing the door behind us.

"Get in the tub," he said.

"Look, mister, I just wanna leave. I don't want any trouble."

"You're gonna get in that tub and get nice and clean," he said. "I don't wanna have to get my doll and her sharp blade."

I looked down into the tub. It was full of cigarette ashes and buds. It always seemed like even when Welt cleaned a room, he left something untouched.

"Get in." The john shoved me forward until I stepped into the tub. Once I was lying down, he pushed the plug into the drain and turned the water on.

"Warm enough?" he asked, adjusting the hot and cold until I said it was okay.

When the water was up to my chest, he turned it off. I didn't blink the whole time he unbuttoned his shirt.

"This is where my wife dragged my soul outta me," he said, pointing to the long scar across his chest. "I've been lookin' for a new soul ever since." He dropped his hand into the water. "Finish this sentence for me. I am . . ."

"I am?" I tried not to stare into his eyes. "I am Arc."

"No." He dragged out the word. "Try again."

"I am in the bathtub?"

He slammed his fist into the water, splashing it up into my face.

"Try again," he said.

"I am . . . here?"

"Goddamn it." He threw the water up into my eyes. "What are you? What are you?"

"I am—am—a person. I'm Arc. I'm a woman?"

"What?" He stopped splashing me. "Say that again."

"I am a woman."

With his lopsided grin, he said, "Let's find out."

He pressed down on my shoulders, pushing me under the water as I kicked against the faucet. Seconds passed, but they felt like minutes before he yanked me back up.

Spitting out the water and inhaling, I screamed, "Are you fucking crazy?"

He kept his hands on my shoulders, preventing me from standing.

"Did you know souls are red?" he asked. "It's because of the blood from the animals at the slaughterhouse that I first learned it. I saw the souls trailin' out of 'em, all red. But not just any red. A special red. And if I see that special red, I know you have a soul. Only those who have a soul are whole. Without one, you're just a sliver."

"A sliver of what?"

"Of a woman. Now you're not gonna like to hear this, but you've got to go back under the water."

I tried to push up from the tub, but he was standing over me with all his weight pressing down.

"Souls only come out on the verge of death," he said. "So you have to go back under until I see the color red. I have to see if you're a demon like the others."

I kicked hard, trying to move the water out over the edge of the tub and make the tile floor slippery enough beneath him that he'd lose his footing, but it wasn't enough. I took a deep breath just before my head was submerged. While he held me down, he watched the rippling water as if he expected something to come trailing out of my ears. I grabbed his wrists and dug my nails in deeper, but he didn't so much as flinch. My lungs started to lose what air I had saved. I shook my head from side to side, the pressure building in my chest.

Through the blur of the water, I saw another figure. They had their arm around the john's neck until he removed his hands from me. I heard grunting and shouting the second I surfaced, the water pouring down my face as I took breath after breath.

"Get off me," the john was yelling as he was thrown against the toilet, his head getting slammed into the bowl by a man wearing a red leather glove.

As I climbed over the side of the tub only to fall onto the tiled floor, Welt gave one final punch to the john. After he fell down, he crawled away, getting up to run once he was out of the bathroom.

The floor was so slippery, I had to use the tub to help me stand. Still I fell back down.

"You okay?" Welt asked, helping me up.

I couldn't be sure what startled me more. Having nearly been drowned, or hearing the sound of Welt's voice. He looked at the water on the floor as if thinking about how much cleaning there was left to do.

"How did you know he was attacking me?" I asked.

"I heard you screaming." He kept his eyes on the water, moving the toe of his boot through it.

"You heard? You mean, you're not really deaf? You've been pretending this whole time?"

"Folks ignore you if they think you can't hear." He reached into the tub and pulled the plug up, releasing the water. "You gonna be fine to leave now?"

I nodded, still getting my breath back.

"You're shaking." He reached into his pocket and pulled out a cigarette. He lit it and smoked on it a couple of times before passing it to me.

"You better get out of here now," he said. "I got a lot to take care of with this mess."

I handed the cigarette back to him. As I was walking out, he asked, "Why'd that fella have them paper eyes taped to his forehead?"

"To see if I had a soul or not."

After I left the room, I wrung water out of my hair on the sidewalk. I looked for the john's van and saw it was still parked in front of the Blue Hour where we'd left it. He was sitting in the driver's seat with his door open, blaring music and staring right at me. I recognized the song as Blondie's "One Way or Another."

As the music blared, he kept his eyes on me and mouthed the lyrics, "'One way or another, I'm gonna find ya.'"

He slammed the van door shut and sped off.

"What happened to you?" Daffy asked. She was sitting on the curb, eating a slice of baloney. "You go swimming without me?"

As I sat down beside her, the water dripped off the fringe of my cutoff shorts.

"If you see a john drive up in a van the color of blood, don't get in," I said. "He tried to kill me in a tub just now. I don't know what would be worst. Drowning, or knowing the last thing I saw in this world was the white cracked ceiling of the Blue Hour."

She studied my face. "Well, the world is full of spiders," she finally said, shrugging. "We know that, Arc. Besides, you got something out of it at least. How much he pay you?"

"I didn't get nothing."

Daffy reached into the deli bag for another slice of baloney. She was now so thin, her clothes were falling off. She had to tighten her pants with a belt and keep pulling up the shoulders of her shirts.

"You're getting as skinny as Mom," I said, shivering despite the heat.

"I know. But I don't feel like eating most of the time. Most of the time, I feel like something is eating on me."

She offered me the slice, but I shook my head, so she folded it up and began to take tiny bites along its edges.

"You remember when we were kids?" she asked. "Mom and Dad had just picked us up from Mamaw Milkweed's. We were going back to live with our parents. We'd be happy and everything would be okay. Remember the promises? Mom tried to keep them when she took a piece of baloney and made a snowflake."

Daffy unfolded the meat and revealed what her bites had made. Little holes here and there, cutting out the shape of something we imagined fell from the sky.

"Baloney snow, Momma called it." Daffy held the slice up, the sunlight shining through the holes. "She would tack the baloney snowflakes to the wall. When Daddy came in, he said she was crazy, but he laughed. Remember?"

"Dad never laughed," I said.

She looked at me, a frown on her face. "What are you talking about, Arc? Don't you remember him laughing?"

I shook my head.

"I feel sorry for you then, because I remember." She stared down at the baloney. "We couldn't bear to eat it after we'd turned it into snowflakes. We'd made it something special by putting holes in it. I wish we were so special. The more holes we get, the less we become."

She looked up at the car honking toward us.

"You need a ride?" The man was looking at Daffy.

She handed me the baloney snowflake and stood up.

"I'll have to get the money you didn't," she said. "I won't be gone long, then we can make more baloney snowflakes. Enough for a blizzard in this hot summer."

Just before she got into the man's car, she stopped to tell me another one had been found.

"Another what?" I asked.

"Another woman."

OFFICE OF ROSS COUNTY MEDICAL EXAMINER
CHILLICOTHE, OHIO
REPORT OF INVESTIGATION BY COUNTY MEDICAL OFFICER

DECEDENT: Indigo

OCCUPATION: Speaking a lost language

BODY TEMP: Unraveled

DESCRIPTION OF BODY: Unclothed

GENDER: Wilderness

AGE: A woman times the river divided by the edge equal to the smoke from the paper mill above her head

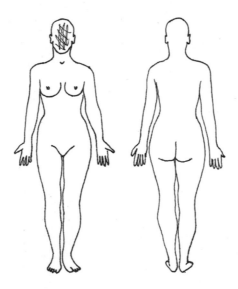

WOUNDS AND MARKS: Right hand missing. Vagal inhibition, consistent with shock of cold water on a hot day. Old fractures suffered previously and unreported. Maybe no one believed her. Two-inch abrasion on forehead. Facedown position. Bruising on outer thighs. Gravel found in abrasions on feet. Sand found in mouth, her words buried. Skin discoloration on inside of right wrist. Large cut across stomach. Two rib bones removed. A wound to the back of the head. Throat slit, like a second mouth. On the top of her head, a crown of thorns, twigs, and grass.

PROBABLE CAUSE OF DEATH:

Being tethered to the hunters.

P A R T

VIII

CHAPTER 37

Some sins are hard to name.
They are even harder to claim.

—Daffodil Poet

WHEN THEY REACHED INTO THE WATER, IT REACHED BACK AS THEY
pulled Indigo from it. A scratch above her heart. Vines and leaves
caught in her mouth. A mark on her left buttocks. A wound to the
back of her head. She was found by a guy who had pulled over to
pee in the tall grass. As he was laughing at the way his piss landed
on a beetle walking by, he saw something out on the river. He would
later tell authorities he thought it was a bag of garbage floating by.

He walked down the bank, not enough heel in the sand, so he
slipped down into the water with a splash that gave him the taste
of the river in his mouth. That's when he saw her hair. Blowflies
kicking off the strands swaying gently under the water like grass in a
pasture. Her arms were outstretched, her fingernails full of dirt and
the terrible certainty. He knew then it was a woman, her body cool
to the touch.

When I told Daffy I wished I'd pulled Indigo out of the water, she
said it was a good thing I hadn't.

"Imagine if you'd found a third woman, Arc," she said. "You would
be damned by the river. Your guilt whispered about. You'd have to
pray for another body just so you don't find it. Just so it falls away
from you. Spider has already said too much. Says the heart of the
beast is in Arc Doggs. In the way he looks at you. In the way he gets
other people to." She sighed. "Poor Indigo. Won't be going to the
wilderness with her now, will you, Arc?"

Indigo's hat was never recovered. If it unraveled her fire, we'd
never know. Her car was found in an abandoned parking lot the next

county over, stiff brown grass growing up in between the cracks in the concrete. The contents of the car weren't disturbed. Her purse was untouched. Those with a badge said she'd parked it there herself. No signs of foul play.

"Probably went to get high and ended up in the river. Nothing more to their story."

I took the archaeology book Indigo had given me and touched the pages in the last places she had. I discovered she had written along the spine of the front flap, *Destruction is just a phase. Sometimes we have to break like an artifact in order to be discovered whole. I see you, Arc. And I hope you find the future you have hidden from even yourself. Come find me.*

In the back of my mind, I imagined I would get clean. I'd surprise her on the Fourth of July, so there'd be fireworks. Then we'd go to the wilderness, speak a lost language, and leave the rinds from fruit on the ground so we could feel them with our bare feet as we walked beneath the stars.

When I looked up at my father's clothes on the windows, I thought I might have done the same with Indigo's if I'd had them. Her floral denim. Her pink blouses. Her socks that flopped down over her sneakers. Most I could do was to reach in under my mattress for the piece of paper Aunt Clover had once torn off an old cookie box. Flattened from years hidden away, I wrote Indigo's name on the corner, not once but twice in little spirals.

Like the other women, Indigo had been found naked, but Thursday told folks on the street that Indigo had been found wearing emerald gloves, a garnet-colored dress, and a veil that made her look like she had red rhinestone eyes.

"This fucking killer thinks he can undress us," Thursday said, "so we'll create our own myths that outlive all the goddamn things he's tried to take away."

I thought the river must now look like a woman lying on her side. One curling up into a tight ball, her fear taking over the woods and flooding out the trees, before vanishing, still holding their roots. Sometimes I thought the whole of Chillicothe on a map would be but a bruised mark, like it'd come into contact with a difficult thing.

By the time Indigo's body was being filed in the morgue, the killer already had a name on the street. We called him River Man because of his setting of choice. He was always supernatural, this River Man.

Oftentimes he had wings, clear as a windowpane, the edges dipped in blood and haunted with sin to match his heart made of ashes that was said to smoke and seethe at night. He had a single claw extending from each cheek. At one time he had been split in two, for there was large stitching, drawn as little *x*'s, going up the middle of his face.

He would perch only on sharp corners, and the rain followed him, pooling at his bare feet, their soles so dirty, it was said he stomped rotten acorns or plums, depending on who you were talking to. Some said he had two arms, but I said he had eight legs and smelled like hot leather and bitter apples. He would fly above us, turning into dust the moment we looked up, only to materialize when he was ready to claim us. He was an exceptional drama. A found fantasy that coursed through our thoughts and was dressed for those brave enough to say the words *serial killer*.

"How many do you have to murder to be considered a serial killer?" Daffy asked me as she rolled on some deodorant.

"I think if you lay down more than one person, you're as close to being a serial killer as one can be," I said, putting lipstick on my bottom lip. "You ready? We don't wanna be late."

We were going to meet up with Violet at Thursday's trailer for a little ceremony. It wasn't going to be the official funeral. Indigo's brother was having her body shipped to Iowa for family out there, so we decided to have a little something of our own.

On our way out the door, Aunt Clover said, "They're gonna come to hate you, Arc."

She was watching a show about Australia and the Sydney Opera House.

"Hate me for what?" I asked.

"For you putting all of them in the river," Aunt Clover said, wiping the sweat of her forehead off with the end of her nighttime scarf. "For putting all of them in the river. *Tsk-tsk*. Spittle, spittle spider, where you gonna hide her? Huh, Arc? Where you gonna hide her?"

We watched her sort through a new batch of twigs, her fingers shaking as she did.

"C'mon, Arc." Daffy grabbed my arm. "She's been staying up too late. Don't know what the hell she's saying half the time."

Aunt Clover started to speak, but held her lips tightly together instead.

Out on the porch, I did the button Daffy had missed on her shirt, as she asked me if her ears were still on her head. After Indigo was found, Daffy started to ask even stranger questions. First, she asked if she still had eyes. Then she asked if her nose was still there, her eyebrows, even the skin on her cheeks. She asked about things she herself could see, like her fingernails and toes.

"Yes, Daffy, your ears are still there," I said. "If they weren't, you wouldn't be hearing anything."

"I just wanted to be sure," she said, heading out to the truck. "I'm not sure of anything. Not even of the color of the sky. Sometimes it just looks as brown as the river to me."

The July heat had made the air inside the truck the same temperature as fire. The leather seats burned the backs of our legs. We found some old junk food bags to put down to sit on.

"Drive like the wind, Arc," Daffy said. "But not so fast it blows my face off. Sometimes I think it's only holding on by a thread."

As we drove past the paper mill, I saw a familiar car parked on the street in front. The dent in the side was facing toward us.

"What's John Theresa doing here?" Daffy asked as I pulled into the spot behind him.

I left my shoes in the truck as I walked across the hot gravel. My shirt stuck to the sweat on my lower back as I passed the dent in his car.

He was leaning against the hood. "Hey, Arc." He watched the smoke pour out of the stacks. "I was on my way to your house. The closer I got, the more I felt like I had nowhere to go. Then I saw the smoke. Thought I'd watch it for a bit. What is it about the smoke from the mill? Why does it captivate us?"

"Maybe we only watch to see if God's on the other side once the smoke clears," I said.

"They say it's the smell of money." He took a deep inhale.

"It ain't ever given us no money." I slipped my hands in my back pockets.

"Daffy with ya?" he asked.

I nodded back to the truck. He looked, but quickly turned back to me.

"Why were you coming to my house?" I asked.

"Because of Indigo," he said. "I was just coming by to tell you how sorry I was. I saw how close the two of you got at Evergreen Daughters."

When he removed his eyeglasses to wipe the sweat from his eyes, I saw that a new antenna had been added to the butterfly tattooed on his palm.

"Another one?" I asked.

"Oh, yeah." He chuckled, dry like the dirt on the road between us. "I make a new antenna every time I break a violin string. To remember what I've lost."

"It's just a little odd that you added a new one at this time. Right when Indigo has been found."

"You think my hand is the hand of River Man?" He frowned. "Keeping track of my victims?"

"Before Indigo left, she said she was going to see you. That you had something to tell her. What was it, John?"

"I had to tell her she would be floating down the river." He bit the inside of his cheek, sucking it in. "That's what you wanna hear, isn't it?" He folded his arms and rested them against his chest. "I suppose I don't blame you. I did kill one woman in your life. Maybe I've killed another. But before you go spreading your rumors, you forget, Arc Doggs, I know something about you. That's what happens when you share a history. We've shared a history, haven't we? The two of us? You wouldn't want your secret getting out, would you?"

He looked over my shoulder. When I turned to see why, I saw there was a black car stopped in the road. Only when another pulled up behind it and honked did he drive on.

"Friend of yours?" John Theresa asked.

"No friend," I said. "Just a spider."

When I got back in the truck, Daffy asked what happened.

"I was only loosening the soil some," I said as we pulled away.

She sighed as she looked back at the mill.

"You can tell men founded this town," she said. "Because here things get cut down, cut up, and smoke fills the air. Arc? Sometimes I have to take a breath. A real deep one. I feel like I ain't breathed in so long."

As the buildings we passed turned into trees and hills, I asked, "Do you remember Mamaw Milkweed in her yellow apron? Her hands would always be glistening from the juice of the sliced persimmons. If you take a deep breath, you can smell them now."

Every time Daffy inhaled, her shoulders would rise, and she would hold on to the breath for several seconds, then release it. By the time I turned into Thursday's drive, Daffy said, "Sometimes you're nothing but a liar, Arc. I don't smell anything but the smell of shit."

She got out, slamming the door behind her. Still, she waited for me so we could walk across the yard together, kicking dandelions and scattering their seeds. When we got to the front door, we saw a piece of paper taped to the screen. There were no words written on it. Just a pair of wavy lines.

"The river," Daffy and me said at the same time.

The bright green stalks in the cornfield were taller than us, the tassels blowing in the gentle wind as we walked through. A group of beetles had found the leaves. They flicked into the air above us, in a series of clicks that popped against the heat.

"Keep your eyes down," I told Daffy as we stepped along the narrow path. "The corn leaves will cut them if you're not careful."

"I'm not sure I have eyes to cut," she said.

Once we got through, we trekked the tall grass, leading down through the woods.

"Her bark is like a map," Daffy said, touching the trees. "Because she lives alone."

"Her grapevines swing a long time," I said. "Because she lives alone."

Daffy pulled the burrs from the fray of my jean shorts as she said, "You've got whispers on you, because she lives alone."

She laughed as she walked ahead.

We heard Violet's and Thursday's voices before we saw them. Thursday was sitting in Cleopatra's time machine, pretending to drive. Violet was on the bank, her legs crossed beneath her.

"And do you remember," Thursday was saying, "how she'd write her sins on the leaves?"

"So they'd fall in the autumn," I said as Daffy and me stepped out of the tall grass.

"Yeah," Thursday said. "So they'd fall in autumn and she never be a dope queen again."

"Why we talking about Sage Nell?" Violet asked. "We should be talking about Indigo."

"You talk about one, you talk about 'em all," Thursday said, getting out of the time machine.

The four of us looked at the water. It was Violet who asked, "When there's no body to bury, no ashes to scatter, what do we do?"

"I read about an ancient custom in Madagascar known as the turning of the bones," I said. "Maybe we do a returning of the bones. A returning of the body."

"Show us how, Arc," Violet said.

Using the flat edge of a rock, I dug in the sand on the riverbank. They each picked up their own rocks and dug with me until we had a shallow hole the length of a woman and the width of her hips.

We walked back into the woods, gathering sticks of different sizes and picking our own pieces of the earth.

"Look what I found." Violet held up a long black feather. "A gift from the hawks."

We carried our piles back to the shallow hole. I pulled out two thick sticks and laid them down as I said, "These will be the femur bones."

The small ones, almost even in size, made the ribs. I connected them to give a curve to their straight lines. Small twigs out of Thursday's pile were used for finger bones, while Violet had the right size for the clavicle.

"The shoulder bones," Thursday announced, careful in her selections.

"A bone for each toe." Violet broke a long thick stick into ten pieces.

For the vertebrae, we laid down rocks and for the pelvis we made a fan of small sticks, connecting to the pubic arch, which was made of pebbles we linked in a circle.

"What do we do about the skull?" Violet asked.

"We remember her face," I said, "and give it back to her."

I took handfuls of water and let it pour between my fingers into the hole and above the topmost bone. Getting on my knees, I molded the sandy mud, sculpting a forehead. Thursday used more water and formed a nose. Violet made the lips while Daffy made sure the cheeks were as much like Indigo's as they could be. Then Thursday gathered some leaves and long blades of grass that went to seed on the top. She laid them down to be Indigo's hair, then she put wildflowers in between the ribs, and I made two holes in the mud.

"Indigo's eyes," Daffy said.

As we stared down at the skeleton of sticks and rocks, Thursday said, "You never really think about how many bones you've got in your body. That is until one day you have to lay them out. There's enough bones to put one down in all the damn counties in Ohio and then some. My God, there's a hell of a lot that goes into making each one of us, huh?"

She put her hands on her hips, but they slowly went toward her belly. Caressing her unborn child, she said, "They say women like us walk ourselves into our own deaths. I say they fucking chase us into it. But they don't get all of us." She reached for Violet's hand, who grabbed the one of mine that wasn't already holding Daffy's.

"No," Violet said. "They don't get all of us." She smiled at me. "Say something we'll always remember, Arc. Something about your ancient civilizations."

I thought of the broken fragments of pottery. Urns with their art on the side. Flint and fossils. Scraps of linen and bone.

"There is nothing more human," I said, "than that which will not go away. Than that which will stay. Her bones will stay here long into the future. When someone comes along and digs them up, they will see that she knew her way in this world as sure as a woman revealing her life and all the rivers she took to get here."

Daffy picked up the hawk's feather. "And when the world tried to break her," she said, laying the feather down where the womb would be, "she gave birth to wings."

In the quiet of the world around us, as quiet as nature can be with its chirps and squawks, we stared at what was left of the woman we called Indigo, One of Unraveling Fires. In the arrival of the wind, we felt her spirit descend until we were awash in a deep and certain belief that we, as women of Chillicothe, Ohio, were as important as the queens of valleys richer than our own.

"We bury her now?" Violet asked.

"We don't ever bury one of our own," I said. "We reveal them."

We took the dirt we had dug up and let it fall through our fingers down upon the bones in a layer of the earth we knew in our hearts to be translucent. Something that would cover but never bury. Then we walked out into the water. It was as though the river was expecting us. At times it seemed to climb up our calves and reach toward us, only to ripple back to depths we could not see.

Violet leaned over and dipped her fingers as she said, "The last time we were all here, I baptized her. I only hope it was enough."

As I watched the river, I began to think of her as a woman in a distant landscape. A woman in a white dress, a lizard at her brow, and a strange custom that saw her surrounding herself more and more with wet land she floated over. Her loneliness something she waited by, and with. Her language done in by that wait that had turned time upside down for her.

"It was enough," Thursday said as she laid her hand back on her growing belly.

As she sang, we stood close, watching the dark water move steadily past, knowing that just a few short days earlier, those same currents had carried our friend.

CHAPTER 38

There is something to be gained by standing in the
rain. There is something to be gained from the pain.

—*Daffodil Poet*

IT WAS AFTER MIDNIGHT, AND THURSDAY HAD ANOTHER EMPTY TOI-
let paper roll in her bruised hand. She pointed one open end toward
the sky and slid the other across her belly.

"So my little girl can get an early start on seeing the universe,"
she said. "Maybe then she won't spend her life on the ground like
me. Maybe on a diet of stars, she'll reach for a little more and won't
end up in the fucking river."

Thursday had driven Daffy and me to the Blue Hour. We'd hoped
to run into Violet. No one had seen her since we had the ceremony
for Indigo at the river. It had been a couple of weeks, and there was
no sign that she had been back at her house either. Added to that,
she hadn't returned any of our calls. The silence was the worst thing
to hear.

"Here comes the killer," Thursday whispered, as Welt passed by
with his cleaning cart.

"I'll be back," I told her.

I ran to catch up to Welt. He was going into an open room, a small
Bible in his hand. As I stood in the doorway, he said, "I put these in
every room. Someone must be finding them helpful. I always have
to replace them."

"That day in the bathroom with the john," I said, "I never told
you thank you."

He stepped past to return to his cart. As he reached in for a stack
of clean towels, he looked at Thursday and Daffy, who were staring
at him.

"The others don't trust me, do they?" he asked.

"They're just a little hesitant," I said. "After I told them you can hear and speak, they thought you might have even more secrets."

"Doesn't everyone?" he asked. "Don't you?"

When I looked away, he said, "I know folks think I'm River Man. I don't mind. I've always been tied to death. Growing up, my old man cut grass for a cemetery. Anytime I was bad, he'd take the key, unlock the gate, and tie me up to a grave. He'd leave me there all night, tied to death. I've been tied to it ever since. When our dog died, Mom looked at me as if I'd been the one to hang him from the tree. Even though I swore I hadn't, she never believed me. I've gotten used to people thinking I've done something."

He rested his gloved hand on top of the towels as he walked inside the room.

"You need to stop talking to him, Arc," Thursday said when I got back to her and Daffy. "He's the type of man who puts cigarette burns in your panties."

"He saved me from the john," I said.

"You think he saved you?" she asked. "Or you think he saved you for himself? It's like standing at the wood line. One wild animal ain't gonna want another one dragging you away before he does. Now, come on. Let's go look for Violet."

We only planned to walk around the block but found ourselves walking farther when there was no sign of Violet. Thursday kept sliding the toilet roll over her stomach, pointing out the stars to her unborn child. Her belly had grown, but not nearly as big as she should have been that far along.

"What can she expect?" Daffy had said earlier to me. "She can't keep wearing crowns and think they're not gonna break the head of her child."

The holes in Thursday's clothes were everywhere except for in the area on her stomach. She kept the fabric there intact, as if she feared the child might slip out one of the holes when she wasn't looking.

"C'mon let's go back. We're not gonna find her," Thursday said, raising her voice as we crossed the street on a green light, the cars honking and jerking to a stop. "Violet's already floating in the river. Why the fuck are we even bothering?" She slapped the hood of the car that nearly hit her. "We're born, then we die. In between we bleed, we bruise, we fuck strangers, and we go missing. Well, I'm tired of waiting for it. C'mon." She opened her arms and screamed in the middle of the street. "Come and get me, River Man. You fucking coward." She threw the nothing she had in her hand as the cars honked and screamed for "the bitch" to get out of the way. "Come and get me, you piece of shit."

I grabbed her by the sleeve, pulling her up onto the sidewalk. As the traffic sped past, she dropped to her knees and cried into the concrete. Daffy and me picked her up. We didn't speak as we returned to the Blue Hour. The words were too hard to find.

In between wearing our crowns and lying beneath johns, we hoped to find Violet. The days passed. On the night of the last big thunderstorm of the summer, I was driving Thursday's car. She was lying in the back seat, the toilet paper roll up to her eye, looking at the night sky. Daffy was riding shotgun, her feet on the dash and tapping to the beat of the music from the radio.

As the thunder gave way to lightning, Daffy pointed to a woman standing on the sidewalk in the rain. "Ain't that Violet?"

"Violet?" Thursday sat up in the back seat as I slowed down and parked. "What the hell is she doing right there?"

Violet was facing the old store she'd shown me before. The one she said would be the future site of her bakery. The FOR SALE sign had been removed. From the lights inside, we could see workers renovating the area.

"Violet?" I wiped the rain out of my eyes. "Where the hell have you been?"

"We thought River Man got you." Thursday held the toilet paper roll over Violet's head as if it could be an umbrella as much as a telescope.

"Someone bought it," Violet said, staring through the window at the workers.

"I'm so sorry, Violet." I tried to pull her away, but she wouldn't budge.

"That's where the cupcakes would have sat." She pointed through the window to an area by the back wall. "The cookies would have been laid out on little paper doilies. Shamrocks for St. Patrick's. Hearts for Valentines. Reindeer for Christmas. Grassy would have come here after school. She would have snuck brownies from the tray and licked the batter from the mixer. But I wouldn't have let her use it until she's older." Violet wagged her finger in the air, the rain flicking off. "She has a habit of reaching for things that spin around. She don't yet understand that not everything that swirls and twirls is good."

"Let's go home, Violet." Thursday tried to wrap her arm around her.

Violet finally looked at us, her eyes widening. "Don't you understand?" Her tears mixed with rain. "I don't have a home."

She ran across the street. The honks filled the air, as did the squealing tires. If the van hadn't stopped in time, Violet would have ended up beneath it.

"Violet!" We each screamed her name. At the front of the van, she paused to look over at us before running off.

As we chased after her, I stopped at the hood of the van and looked at the driver. It was the john who had tried to drown me in the tub. He was watching Violet run off. When he turned and met my eyes, he smiled at me, showing all his teeth, and said something I couldn't hear.

"Arc, come on." Thursday yelled for me.

I slammed my fist down against the van's hood. The john's eyes grew colder and I backed up in the rain, then ran to keep up with Thursday and Daffy.

We chased after Violet, but she disappeared around the corner.

"Where has she gone?" I tried to see through the rain, now falling even heavier.

Thursday gripped the toilet paper roll. It was so wet, it was unraveling. She dropped it to the ground and said, "Let's get the fuck outta here."

Thursday cursed the whole way back to her car. She drove, the windshield wipers kicking the rain out to either side, as we held our thoughts like a piece of hard candy. Something we could turn over with our tongue and make room for against our gum line and cheek. The bulge in our mouth, the hard feeling against soft places. And the hard feeling was River Man. Violet wasn't just an addict who had relapsed. She was a woman running barefoot on the streets of Chillicothe in the rain, and that made us believe in the boogeyman that much more.

As Thursday pulled into the drive at Violet's house, there was a stillness in the air. It seemed like her place was but a snapshot, the silence almost overwhelming. I thought about dropping to my knees and digging. Digging until I found the sound, jingling like the silver spoons she pierced her ears with.

The three of us walked past the bag of trash in her yard, torn open by wild animals. The remnants were scattered across the bright green grass and soaked into the ground. Her front door was closed but unlocked. When we got inside, we found nothing more than a mess. We kicked the trash out of the way.

Using the black marker from Thursday's purse, we scribbled notes on the white fridge door. *Violet, don't walk along the crack. Remember some men have twisted veins and a wolf for a heart. Run away when you hear the howling. Remember the smell of knives. They smell like blood. Stay away from the puddles full of night. Listen for River Man. He sounds like hunger.* We drew a heart big enough that we could write inside it, *From the Chillicothe Queens.* Around the heart, I wrote a field spell like I thought Mamaw Milkweed would have: *bee balm, mustard seeds, witch grass, come home. We left the porch light on for you.*

Daffy then took a piece of the red yarn from her pocket and used one of the fridge magnets to hold it in place over my words. "That way," she said. "The bird will fly down and read our prayer."

We were silent on the way to Thursday's trailer. Once we were in the drive, she looked down at her stomach and rubbed it for several moments. She sighed. "Do you think when she's born, she'll know I'm her mother? Or do you think she'll believe I'm just a stranger holding her until her real mother comes back into the room? Sometimes, I think it'll be so fucking nice to walk hand in hand with her down the street, but what if one day, I'm making her a grilled cheese sandwich and I leave the pan on the stove and the whole place burns down? What if one day I'm Violet staring into the window of the life I wished I had but was too fucking late to get?"

"Why don't we go back?" I asked.

"To look for Violet?" Thursday raised her eyes to mine.

"No," I said. "Back to rehab. Not one in Chillicothe either. One farther away. One far enough away that when we get out, we can't smell the mill or the Blue Hour or—"

"The river," Daffy added.

"Yeah," Thursday said, her voice low. "I like that idea. But we might as well finish the shit we have left."

The rain beat down on top of our heads as we ran into the trailer. Inside, the blue carpet still had crisscrossing vacuum lines from her mother's weekly cleaning. The bloodstains remained, though.

"Did I show you what Mom got for the baby?" Thursday asked, heading to the table where there were folded piles of tiny shirts and onesies. She held up a small pair of yellow socks. "Ain't they just the cutest things. Can you even imagine feet this small?"

She reached into her purse and pulled out a baggie, which she gave to me.

"Shit's in the bottom drawer there." She pointed to a chest against a wall.

As she talked about the diaper bag, with the little yellow ducks on its side, I pulled open the drawer and got out a spoon and needle.

"Mom's already got all my bottles and everything," Thursday said. "You've got to sterilize the bottles. You know that?"

Daffy shook her head while I held the lighter beneath the spoon.

"This is for diaper rash." Thursday held up a tube of cream. "Special shampoo." She grabbed an amber-colored bottle. "Just for babies. It's safe to get in their eyes. You know you can't put a stuffed animal in the crib with a baby? They could suffocate. Hey, Arc, that shit almost ready?"

Thursday sat on the floor by me and wrapped the strap of the diaper bag tightly around her arm. I pushed the needle in and emptied it inside her. As she laid her head back on the edge of the sofa, she closed her eyes, and Daffy said, "I hope she has daughters who are twins. I wouldn't want her kid to have to imagine a sister. I'd want her to have what we have. You know, Arc? I couldn't have lived without you."

As I stabbed the needle into our veins, Daffy said her toes were dry. "And my shoulder and my knee and the pinkie on my right hand. Am I turning to dust, Arc?"

Together we closed our eyes. I dreamed of being inside the paper mill. Sawdust filled the air and the loud sounds of the saw hurt my ears. There was no one in sight. The machines seemed to be running on their own. As I walked through, my bare feet left footprints in the sawdust on the floor.

When the conveyor belt jumped to a start, I saw that instead of logs about to be cut, there was Harlow, Sage Nell, and Indigo. They didn't move. Not even when I tried to pull them off. They lay perfectly still and straight, like pieces of wood. Harlow was first to the spinning wheel. It cut her up the middle, the blood flying through the air like more sawdust. I screamed, trying to pull Sage Nell off, but the saw took her, too, her face dividing under the blade.

"No," I cried. "No, please."

When Indigo was thrust forward to the spinning blade, her blood sprayed my face and the white dress I was wearing.

There was one last body heading toward the saw.

"Violet?" I tried to take her away with me.

She screamed as the saw cut up her stomach. I ran out of the mill, then turned to look back. The smoke barreled from the stacks. At first it was gray, but it turned a bright red that took over the white sky. I pressed my hands tightly over my ears. The screams only got louder.

When I opened my eyes, I realized the screams weren't in my dream at all.

Feeling the warmth on my hand, I looked down and saw what appeared to be coffee grounds on my palm. It was so brown, I didn't realize it was blood at first. Until I saw the puddle of it leading to Thursday.

"My baby." Thursday's scream was louder than all the thunder outside put together. "No. Please no. Oh, God."

She clutched her stomach, her fingers going through the holes cut in her long sleeves, the blood clotting down the inside of her legs.

CHAPTER 39

The scar of a star, stretches far.

—*Daffodil Poet*

AFTER THURSDAY LOST HER BABY, SHE LOCKED HERSELF IN HER trailer. The closest I got to her was sitting on the other side of the door. At times she would ramble.

"Maybe we're like the elephants, Arc," she said. "An endangered species being poached for our tusks."

Other times she was angry, screaming out her words.

"We said we were wearing crowns. What a fucking laugh. We should have said what we were really doing. Maybe we could have been queens in a different parade. But not here. Not here in the land of smoke and dope."

Her parents would leave groceries at the front porch and plead with her to let them come in. The mom always wearing something dark blue. Always with some dessert in her hand. When they came with a chocolate cream pie, she offered me some.

"That's okay." I stared at the meringue smashed beneath the plastic wrap.

"Thursday?" She knocked on the door with her free hand. "I've baked your favorite. Over the moon pie. C'mon, sweetie. Open the door."

I passed her dad on the steps. He asked if I wanted a piece of pizza from the box he was holding.

"No, thanks," I said.

As I pulled out of the drive, her dad was opening the box in front of the window, saying, "It's your favorite, honey. Mushroom. Please let us in."

The door remained closed and locked.

When I got home, I thought I'd find Daffy in her room, but it was empty. I'd made her promise that she wouldn't go out by herself with a killer on the loose, and yet I found myself driving to the Blue Hour to look for her. There were two women I didn't know on the sidewalk. I asked if they'd noticed a woman who looked like me around that day.

"Naw," the tall one said. "Ain't seen no one who looks like you."

"Except for you," the other one added.

I went around to a couple of rooms and knocked but got no answer. When I saw the maintenance door ajar, I pushed it open. The room was narrow but long, with several rows of metal shelves that housed cleaning supplies, tools, and boxes. At the end of the room was a desk pushed against the wall. Beside it was a stand with an old box TV and a VHS player. The TV was paused on a close-up of a woman's face. I picked up the remote and pressed play.

The movie, *What Ever Happened to Baby Jane?*, was in black-and-white. The actress, Bette Davis, was crying in the scene. I was about to pause it again when the picture changed, this time in color. Static cut through the image. Like Bette Davis, this woman was crying and wiping her tears on her baby blue sweater. The clip was clearly home-made and the date, 1990, hovered in the upper-right-hand corner.

I ejected the tape and found TEXAS written on the label. The crate by the stand was full of more tapes, all with names of states. I picked up one that said TENNESSEE and put it in. It was a series of home videos mashed with movie clips, all of women and all of them crying. Tape after tape, I fast-forwarded over their faces. Some sobbed and wailed, holding their hands up to the sky. Others sat quietly, tears rolling down their cheeks. Some of the homemade movies were filmed on a street with some inside homes, the dates ranging from various decades.

"You found me out."

I dropped the remote and turned around to see Welt. He held a hard look in his eye.

"You found me out," he said again.

"I'm sorry," I said. "I didn't mean to go through your things."

"I'm a collector of tears." He nudged the box of tapes with his shoe. "You won't believe how many people get rid of their family memories." He picked up a tape labeled KANSAS. "I've found them in yard sales, dumpsters, thrown out like trash. Sometimes you get one, and it's a family laughing at amusement parks." He ran his gloved finger over the edge of the tape. "But sometimes they film the sad parts, too. Those are the ones I take and put in my collection. What do you think about it? My collection?"

"Why do they have states written on them?" I asked.

"To mark where I got them from," he said. "I move around a lot." He ejected the tape in the player and replaced it with the one in his hand. "Momma always told me to keep moving around. She said I had a concrete heart and I'd sink to the center of the earth if I stayed in one place too long."

As the video played, I started to step backward, toward the door.

"Don't you wanna stay and watch?" he asked. "We could ruin our eyes together."

"Maybe another time," I said.

When he smiled, his broken teeth showed. "I always doubt it when people say things like that." He turned back to the TV. "This one is one of my favorites," he said of the woman sitting at the table, wiping her eyes on the sleeve of her pink sweater. "God, I'd kill to drink her tears."

I ran to the door, pushing it open. Only when I was in the truck with the door locked did I look back. Welt stood in the doorway, his gloved hand up to his ear, as if listening to it.

"He reminds me of the monsters in Mamaw Milkweed's old stories," Daffy's voice echoed in my ears as I drove away from the Blue Hour. "The ones who set the fires and steal the dreams."

My body shook in its own chill as I gripped the steering wheel over the rhymes Daffy had written on it and prayed she would be home.

When I got to the house I nearly hit the mailbox speeding in. Running inside, I asked Aunt Clover if she'd seen Daffy.

"Sure," she said. "I see her there." She pointed to the corner of the room. "There." She pointed up to the ceiling. "There and there and there." She pointed at the floor, TV, and coffee table. "And of course, here." She held her middle finger up at me.

I knocked her loose twigs off the sofa cushion, scattering them on my way down the hall.

"You fucking bitch," she hollered after me.

I opened Daffy's closed door. The room was empty. I walked over and stood at the window we'd stared out of that day at John Theresa, when he was still just the violin man. When I looked down, I saw I was standing on our drawing of his face, faded from the long years.

I got down on all fours and placed my ear against the violin strings that we had tried our best to draw straight. It was then that I saw my sister beneath her bed.

"Hey, Arc," she said.

"What are you doing under there?" I asked.

"My feet are disappearing."

"What are you talking about?"

"Sometimes," she said, "I look down, and I just see dirt and rocks."

"I was scared to death, Daffy. I didn't know where you were."

I crawled under the bed beside her.

"No Happy Meal, Arc?" she asked. "You brought me a half-eaten Happy Meal that night you found me under the bed. Where's my Happy Meal now?"

"Where have you been?" I asked. "I told you not to leave the house alone. Not with River Man out there."

"Funny how they call it a Happy Meal. As if happiness were that simple it could come in a small red box."

I broke the silence that followed and said, "I have a secret to tell you, Daffy. There *was* a toy in the Happy Meal. I took it and kept it for myself. It was a princess."

"I know," she said. "I got one in my Happy Meal."

"You got a Happy Meal?"

"He brought me one, too."

"You mean, you got a Happy Meal and you didn't save any of the food back for me?" I looked at her. "What if I hadn't gotten one? I was hungry, too. You knew that. You were just gonna let me starve?"

"I didn't think about you."

The words hung heavy in the air before Daffy grabbed my hand and squeezed it.

"I suppose I'm our mother's daughter after all, huh, Arc?"

She scooted over closer to me and laid her head against my shoul-

der as she asked, "Do you know why I was under my bed that night?
I was hiding from the spider."

"Spiders crawl on the floor, too, Daffy." I stared up at the underside of the box spring. "Why are you under here now?"

"I'm hiding from him again. He's been driving up and down
the street." She smiled and turned to me. "Tell me about the
Trung sisters, Arc."

Her once-bright red hair had thinned so much around her face,
it made her forehead loom larger, the shadow cast down across her
nose. She looked older than she was. In a certain light, you might
think she was a middle-aged woman who had no prayers to spare
from her own needs. The sores on her skin returned in the same
places they had already scarred over, and even her hands appeared
to be shriveling.

"In ancient Vietnam," I said, "the Trung sisters formed an army
of women. They found their independence and became queens."

As I spoke, she mouthed the words. She asked me to tell her the
story twice more. I did as I ran my hand through her hair, the strands
coming out in between my fingers.

"Maybe we should get you some vitamins," I said, "so you don't
fall apart so much."

She stared out at the twigs glued to the wall. "I know what Aunt
Clover is making."

"What is it?" I asked.

"Her reflection."

CHAPTER 40

Yes, I am certain at last, I am but the past.

—*Daffodil Poet*

WHEN WE DISCOVERED CLEOPATRA'S TIME MACHINE, IT HAD BEEN buried for decades. The only thing visible was the top of the cracked windshield. Sage Nell had been the one to see it when the four of us first went down to the river together and discovered our Distant Mountain.

"There's something shining over there." She had pointed to the chrome edge of the windshield reflecting the light of the sun.

We didn't know at the time that the entire car had been buried. All we knew was that there were enough parts showing to tell us it was from the 1950s.

"Look at these tail fin wings," Sage Nell said as she ran her hands over the tips sticking up from the ground like shark fins. The red taillights had been broken, leaving shards stuck in place like broken rubies, or so Thursday said. Over time, as we returned to the spot, we would dig out the car little by little until we had shoveled out the leather seats, exposing the rearview and side mirrors, and saw that the color of the metal body had once been blue.

"The color of lapis lazuli," I told them.

Splintered from the hood was a sharp piece of metal that stuck up toward the sky, its end pointed.

"It's like a medieval sword," I said, running my hand down the length of it.

On the leather seats were fossilized marks. Thursday said she knew what they were.

"Leaves," she said. "But not leaves from now. Leaves from the past. Leaves that don't fucking exist no more."

Sage Nell announced the car's tires were gone when we dug out enough to know that. Daffy would come to find a cat's skull in the trunk when we finally pried it open. The skull had gotten stuffed with mud, the rounded side of a small blue marble showing through in between the fangs.

"I bet when this car was on the road," Sage Nell said, running her hand down one side, "she took the moon's breath away."

Scratches now marked the metal and were what Daffy said was the fury left over from a woman with claws.

The four of us got in. Daffy sat in back with Sage Nell, while I sat in front with Thursday. She slid in behind the wheel, pretending to drive as she knocked dirt off the dashboard and said, "This car has got time all over it."

"That's because it's a time machine," I said. "It's been to the age of the dinosaurs." I pointed to the fossils on the seats. "It's been to Egypt." I held up the cat skull. "It don't have no tires because it never needed any. It was pulled like a chariot by winged horses made of fire and ice."

"What type of gas do you put in a time machine, Arc?" Sage Nell asked.

"River water," I said. "That's why it's parked here. A fueling stop."

We all laughed as Thursday pretended to drive through the portals of time and space, making a squealing sound as she pressed on the brake.

"Who the fuck you think this time machine belonged to?" she asked.

"The last queen of Egypt." I stared into the eyes of the cat skull.

"Who was the last queen of Egypt?" Sage Nell asked, holding her hands up in the air as if Thursday were driving us down a hill.

"Cleopatra, of course." Daffy smiled.

"Well, let's fill this baby up," Thursday said. "See if we can't visit a little of the past."

I knew after Thursday lost her baby, it was to the past that she'd try to go. Her phone call came a little after one o'clock in the morning. She said she'd gone out to Cleopatra's time machine with a bucket.

She filled it with water from the river, then dumped it down over the car and got behind the wheel.

"But it wouldn't start," she said. "No matter how much river water I tried to fill it up with. No matter how many times I pleaded."

It had been a couple of weeks since she'd lost her baby. It was the first call I'd gotten from her since. I had still been going over to her place, sitting outside the door, asking her to let me in. But I'd only been answered by silence.

"I thought I could go back to the past," she said, "to when I found out I was pregnant. I'd do it right. No more using. I'd eat the things I was supposed to. Not drink any of the things I wasn't. Turns out the time machine is broken, Arc. No wonder Cleopatra abandoned it in Chillicothe, Ohio."

Thursday hung up as immediately as she had called.

When I got to her place, the front door was locked. "Hey, Thursday?" I knocked. When she didn't answer, I banged. "C'mon, open up."

I went to one of the front windows. It was open, so I punched out the screen and climbed inside. The trailer was dark, but I saw a sliver of light around the bathroom door. I pushed it open and found Thursday, scissors in hand. She was cutting so many holes in her clothes, she was nearly naked.

"Get the fuck out of here, Arc." She held the scissors up like she was going to stab me. But instead she dropped them and fell down against the bathroom cabinet.

"I'm sorry, Arc. I didn't mean—I'm so sorry."

"It's okay." I held her in my arms. She had cut her clothes so quickly, her skin had gotten nicked and was bleeding.

"I want my baby back, Arc." She buried her face in my shirt. "I knew what I was doing wasn't good, but I didn't really believe I'd lose her. I thought I had time to get better."

I rocked her, her shirt sleeves cut so much, they fell to the sides of her arms.

"Why do you keep making all these holes in your clothes, Thursday?" I wiped the blood off her arm.

"All the things we've done, Arc, it's cost us emeralds and sapphires and rubies. But it's also cost pieces of ourselves. That's all this is." She picked up the cut fabric off the floor. "Pieces of myself cut out to pay the devil." She let the bits fall through her fingers. "I hate thinking about my daughter buried in the ground with the worms who eat everything to bone."

She stared at the used needle on the floor behind the toilet.

"What if she ain't buried in the ground?" I asked.

Thursday looked up at me, her eyes darkened by the tears.

"What if we bury her in the sky?" I wiped her cheeks until she smiled.

She let me pull her to her feet and lead her through the house, out the back door. The night sky was clear. Hours of darkness were settling in while the stars sparkled like the jewels Thursday always swore she had.

She used me to lean on as we stepped into the tall grass.

"Where should we bury her?" I asked.

She scanned the sky with her eyes.

"That cluster of stars." She pointed up. "They look content. Like they're the lights at the front of a house that is warm when it needs to be and nice all the time. That's the spot."

Sitting down, she said, "I don't have my baby's body, Arc. They fucking took her from me."

"What if I have her right here?" I said, holding my arms up.

Thursday gave her eyes to the tall grass, blowing in the wind. She watched it as she softly chuckled and said, "I'd say, give my baby to me."

She reached her arms up, the tears slipping down her cheeks. I cradled the air and handed it off to her. She took it like there was a blanket wrapped around her child and the blanket was so long, she had to hold it up. As she looked down into her arms, rocking them side to side, I went back inside.

In the dim light of the bathroom, I scooped up the pieces of fabric off the floor. I could hear Thursday's voice from where I was. She was singing, but it wasn't a song from the radio. They were her own lyrics. The ones a woman creates after she's long gone in the mountain mist.

"'I'll give you a reason to buy me some flowers,'" she sang. *"'A life is a clock, the minutes they tick and they tock. At one, you were born my little girl, at two, you sprouted and grew. Come eleven, I finally found heaven. And at midnight, I cried in the light. Now won't you buy my girl some flowers, for she's no more hours. Won't you buy her some flowers, for she's no more hours. Buy some flowers, she's no more hours. She's no more.'"*

When I sat down beside her, she said, "I'm glad it's you who's with me for her burial, Arc."

She kept her eyes on what she cradled. For her, it was the something she had lost. For that moment, she was able to find it again.

"I'll bury her by my firstborn," she said, raising her arms.

We both looked up, and as the wind blew her sleeves, they swung like a blanket lifting into the air.

"Help me dig, Arc." She lay back, her hands still up and taking clumps of the sky.

I placed the pieces of fabric on the ground and lay back beside her, our fingers snatching the air until she said the hole was deep enough. She put her hands on each of her cheeks and smiled as she counted.

"One star leaving, two stars going away, three stars already gone." She released a long exhale that surrounded us. "She's in the hole now, Arc."

I stood, taking a handful of the fabric and cast the pieces up to the stars. Though they fell back upon us, Thursday said, "Give me a handful of that dirt, Arc Doggs."

When I let the pieces of fabric drop from my hand into hers, she stood, throwing them up with a cry that lasted far longer than the time it took for the fabric to fall back to earth. The pieces that had fallen, she picked back up, grabbing grass with them, until she was throwing handfuls of the ground up to the sky, grunting with each pitch. Her fury, a match for her grief.

Out of breath, her final cry came from deep within her. A roar, really, that burst forth and disappeared into the darkness. Her arms hung down by her sides, and tears puddled on her cheeks.

"She's buried in the sky now," she said. "There are no earthworms up there. Nothing that will eat her down to bone. There are only the stars, and they'll teach her how to be one of them, until she shines like a meadow in the distance."

"You're the mother of that meadow," I said.

"Yes." She smiled.

"You are the mother of that star," I told her.

"Yes." She raised her chin and squared her shoulders. "I am the mother. I am. I am. I am."

OFFICE OF ROSS COUNTY MEDICAL EXAMINER
CHILLICOTHE, OHIO
REPORT OF INVESTIGATION BY COUNTY MEDICAL OFFICER

DECEDENT: Violet

AGE: As old as the herons

EYES: Butterflies

HAIR: Like the flower

DESCRIPTION OF BODY: Unclothed

GENDER: Mother

BODY TEMP: In need of a flame

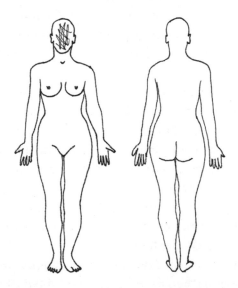

WOUNDS AND MARKS: Poorly nourished. Distinctive pattern of bruising on back of right knuckles as if she fought back. Fingernails broken. Been in water a long time. Dirt found beneath eyelids. Plant material in the nostrils and between the legs. Present in the smaller air passages. Severe abrasions on the breasts. Nothing unexpected. Bruising found prior to drowning. Heart had already stopped pumping when they were suffered. Areas purple in color were, however, made when she was still alive. Blunt impact to the back of the skull. Bleeding present over the surface of the brain. A crown of twigs and stems. Lungs are full, like a woman taking a deep breath, about to sing us her song.

PROBABLE CAUSE OF DEATH:

Stood too close to the edge of the water.

CHAPTER 41

On the way down, she reaches for her crown.

—*Daffodil Poet*

TWO TEENAGE BOYS WENT FISHING. THEY FIRST STALKED THROUGH their backyard to find grasshoppers to fill the old pail with them. Jumping and trying to escape, the boys trapped the insects in the pail with its lid. Then they propped their fishing poles against their shoulders and swung the pail by its handle between them as they walked down to the river. They each chose a grasshopper.

As they pierced their squirming bodies with the cold hook, one of the boys looked up at the water.

"The current is moving fast today," he said.

As the other cast his line, it landed with a splash, just as the body of Violet floated by. By the time the two boys got the police, she had gone farther downstream. They eventually found her, caught in the branches of a fallen tree, like an unfinished song.

"River Man," the whispers on the street said.

Silence was what the sheriff's department said.

In her absence in our lives, we spoke of Violet and all the ways she had made us feel seen.

"She'd always bring me the custard-filled doughnuts," one of the women said. "She knew I liked them best."

"She'd make the strawberry-filled for me," another one added.

They would remember how Violet always got enough napkins to wipe the glaze from our faces and fingers, like a mother cleaning her children.

"Violet's death makes me think about Mamaw Milkweed's fruit cellar," Daffy told me.

I myself thought of it. A skinned dwelling of cinderblock walls. Crates of fruit and puddles on the floor of something wet that silvers in the moonlight. There among the pale, dim walls, a bright purple ribbon on the table. A single delicate thing left to be remembered.

"I'm scared we'll never see the color violet again," Daffy said.

A couple of days after Violet was pulled from the river, Daffy and me were standing in front of the Blue Hour with Thursday. Ever since that night we buried her daughter in the sky, Thursday had returned to the street. She made no mention of the child she'd once carried. If someone were to come up to her and say, "I'm sorry, Thursday. I heard what happened with your baby 'n' all," she would say, "I'm still a mother," and look up at the sky.

For the first time since we'd known her, she was wearing none of the plastic beads she swore were opals or turquoise or peridot. No rings of amethyst or emeralds. No bracelets of malachite, amber, or jasper. Not even her stud in her nose. Her skin was unadorned. When I asked her where her diamonds and sapphires were, she said, "Oh, you mean those cheap plastic things? Wasn't worth nothing at all. There comes a time we gotta stop playing pretend, Arc."

Her clothes still had the holes in them, only they had gotten bigger. She cut out the elbows, one at a time until the fabric flapped like wings. The shredded hole on her shoulder was big enough to look like something had tried to take a bite out of her while her knees were exposed along with the length of her legs. Between the hours of herself and the next day, she could blur all on her own until the next crown made her forget for just a moment why she held the scissors.

"You okay, Thursday?" Daffy asked.

"How can any of us be?" she said. "They're killing our friends. Everything seems like a deeper abyss now. I'm not surprised it's happening though. In a town like this, monsters feed on the smoke. If you look closely, some women always have the shadow of a man following them." She raised her eyes to the stacks of the paper mill. "Do you think when we buried that time capsule, we buried us, too? Do you think we brought this curse upon ourselves?"

She opened her hand, showing a small tattoo on the underside of her left wrist. It was the body of a wolf.

"She don't have a head," Thursday said. "It was eaten off."

"By what?" Daffy's eyes widened.

"By my fucking secrets." Thursday reached into her purse and pulled out a wad of money. "This is to get me to my faraway place." She shoved the money back down into her purse.

"You didn't steal that money from Highway Man, did you?" I watched her rub over the tattoo.

"He won't notice for a while," she said. "By then, I'll be beyond the Distant Mountain. You should leave, too. At least until River Man is finished trying to fill the river with blood."

The three of us turned to the sound of something rattling. It was cans tied to the shopping cart and the hem of the wise old one.

"She can climb like a cat," I said, staring at the old woman pushing the cart.

"She flies like an owl." Thursday wrapped her arms around herself.

The woman's faded scarves blew up in the wind like smoke rising out of her head.

"They say if you get inside her shopping cart," Thursday said, "you get inside her cradle. For a little while, you get to be carried. When life gets too fucking hard and you feel you can't go on, she pushes you. Only an old woman would have such kindness."

As she walked by, Thursday gripped the side of the cart, getting inside. The woman took no notice and pushed the added weight in the cart with the same look in her eye as when there had only been the dirty blanket and the tattered teddy bear.

"It's awful nice," Thursday hollered out. "Hey, Arc?" She held the teddy up into the air. "Don't let the devil know."

"Know what?" I hollered back.

"Your name," Thursday said, holding tight to the bear. "Don't let the devil know your name, too."

Just before the woman pushed her around the corner, Thursday yelled, "Hey, Arc? Caught you." She screamed the phrase out the way I imagined her brother once had. Then she laughed, but it wasn't real. "I guess I'll disappear now, huh?"

The wise old owl pushed the cart around the corner. The cans tied to the hem of her skirt, rattling into the distance.

CHAPTER 42

In a dream that fades away, we are but the prey.

—*Daffodil Poet*

"TO BE A WOMAN IS TO BE FROM THE BEGINNING OF TIME," MAMAW Milkweed would say as she stared at herself in the mirror. "It is God's greatest challenge posed to us. If we fail, we'll be promised nothing but an eternity of that failure, lost in the mist at the edge of the county. If we find our way out, thank the women before who left the light on against the dark."

I thought her words were the reason the mirrors in my dreams always reflected the curve of a woman's lower back, perhaps even my own. But as the curve thinned, I knew it was Daffy I dreamed of. By that October, she had lost so much weight, her clothes were too big. She'd started to pull things out of her closet. Clothes we wore when we were younger, like overalls and jumpers, things that could stay up on her bony frame. Much of her hair had fallen out, the bald patches more noticeable in the braids she pulled tightly back. Most days she seemed to have a layer of dust over her eyes, dimming the light. New sores covered her skin as if they would never heal, and she said she thought there were craters in her heart like the moon.

"Sometimes, Arc, I look in the mirror, and I don't see a reflection."

"It's only because of the tape on the mirror," I told her. "No one can see their reflection in this damn house."

It was our birthday. We were turning twenty-one. We were in her room and she was back to getting more clothes out of the box in the closet. I was sitting on her bed, reading.

"What book are you reading, Arc?" she asked.

"It's Mom's." I held it up. The word *diary* written in gold across the satin cover.

"Mom's writing looks so young, don't it?" Daffy peeked at the page. "Makes ya remember she wasn't always an aged woman in a back bedroom."

Daffy reached into the box. She pulled out a sweatshirt and slipped it on. It was cream-colored, with powder-blue sleeves. The image on the front was of the old book character Holly Hobbie, a little girl with a patchwork dress and a large floppy bonnet that hid her face from the side. With the sweatshirt, Daffy wore a pink slip, edged in lace, and chocolate-brown knee socks.

"You wore that when we had the flu," I told her.

"You don't think the germs are still on it, do you?" she asked. "Make us sick again?"

"I'm not sure that matters anymore, Daffy. You already look pretty ill."

She ran her fingers over her face. "I'm losing a fingernail."

I took her hand in mine. The fingernail was still there, but it was black.

"I'm turning into Momma." She smiled, her eyes glazed. "Soon you'll have to put my mattress on the floor. I'll stay in the dark and the cold, and we'll speak by cans tied to a string."

She dropped her eyes and noticed the animal carrier at the front of the closet.

"It's to hold something small and lost," I said. "I picked it up at the discount store."

She didn't ask what I was going to put in the carrier. She merely came over and flopped down onto the bed, too weak to stand any longer.

"I have something for you, Daffy." I unfolded a white piece of paper from my pocket. Sticking on the bottom corner was a small square of bright yellow. "Did you know if you stare at the color yellow, then look at a blank sheet of paper, you'll see a color that's not yellow at all?"

She stared at the yellow square and counted down the seconds. When she moved her eyes to the white space, she smiled.

"Oh, Arc. It's the color violet. I was worried we'd never see it again."

"Yeah." I hugged her as she leaned back into my arms. I nuzzled my face in her hair. It smelled like the wet rocks on the riverbank.

"Is this my birthday gift?" She looked back at me.

"No. This is." I picked the plastic grocery bag up off the floor.

As she opened it, she asked, "You think Momma remembers it's our birthday?"

"What matters is that we remember," I said.

"It'd be nice if she did, too." Daffy opened the bag and pulled out a plastic lid.

"I got it off a can of cornmeal," I said.

"What is it?" She ran her finger along the piece of red yarn tied through the hole I'd cut in the side of the lid.

"It's a river compass," I told her, pointing out the directions I'd written in black marker on the top side. I turned the compass west and said, "This way out of the flood. And this way to keep from drowning." I turned it east. "But to never be lost again, head north." I turned the compass toward the stars.

"What about south?" she asked.

"Don't head south, Daffy. It's where all the ghosts are."

"Let's go to the river, Arc," she said. "Try it out."

"It's not safe, Daffy. Not with River Man out there."

"That's exactly why we have to go."

She stood and walked out the door. I paused in the hallway to put on my shoes, but when I saw Daffy hadn't, I left mine off, too. Together we walked by Aunt Clover sitting on the floor in front of the TV, her eyes on the floating shots of the Eiffel Tower.

"France," she said, placing her hand on the screen. "That's where the *Mona Lisa* is. Spittle, spittle, spider, where you gonna hide her?" Aunt Clover spit into her palm and smacked it against the TV screen over Mona Lisa's face. "Right there."

Daffy tugged on my arm, and we walked out, not letting the screen door slam behind us.

I drove to Thursday's trailer. It was dark. She hadn't been seen in weeks. Her parents had put up posters, even had a cash reward. And though they had gotten calls from folks claiming to know exactly where Thursday was, none of the tips led them any closer to their daughter.

Daffy and me glanced back at the trailer as we walked through the cornfield. It had not yet been harvested, but would be soon, the tall stalks cut down for the winter months ahead. Daffy walked backward through the leaves, the compass spinning from the red yarn in her hand.

When we got to the small patch of woods, Daffy said, "The trees are damp and mysterious and naked."

"Because she lives alone," I said.

"And they sing and sing and sing," she shouted.

"Because she lives alone."

At the Distant Mountain, we passed the time machine. For a moment, I thought we might find Thursday there, still trying to fill the gas tank with river water and go back to a time she could start from the beginning again. Left with only ourselves, I watched Daffy stand on the bank, staring out at the brown water.

"I have a gift for you, too, Arc," she said, opening her hand.

Lying in her palm was the princess from the Happy Meal all those years ago. Her face was dirty and her crown was missing one of its sticker jewels. Daffy had used tape and glue to carefully piece the plastic back together.

I took the princess and closed my fingers around her as I held her to my chest.

"I've missed her," I said, remembering who I used to be.

"Why didn't you ever do anything more, Arc?" Daffy put her finger beneath my chin and lifted it until our eyes met. "Get out of this place? Go away? Do something great? You were the smart sister. How'd you end up with a stupid life?" She stepped away and looked down at the compass. "I'll tell you why, Arc. Because you're my sister. I held you back. I know that now."

"You haven't held me back," I said, my tone giving something more away.

"Do you know why I call you Arc?" She smiled out upon the river. "It's not because you dig in the dirt like an archaeologist or like why Mom calls you Arc. I call you Arc not with a *c* but with a *k*. Like the ark that saved everyone from the flood. You're my ark, you always have been. There to save me when the flood has come. But the thing about saving someone in the flood is that you have to get in the water, too. Sometimes you don't get back out. I drowned you with me, Arc. Just like Daddy did to Momma. And Momma did to Aunt Clover."

She picked up a rock and threw it into the river. "Tell me the story of the Trung sisters."

"Daffy—"

"Tell me the story of the Trung sisters, Arc."

I hugged the princess and closed my eyes.

"In ancient Vietnam," I said, "there were two sisters who revolted against the power that tried to steal their home. The sisters formed an army, comprised of women. This army pushed the forces back. The sisters were announced as queens."

"Now tell me the ending," she said. "The one you always leave out. I wanna know the whole story this time."

I opened my eyes and watched her take off her clothes. When she was stripped to her underwear, I said, "For three years, the sisters ruled. For three years, they were queens, until the enemy returned. Rather than face defeat, the two sisters walked hand in hand out to the point in which the Day and the Red Rivers met. They drowned themselves."

"Now that's the whole story." She stepped toward the water, the compass with her. "Let's see if this thing works."

She held it out as the river rose up over her feet. When it got to her waist, she said, "I can feel their spirits in the water. Harlow's. Nell's. Indigo's. Violet's. I can feel their spirits. They make the river cry now."

She dove under as I shivered in the cold air. When she surfaced, her arms shot up, smacking down on the water.

"Help me, Arc. I can't—" Her head went back under.

I dropped the princess to the bank and ran out into the water, splashing it up as I dove in and wrapped my arms around my sister's thin waist. She was limp in my arms as I swam her to the bank and pulled her from the river.

"Daffy, don't die. Don't leave me."

I gave her mouth-to-mouth, the way I'd seen lifeguards do on a TV show once. As I started pumping on her chest, she laughed.

"I got you, huh?" She laughed louder, stopping when she saw my face. "I'm sorry, Arc. But you see what I mean? You always save me."

I slapped her hard across the face. "That was a stupid thing to do, Daffy."

"The stupid thing was you jumping in after me," she shouted as I tried to cover my ears. "You're gonna have to let me go, Arc. I'm only dragging you down with me. Let me go."

"No, I can't." I got up and ran into the darkness of the trees.

When I was at the edge of the cornfield, I felt her hand in my own. She had put her clothes back on, though she let her chocolate-brown socks drape over her shoulder. She didn't say anything. She just squeezed my hand, and I let her.

Together we walked through the field. We shivered the whole ride home.

Only when we were going inside the house did I suddenly remember. "I left the princess on the riverbank, Daffy."

I started to turn back, but Daffy kept me from it.

"You can't go back, Arc," she said. "No matter how hard we try to hold on to the past, you can't ever get those things back."

She let my hand go as she stepped into the house. Looking once more out on the night, I followed her.

Dear Diary,

Me and Flood have brought our girls home with us. I'm touching heaven, I'm so happy. They'd been living with Momma in her big old farmhouse. No doubt she fed them stories of witches and purple skies, of dreaming of shells and cast-iron skillets and of muddy water. But they don't have to live with her no more, so I can tell them all about purple skies and blue moons myself.

Flood ain't on the stuff no more and I ain't either. I feel really good. I told Flood I feel fancy and lit up. Nice like that.

I'm so happy to have Arc and Daffy, Diary. At first all they did was cry and ask for Momma. I told them I was their momma, but sometimes they still look at me like I'll bite their hands off if given the chance. Sometimes Arc frowns at me so long, I don't think I could ever feel more unloved.

Sometimes I don't think God hears prayers in this wilderness.

Flood got a job at the paper mill, did I tell ya? I hope he keeps this one. I have to watch him closely. I worry he might go back to—(don't wanna say its name and give it power).

I hate how the girls look at me like they don't know me.

I dug a hole in the backyard and put some things in it. A few marbles. A spoon. A hair barrette. I covered them up and told Arc it was a good place to dig. You should have seen her face, Diary. She thought she'd found a buried treasure.

I sat in the grass and held Daffy on my lap while we watched Arc. It was so nice.

I'm scared. I'm scared I might ruin everything.

I brought a dead leaf in on the bottom of my shoe today. I should have looked before I went inside. Arc's the one who saw it. There's bad luck in the house now, we all know it. I'll have to ask Momma for her old glass bell. Fill it with something dark and drink out of it until the devil is banished from our house.

⟶

CHAPTER 43

Whirly, whirl, said the woman as she twirled.
Whirly, whirl, I am but a girl.

—*Daffodil Poet*

I HEARD THE SOUNDS OF HORSES GALLOPING. I COULD SMELL THE
dust being kicked up by their hooves. I felt the touch of their manes
on my cheek. Their heavy breathing on the back of my neck.

The last thing I remembered was being with a man at the Blue
Hour. Daffy had gotten her own john. A familiar one, who liked to
watch her dance. Mine was the type who liked to pee in the corners
of the room and on me, to mark his territory. Pisser John, I named
him.

After the piss and the fuck, I felt light-headed, so I lay back while
he snorted a line and laughed at some late-night comic on the TV.
When I next opened my eyes, I did so to the face of a horse. Her
mane was black, her body was dark brown, her chest was bright white.
She blinked her large eyes at me as she chewed on a mouthful of
grass.

Something slithered across the top of my bare foot. I looked down
and saw the tail end of a garter snake disappearing into the tall weeds.
I was in a field. The unplowed ground rocky beneath me. The land
had once been for corn. I could tell from the random stalks that had
sprouted from old seed. As the horse took a few steps over to grab
some cattails, I saw the land stretched for miles until it met the hills
that rolled behind Mamaw Milkweed's old farmhouse. I was in the
overgrown field Daffy and me used to play in as children.

The house looked as it always had. The same front porch with
its white-painted spandrels. The same wooden shingles. The same

ash-gray roof. Even the same blackbirds perched there. The child wasn't the same, though. A child of short black hair, standing in the mowed yard. She watched me stand and walk across the road, the gravel sticking to my bare feet at the mailbox. When I opened it, I half-expected to find one of Daffy's bulb catalogs, but it was empty.

"Where's your clothes at?" the girl asked in a singsong voice.

I looked down to see I was naked.

The mother came quickly out of the house, drying her hands on a bright blue kitchen towel. "Andie, come here." She waved the blue towel like a flare calling her child in.

As she ran to her mother, I looked around for any sign of Daffy or the truck. There was little there in the comfort of the emptiness of the road, which seemed to lead to nothing in both directions. It was as if there was only that field and the house left in all the world. I tried to find the memory of what had happened between the time I lay on the bed in Pisser John's room and the minute I awoke in the field. But all I could feel was my own flesh shouldering the moment as best I could. I watched the dark brown horse pace in the field, her nostrils flaring.

"Can we help ya with something?" the woman asked.

I knew she was a wire wife, like a screen door, opening and closing a million times before noon. Perfect for an old farmhouse.

"Mamaw Milkweed used to live here," I said, sitting down in the grass. I felt less naked that way.

The woman looked both ways down the road, perhaps just then understanding I was alone.

"Momma." The little girl tugged on her mother's hand. "Look at her eyes. They're pretty like the sky. Pretty like the grass."

The woman turned back to me. "Yes," she said. "I've never seen eyes like yours."

"They're witches' marbles," I told her.

She nodded and held on to the towel with the same forceful grip she had on her child. "Do you need to call someone?"

"My sister." I was peeing in the grass and hoping she wouldn't notice.

"You're welcome to come in," she said.

I used the grass to wipe. When I stood up, I tried to cover myself as best I could with my hands. Once I was on the porch, I stopped to stare back at the horse.

"Is she yours?" I asked the woman.

"Is who mine?"

"That horse in the unfenced field." I pointed. "Won't she run away?"

"What horse?" the woman asked. "Are you okay?"

"I'm sorry I'm naked," I said, turning my eyes down.

"I'll get you something," she said, stepping into the house first.

It had been a world of time since I'd been inside Mamaw Milkweed's old house. The same staircase was there, but gone was the floral wallpaper, replaced by walls painted in a shade of pale blue that made for a young family's nest. The floor had been ripped out as well. Instead of the thin oak boards my sister and I knew, these wider, darker boards smelled like the lemon-scented cleaner the woman had used when she last mopped. In the places on the walls where Mamaw's watercolor pastures and flowers used to hang, there were black-and-white photographs of tall trees. A monochrome reversal of the bright colors Mamaw had lived by.

I wondered if the tortoiseshell barrette Daffy and me had hidden in the scroll vent in the living room was still there, or if the two pink moons we'd drawn on the inside of the bottom kitchen cabinet had been kept safe. It was curious to me that the house could still exist as differently as it was. Before, it had been an old woman's home of doilies and ruffled lampshades that represented her delicate love of moths flying on the porch in the evenings and a sense of worshipping the slightest sign of a good day and night. Though the windows were still in the same place and the rooms had not changed their locations, Mamaw's home of old-time florals had been transformed to a young woman's house of clean, white cotton.

"My mamaw Milkweed used to live here," I said again, if only to remind myself, as the woman wrapped a light blue quilt around me. Her touch was gentle, yet my skin hurt. I felt an ache in my jaw while my skeleton expanded and contracted. I was light-headed and certain I was about to vomit up something that would take away everything nice in that house. I was being pushed through the keyhole and was amazed my skin was still on my bones.

"May I use the bathroom?" I asked, swaying from side to side.

"Sure." The woman tried to steady me. "It's right down the hall, to your right."

"I know where it is," I said.

"I'm sorry. I keep forgetting you know this house." She let me walk on my own.

After I got inside the bathroom, I locked the door and headed straight to the medicine cabinet. There was nothing but poison ivy cream, bandages, and various other ointments you'd take with you on a walk through the woods. There was a bottle of cough syrup pushed in the back. From the label, I saw it had been prescribed for little Andie and her cough last April. I drank the little bit that remained and put it back in its place.

When I closed the cabinet, I stared into the mirror. It had been a long time since I'd really seen myself. The mirror at home was covered in tape from Aunt Clover. Any image reflected in it was blurred and distorted. Now, in the clear mirror that the woman made sure to keep clean, I saw my hair had thinned, like Daffy's. The hue, once a bright red, had dimmed. New scars over old sores tore through my cheeks. I was unlit. My earlier face, forsaken for this new one. I had a sudden hunger to be pretty. To bare a different heart. I felt it would be a miracle to alter the image of myself. The drooping gaze, the unkempt soul, hanging there on my face, so numb.

I laid my head against the bathroom door. When I opened it, a little girl stood on the other side. It was Daffy, as she had been when she was nine years old.

"What are you doing here, Daffy?" I asked her.

She giggled as she skipped off and faded into the wall.

I heard the woman in the kitchen and stared at their family photos framed on the wall as I walked down the hallway. I pushed the corner of the last frame down.

In the kitchen, the daughter was sitting at a plastic child's table beneath the open window. She was coloring in her book.

The mother was standing over her and telling her how nice her art was. "Stay inside the lines now." She patted her daughter on the head. "Good girl."

Unlike the changes in the rest of the house, the kitchen still had its white steel cabinets and its yellow tile, as bright as the center of a daffodil.

"You can use the phone." The woman pointed to the yellow phone that was on the wall by the pantry. I used to reach up to it as a child, twisting the spiraling cord around my tiny fingers.

"I'm surprised to see the kitchen left undone," I said. "You've changed the rest of the house so much."

"We did freshen up the paint job in here." She started to wash the dishes she had left in the sink. "But kitchens are so expensive to knock down and build back up."

She seemed to be tallying the cost in her mind.

"It's on our to-do list, though," she said. "My husband's father got this place as an extra investment property back when it went on the market. Must have been after your mamaw died. It sat empty for so many years. The old man died about a year ago and passed it to my husband. We've been here for about eight months now."

"She was killed," I said as I picked up the phone. "Mamaw Milkweed."

"My God. In this house?" The woman dropped the mug into the water, splashing the front of her pale green dress.

I hesitated answering her. I wanted her to imagine blood on the walls and a skinned body being dragged from room to room.

"No," I finally said, "she was killed in the road. A car hit her."

"I'm sorry." She laid her wet hand on her chest. "Vehicles go by so fast out there. I always tell Andie to never play by the road. Isn't that right, honey?" She turned her gaze on the child, who was coloring with so much pressure, she broke the crayon.

"There used to be yellow curtains." I pointed to the windows where white cotton curtains now blew in the breeze.

"We thought white curtains would freshen up the place," the woman said.

I don't like them, I wanted to tell her, but didn't.

"Well, don't mind me, I'll just be over here." She turned back to the dishes, thankful to have something as simple as soap and water.

As I placed the phone against my ear, I expected to hear Mamaw Milkweed's voice.

"Is that you, Arc? In my kitchen?"

"It's not your kitchen anymore, Mamaw."

"Is it still yellow?"

"Yes, but it's a different yellow. Like the yarn skeins. It's a different dye lot. It looks the same but it's not."

I pressed the buttons to call home. When there was no answer, I hung up.

"My sister's a late sleeper," I said to the woman as she watched me call the number no less than five times. "She never picks up when you need her."

Aunt Clover's voice finally answered. "Who the fuck is this?" she hissed into the phone.

"Thank God." I sighed. "It's me. Arc. I need you to come pick me up."

"Where the hell are ya?"

"Mamaw Milkweed's," I said, looking at the woman. "I mean the house she used to have. Come pick me up." I held my hand over the mouthpiece, whispering, "I'm naked."

The little girl laughed until her mother shushed her with the dish towel.

"What the hell you want me to do about it?" Aunt Clover raised her voice loud enough to be heard around the room. "You got yourself in trouble. Get yourself outta it. You stupid bitch."

"All right, it's time for you to go upstairs." The woman lifted her daughter from the chair.

"Mom, I wanna stay. I like her," the girl said just before her mother carried her from the kitchen.

I could hear them out in the hall. "Get up those steps. Keep walking, young lady. Play in your room until I call for you."

I tightened the quilt around me before the woman came back into the kitchen.

"Please, Aunt Clover," I said. "I need you."

"I can't come get ya," she said. "You took the truck with you, ya dumbass."

"Where's Daffy?" I asked. "Is she there?"

"Fuck you, Arc."

"Can you just come get me?"

She sighed heavily. "I'll see if I can find a ride. Dumb bitches always—"

The line went dead. I hung up and turned to the woman. "My aunt's coming to pick me up."

"Can I make you anything while you wait?" She gestured toward the stove.

"I actually don't feel very good."

"You want something to drink at least?" she asked. "Fresh coffee? Orange juice?"

"I think I'll wait outside on the porch for my aunt."

She nodded, her eyes on the sweat on my forehead.

When I was out on the porch, I flopped down in the swing. I wrung the quilt and bit it so I wouldn't grind my teeth to pieces. I could feel myself getting pushed more and more through the keyhole. I looked out, wishing to see the front of our truck coming down the road. I even imagined the little baggie and needle waiting on the seat for me.

I curled up with a twisting ache in my bones. As I laid my head back, I closed my eyes as the horse across the road in the field kept hers on me.

The dream I fell into was of the river. Violet, Sage Nell, Indigo, and Harlow were on the sandy bank. They were naked, standing in puddles made from their dripping hair. Their blue-green veins glowed beneath their skin. Their mouths were on each of their right knees. I watched as the lips slowly traveled up their legs and across their stomachs. They slid over their breasts and up their necks, finally settling on their faces.

"Hello, Arc," they said at once. Sage Nell's mouth slightly hung toward the right as if it might once again fall down her body.

"Hello," I said.

Violet held her hand up. Brown water poured from the blue vein at her wrist. I stared at the way the water splashed onto the ground. I saw then that they had webbed feet. There, in the stretched and taut skin, were tiny fish and turtles, swimming as if it was where the river had collected on their bodies the most.

I caught sight of a small black spider crawling out between Indigo's legs. I watched him walk across her foot to cast a web over to Harlow.

"Don't let him in," I said to her, but she didn't stop the spider from crawling inside her as Thursday stepped out of the river and joined them.

Her stomach started to grow, expanding bigger and bigger until her skin tore open. What was born from her womb were daffodils. They fell onto the water.

"River Man eats these," I said as I picked up one.

"Don't say anything to anyone," Violet said, every word spilling dirty water from her mouth. "Don't say what you did, Arc."

"I didn't do anything," I said.

"Arc?" Sage Nell said my name.

"Yes." I turned to her.

"We're River Witches now," she said. "We live by the twilight. The water is our magic. We can flood the world if we want. We can drown things, too."

"My great-great–a million greats–mamaw was a witch," I said as I let the daffodil drop back into the water, rising higher and higher.

"We know," Indigo said. "It's why you understand all this shit and blood. You've got magic in you. You can mother claws and move bones. Don't say anything to anyone about what you've done. They won't understand. They'll call you River Man."

More water spilled out of Violet's wrist until it was a flood we were in. As I struggled to stay above the water, Violet said, "Be careful, Arc. There is danger coming. Be careful."

I took one last gulp of air, slipping under as their mouths fell back down to their knees. With the water all around me, I tried to find a way out, but no matter the direction I turned, there was nothing but more of the flood. As it rushed into my mouth, my shoulders shook.

"Excuse me, miss?"

I followed the woman's voice toward the light.

"Hello?" she called. "Please wake up."

When I opened my eyes, she was standing over me. The little girl was behind her, bouncing a ball. The quilt had fallen off me and onto the porch floor. The woman picked it up and tried to wrap it back around me.

"Is my aunt here?" I looked past her, expecting to see the truck in the driveway.

"No," the woman said. "I don't think she's coming. Do you have someone else to call?"

I closed the quilt tighter as I shook my head. The little girl bounced her ball harder.

The woman suddenly turned to her daughter to say, "Don't

bounce the ball so hard, Andie. It'll bounce up into your face. You'll get hurt."

"Sorry, Mom." The girl dropped the ball and ran out to the tire hanging from the large tree in the yard.

"You're a good mom," I said.

"What?" The woman turned back to me.

"I said you're a good mom."

"Oh." She smiled and wrung her hands. "You got any kids, honey?"

"Naw." I coughed until my throat hurt and watched the girl swing on the tire, higher and higher. "I did find a baby in the dirt once. A plastic doll. Its face was caved in on the side. I'd rock it and cradle it. But I lost her. A long time ago. I lost her. Hey," I called to the girl. "You're swinging too high. You'll get hurt."

"Sorry, M—" The girl looked from me to her mother, unsure of who had spoken.

"I can drive you home, sweetie," the woman said, "if you'd like?"

She carefully watched me use the end of the quilt to wipe the sweat from my face as I said, "Okay."

I waited for her to go inside to get the keys. She called her daughter in with her. I heard their whispers inside the house as I looked across the field. The horse was gone. I ran to the edge of the porch and vomited.

"Ready." The woman came through the door, locking it as her daughter held on to her leg.

I wiped my mouth and saw the yellow curtains beneath the woman's arm.

"You still have them?" I asked.

"I boxed them away in the attic," she said. "I could tell they were handmade. I didn't feel right about just throwing them out. Not with the names stitched in the edging."

She let the screen door slam behind her, as she unfolded one of the curtains and showed Daffy's, Aunt Clover's, Mom's, and even my own name embroidered in the fabric.

"Mamaw Milkweed made those," I said, trying to smile.

"You should have them." The woman handed the curtains to me. As she stared at my face, she said, "Maybe I should drive you to the hospital. You look really sick."

I shook my head and took off the quilt. I laid it across the porch swing, then unfolded a curtain panel.

"My mother wore the same thing once when she was a dandelion queen," I said, wrapping the curtain around my body.

The woman held tight to her daughter's hand as they walked down the steps. Her car was parked at the side of the house. A four-door, in the color of coffee. She buckled her daughter in, as I got in the front, immediately rolling the window down.

When the woman slid behind the wheel and started the car, country music shot out from the radio. I grabbed my pounding head and screamed.

"Sorry." She quickly turned the volume down. "I'll need to know where to take you."

Once she pulled out on the road, I gave her directions and watched Mamaw Milkweed's house disappear in the side mirror as I held my face out the window.

"When you smell the paper mill," I said, "you'll know you're getting close." I hunched forward and coughed, hitting my face against the dash. "We live in the shadow of the mill."

"Well." She cleared her throat. "Must be nice getting to see the smoke from the stacks."

She watched me from the corner of her eye, in between checking on her daughter in the rearview mirror.

"It's from the horses underground." I looked out the window to see that the dark brown horse had returned and was galloping beside the car. "The smoke is the dust they kick up."

"Oh, that's a nice thought." She smiled. "Where'd you hear that from?"

"My father," I whispered, pointing her to the street that would take me home.

When I opened the car door, I fell out to the ground, retching.

"Are you okay?" she asked.

"I'm fine." I got up, my legs shaking beneath me.

"Don't forget these." She reached the stack of curtains to me. "You never told me your name?"

"Arcade Doggs." I wiped my face with the curtain lying on the top. "But everyone calls me Arc."

"Take care of yourself, Arc Doggs," she said. "And if you ever want to pay a visit to your grandmother's house in the future, you would be welcome."

The little girl waved goodbye as they pulled out of the drive. I fell down again, finally crawling to the front door. The curtain I was wearing slid off my body and onto the grass.

When I got inside, Aunt Clover was spread out on the sofa.

"I thought you were gonna come pick me up?" I asked.

"Oh, shit." She laughed. "I guess I forgot."

"Is Daffy here?" I pushed her over and fell onto the sofa, reaching for one of the needles on the coffee table.

"Daffy?" Aunt Clover looked from the TV to me. "Naw, she ain't here, Arc. You smell like the river." She reached over and grabbed my hand, holding it against her cold nostrils, flaring like the horse's with every inhale. "You stink of it."

Dear Diary,

It was a really wonderful day with the girls. Flood made us pancakes this morning. It's a Saturday and he got a day off from work.

His clothes stink like the mill. His hair stinks of it. His skin stinks of it. I hate it, but it's good money. I'm scared of what he might buy with it, though. I'm scared of what I might buy with it.

The delicious sin.

We made baloney snowflakes. Daffy laughed and laughed. She's starting to come around. She's calling me Momma now. Daffy gives love a little easier. She don't hold so hard to my mistakes.

Arc is more difficult.

She's a wide eye. She watches everything. She checks mine and Flood's pockets, the inside of our shoes. I caught her going through our dresser drawers, searching.

I don't blame her for not trusting us. She's a smart girl. Too smart.

After the baloney snowflakes, we went for a walk. Flood dropped chicken bones. Told Arc she had "discovered" dinosaur bones. She said they smelled like fried chicken and we laughed and laughed.

I lost my earring on the way back home. We looked for it, but couldn't find it.

I loved that earring. It was shaped like a horse. Flood had given it to me when we first met and he told me there are horses in the ground of Chillicothe, just a running and a running and a running . . .

I wish we lived in a house with our initials monogrammed on the towels and airplane tickets in the drawers and a way to escape each other without leaving.

The mill is good money. I know what he buys with it, though.

CHAPTER 44

I cannot say that today I will not fray.
It is my nature to go away—to go away and stay.

—*Daffodil Poet*

I AM AWARE OF MY SOUL HERE IN THE AFTERLIFE IN WAYS I WAS NOT before. I can see it. I can feel it. I can smell it. I know it swims. I know it flies. I know it is noon and midnight and all the times in between. And what of my sister's soul? All I can say is that I detect it. The way one detects a weak signal coming from somewhere in the distance. A light, flashing in brief intervals that directs me toward no specific course. I am without a compass. Yet haven't I always shared something with my sister? The soul of twins, born the same day in this infinite span. They say a twin knows when their other half is gone. I say the best thing a sister can do is hope she's still here.

I waited all night for Daffy. When she didn't come home the next day, I walked to the Blue Hour. Our truck was parked in its usual spot by the side lot. The keys weren't in the ignition. I found them under the mat in the place we always put them for one another. I ran my fingers over Daffy's rhymes in black marker inside the truck. On the top of the leather seat on the passenger side, I found her newly written words.

I cannot say that today I will not fray. It is my nature to go away—to go away and stay.

The neigh was high and long. I turned to see the dark brown horse galloping down the sidewalk in front of the rooms. Standing in one of the open doors was a john I recognized. The one who liked to watch Daffy dance. He wasn't wearing a shirt. His chest hair was exposed, as wet as the hair on top of his head. He was leaning back against the doorframe, scratching his tattooed arms and watching a group of women across the street. The more he watched the women, the closer his hand got to his open fly.

I slammed the truck door. When he saw me, he grinned.

"Hey, there you are, baby." His voice was aged by the packs of cigarettes he smoked. "Where the hell have you been? When I called ya, you said you were on your way." He opened the door to his room wider. "How about we go in and have some fun?"

I quickly pushed past him and walked into the room. The bed only showed that someone had slept in it. I went into the bathroom. The shower curtain was closed.

"Daffy?" I yanked the plastic curtain back to find nothing but a tub of water.

"I made a hot bath earlier." The john came in behind me. "Cold now."

He pulled up the stopper to let the water drain out. I turned to see a white undershirt soaking in pink water in the sink. When I lifted it up, I saw bloodstains on the front of it.

"Damn nosebleed." He took the shirt from me and pushed it back down.

I headed to the bed where I got down on all fours to look under it. All I found was a couple of dirty needles and cigarette butts with lipstick smears.

"What you looking for, babe?" He leaned down to see under the bed himself, stretching the broken heart tattooed on his back.

"Where's my sister?" I shouted.

"Hell, if I know." He brushed his thin hair over with his hand. "We gonna get this party started or what, Daffy?"

"I'm not Daffy." I searched through the items on the dresser top.

"You sure the fuck look like her." He ate me with his stare. "Same eyes and every—"

"I'm her sister," I said, picking up his camouflage jacket. I checked the pockets but only found a lighter and a candy bar wrapper. "We're twins." I stepped over to the small closet and threw open the door, finding wire hangers swinging on the wooden rod. "I know she was here."

"Hell, she was not," he said.

"She was coming here to see you."

"She never showed up." He reached to get his pack of cigarettes from off the bedside table. As he lit one, he said again, "You look just like her. I wouldn't mind fucking you instead." He reached into his open fly and grabbed himself. "I assume the pussy and price are the same?"

"Where's Daffy?" I pulled the sheets up off the bed, as if she'd left a note for me on the mattress.

"I told ya, honey." He pointed the cigarette at me, the roughness in his voice vaguely human. "Now you gonna play nice?"

I ran into the bathroom again.

"What did I tell you, you little cunt." He grabbed my arm and twisted it behind my back. "She ain't here."

"What have you done to her?" I jerked out of his grip. "You've done something to her, you fucker."

I pushed him back and ran. In the parking lot, I yelled her name. If she was in one of the other rooms, perhaps she'd hear me and come out.

"Daffy? Daffy, where are you?"

Blinds moved in some of the windows. A few people opened their doors just wide enough to peek out, their bloodshot eyes glazed and frightened of the light. Eventually someone called the cops on the woman who was screaming herself hoarse in the parking lot. When the cruiser pulled up beside me, I still didn't stop screaming until the officer approached with his hand on the gun on his hip.

"Just calm down now," he said. When he turned to spit off to the side, I saw the scar on his left cheek that looked like two fishhooks tangled together. The rippling, thick skin was just as I remembered it when I was a kid and he had held me tight in his arms while my father was being carried away beneath a white sheet. I remembered his words, too.

"Give it a few years," he had said all those years ago. *"We'll be arresting this kid for the very same thing."*

I waited for him to recognize my eyes, but he only stared at me in disgust, as if I could never have been a child who had better hopes for herself. Never been the little girl he had held in his arms and told everything would be okay.

"Why the hell you gotta be out here causing problems?" he asked.

Before I could answer, the dispatcher called him on his walkie-talkie.

"I got it handled," he told her. "Just another junkie here at the Blue Hour. Now." He turned back to me. "What's the trouble? Run out of maxi pads?"

"I can't find my sister," I said. "Help me. I can't find her."

"Where'd you see her last?" He looked past me at the vehicle cutting through the parking lot, as if it were more important than me standing with tears in my eyes right in front of him.

"She was coming here to see him." I pointed at the john leaning against the open doorframe of his room. The cigarette glowed red between his lips.

"All right." The officer cleared his throat as he looked up at the blue sky, perhaps thinking it was too nice a day to be in uniform. "I want you to stand right there." He pointed toward his car hood. "Stay put while I have a little chat with him."

I stood against the hood, scratching my arms until I was leaving long red marks. The officer shook his head and cuffed me. He gave me a big push into the back seat of his cruiser. From the window, I watched him and the john chat for what felt like the whole afternoon. They laughed like two old buddies. When the officer was leaving, he even held his hand out for the john to shake. I laid my sweating forehead against the window glass and shouted, "C'mon, man."

As soon as the officer finally came over and opened the door, pulling me to my feet, I asked, "Where's Daffy?"

"You're free to go" was all he said as he removed the handcuffs.

"Wait. What'd he say to you? Where's my sister?"

"He says until you started shouting you weren't Daffy, he thought she was you."

"We're twins," I said. "He's done something with her. I know it."

"Your sister was selling herself, wasn't she?" He sighed as he opened his door.

"What's that matter if she's missing?" I asked.

"It matters because prostitutes ain't expected home by dinnertime, now are they? Maybe she's with another john." He patted his privates, then got into his car. "Give her some time to show up. Hell, maybe she's home right now, showering so she can smell all nice when she next sees ya."

"There's a murderer on the street." I grabbed the top of his car door before he could shut it.

"What murderer?" he asked, as if it had never crossed his mind.

"River Man," I shouted. "The one killing all the women. And now my sister is missing. River Man could have her, and you don't care."

"You wanna remove your hands from my vehicle?"

"I'm trying to get you to take this seriously." I let go of the door. "My sister is missing. You gotta help me. Please."

"She's an adult, right? As old as you, if she's your twin? Well, hell, you look pretty overripe. Let her come home on her own. It's her right to come and go as she pleases. Maybe she's with one of her boyfriends or at a party somewhere that you weren't invited to. I'm sure she'll show up. And by the way. Ain't no River Man killing your kind. It's your own selves."

He stared into my eyes the longest he ever had. A moment of recognition. Somewhere in his mind, he was remembering the little girl I once was.

"Have I seen you before?" he asked.

I shook my head, too ashamed to revisit the past.

He looked away. Maybe it was his own shame as he shut the car door. After he pulled away, I stared at the john. He gave me the middle finger on his way back into his room.

I walked around the Blue Hour for the next several minutes looking for my sister and calling her name.

When I saw the blood-colored van parked on the corner, I stopped. His door was open, but only his leg was out, swinging up and down against the pavement. He turned the volume up louder, Blondie's "One Way or Another" blaring on full blast.

The music suddenly stopped, and the john stuck his head out of the van, staring at me.

" 'I'm gonna get ya, get ya, get ya, get ya,' " he said.

I turned and ran back to my truck, locking the door behind me. Welt was watching from the open door of the maintenance office. He disappeared inside, returning seconds later with a fishing pole over his shoulder. He kept his bare hand in his pocket as he walked toward me. He used the handle of the fishing pole to knock on my window until I rolled it down.

"Give me a ride to the river?" he asked, pulling a small baggie of dope out of his pocket. He laid it in my hand as he said, "I'd like to go fishing."

After he got in the truck, he looked out the window and watched the birds fly in the sky while I got a needle out of my purse and searched for a vein.

"What's that stuff feel like?" he asked, not taking his eyes from the birds.

"It feels like I'm wasting my fucking life," I said, pushing the needle in.

He turned to watch me lick the blood off my arm.

"Where at on the river?" I asked.

"The Distant Mountain," he said.

I pulled onto the road, for a moment forgetting where I was.

"Did you say the Distant Mountain?" I turned to him. "How do you know that name?"

"I heard you and the other women talking about it one time. That is the name, isn't it? Your place at the river?"

I reached for the pack of cigarettes on the dash. Taking one for myself, I offered the pack to him.

"I don't smoke," he said.

"You gave me a cigarette after the john."

"Only part of me smokes," he said. "The bad half. Momma used to say she'd bury it in the basement. She could be indifferent like that."

"Your bad half?"

"I don't wanna talk no more about it. It's what it wants. To be acknowledged. One word is never enough. It desires to be described in great detail, but if I refuse, then all that bad will keep out of sight."

He watched the way the smoke left my lips.

"Don't be scared, Arc," he said. "Don't you know every living creature has a side that's indistinguishable from the darkness? Why else would we make such an effort to smile?"

He himself smiled until his thin lips disappeared.

"Have you seen Daffy?" I asked, trying to keep my fingers on the cigarette from trembling. "She didn't come home last night. I'm worried."

"I heard you calling for her at the Blue Hour. 'Daffy. Daffy.'" He reenacted my screams, but in a hoarse whisper. He fell quiet as he looked down at the writing on the glove compartment. "Daffy write all these things?" he asked.

"Yes," I said.

"Was she a poet?" he asked.

"At home she was."

"Daffy." This time when he said her name, he said it as though he were addressing me. "It might last forever, you know."

"What?" I asked.

"Your sorrow."

When we got to Thursday's trailer, the place was still dark and empty. Her parents had made posters with Thursday's photo on them. They put the posters all over the property. They flapped in the breeze like broken wings.

"That's Thursday's place," I told him.

"I know." He got out of the truck. He put his fishing pole on his shoulder without looking at the trailer and walked quickly to the cornfield.

"You know where she lives? Have you seen her?" I struggled to catch up to him.

"You are unswervingly fearless, Arc Doggs," he said. "Asking about missing women in a time when you don't yet know who has made them go missing. Don't you figure the next person you ask might be River Man?"

"Do you know who that might be?"

"River Man?" His voice deepened. "I suppose he'd be someone who must have been asked, 'Who are you?' Him being River Man is the answer to that question. The bloody and brilliant announcement of identity. The dead women are just what is there when he's allowed to be who he is."

As we entered the woods, I stared at the red leather glove on his left hand. A flying beetle landed on it. I went to touch the beetle, but Welt jerked away as if I were raising my hand to him.

"I wasn't going to hurt you," I said.

He carefully let the beetle crawl from the glove and onto a leaf.

"Each morning when I was a kid," he said, "I would ask the rising sun to bring me a friend for the day. Someone to play with. To share secrets with. Someone who would not turn away from my smile. But no friend came. The loneliness has never left. So now, when someone reaches out to me, I don't ever see the gesture as coming from a friend, because I've never had one."

He walked ahead. When we got to the riverbank, he put his pole among the rocks, and sat down.

"What was it like?" He looked out on the water. "Finding the bodies?"

"It made me unsure," I said.

"Unsure of what?"

"If women ever really outlive men."

"River Man could be a woman," he said. "The devil is in them, too, you know."

"An anger floats in those bodies of the women," I said. "The anger of a man. It's what he gives them before he gives them to the water."

He looked up at the sky so deeply, I thought there must be something there. But all I saw were the clouds.

"The water is as cold as a grave," he said.

When I looked down from the sky, I saw he had removed the glove when I wasn't looking. His bare hand was now hidden in the river. The water was too brown for me to see anything.

"I like to stick my hand into the river from time to time," he said. "You never know who might grab hold, wanting a little help out."

"Have you seen Daffy, Welt?" I asked again.

"I don't believe I have." He began to softly sing, *"'Won't you buy me some flowers, I've no more hours. Buy me some flowers, I've no more hours. I've no more hours. I'm no more.'"*

"Where did you hear that from?" I asked, the river suddenly feeling so close, I was sure my feet were wet.

"I hear all your songs," he said.

I felt certain I'd dreamed of him before. As he was now, kneeling by the river, his hand in the water. Only in the dream, I was running. *Run, Arc, run.*

Hearing Mamaw Milkweed's voice, I ran. The low tree limbs slapped back into my face through the woods. The rocks nearly tripped my feet. The cornfield like a maze, back to the truck. I stole every red light I could as I sped home.

"Daffy?" I threw open the front door. "You here?"

"What's going on?" Aunt Clover came from the bathroom, blood on her fingers.

"Is Daffy home yet?" I asked her.

"Addie?" Aunt Clover stepped back into the bathroom. "You're gonna have to do something about this. It's getting outta hand."

I looked into the bathroom and saw Mom slumped on the toilet, a tissue stuck up her nose, stopping the blood. She had two new black eyes. I found myself wondering what trinket she had stolen from the john who gave them to her.

"She'll show up," Mom said, her voice getting lost at times. "Daffy always comes home with you, Arc."

"This is different," I said, as Aunt Clover put the blood on her white belt.

I wanted to tell her the belt was only for her own blood, not for Mom's, but instead I tore into Daffy's room, looking for something she might have left behind for me to find.

"Well, what's so different this time?" Aunt Clover's voice carried into the room.

"I feel it," I said as I got down on all fours. I knew I wouldn't see Daffy under the bed, but I still looked. I saw only the spiders she'd drawn on the floor as a child.

"What do you feel?" Mom was up from the toilet seat and leaning against the bedroom wall.

"I don't feel her." I stared into my mother's widening eyes. "I don't feel her anymore."

Mom collapsed onto the edge of Daffy's bed and said, "No, not my baby."

"I'm sorry, Momma." I crawled across the floor to her. The brown water of the river was spilling out from between my mother's legs. She splashed her toes in the puddle it made.

"I should have come in here and checked on you more," she said as she rubbed Daffy's pillow. "When you girls had that flu. I should have come in, I should have . . ."

I sat against my mother's legs and laid my head on them.

"Where is she, Arc?" Mom asked, her eyes rolling back. "Where is your sister?" She grabbed the hair on top of my head, nearly tearing it out by the roots. "You fucking bitch, Arc." She let out a scream. "It's your fault. You killed her. I know it."

Dear Diary,

I took the girls down to the river today. The brown water like a wild thing. Daffy loves swimming. She's the fastest fish in the world. That's what Arc says.

Arc pretended to dig the whole time, but really she was watching me. I just kept smiling. I told her I wasn't doing anything bad. I know she didn't believe me.

I hate it, I hate it, I hate it . . .

I took pawpaws to the river with us. The girls like them. Like how they smell like bananas. Like how yellow they are. Arc kept asking me to take off my sweater, but I told her I was cold. She tried to pull up my sleeves, but I pushed her back. I didn't mean to do it so hard.

She threw rocks into the river. The water splashed back on her frown.

Daffy told me she needs more construction paper for her flower bulb catalog. I told her I'd get her some. Remember to get some, Adelyn. Remember. Remember . . .

And some spaghetti sauce for dinner, a loaf of bread, laundry detergent, chocolate for the girls . . . remember, Adelyn. Remember.

Flood got in trouble at the paper mill. They told him if he misses one more day, he's gone. Gone like his smile. Gone like his clean shirts. Gone like him each night.

Remember to pick up some chocolate for the girls. Remember, Adelyn. Remember . . .

CHAPTER 45

Which witch was a snitch?

—*Daffodil Poet*

TITANS WERE THE FIRST GODS OF GREEK MYTHOLOGY. BEFORE THEM, the universe was empty. The emptiness was called chaos. From the chaos, a woman emerged. Gaia. She was the earth. But if you ask me, there wasn't emptiness before the titans. There was a river. There is one here now. It sometimes flows by without me even seeing it. I only know it is there when the horses splash as they gallop. They run so fast, they put a flood at my feet that ripples up to my ankles, like the river I came from. The one I look over my shoulder at and try to see in the distance. But all I see are the bodies, floating facedown toward me.

It had been over a month since Daffy disappeared. Thursday still hadn't been seen either. I drove to Violet's and sat in the truck, thinking if I was there long enough, I might see Thursday and Daffy holding hands and walking down the road like there wasn't anything more to their disappearance than a stroll across the gravel. But the only movement at Violet's was the loose screen door, flapping against the frame in the wind.

The landlord had already cleaned out the trailer and dumped the things he couldn't sell in a pile in the yard to be burned. There were her wooden spoons, clothes that were too stained to save. All the things one accumulates in life before that life accumulates mud. I picked through the items, seeing a dented can of pears, the juice slowly trickling out from under the lid. There was broken glass and cookbooks with their covers smashed in. Beneath the tins of spices, I saw a blue and white paper bag. I pulled it out. *Flour* was written across it in a cursive script that reminded me of the writing in my mother's diary. When I held the bag up, I felt something slide to one side. I reached my hand in. With the last bit of flour, there was a cassette tape in a sandwich baggie.

Written on the white sticker was *For Grassy*. I dropped the tape back into the flour bag and carried it close to me as I left. I found myself driving behind the galloping horse. She led me to the swinging sign, shaped like a skull. Even though it was business hours, the tattoo shop was empty. I walked inside and to the back but found no sign of Highway Man. I stared out the open screen door at the pieces of snakes on the sidewalk. Some had thawed completely, leaving little puddles. I stepped out onto the concrete and picked a rock off the ground. I slipped it into my pocket and went back inside as I called out, "Highway Man? You here?"

In the emptiness, I returned to the front of the shop. The tattoo gun was on the metal tray, filled with blue ink. I picked it up and held it to my forearm. My hand wasn't steady enough, so the tattoo I gave myself had crooked lines. It was no larger than an inch in length. Looking at the bareness of my other arm, I switched hands and gave myself an identical tattoo on that side.

"One, two." I counted the tattoos aloud. "Three, four, five, never die . . ."

Switching hands more than once, I gave myself several small tattoos from my shoulders to my wrists, all of the same image, the blue ink bleeding down my skin.

"What the hell you doing?"

Highway Man stood in the doorway. The little bell ringing above his head.

"Nothing." I laid the tattoo gun down, trying to hide my arms.

He had a sandwich. I recognized the wrapper from the diner a few doors down. He threw it onto the counter.

"This ink ain't free, you know?" He grabbed my arm and smeared the blue color beneath his thumb. "What the fuck are these even supposed to be?"

"Daffodils," I said.

"Daffodils? Anyone ever tell ya, daffodils ain't blue, you stupid whore?"

He stared into my eyes like he was concentrating on something in the distance.

"Let me show you how to do it." He picked up the tattoo gun and pressed the needle into my skin, running it over the crooked lines to straighten them.

As he worked, I stared at the scars pitting his cheeks. "You know when tattooing first started?"

"A long fucking time ago?" he said.

"Yeah," I said, "a long fucking time ago. Thing is, no one knows when that might have been."

He only glanced up at me.

"They found Egyptian mummies," I continued, "with blue tattoo marks under their skin."

He used a tissue to wipe the run of ink.

"A mummy from 700 C.E. was found to have a tattoo of the archangel Michael on her inner thigh," I said. "It's thought she put it between her legs to protect herself."

"From what?" he asked.

"From men trying to take what is simply not theirs."

His brows pulled tightly together as he redrew the daffodil petals. "What you doing here, Arc Doggs?"

"I came to see if you've seen Thursday around."

Before I could say Daffy's name, he laughed so loud, it bounced off the walls.

"Thursday? Thieving whore." His voice deepened. "You'll know when I find her. I'm gonna pitchfork that bitch."

He wiped my skin, counting the daffodils.

"One. Two. A million and three. Why'd you give yourself so many?" he asked.

"Maybe I'll keep getting them," I said, "until the killer is found."

"Then you'll end up covered in more daffodils than your own flesh." He started to make a new one on the back of my right hand.

"You don't think the killer will be found?" I asked, staring at the way he made the daffodil's stem into a needle.

"Naw." He half-smiled when he saw my face. "You think I'm saying that 'cause I am the killer? I hear the word on the street. I know everyone thinks I'm Riiiivvvvver Man." He sang out the word. "It's why you came here, ain't it? To see who I am up close? I'm River Man. I'm River Man. And yet I ain't never been to the fucking river."

He finished the last daffodil, the needle of the syringe making the stem extending up through the petals. After he laid the tattoo gun down, he licked his lips and looked at mine, rubbing his thumb over the lipstick on the bottom half of my mouth.

"You think it's me?" he asked.

"No. You would burn the bodies," I said, "not put them in the river."

"You don't think whoever is killing 'em and dumping their bodies is doing it to be intentional?" he asked. "Don't you know a man knows how to murder a woman by now and let her body be found, only if he wants it to be? Naw, the person doing this, they want the bodies to be seen. Like they're on display. That's why River Man kills them before he puts 'em in the water."

"How do you know they're killed before?" I asked.

"If you die outside of water, Arc Doggs, your lungs are filled with air, which means the body will float until the water fills 'em back up again. River Man wants them to float so they're easier to be found. It's all for looks."

"Like the crowns?" I asked.

"What?"

"The bodies," I said. "The killer gives them each a crown made of twigs and leaves. He puts it on their heads, ties it tight to their hair so the crown won't float off. Because they're queens. That's how I know the killer isn't just a stranger passing through. He's someone who knows us. Knows us as the Chillicothe Queens. Like you."

He touched the tip of my nose with his finger.

"It's an old nose," he said. "Like a woman's from a long time ago. A shape you don't see no more except in one of them old paintings rich people hang on their walls. And your eyes. Blue and green. You got widow eyes."

"I've never been married."

"It ain't about being married, Arc Doggs. It's about losing love to death. You don't have to be married to do something like that." He ran his fingers along my chin line. "It's like seeing everything in reverse. You know how you drive down a road and you think you see a tree in all the ways it is. You see its trunk, its leaves, its branches. Then you put the car in reverse and see the tree on your way going back. It's still the same tree, but it's different. That's what you are when I look at you. The same tree, but different."

He tapped his fingers on my face in a gentle rhythm.

"What do you think about me?" he asked. "Aside from me being River Man."

"I don't think about you."

"Sure you do. You think about the way I punched you in the face that day at Thursday's. The way I scraped the skin off the bottom of her feet. Same as most folks. They think of me and my big bad boots. My tattoo on my chest. The gun in my back pocket. They think just what I want them to. I control the narrative."

He looked over at the upright piano against the wall.

"I once won a bet against a guy who swore I couldn't play that thing," he said.

He walked over and dragged his fingers along the fallboard before lifting it up. He sat down on the bench and played an arrangement that seemed to please him more than it did me.

"Growing up," he said, "we were too poor to afford a piano. Momma taught us to play on her skin. She'd use a black marker and draw the keys of a piano on the length of her arm. Then she'd hold her arm out for me and my brother. She taught us notes and chords and how to play skin as if it was ivory. Little did anyone know that in the trailer they all thought nothing but trash lived, a woman was teaching her two sons how to be more. She's why I turned to tattoos. She showed us that you can draw on your flesh, and it can mean something."

He ran his fingers over the keys, playing them deliberately out of tune.

"She thought it would save me and my brother," he said. "Music."

"Where's your brother at now?" I asked.

"Somewhere in a prison between here and the Mississippi River. He's the nastiest kind of brother, but the best kind, too. He's got what Momma used to call blue devil edges. Means he burns cold. Worst type of person, 'cause the bad they gonna do to you, you don't see coming. It just one day happens, and you're damn near perfect in hurt but not much else."

"What'd he do to get sent to the pen?"

"He ain't no River Man," he said. "Not like me, huh?" He laughed, putting an extra flourish on the high keys. "He got sent in for killing one of his own. One day Daddy said he had a headache. My brother just picked up the shotgun and blew Daddy's head off. After he done it, he said, 'There, now it don't hurt no more.' Daddy didn't see it coming. Momma said my brother had blue devil edges, and she was right."

He stopped playing, the key he ended on, sending a shrill sound through the shop. He rose from the bench and slowly walked back to me, taking off his shirt.

"Momma said something about me, too," he said. "Said I was dipped in evil." He took the cigarette from behind his ear and lit it. "Take your shirt off, Arc. It's time to pay for that ink you got."

When I didn't remove my shirt, he removed it for me, slipping it over my head and dropping it to the floor. Standing in only my bra, I didn't look away from his cold stare as he stepped close enough, his smoke exhaled on my throat. He ran his eyes over my collarbone, along with his fingers. Leaning forward, he kissed the side of my neck, biting it beneath my ear.

He held the glowing end of his cigarette to my bra strap and burned the fabric until it fell down.

"I know why you do it," I said.

He took a long drag on his cigarette. "Do what?"

"Why you break the snakes."

"Tell me, Arc Doggs. Why do I break the snakes?"

"This place wasn't always Chillicothe. It wasn't always Ohio. It belonged to cultures who knew its real name and they dreamed of brown crickets and muddy water. They knew the world is just a snake, eating her own tail. You know this, too, don't you? Heard it whispered in the ripples of blood. You think if you break the world, she's yours. But you're *nothing* but a tin god. And no matter how many times you try to break the world, she will never be yours. She will, until the end of time, belong to only herself. And for every snake you break, one of her sisters takes her place. Do you know anything about sisters, Highway Man? They are a whole hell of a lot stronger than any man, and they will outlive you."

When he smiled, his lips twitched and his eyes hardened with his stare.

"Well, the bitch done got it figured out, huh?" He leaned in closer.

"I know you let my snake out of the freezer." He held the cigarette to my other bra strap long enough to burn my skin beneath. "Don't you know by now, Arc? Nothing gets away from me."

The horse walked up behind him. She stood on her hind legs, raising her front hooves into the air, her mane blowing back.

"You hear me, whore?" He grabbed my chin and jerked it toward him. "Nothing gets away from me. Especially not some prostitute junkie."

I slipped my hand into my pocket, wrapping my fingers around the rock as the horse clacked her hooves against the floor.

"Is that what you said to the other women?" I asked. "Before you put them in the river?"

He smiled just before the rock hit him right where I'd aimed. At the center of his face.

"You fucking cunt." He fell back on his heels, his hands going to his forehead, the blood spilling out over the backs of his fingers. "I'm gonna kill you."

By the time he lunged, I was running out the door, the horse running right beside me, the same frightened look in her eyes as in mine.

Dear Diary

   It's been a while. I . . . I'm sorry I lost tracke of timmme.

   The girls lockd themsefes in Arcs room. Floood banged on the door, but they wouldn't open ittt for him. not even when he started crying.

   He told mi if I luved him, Id do somme with him. he sayed we d only do a litle.

   I hate him. I HATE hiim.

   I took one of Momma's floewr catalogs that Daffy liked so much and ordered one of every bulbe. I put a check in side with it. I hope they send the bulbs before they caxsh it. I already told Dafy the flowers were coming. Arc ruined it. She told daffy I was lieing.

   I called my sister cclo. Clove, Clover . . . Clo.

   I pt some old roots under my bed. Momma alwys said to kep a footing on the ground, one should always selep with roots beneth them. I pulled thm from the backyard. Left the dandelins on the ground. I couldn't rememburr if Momma said to snake the dirt off or not. I left it on.

   Sometimes I think I should just take the girls back to Mommas. She can bee their rootz . . . be their ro . . .

   I'll make them pancakes in the mornin. I promixe.

CHAPTER 46

Listen to the boys play with their toys.
What noise. What noise.

—*Daffodil Poet*

I CATCH GLIMPSES OF MYSELF AS A CHILD HERE. NO TALLER THAN THE wild milkweed I run by between the horses' legs. The deep bellowing hoots of owls. The piercing coyote squeals. The naked screeches from unnamed beasts on their four-legged hunts. I chase myself, trying to catch me. But the child runs fast. I know I will be here in this pursuit for as long as the river flows, in this mess behind heaven. A place that is not blue but is beating and empty. I whisper into the space before me, hoping that in there my voice is not distant to my sister, for her voice is distant to me. Not blue, but beating and empty. Mostly primal droppings. Blood and filth, shit and piss, too. I know I am standing in that which I lived. The end possesses me now. All I can do is speak and hope that my voice is not so distant to her or to the other women who have gone before me.

I tried. Let it be known, I did try to find who killed them. Who would soon kill me. As the cold wind rushed against my face, I stepped close to the edge of the river, through the tall hardened spines of overgrowth. I walked along the edge, looking into the water. I was searching for anything. The Holly Hobbie sweatshirt Daffy was last wearing. Her dirty pink slip. Her body floating on the water. As if it'd be as simple as her swimming laps from one end of the river to the other.

I looked up to see the horse—the color of the socks Daffy had last been wearing—galloping across the overpass. Watching her mane, I climbed back up the bank and got into the truck. As the horse's hooves clacked against the gravel, I looked at the flour bag on the passenger seat.

The horse stayed with me as I drove home. It was the end of November. Frugal in its vanities. Quiet and clear, the clouds not visible against the white sky. The final days of autumn. No more leaves to write sins on. The air colder than it should be. The type of afternoon that reminded me of day-old bread, soft yet starting to get hard around the edges.

Inside the house, Aunt Clover was still sitting on the sofa. Her side of it was lower, the cushion beneath her sunken from the years, like a hole she was falling into. There was a bag of twigs in her lap, but she wasn't sorting through them. She was staring at the TV. For the first time I could remember, it wasn't on. The screen was blank. Without the bright light, I saw how dusty it was, covering the gentle curve of the glass. I wondered how she could have ever seen through the dirt and grime.

"Why aren't you watching one of your travel shows?" I sat down beside her, the flour bag on my lap.

"In the last one, they were in South America," she said. "At the Amazon River. I got scared if I stared at the water long enough, I might see Daffy floating in it."

She slowly looked at me, her eyebrows turned up, making the lines between them deeper.

"You find her yet?" she asked, her tone the softest it'd been in years.

I shook my head.

"I always knew she'd die young," she said. "It was the only fate for her after she broke the hourglass when she was a little girl."

"What hourglass, Aunt Clover?" I asked.

"The one Momma had on her kitchen counter to time her biscuits."

All I could conjure in my mind was the tin of baking powder on the yellow tile of Mamaw Milkweed's counter, the large cream bowl, her wooden spoon, the jar of honey, the can of shortening, measured one teaspoon at a time.

"I remember the biscuits," I said, wiping my nose. "I don't remember no hourglass."

"That's because Daffy broke it." Aunt Clover stared at the floor. "You can't break time and expect to get away with it."

I studied my aunt, a woman who still wore a leopard collar like she had a good story. She no longer feathered her bangs, though. She let them string down into her eyes, which had little color left to them. Her shirts were still low, but her breasts had fallen lower, the cleavage nothing but a deep indentation that ran toward her belly button. The belt she wore looped into her skirts had given the last of its white leather to be the color of her blood, dried brown.

"Aunt Clover? Can I ask you something?"

"Mmm-hmm." She sucked her lips back into her face until they disappeared, her eyes still on the floor.

"Why you put your blood on your belt?"

She took a deep breath as if building the strength to say, "When your skin cracks open, you bleed. Even though I tape the cracks, the blood still comes out. This world has almost bled me dry." She ran the backs of her dirty fingernails up and down her arms. "If I don't keep some blood, I won't have nothing to put back in the cracks. I gotta keep some extra blood on me."

She raised her eyes from the floor.

"Can I ask you something now, Arc? Why you always wet?" She laid her hand on top of my head, her fingers hanging down on my forehead. "Why is your hair always like a wet pile of weeds, and why you always smell like the river?"

"I was looking for Daffy," I said.

She squinted like she was searching for something. "Spittle, spittle . . ." She turned to the bag of twigs. "I'm almost done with it," she said. She quickly looked behind her shoulder, her eyes desperate, like someone had just called her name.

"Almost done with what?" I asked.

"Daffy's wall." She held the last word, her deep tone like an echo. "I just gotta find the final twigs. They have to be perfect. Then I'll be finished. Can I have some of that flour?" She pointed at the bag on my lap.

"Ain't no flour in it," I said.

She rolled her eyes slowly. "Liar, liar, pants on fire," she said, careful to speak each word clearly.

I left my aunt to sort through her twigs and went back out to the truck. Exhausted, I sat for a few minutes, wishing the heater worked well enough to warm my hands at least. I tried to think of all the places Daffy might be. But most of them no longer existed. Mamaw Milkweed's kitchen, our father's lap, the large hole dug in the back of the colonial house we'd found when we were kids. I thought of all the roads we'd walked to get to and from the Blue Hour. Was she there? In the gravel? I thought of every place she'd ever planted a bulb. In the backyard. By the discount store. In the narrow path behind Big Gray. Then I thought of our little apartment. The one we believed would be the start to the rest of our lives. I thought of our small kitchen. Of the cubbyhole we filled with the blue and white dishes.

I put the truck in gear.

On the drive, I kept my eyes out for anyone who looked like Thursday or Daffy. Sometimes I would think I saw them, but whenever I slowed down and saw their faces, they turned out to just be other women on their way to the night.

When I pulled into the grocery store's lot, the horse waited until I parked. She walked into the store with me. As soon as I saw a woman with red hair, I grabbed her by the arm.

"Sorry," I said as she frowned. "I thought you were someone else."

The horse's deep neighs cut through the sound of the shopping cart wheels and the mothers checking off their lists. I got turned around and ended up in the dairy aisle, when I'd been looking for housewares. I finally found it, the dishes in the same place they had been when Daffy and me first saw them. I can't say why I thought I might find her standing there, perhaps one of the blue and white plates in her hand, but I did. When she wasn't, I thought about knocking the whole display down, making a beautiful mess on the floor.

Instead, I picked up a plate and turned it over to the crown stamped on the underside.

"'Maybe we'll get the whole set,'" I repeated Daffy's words, as I put the plate back on the shelf.

I followed the horse, her tail twitching back and forth, flicking out in front of faces that never saw her. I followed her through the aisles but stopped when I saw him by the shelves of canned fruit. He had his back to me and was talking to someone he had to lean down to. He kept tapping his long yellowed fingernails on a can of persimmons.

As I stepped closer, I saw he was talking to a little girl around the age I had been. She had a basketball in her hand. On occasion she bounced it.

"You're good at that," he told her, reaching out and plucking a strand of hair from her head.

"Ow." She touched the place she'd felt the pinch.

As he wrapped the hair around his gold chain, I came up behind him.

"Adding another strand to your web?" I asked.

If he was startled, he didn't show it. He merely turned to me with a grin as the little girl looked into my eyes.

"Who are you here with?" I asked her.

"My mom's waiting for me in the bread aisle," she said. "I'm supposed to get a carton of milk and take it back to her."

"Then you better go on and get it," I told her. "And if you ever see this man again, run away. Run as fast as you can, and tell your mom, your dad, or whoever you have to tell about him. Tell them that he's a spider and that he attacks little girls at night in their beds. And that he'll never stop unless he is stopped." I grabbed the girl by the shoulders and shook her. "If you don't, he'll come for you. He'll come for you."

"What's going on here?"

I turned around to see a woman quickly pushing her cart down the aisle toward us. "What are you doing to my daughter?"

The girl dropped the basketball and ran toward her mother, grabbing onto her and pointing at the spider.

"You fucking bitch." He reached out to grab me, but I ran down the aisle, past the woman and the girl, both staring at the man chasing me. The horse galloped beside me as I ran into the parking lot.

Just before I opened the truck's door, the spider threw me against it.

"You think you can fuck with me?" he shouted. "Think you can follow me?"

"I'm not following you," I shouted back. "I'm looking for them."

"Looking for who?"

"You fucking know who, you bastard. Daffy and Thursday. My sister and my friend."

He forced a smile as he stepped back, waiting for a shopper to pass by to their own car. After they'd gone, he said, "There ain't no one to look for, you dumb whore."

"No one?" I threw open the truck door and reached inside, grabbing the photo of us off the dash. "Her." I pressed my finger over Thursday's face. "And her." I did the same to Daffy's.

He snatched the photo out of my hand. "You wanna know what happened to these women? This is what happened." He tore the photo in half, ripping Violet's face.

"No, don't." I tried to get the photo back, but he held it above his head.

"And this is what happened." He tore the photo again, severing Sage Nell's head from her body. "And this," he said, splitting Daffy into two. "And do you know what?" he asked, tearing the photo again until none of their faces were left whole. "No cars have suddenly squealed their brakes and stopped in shock. People are still walking about. No one is shouting at the top of their lungs. The world is still spinning. Why? Because no one gives a damn what happens to any of these whores. Or to you."

He threw the pieces, scattering them across the asphalt. As they blew in front of the tires of the oncoming traffic, he delivered a punch to my lower gut, causing me to fall to my knees.

"The day I pull you from the river," he said, "ain't a day too soon."

As he turned to walk away, I grabbed the door handle and used the truck to help me stand back up.

"I hate you," I screamed for all the women I'd ever known and jumped onto the spider's back. He spun around, trying to fling me off, but I held tight. When I grabbed his gold chain necklace, he threw his fist back, knocking me in the face. I fell off him but kept hold of his necklace, breaking the latch. I laughed as the chain swung in my tight grip.

"You fucking bitch." He punched me again in the face.

I laughed more, feeling the warm blood on my skin as I ripped strands of the hair from the chain, finally freeing them and releasing them into the wind.

"You won't catch any more butterflies in your web, you son of a bitch." I threw the now bare and broken necklace at his feet. "I'm not scared of you anymore. You hear me? I'm not fucking scared of you."

As shoppers gathered, their carts full of bags of groceries, he smiled at them, running his fingers through his hair until it was carefully combed back.

"Nothing more to see here, folks," he said, showing his badge. "I've got things covered. Just another junkie looking for a high."

He stepped closer to me but kept his smile for the people as he leaned forward and whispered, "You think you can fuck with me? You are nothing, Arc Doggs. Your disappearance has begun."

The horse reared up behind him, her whinnying, sharp and high.

Dear diarey,

Flood's not working at the miillll anymore. Hes not workkig anywere.

I got the girls ready for sckool. I don't know if I can do . . . I dont knowe if I can bee Adelyn anymre. If Im knot her, am i still a mother??

Or am i like a wyld bird now who will fihgt with the snakes

It wasn't supposed to be like this.

I failedd i fall i fall i fall

Theyll always h8te me. arc and daffy. I wish they would've have had a bettter mother than me. I wish they would beleve me whn i tel them I luv them.

CHAPTER 47

I'll leave a note in the back of my throat. You'll know
it's from me, you'll know it's what I wrote.

—*Daffodil Poet*

THERE ARE EXCEPTIONAL DEMONS THAT WAIT FOR US ALL. AN INFI-
nite pulse that insists we float down the river that has been made
for our drowning. In shallow water, rocks mutilate our truths. In the
deeper depths, it is our own dying that forms an opinion of us. I wish
I could vanish from my death. I wish I could run free with the horses
and never again be the daughter of dropped miracles. I wish I could
emerge pretty in a dream that fades away every part of myself I have
ever hated. My mother hates me. My father hates me. My sister hates
me. But the needle loves me.

After I injected, I laid my head back on the truck seat. I don't
know how long I stayed there before I reached into the flour bag,
pulling out the cassette. I dusted it off, then slipped it into the tape
player on the radio. At first, I didn't think the volume was turned up
enough. All I heard was silence. Then Violet. She sang. Lowering and
raising her voice until she started to hum. When she finally spoke,
she said, "Grassy, this is your mother. I hope this recording sounds
good. Not too much static. Um." She cleared her throat and coughed
a couple of times. "I just wanted to tell you how proud of you I am.
I've made enough mistakes in my life than I care to think about, but
you were not one of them. I hope you won't hate me, the older you
get. There's gonna be people who say things about me. They'll call
me names. They'll say the word *addict* a lot, and they'll try to carve
all my offenses into stone. Worst, they'll try to pass that heavy burden
on to you to carry. But I want you to cast that stone away and think
of me always as Mom.

"Some days I might be gone so long that you remember me as just another dream. You might forget all those times we licked the buttercream frosting off the spatula or dyed your doll's hair with grape juice or laughed until we peed our pants." She laughed herself. "The last time we spoke, you told me about how you picked the dandelions. You told me that you wore the flowers in your hair and that your daddy gave you crushed seashells to put around the tomato plants. You said a butterfly came and landed on the back of your hand and you told me you wished I had been there with you. I want you to know, Grassy, that I was there. I was the one who landed on the back of your hand. I saw the wonder of each and every thing you have ever done.

"Life comes with heavy silence at times, baby, and you might be tempted to shut your eyes and be invisible. But I want you to know that you always have a song. It's inside you. You're powerful, you're smart, you're creative, and no one can take those things from you." Violet paused with a sigh. "Listen to your father. I know he can be tough, but he wants the best for you. He's a good man.

"There'll be some things he can't teach you. You just listen to your own song. You'll find your way. Don't let the bad times get you down. You have to have some of those moments where life tells you, it's time to cry. Without those, what would fuel the poets? I want you to look in the mirror every day and remind yourself that you have wings. Sometimes to say you have wings is no lie. It's to say that when you take off, you'll fly. And you are gonna fly a long life and become an old woman whose time has brimmed with fearless magic. I love you so much, Grassy, it hurts. A mother's hands are hourglasses to her children. Our lives fall into yours as we pass the sands of time to you. I give you the grains of my unspent days and enough time to look back on a moment we both remember with love. My destiny was always this, so I have nothing to be sad about. And if anyone asks, my name was Violet. One day, I had been. And now I live with the butterflies who flutter through the meadows, hungry for nectar and nothing more. To be your mother has been the greatest joy of my life. And I want you to know that anytime you see a butterfly, it's me, always with you. How lucky am I?"

Violet sang a few more notes, before the tape went silent. I sat there for several minutes, laying my head against the steering wheel.

After I ejected the tape, I put it back into the bag, and turned the truck's ignition on.

Violet's ex-husband lived in the house they once shared. A brick two-story in Victorian architecture. Garland was recently draped on the white posts of the porch, and the front door had a fresh coat of paint, the color of cranberries.

It was Grassy who answered my knock.

"Who are you?" she asked.

"I'm a friend of your mom's," I said.

"My mom's gone." She looked down. Her hair was in pigtails. The small snowflakes printed on her turtleneck matched the ones on the cuffs of her corduroy pants.

"She left something for you," I said.

"What?" She looked up, her eyes the color of Violet's.

"This." I handed over the flour bag.

She pulled out the cassette.

Just then her father came, draping a dish towel over his shoulder. "What is this?" he asked, taking the cassette from her.

"Violet left it," I said.

Grassy reached into the bag and pulled out the photo of herself and her mother.

"I didn't realize she'd put that back in there," I said, smiling. "Keep that photo safe, Grassy. Don't let anyone tear it up."

"No one would tear up a photo of my mom," Grassy said, holding it tight. "The world would stop spinning."

She didn't miss a second taking the cassette back from her father. "Daddy? Can I listen to it?"

"Yeah," he said. "Why don't you go on into the living room and put it in the player?"

She ran off down the hall.

Before she disappeared, he added, "Don't start it until I'm in there."

She said okay, but I had a feeling she'd press play as soon as she could.

"Thank you for bringing the tape by," he said, turning to me. "Violet would have appreciated it." He wiped his mouth softly with the backs of his fingers. "I always thought with enough patience,

Violet would make it, you know? That she'd come back home and everything would be the way it was before."

I noticed he was still wearing his wedding ring. He twisted it around his finger as we listened to the sound of Violet's voice fill the house. Grassy had turned up the volume as loud as it could go.

"It's a beautiful war, isn't it?" He looked up at me.

"What is?" I asked.

"Life." He grabbed the doorknob. "She cared a great deal for you women on the street. I hope you can do what she couldn't. I hope you can find your way out."

He closed the door. The wreath on it swung, then fell still.

Dear Diery,

    I'm srry Daffy. I'm sorry, Arc.
    I thought about giving theme back to Moma. They loove her. not me. but I think if they se everything it does. Everthing it takes away, theyll know they dont wanna this life for themselves. I don't want to send themm away and they think I abadoned them for something realy great. When its shit. Its all shit.
    They need to see it so they kno not to do it themselves. I'm skared. I'm scared theyll be liike me and flood.
    I wouldn't be able to live with miself if they livvved with the nedle. Not my gurls. Not my babyies. I lo . . . I love them.

CHAPTER 48

Bless this mess.

—*Daffodil Poet*

EVEN HERE, PUSHING AGAINST THE NEBULOUS TIDE, I FEEL AS IF I AM in Chillicothe. I am only looking at it from a different angle. The hills that bear a second look from this perspective. They seem to be merely land that is floating, sailing with the fumes from the paper mill that billow up toward the sky like a feather of the morning.

Hold down the kingdom and spin for miles, the angels here sing. Or maybe they are demons in broken halos. Am I in heaven? Or am I in hell? I can only go by the sins of my earthly life. Were they sins I had? I recall thinking I'd prayed long enough to be forgiven. Forgiven for the lie, the truth, and forgiven for the cold.

Winter in Chillicothe, Ohio, was a gray sky. It was a bare branch. It was a freeze on the windowpane. A collection of snowflakes that melt too soon in the hand.

The first snow of that last winter, I drove to Thursday's trailer for the final time. I planned to use the orange marker in my pocket and draw a fire. It was something Mamaw Milkweed once said to do.

"When you feel like you're on fire," she'd said, "draw one on the wall in between the windows facing east. Draw the flames tall and open the windows to let out the smoke. Your house will be on fire, but will not burn down. The blaze will rage, but you will not. Whatever had tried to burn you down, will have only burned you up onto your feet. And a woman on both of her feet has inherited the ancient hope that all will be okay."

I knew after I drew the fire, I would go to the Distant Mountain, stand on its peak, and scream the names of all the women I have known in my life.

But when I got close to the trailer, I saw a figure sitting on the bottom porch step. She was hunched, the snow falling on her back.

"Daffy?"

I held my foot down on the accelerator, the windshield wipers kicking the flurries to either side. By the time I pulled into the gravel drive, I knew the woman wasn't my sister. She wasn't the shadow of the roof, even though she sat as still as it. She wasn't a drift of the snow, no matter how cold she looked. She wasn't a missing woman, and yet she was missing something. The daughter she hoped would come back to her. I hadn't seen Thursday's mom since I'd passed her on the street where she was putting more posters up with Thursday's face on them.

"Sometimes I think this winter is the coldest it'll ever be," I said to her once I was out of the truck. I stared up at the snowflakes. "Thursday always said whenever a bracelet or a ring or a necklace broke in the world, the broken pieces would lift up into the sky and become snow the first chance they got, so they could be something falling but still beautiful."

Her mom didn't take her eyes off the poster of the Monarch butterfly she was holding.

"I tore it by accident," she said, "when I was getting it off the wall." She ran her finger over the new tear on the left wing, as if she thought she could glue it with her flesh alone. "Do you think Thursday will ever forgive me, Arc?"

When she looked up, her eyes brought the ache in her voice with them.

"She'll forgive you." I sat down on the step beside her. "The wings were already torn."

"But this tear is what I made," she said. "It's the biggest one of all."

The front door was open. I could hear things clattering inside.

"Is that her dad in there?" I asked.

"We're moving her things out," she said. "Taking them home so they'll be safe." She wiped the snowflakes off the poster. "I'll put this up on her bedroom wall. She can see it when she comes back home. Why are you here, Arc?"

"When I was a little girl, my mamaw Milkweed told me that when-

ever I felt the world was burning too much of me away, to draw a fire
on the wall and claim the flames for myself. I figured I'd come here
for Thursday, find her windows facing east, and claim them for her
so maybe she wouldn't burn."

"But it's not a fire taking the women," she said. "It's a river."

"Drowning is just another way to burn us," I said.

Clear snot was running out of her nose, over her lips. She didn't
try to wipe it away.

"There's something inside I think you'd like to have," she said.

She stepped into the trailer for a moment. When she returned she
had the photo of the group of us that had sat on Thursday's shelf. It
had been removed from the frame.

"Thursday would want you to have this," she said, sitting back
down and handing the photo to me.

"Thank you." I tucked the photo inside my coat to keep the snow
from getting on it.

"Have you heard anything?" she asked. "Who might have taken
her?"

"There's rumors," I said. "The same ones you hear about River
Man. But I haven't met anyone who can say who he actually is."

"I call the cops every day," she said. "They say she's with a dealer
or a john, like she deserves to be lost. They act like I'm taking up
their precious time. Like I'm calling in about a lost sock. Something
as replaceable as that." She laid the butterfly poster on top of her
knees, then used both hands to rub her face. I knew she hadn't slept
in some time. "Did they question you about her, Arc?"

I shook my head.

"See?" she said. "They don't talk to her friends. Don't try to find
any witnesses. To them she doesn't matter. A rock. A stick. A pile of
dirt. What do they all have in common, Arc? I'll tell you what they
have in common. The police don't look for them when they go missing. Women like my daughter. Like you. You are a rock. A stick. A
pile of dirt. And you are allowed to disappear as if you never even
had a name. But she has a name. They refuse to say it, so I'll have to
say it for them. Thursday, Thursday, Thursday." She cried out her
daughter's name until she went hoarse. "I wish they knew how hard
it is to love a child you can't find. You love her for everything she
was. Everything she wasn't. Everything she might never get to be."

She looked out at the barren cornfield across the road.

"I keep waiting for it," she said. "The call telling me they've found my baby's body in the cold river. I don't know if it's best to know she's dead, or have hope she still lives. That she went off someplace. That she's happy. Sometimes I imagine she didn't lose the baby and that she had a little girl. If I shut my eyes tight enough." She did so until her eyelashes disappeared. "Then I can imagine the two of them surviving this."

She reached in under the poster and pulled out a used needle.

"Just when you think you cleaned up the last one," she said, "you find you haven't. I keep thinking about what it was I did that made her turn to this life. Then I think, maybe it was something I didn't do. Maybe I didn't love her enough or say the right words, or I wasn't quiet when I should have been or loud when I needed to be. It's like something burnt in my mouth. Everything I eat, tastes of it. Everything I smell, smells of it."

"It wasn't your fault," I said.

She studied my face in a way it hadn't been for a long time. Tenderly.

"You don't blame your mother?" she asked.

My eyes gave something away, and she closed hers.

"It's always the mother who has the reasons inside her hands," she said. "You know what I keep thinking about? When she was a little girl, she'd take my hands and hold them up to her eyes. She'd look through my fingers and say, 'You're the best telescope in the world, Mommy.' I don't know when that stopped being true." She opened her eyes and looked down at her shirt. "Now I only wear her favorite color."

"Midnight blue," I said.

She nodded. "I got it in my head, if I wore her favorite color all the time, maybe I could become her favorite thing."

I took the needle from her while she quietly cried. As I turned it over in my hand and stared at it, I said, "The first hypodermic needle was invented in 1853. The persisting story in the annals of history is that the wife of the man who invented it, died of the first injected drug overdose. Some say this is a myth and that it's better truth to say the woman outlived her husband in ways that make her ordinary and sober. I wanna believe her addict death was only a figment, something to romance still waters, that she was no junkie after all, but a woman who had survived long enough to prove she had her own life to live."

The tears were warm on my cold cheeks.

"Oh, Arc." She reached for me, but I jerked back. "It's okay," she said, gathering me in her arms. "It's okay, honey."

I let her lay my head on her chest and hold me tight as I looked up at the snow, trying to remember the feeling of my own mother's arms around me. I could not.

"It's okay. *Shhh*." She stroked my face.

"I gotta go." I pushed away and ran toward the truck.

"Please stay, Arc. Stay. It's not safe out there. Stop."

But I didn't. I got in the truck and pulled out so fast, it slid sideways. Straightening the wheels, I looked one last time in the rearview mirror. She was standing in the middle of the road, her arms waving in the air, her voice telling me to come back. It felt nice to have a mother calling me home, even if she wasn't mine.

The horse ran alongside the truck as I recited the rhymes Daffy had written across the steering wheel and turned into the Blue Hour. I reused Thursday's needle as I watched women go in and out of rooms, their eyes as vacant as mine. The snow fell harder, landing on their shoulders and on the back of Welt as he pushed his cart inside the maintenance office and disappeared.

I found the door unlocked. The light at the front of the room was off, but there was one on in the back. I stepped softly. Peeking between some sheets on a shelf, I saw Welt sitting at the small table pushed against the back wall. He had a thick book opened and was reading aloud. Off to the side, I saw the red glove lying on the tabletop. I followed the light until I could see the white pages, his bare hand marking the lines he was reading.

The hand was not disfigured or scarred or artificial. The fingernails were not broken or cracked or as yellow as the rumors. They were, however, long and painted red. A gold bracelet hung from his large-knuckled wrist, the charms sliding across the page. For all the frightening things I had expected, it was nothing of the sort. It was merely a hand.

Beside him, the TV was on but muted. More of his homemade

videos. This time I knew the woman on the screen. Thursday. She had been filmed sitting on the curb, hiding her face in her folded arms, her shoulders shaking. The next scene was of Sage Nell wiping her cheeks and standing outside one of the rooms. He filmed Violet leaning against the brick wall. She raised her eyes to peer off into the distance, her tears making her cheeks shine. When I saw Indigo, she was walking to her car. Unlike the others, she was not crying. She was leaving. But she stopped suddenly. When she turned and spotted the camera, she stared directly into it before the scene cut to a black-and-white movie, the actress crying until her mascara ran.

As I took another step, I slid my hand down the shelf, accidentally knocking over a can of moth balls. I tried to catch it, but it hit the floor with a loud rattling sound.

Welt shot up from his chair. He lunged toward me and grabbed my arm before I could move.

"Wander in the wilderness where there is no way," he echoed the Bible.

"Let me go." I tried to pull out of his grip tightening on my arm. "Let me go, Welt."

"Do you think there are ever ordinary journeys, Arc?" he asked. "Or do you think each one is as dazzling as a comet blazing across the sky? I believe our paths have crossed for a reason."

"And what reason is that, Welt?"

"So we can remember our humanity, Arc." He let my arm go and stood back.

When he saw me staring at his bare hand, he stared down at it, too.

"It's my mother's hand," he said. "It's the last thing she gave me before she went away." He shook his wrist so the charms on his bracelet jingled. "Her angels. They're all here. To guide me through the mist."

Each charm was an angelic figure, their wings ready to fly, their eyes closed.

"She loved reading old-time lines." He looked down at the Bible. After he closed it, he ran his fingers over the gold lettering.

I saw the skin on his mother's hand was softer than his other. As if under the glove, he had layered it with heavy moisturizer. It did not smell of the disinfectants he used in the rooms of the Blue Hour but rather of perfume. The type of perfume that is darkly colored in the bottle and as sharp as a creak in an old farmhouse floor.

He had shaved the backs of his fingers and trimmed his nails. He moved the hand softly, the way a mother would. Ever so gently with the palm open, while his other was clenched into a fist.

I looked over his shoulder at the TV screen, now seeing myself. He had filmed me with my arms wrapped around my stomach. He had zoomed the camera in on my face and the way my tears mixed with the blood running from my nose. With his mother's hand, he grabbed the remote and turned up the volume so I could hear the sounds of cars passing me on the street. Of women talking and laughing in the background. I heard his breathing. I heard the rippling of my cries.

"I told you I was a collector of tears," he said. "There's a lot to collect in a place like this. So many in fact, I fear there are too many rivers in the world."

I took a step back, knocking into a small cabinet.

"Are you afraid, Arc?" he asked. "You shouldn't be." He looked down at his hand. "Mother wouldn't want me to hurt you. She likes you."

I tried to find something inside the cabinet like a crowbar or a hammer. The best I came across was a large plastic bag of the tiny bar soap he put in the bathrooms. I grabbed the bag and swung it toward him, shouting, "Stay away from me."

"You don't think . . ." He took a step. "I'm not going to hurt you. I haven't hurt anyone."

"I said stay back." I swung the bag and hit him in the side.

He only kept his face turned, laying his mother's hand on the edge of a table.

"I saved you," he said. "Or have you forgotten?"

"Maybe you only saved me so you could hurt me. You said yourself, you're a collector of tears."

"Yes." He raised his voice. "So women like you know someone else has seen them in a world where few people do. I may bring shadows with me into a room. I may bring whispers at my back. People who say I'm weird or odd or plain stupid. But I'm smart enough to know that here at the Blue Hour, the women have all turned into sugarcane, to be cut down and fed to the next hungry man. So what if I try to collect something from them so it's not devoured, too?"

He looked at me a moment longer, then turned away.

"How else should I live?" he asked. "I am only me. I'm glad I have my collection, because I don't have much else. And I do not love the river enough to lay my dead down in it. Water is no place for a man with a concrete heart. I'd sink before I ever made it back out."

He faced me and wiped his own tears.

"Before you go, take this." He reached down to the floor and pulled a purse from the shadow of a table's legs. The fake brown leather was peeling from the strap and the flap hung open and loose in a way that Thursday had always complained about.

"She left it in one of the rooms," he said, holding it toward me. "I want you to have it. I think you can use what's inside."

"Thursday wouldn't have left her purse," I said.

"You women leave so much behind, it's a wonder you've still got your skin."

I reached out and grabbed the strap.

He stared at me, before holding his hand to his ear. "What's that, Mother?"

As he listened, he closed his eyes while his lips moved in whispers.

"Mother says she's sorry about all your friends," he said, opening his eyes. "She loved them, too."

I dropped the bag of soap and ran, pushing open the door and racing to the truck. I threw Thursday's purse onto the seat and started the engine. I nearly hit another car as I pulled out onto the road.

On the drive home, I kept seeing the videos of us all play in my head. I thought of Welt holding our tears as if they were something solid, like clear rocks he could pick up from the ground after they'd fallen from our eyes, and pass from hand to hand, measuring the weight of each against another. Would Violet's tears weigh less than Sage Nell's? Would the edge of mine be rough or smooth? Would they be judged against our hearts? Would they be as cool to the touch as the waters of the river? Did the man who collected them know a woman's tears can never truly be owned?

As I drove past the paper mill and got closer to home, the approaching house had never looked so beautiful to my tired eyes. After I parked, I sat in the silence. The flurries fell so heavy, they began to cover the windshield. I opened Thursday's purse. There was a half-eaten candy bar. An old shopping list that had the things on it she wanted to buy for her baby. In the bottom, the used needles piled up. There was nothing that told of where she might be. Of what might have happened. There was, however, a brown paper bag. It'd been opened, but Welt hadn't touched the wad of money, except maybe to count all five thousand of it.

"Shit, Thursday."

I reached inside my coat and took out the photo her Mom had given me. I placed it on the dash where the old photo once rested. Then I wrapped the brown bag back up and carried her purse inside to Daffy's bedroom. The bulb catalog she had made as a child was on the top shelf of her closet. I took the money out and laid the bills flat inside it. After I put the catalog back on the shelf, I made sure to turn out the light. I knew no one else in the house would look inside the pages of what had once been a little girl's dreams.

dear diary,

Ark is angree with me.

She foud my hiding placx. She brok the needle told me she wished I would goo away. I slaped her. I tried to tell her I was sory, but she strikes like lightning.

I had a drem of a treee. I took a knife to its barke and cut it away. But it wasn't the bark I was cuting. It was my own skkin.

I wish I could give arc eveything she wanted. But what she wants is someting I can't giv her. I cant even give it to myselv.

Sometimes I thik I gave birth to a knife and she cuts me, cutts me, cus me, deep, deep, deepp.

My daughter hates mee, but the nedle loves me.

My dauhter hates me,
but the needle, she loves me.

CHAPTER 49

Even death settles in the fresh flower petals.

—*Daffodil Poet*

I DREAMED OF THE LAND AS A GRAY PLACE. EVERY BLADE OF GRASS, every beetle, every crumb of dirt beneath my bare feet was gray. The trees were leafless. The grass was flattened as if something heavy had rolled over it. As I approached the hill in the distance, I saw that the trees were being pulled in toward the center until they snapped and lay fallen on the ground. I stared up at the only tree left standing. A tree that had a big, thick snake wrapped around its bark.

"Devil's decay," Daffy said.

She was standing in a gray ratty dress that fell just above her reddened knees. For all the thought I had in my dream, I was certain our mother had made my sister the dress. It was too tattered and poorly to have come from anyone else. I looked down and realized I was wearing the very same thing.

"We're the Grey Sisters," Daffy said. She reached into her mouth and tore a tooth out with her bare hands. With blood spilling over her lips, she handed the tooth to me. As I placed it in my mouth, she removed her right eye.

"You're missing yours," she said. She placed the eye into my empty socket, then stood before me, one eye blind and one tooth gone.

"It's your turn to have them," she said. "Maybe now you'll finally be able to see the truth. Open your eyes, Arc. Open your mouth. Speak the truth."

She walked away as I saw our house in the middle of a field. Insects buzzed by me. Flies, beetles, spiders, all things that crawl or creep. They flew past in a straight shot toward the house, where they smacked against the sides and the roof as if there were a magnetic force there.

Following the insects was a great swarm of larger creatures. Squirrels, frogs, raccoons, and opossums. Birds were being yanked down from the sky. Deer were flying sideways until the whole house was covered. As I walked up onto the porch, on steps covered in screeching beetles and centipedes, I looked inside the open doorway. My mother, aunt, and sister were sweeping up shards of something broken. After Mom used a dustpan to collect the pieces, I watched the women in my life glue them into cups, plates, and bowls. But they were not just pieces of porcelain or glass or ceramic pottery. They were pieces of our faces. And once they placed the last dish on the shelf, our faces broke all over again, to the floor.

"The devil's decay," Daffy said.

With the tooth my sister gave me, I began to eat the animals off the house. They screamed, but I ate them anyway, until what remained was a single bird, flapping her one good wing against the ground. I ate her, too, my dress drenched in the blood.

I could taste the dream in the back of my throat when I woke. I carried it with me as I drove to John Theresa's cabin and stood outside it the next morning with a shovel in my hand. I thought of Daffy's words in the dream and knew I was soon to speak the truth. As I heard the violin play from inside the cabin, I went around to the backyard and dug the hole as deep as I could without falling in. Inside it, I laid down the yellow curtains Mamaw Milkweed had sewn all those years ago. With them, I buried the windows they did not hang on. The father who never came back. The mother who left her daughters abandoned just outside her bedroom door.

I screamed and caught my screams with my hands, laying them down upon the curtains. I cried, then caught my cries with my hands, laying them down upon the screams and the curtains. I roared and caught my roars with my hands, laying them down upon the screams and the cries and the curtains.

"What are you doing?"

I looked up at the sound of John Theresa's voice, the violin in his hand at his side.

"I'm having a funeral for my dreams," I said.

He looked down in the hole. "What is that yellow fabric?"

"Something my mamaw made a long time ago."

"I thought you said it was a funeral for your dreams," he said. "Are those your dreams?"

"What is a dream," I said, "but something the women before us have made?"

He watched me shovel the dirt in. "Why would you have a funeral for your dreams?"

"They were all of a dead girl," I said. "I figured I should bury them as deep as her. Maybe then I'll get to resurrect a chance."

"A chance to do what?" he asked.

"To live." I laid the shovel down and walked on top of the grave until the dirt was flattened. Then I headed up the porch steps, past John and into his cabin. I stared at the open jars on the table. The muddy water inside was full of floating insects.

John came in behind me and watched as I opened the cabinet and took down the small drinking glass. The pieces of paper were still inside. I sorted through them and dumped the new pieces onto the table, spreading them out. They all had the women's names written on them.

"Violet. Thursday. Indigo. Why are their names in your glass?" I asked.

"They were my friends, too," he said. "Friends are a reason not to drink."

I stepped closer to him, holding his hand open so I could run my finger over each of the antennas of the butterfly tattooed on his palm.

"Harlow. Sage Nell. Violet. Indigo. Thursday." I let their names linger. "A butterfly's antenna for each of them."

"And what about this extra one?" he asked. "If you're proposing I'm River Man, keeping track of my victims, why do I have one antenna more?"

"Maybe it's for a woman you killed a long time ago," I said. "Or for the one yet to be killed."

"You mean like you?"

"Whose blood was on your shirt that night at the Big Gray, John?"

He looked up at the small orange beetle with black spots flying around the ceiling light. When she landed on the counter, he caught her.

"These things try to hide in a house in winter," he said. "Try to hide in the warmth." He opened his hand over one of the jars, dropping the beetle in. When I tried to get her out, he grabbed me, pinning my arms as the beetle struggled in the water. He shoved me against the table. I pushed forward, trying to make the table rock enough to turn the jar over and spill out, but it only wobbled enough to clack the jars against one another.

"You're killing her." I watched the beetle try to climb onto the edge of the glass. "Stop, you're killing her."

"She's just a bug. She doesn't matter." He breathed harder, then I heard the clack of hooves out on the porch.

I saw the horse standing in the open doorway. As she raised her leg, I raised mine and kicked John. The arms he had tightened around me loosened. Entangling my mane with the horse's, I pushed him down to the floor and made sure he didn't get back up. I remembered, and I punched for those memories. I felt, and I punched for those feelings. My fists were my hooves stampeding him into the ground. Not just him but all those who had tried to hold me down.

Somewhere I could hear the breathing in the rooms at the Blue Hour. The harsh breaths of the johns waiting for what their money could buy. The frightened breaths of the women shielding their faces from what money can buy. I tasted their cries on my lips. The taste of rust, fire, and smoke. I blew it out my nostrils as flared as the horse's behind me. She neighed and I opened my hands, no longer full of all that I once carried.

I stood up from John. He had shielded his face best he could, but he still came away with a busted nose, like the ones I had. His lip was cut, the way mine had been. His eyes would soon be blackened, as dark as the bruises I have known. I wished the wounds I gave him to be the last open wounds in the world, but I knew they would only be for the second it took another man to raise his fist.

As John pulled a handkerchief out of his pocket and held it to his nose, he lifted himself up into a chair at the table. His heavy breaths settled in his shoulders as he stared down at the jars, the beetle long since drowned. I took her body out of the water and laid her in my palm.

He coughed into the handkerchief, spattering more of his blood on it.

"I had a feeling the moment I met you," he said, "that you'd one day kick the shit out of me."

I sat down in the chair on the other side of the table and stared at the beetle.

"You haven't just come here for my blood. Why are you here, Arc?"

"Have you seen Thursday?" I gently nudged the beetle's body with my finger.

"I haven't," he said.

"Have you seen Daffy?"

In the silence, I looked up into his eyes.

"I never saw Daffy, Arc."

"You met her at our house," I said. "When you came to say sorry about killing Mamaw Milkweed. Remember?"

"Yes." He nodded. "But I never saw her after that."

"You saw her at Big Gray." I nudged the beetle harder. "You saw her swimming."

"I saw you." He lowered the handkerchief, letting the blood drip down over his lips.

"We're twins," I said, the words played so many times over, they barely had meaning anymore.

"That's true. But the only Dogg girl I saw at Big Gray was you."

"How do you know?" I asked.

"I didn't," he said. "Not at the start. But then I remembered when I first met the two of you at your house. I remembered your right eye was blue and Daffy's was green. Every time I saw Daffy at Big Gray, the eyes were wrong. Her right eye was blue like yours. Just like here when you came to the Evergreen Daughters. I heard you with the other women. Heard the way you said you were Daffy at times, but the eyes were as wrong as they'd been back at Big Gray. It was only ever you. So where is Daffy, Arc? What have you done to her?"

I nudged the beetle until she started to move her tiny legs. Her antennae flickered. She opened her wings. She'd only been pretending to be dead.

"What do you think I've done to her?" I held my hand up and let the beetle fly out. I watched her go around the room, but when I lowered my eyes back to my hand, I discovered the beetle was still dead after all.

"Where is your sister, Arc?" he asked.

"She's in the river," I said. "Has been ever since she was nine years old."

Dear diary

*I havn't written t you ina long time. The yaers . . . theyve hurrt.
Evry part of myself, Ive hated more and more.*
I just wanted to telle you, Daffy got sicke.
*I hate this place. I hate this life. I hte how easly little girls can cry
and cough and . . .*
I just wantd to tell you. daffy got the flu.
She's dead.

Lightning bug, lightning bug you are my drug.
By this time tonight, I will be loved.

—*Daffodil Poet*

1981

THE FLU. IT'S A KILLER. KILLED SEVERAL FOLKS IN CHILLICOTHE, OHIO, that year. Including my nine-year-old sister Farren Doggs. Better known as Daffodil Poet.

I'm gonna be a queen. I'm gonna be a queen and be seen.

I thought that by making myself sick, too, I could save her. Together we would fight the monster and win. No matter how much I wanted that, it did not happen. As we lay in bed, I shook her so hard, I banged her head against the headboard. She would not open her eyes.

"Daffy, please. Please wake up. Mom. Momma?" I shouted for her.

It was Aunt Clover who came into the room. "What's going on?" She stumbled and fell against the doorframe.

"Daffy won't wake up. Help me. Make her wake up." I kept shaking my sister. Her lips were blue. "Make her wake up, Aunt Clover."

"Let me see." Aunt Clover pushed me over, turning on the lamp. "Oh, my God." She grabbed her mouth and fell back onto the floor. "Arc." She grabbed my arm and pulled me into her. "Get out of the bed."

She wrapped her arms around me tight as she rocked us back and forth and muttered, "What do we do? What do we do?" I stared at Daffy's limp arm hanging off the side of the bed.

"What's all the crying about?" Mom stood in the doorway, wiping her eyes.

It took her a moment to see Daffy.

"What happened? What happened to my baby?" She crawled onto the bed, grabbing Daffy up. Her head fell limp over Mom's arm.

"What'd you do, Arc?" She turned to me. "What'd you do to her, you little bitch?"

"I didn't do nothing," I screamed back.

"My baby." Mom lifted Daffy's head and tried to get it to stay up. "Maybe she's got something caught in her mouth. In the back of her throat."

She put her fingers inside Daffy's mouth.

"Addie, stop." Aunt Clover pushed me out of her arms and stood up. "Stop it. There ain't nothing in her mouth."

"They're gonna take me away, Clover." Mom looked up at her sister. "They'll say I'm a terrible mother."

As Aunt Clover grabbed Mom, she let go of Daffy. She rolled off the bed and hit the floor with a thump.

I crawled over to her side and lay down to face her. "It's gonna be okay, Daffy," I whispered.

Aunt Clover kept her arms wrapped around Mom. Together they walked out into the hall. I heard them whispering as I pulled the blanket down off the bed and laid it over Daffy.

"So you're not cold," I told her, moving her hair out of her eyes. "Everything is gonna be fine, Daffy. You're just a little sleepy. When you get up, I'll make us hot chocolate like on the commercials. We'll laugh and fill a bowl with water. Mamaw Milkweed will talk to us in the ripples. So will Daddy and he'll tell you all his best jokes. Every-thing will be okay from now on. I promise."

When Aunt Clover came back, she did so alone.

"Get up, Arc," Aunt Clover said as she started to strip the sheet off Daffy's bed.

"What you doing?" I asked.

"Just help me." She bundled the sheet against her chest as she carried it over, dropping it to the floor at Daffy's feet. "Help me wrap her up."

"No."

"Arc." She grasped my shoulders. "We have to protect your mother. Do you hear me?"

"No." I stepped back out of her hands. "We've got to take Daffy to a doctor, so they can help her and give her medicine and—"

"Daffy is dead, Arc."

"No, she isn't. She's just sleeping." I got back down on the floor by her.

"Look at her, Arc. She's as still as old bones. And she's cold as ice." She picked up Daffy's hand. "Her fingers are getting stiff."

"Shut up, shut up, shut up." I cried and screamed. "You're a dirty lying whore. Shut up."

"Listen to me." Aunt Clover yanked me to my feet. "I'll tell the cops you did it. You hear me? I'll tell them you killed your sister. They'll take your name from you, and they'll take all your memories until you forget you even had a sister in the first place. They'll leave you outside like a chained dog. *Bark, bark, bark. Grrr.* They'll leave you out so long, you'll disappear into the ground. They'll dig you up in the future and find nothing but broken crowns. You want that?"

I shook my head as she shook me.

"Then help me." She picked up the sheet and stretched it out onto the floor. After she laid Daffy on it, she wrapped the sides up around her.

"Get her feet," she told me.

As Aunt Clover lifted Daffy's head, I wiped my nose on my sleeve and picked up my sister's feet.

"Good girl." Aunt Clover, out of breath, grunted as we carried Daffy out of the room.

I looked down the hall at my mother's room. Her door was closed.

"Mom," I cried for her. "Please come out. I don't wanna do this. Say we can take Daffy to the doctor. Momma?" I carefully laid Daffy's feet on the floor, then ran down the hall and banged on Mom's door. When I tried to turn the knob, she held it from the other side.

"Momma, please." I tried to shove the door open. "Help Daffy."

"Go away, go away," Mom screamed. "I don't know you. Go away."

Aunt Clover dug her fingers into my arm as she jerked me back to Daffy's body.

"What the fuck did I tell you?" Aunt Clover slapped me hard before picking Daffy back up to carry her into the living room.

She laid her on the sofa, the sheet falling off her side and revealing the Holly Hobbie sweatshirt.

"Where the fuck are they?" Aunt Clover let loose a constant stream of curses as she searched through the clutter on the coffee table, finally finding the truck keys.

"Hold the door open," she told me.

I lifted up the collar of my shirt and cried into it as I held the screen door open with my foot. Daffy's legs swung as Aunt Clover carried her out and put her in the truck.

"Get your ass out here, Arc," Aunt Clover hollered.

Wiping my face, I let the screen door slam behind me. I glanced back at the cold and dark house, then climbed up into the truck, Daffy in between me and Aunt Clover.

"Can we take her to Mamaw Milkweed's house?" I asked.

"Take a dead girl to a dead woman's house? Ain't no sense in re-uniting the ghosts." Aunt Clover put the truck in gear. She tried to keep the sheet wrapped around Daffy's face, but it kept dropping down with every bump she drove over. When she hit a pothole, Daffy's head fell onto my shoulder. I reached in under the sheet and grabbed her cold hand, squeezing it.

"Where are we taking her?" I asked.

Aunt Clover looked over at me, then turned her eyes back to the road.

"Her favorite place," she said.

We drove a long time, following the river to the edges of the county. I'd never been out so far. The woods we walked through were dark. Bare branches creaked overhead as Aunt Clover carried Daffy across the hard ground. It was so frigid, I could see every breath I exhaled. When we got to the edge of the river, Aunt Clover took the sheet off Daffy and tied it into a bag that she started to collect rocks in.

"Help me, Arc," she said, but I sat down beside Daffy, pulling up her knee socks. They had fallen to her ankles. I knew her legs would be cold. I straightened her pale pink slip and took the barrette out of the side of her hair to pin up her braid, so the tail stuck up like a flame. I thought it'd be enough of a fire to keep her warm.

After Aunt Clover had the bedsheet full of rocks, she tied the corners around Daffy's neck.

It was October, but an unusually cold one. The edges of the river were starting to freeze. Aunt Clover broke the ice away as we pulled Daffy's body out facedown into the water. I had to stop because it got too deep. I could no longer touch the bottom. Aunt Clover alone walked Daffy's body out into the darkness, the bag dragging the water underneath.

When Aunt Clover let go, Daffy slowly began to float away.

"It's a good thing she's a girl," Aunt Clover said. "They always know how to sink to the bottom of things."

We watched as the rocks began to pull Daffy's body below the surface. Before she disappeared completely, I screamed and tried to get to her.

"Stop it, Arc." Aunt Clover grabbed me. "You hush up right now."

She yanked me from the water, dropping me onto the bank.

"She'll like it here, Arc. You know how much she loved swimming. In the river, she'll swim forever. We can't ever say she's dead. You hear me? I want you to say Daffy is not dead."

"But she is," I cried.

"We can't ever tell nobody that. Don't you understand? Your momma will go to jail. I'll go to jail. You'll go to a place that's even worse."

"But someone's gonna find her."

"You think anyone cares if there's one less girl in the world? Ain't no one gonna be looking for her. Cold as the river is, ain't no one gonna be down here. Besides, what if they do find her? Daffy loved swimming. We'll say she went to the river to swim. They'll think she drowned on her own."

"I don't—I don't—"

"Listen to me," she said. "You being a twin is God saying all of this is okay. I mean, we get to go on as usual. When folks see you, we can just say, 'Oh, that ain't Arc. That's Daffy.' That way it's you some of the time, but Daffy some of the other time. You get to be both Daffy and you. Now ain't that wonderful?"

"You mean, like she isn't dead?"

"That's right. Like she isn't dead at all. The best thing a twin can do," she said, "is to let her sister have half of her life. You wanna be a good sister, don't you?"

I nodded, inhaling the snot back up into my nose.

"Well, here's your chance, Arc," Aunt Clover said.

"But people will know I'm not Daffy. My right eye is blue. Her right eye is green. And my—"

"You'll be surprised, Arc, how much people forget, especially about a couple of little girls who ain't nothing to them. You just believe it, and it'll be so."

Our whole childhood when Daffy was alive was spent imagining. Imagining eating birthday cake, hearing violins, and living a life better than the one we had. That's all I was doing after she died. I was turning the savage side beautiful so she could live again. I did the things I loved, but I also did the things she loved, like planting flower bulbs. Daffy dug in the ground to put something in it. I dug to take something out. The artifacts left behind.

It was me who Tam saw swimming in the pool. Me who ran up to John to get thirty-five dollars to be on Big Gray's team. Who Daffy became was the side of myself who first did the drugs, so I could have someone else to blame. Daffy was my addiction, fully formed and personified in a separate entity who was always and forever me.

Dead women take their secrets with them. Dead girls do, too. It became so I could change from being her to being me with little difficulty. In conversation, I spoke and answered for her, those around me not realizing that in my head I had changed identities. That's not to say I was confused, delusional, or textbook insane. I knew my sister was dead and already in the river by the time Harlow first floated her way into our lives.

When the other women kept going missing, only to be found the same way, I knew it was time. Time to have my own life. But I didn't want to just get rid of my sister. I didn't want to let her float away and sink. I felt a responsibility to share my existence with her so I wouldn't feel so guilty for living beyond her. I couldn't remove Daffy from my life.

Maybe River Man could.

As the women ended up in the river, I let Daffy step closer to that current. Only then did I have the chance to survive myself. And even though Daffy had never done drugs, she ended up in the river due to them. Lives lost to addiction are not always because the victim was the addict. Sometimes you die because the person you love is one. In Daffy's case, that was our mother.

ddear dirty,

It's gettin hard and harder to finde a pen.

I wanted to tell you that todday was a pretty god day. I made the girls baloney snowflkes again.

They didn't laugh as hardd as they did before, but Arc still smilled at me, even if daffy made her.

flood was there for a while. Ark didn't yell at him or tell himm he stunk like she usually doees.

He didnt really know what to talk about so he tolld them about the mill. That the smoke was dust from gallping horsess. Then he said he had to go.

daffy wanted him to stay, but he left anyway.

I told Arc I wanted her to have my purrple dress when she was olde enough. I told Daffy I wan her to have my blue one.

Arc told me that she wil find my earing for me. my ering sheped like a horse. I told her that I knw she would, even though I know its gone forever. gallop, gallp away

CHAPTER 51

This is my last chance to dance.
With the mothers and with the aunts.

—Daffodil Poet

MY MOTHER WAS SITTING ON THE EDGE OF HER MATTRESS, HER ONE eye open. She was the county's only cyclops. The other eye, swollen shut. The tones of her skin were purple and blue like the scarves her mother once gave her. Her lips thinned, gone like her husband. Her bony knees were up, her arms lying around them. I stared into the glazed surface of her one opened eye, outlined with black liner to make her appear like she gave a damn. Her hair was now gray. As gray as the smoke that filled her lungs. As gray as the smoke that drifted up to the sky. She'd lost most of her teeth. Her gums, something she would rub with her pinkie every few minutes as if they hurt her a great deal. She coughed and hacked and would never be considered beautiful again. By that time, she had outlived my father by nearly two decades, but she no longer allowed herself to think about things like that. The termites had eaten what nostalgia she had left.

I sat down against her legs and laid my head on them. "Momma? My skin feels hot."

"It's just the witch in you." She had the rough voice that so many addicts her age come to acquire.

"There is no witch," I said.

"Not now. They burned her. Don't you see the big fire still burning in all the corners?" She looked around as if the flames existed. "They burned her, and we've had hot skin and the flames ever since. Never did any of us any good having a witch in the family. Never gave us any spells. Any powers."

"Our powers are in our dreams," I said, as I knew Mamaw Milkweed would have.

"I don't dream no more," Mom said as she leaned down to scratch off the large scab on her shin.

"I do," I said like a girl surprised at what she is still capable of. "I dream."

"What do you dream of?"

"I dream of Daffy," I said. "Of what happened to her."

"Shhh." Mom ran her fingers through my hair.

I listened to her hum for a few seconds before saying, "You lost your earring, Momma. Do you remember?"

"What?" She looked around as if she'd find the earring beneath the covers.

"It was a long time ago," I said. "Daffy and me weren't no taller than your knees. You smelled like perfume then. We were walking from here to someplace else. I can't remember what for. Somewhere along the way, you lost your earring. You didn't realize it until after we'd gotten home. You cried so much for it. Dad said he'd buy you another pair. But you said no. You said you wanted that one because it was yours."

"It was a horse," she said, feeling her naked earlobe. "Brown like a burnt soul, a mane of black. When I moved my head, the horse galloped. Remember?" She moved her head like the horse would appear again.

"I thought if I found that earring," I said, "then you'd be returned to who you were before you lost it. If I found the earring, there'd be no needles. I could save you. I could save all of us. You'd be as you were. Brushing mine and Daffy's hair in the morning before school. Teaching us the alphabet, one letter at a time. Every time I dug in the dirt, it was to find you, Mom. I'm sorry. I'm sorry I never did."

"You found this." She reached under her pillow and pulled out the arrowhead.

"You had it?" I said. "This whole time?"

"It protected me, like it did that day." She laid it in my hand and closed my fingers around it. "You take it now. Let it protect you. I dreamed you would need it. I lied when I told you I don't dream no more. I do. Now, where's my blue-eyed girl?"

I shut my green eye, leaving my blue one to stare up at her.

"Where's my green-eyed girl?" she asked.

After I closed my blue eye, she rubbed her hand on my cheek until I opened both eyes to her.

"There you are," she said. "There's my girl with the blue and green eye."

I looked up into her face, aged like something that had been blamed for years. There in the fading span of her eyes was a love, briefly visible, behind the high. I craved a miracle. One where she'd shake from her fog and be as certain and clear as a good day. She would smile, and her color would come back. She would laugh and say it wasn't anything at all, these years. Just her, turned away for a second, and nothing more. Her hair would brighten, and her greasy roots would disappear beneath the shine.

But that did not happen. She merely lay down. "I'm tired, after all," she said.

She had stuffed so many things she'd stolen from the johns into the mattress that there was no level place to lie anymore. It bulged and rose, pushing against her body. She winced as she tried to find a comfortable place to rest.

"Let me take the things out for you, Momma." I reached into the mattress, but she said no.

"My momma said I'd made my bed and I'd have to lie in it," she said. "Well, I didn't make myself a comfortable bed, Arc."

She covered up the hole with her hands in case I were to reach back inside.

"Momma?" I called for her like I did when I was a child.

"Yeah, baby," she spoke softly, like she had so long ago.

"Would you come away with me?" I asked. "Come away with me to get better?"

Her eyebrows twisted up as she tried to understand.

"We could get better together," I said. "You wouldn't be Addie the addict anymore. You'll be Adelyn, and Aunt Clover would be all four leaves of something lucky. We'll live by the ocean and watch the whales and be too far away to see any more smoke from any more paper mills."

"I'm too old to climb a ladder." She stared at her husband's clothes hanging on the windows. "You'll have to do it, Arc. You'll have to hang Daffy's clothes with his. I should have done it right after she . . ." She let her words fade. "Arc, promise me you won't die, too. Please, please." She grabbed my shoulders and shook me with all the strength she had left. "Please promise you won't die. That you'll always come back to me."

"I promise, Momma."

"Good girl." She dropped her hands.

I watched her close her eyes. I thought she had fallen asleep, but then she spoke.

"Do you remember when I brought you back home from your mamaw's?" she asked. "I got you and Daffy each a pair of new yellow shoes. Do you remember them? They were yellow and shiny and had a strap that went across the top of your foot. They were special shoes. The type you wear with frilly socks on your way to Sunday. You both wore them until they began to cramp your toes as your feet got too big. Knowing you could never wear them again, I buried the shoes in the backyard so that someday, someone can dig them up and they'll know someone loved you because they gave you dancing shoes."

She closed her eyes again.

I kissed her on her sweaty forehead and told her I loved her.

"I'll be back home later," I said because I didn't want to worry her.

"Promise?" she made sure to say.

"I promise."

I stood up, staring down at her and taking in every last look I could. I closed her door slowly behind me. As I walked down the hall, I saw Daffy's bedroom light on. Aunt Clover was standing in front of all the sticks on the wall.

"I'm finally finished with it," she said.

The twigs had completely overtaken the wall. Some were only as big as my thumbnail, others as long as an arm. In some areas, they rose several inches thick. In others, they lay as single layers.

"This is the first one," she said, laying her hand on a small twig that was gray against the brown ones surrounding it. "I picked it up from the ground that night we took Daffy to the river."

She had placed the twig vertically in the center of the wall. No other stick touched it.

"I can't believe I'm finally finished," she said.

"What is it?" I asked.

"Don't you know?" She faced me. "It's the *Mona Lisa*." She turned back to the wall with the biggest smile I'd ever seen on her face. "Can't you see her? Can't you see her?"

I looked up at the wall and saw the decades of our lives. All the jumbled truths, tethered to space and time and each other.

"Yes," I said, "I see her."

"And you thought I'd never see the *Mona Lisa*." She laughed, and it was pure joy. "Spittle, spittle, spider, where you gonna hide her?" Aunt Clover spit into her palm and smacked it against her own chest. "Right here."

I wrapped my arms around her and hugged her tight.

"Bye, Aunt Clover."

"Bye-bye." She pulled back and sat on the floor. When she stared up at the twigs, she reached her hands out toward them but did not touch.

I stepped over to the closet and grabbed the small animal carrier. I already had a can of tuna inside it. I reached up to the top shelf and got Daffy's old bulb catalog. Opening its pages, I collected the money out of them and slipped it into my pocket, but left the catalog on the shelf. It was time to leave some things behind.

"Arc?" Aunt Clover called to me just before I stepped out of the room.

"Yeah, Aunt Clover." I turned to face her.

"What, if anything, am I?" she asked, keeping her eyes down. "If I am? Sometimes I give a second thought for the young woman I used to be until I fall to my knees. Every time I am astonished at how lonely I can be. Because it is so very lonely being a coward. And I am a coward. I'm sorry, Arc."

I thought she was talking about Daffy, but then she said, "I'm sorry I left you when that man was hurting you. You were just a little kid. You couldn't fight him off. You could only hope I would. But I let him have you. I went out to the sofa and I sat down and I let him have you because I didn't wanna get hurt, too." She raised her eyes to mine, her tears spilling down her cheeks. "I'm sorry I left you. I should have—I should have gone back in. I should have saved you."

"On the beautiful side you did," I told her as I knelt beside her and wiped the tear off her cheek. "You came in and saw the spider in my bed attacking me. You yelled at him and hit him and—"

"And he hit me back, and I ran like the coward I am," she said.

"Only on the savage side," I said. "But on the beautiful side, you pulled off each of his eight legs. Then you took him by the mouth and you screamed our names until they filled his throat and he choked to death on them. And you took his body and you turned it into sand and we let it fall between our fingers until not even a grain of him was left in this world. Then me and you got in a boat and paddled it down the river, and we went to Brazil and Japan and—"

"Italy?" she asked. "And France?"

"We went everywhere in the world you've ever wanted to go," I said.

She turned back to the wall, wiping her eyes on her sleeve.

"Isn't she beautiful?" She sighed, staring at the twigs. "The *Mona Lisa*."

I smiled at my aunt one last time. Out in the hall, I set the carrier down and went into the bathroom. I stood in front of the mirror. Tape completely covered the glass. The image I saw reflected back was no more myself than the glare reflected from the ceiling light. I pulled the tape off until my face was staring back at me. Reaching into my pocket, I took out my lipstick. I applied it to my whole mouth, then went into my room and looked around for what I wanted to take. But there was nothing I wanted to hold on to. Before leaving, I dragged the old plastic stool over to the corner of my room. I stood on it with the broom that hadn't been used in ages and dusted the spiderweb down.

I stared at the thin strands, caught in the stiff bristles, as I got off the stool. Carefully collecting the web with my fingers, I laid it on the floor. Letting the broom fall from my hand, I raised my foot above the web, holding it there a second, before bringing my heel down upon it, crushing the web beneath my foot. Dusting off my hands, I left my room and the old spiders behind.

I took the tuna can into the kitchen and opened it. Then I went into the backyard with the carrier. I put the can of tuna inside it and waited. Petticoat looked over from the broken chain-link fence. She had been lying on it, curled up. When she smelled the tuna in the air, she rose and sat for several seconds, eyeing me. I stood silently as she took slow steps toward the carrier. She peeked inside, smelling the air in hungry sniffs. She hissed at me, but I only stared back at her. Pacing in front of the carrier, she finally entered it. I quickly closed the door. She spilled the tuna inside, growling and fighting to get out.

"I'm not gonna leave you here," I told her. I carried her around to the truck and put her on the seat. As I started the engine, the horse paced in the yard, neighing, her hot breath turning to smoke in the cold air.

Petticoat let out a long howl as I pulled out of the drive. The horse galloped beside us until we got to the paper mill, where she disappeared into the smoke.

"It's okay, Petticoat," I told her. "We're gonna leave this place and never come back. I know you don't trust me now, but I'll make sure you have a good life from here on out. I promise."

I turned out of town, heading to the Distant Mountain. After I parked on the side of the road, I reached into the glove compartment and told Petticoat, "I won't be gone long. I just have to do something before we go." I got out and walked through the cornfield down to the river. It was starting to freeze in places, the current sliding over the ice. I knelt and placed the compass I'd made for Daffy on the water. As it floated away, I said, "Find your way home, sister."

As I stood and stared up at the bright white sky, a hand came from behind and covered my mouth until I could no longer breathe.

OFFICE OF ROSS COUNTY MEDICAL EXAMINER
CHILLICOTHE, OHIO
REPORT OF INVESTIGATION BY COUNTY MEDICAL OFFICER

DECEDENT: Arcade Doggs

OCCUPATION: Archaeologist/Sister/
Finder of the horses

EYE COLOR: The earth and the water

HAIR: Red as a flame

DESCRIPTION OF BODY: Unclothed

GENDER: Witch

BODY TEMP: As cold as her house

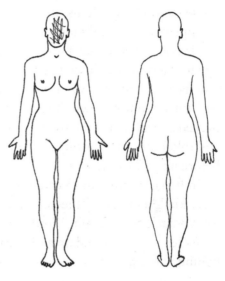

WOUNDS AND MARKS: Daffodil tattoos on back of hand, inside of arms, wrists, and shoulders. Green stems. White petals. Gag around mouth. Leaves stuffed into her throat. She couldn't scream. Body was dragged for some time. Skin along backbone scraped off. Spine exposed. Heart had already stopped pumping when kick marks on face and rib cage were made. She was beat for a long time after death. There was anger for her. Numerous fractures to the right and left side of the chest, consistent with heavy object being placed upon her. Daffodil tattoos on backs of fingers. Old rib injury healed on its own, scar tissue left over from previous burns, and crescent-shaped scar on foot, likely suffered from childhood.

Roots, butterfly larvae, and mud found in air passages. Rocks like jewels. Slashes along backside, consistent with the laying down of a woman. One eye gone. All teeth but one missing. There are daffodils tattooed upon the skin. Unsure if they are things that have been given. Or things that have been taken. A crown of twigs and leaves upon her head. The last queen of Chillicothe.

PROBABLE CAUSE OF DEATH:

Living on the savage side.

CHAPTER 52

Her frown will be her crown.

—*Daffodil Poet*

MY NAME IS ARCADE. I WAS NAMED AFTER THE BRIGHT FLASHING lights of the game my mother played with my father. My naked body was sent out onto the river on a Sunday. The water rippled around me when he gave me that last shove with his foot. Later that night the river would begin to freeze, trapping me in the ice until the thaw. I would sink to the bottom where the gases filled me, pushing me back up to the surface, where I continued to decompose. I floated facedown for weeks until I was discovered.

River Man not only found me. He found Petticoat. The creaking of the truck door opening and another promise broken. I don't have to tell you what happened next. Sometimes I see her here with the horses, when she allows me to. At least here I know she's safe.

No one claimed her body. And no one claimed mine, until Thursday's parents did. They gave me a nice funeral. I suppose the funeral they would have given their daughter. When they got word a woman had been found in the river, they thought it was Thursday. They didn't know at the time that her body would never be found. Maybe years from now, some little girl will come along and dig up what remains of her. Maybe that will happen. Or maybe she will stay the one never found, like my sister.

Aunt Clover had been the one who was called to identify my body. I wasn't surprised when she said it wasn't me and left. It was easier for her and Mom to survive by not having another dead daughter and niece to bury. Maybe if I were still alive, I'd hate them. But not here. Here I understand.

I will say my mother has never stopped talking about me. As the years come on, she'll tell people I was born in a small cinderblock house with concrete floors my sister and me would draw on. Mom will walk on these drawings, faded by time and by the years they have been stepped on, as she tells them I was a small kid, destined for big things, or so she thought.

"This house will be on fire and burn until my Daffy and Arc come home."

Sometimes folks have a hard time understanding through the slur what she's saying. Drugs change the way people listen to you. They discount what you say and will oftentimes force a nod, if only to escape having to ask a million and one times for you to repeat it and to speak clearer. Worst yet, they'll laugh at you. At the way you saunter, at the way you talk.

Damn junkies. Fucking idiots.

But she'll start to cry as she says my name. They seem to understand that.

Then they'll talk to her about the drugs. She'll sit up straighter and pretend that the Ohio and Chillicothe of her youth was as pleasant as a bowl of her mother's persimmons on the counter. She'll say back in those days, she'd walk the streets, not to turn a trick but to laugh with her friends. She would kiss a boy, not for money but for heart's instinct. She could walk outside at night, not in fear but in quiet awe of the stars above.

"We thought drugs were the problems of big cities, not small towns like ours. Times have changed. Now when folks talk about Ohio, they talk about it as something lost. We have dropped the kingdom we were given." She says this in clear ways that make people wonder if she wasn't smart after all.

She knows a thing or two, this mother who sits alone in a house that once had two daughters and a husband. Death can be life-changing for a woman. She is left with a string tied to a can and her sister's voice floating toward her in a house now empty of any love, like the pastures of their youth. All that innocence and good ol' small town industry and safe streets are gone. Replaced by something that is killing entire generations who could have been more.

They will look back on this land years from now when the next generation has gotten control, and they will talk about the demons of the hills. The almighty poverty, the almighty abuse, the almighty surge of addiction. They will banish these demons until we are all captured in this myth where stories have been entangled for destinies to matter.

They'll say our true killer was addiction itself. *Addiction.* Defined as giving in to something that is known to be harmful. Books will be written about it. Important voices will go on TV, documentaries will be filmed, and someone will win a Pulitzer Prize for humanizing what was already human. Who we were as women will be lost to a whole conversation about addiction itself.

You remember when drugs were so bad, we were finding needles out on the sidewalk? someone will ask, in expectation of opinion, while someone else will say so-and-so died of an overdose, and that they knew them, but only for that reason.

To give that much to something as stupid as drugs. What dumb hicks. Glad I was never that dumb.

I won't make excuses. I made the choice to take the needle, but I will say an addict was a child once, too. We had hopes and dreams of being something more. Our dream wasn't to give ourselves away. That much is true.

Mamaw Milkweed once said, "A shotgun don't fire softly."

It took me a while to figure out what she was saying. Then I realized what she meant. Life hurts. When you're in front of the gun, it hurts a hell of a lot more. For some of us, to stand in front of the gun is less of a choice and more of the place we were delivered to here on the savage side.

Whatever the origin of addiction, the ending is usually the same. Sirens going down the road. A body lying close to another one. White crosses on the highways. Overhead, the sound of wings or maybe just silence.

Somewhere in that very conversation, someone will say our names. The names of the women whose bodies spent their death in the river, like me, disappeared in the unsolved case that today is known as the Chillicothe Six. For a moment there will be a hush that follows our names, until we are forgotten, dissolved to the risen tooth of time.

Will they find out who did this to us? I used to wonder.

Conspiracy theories will eat us out of body and bone. Was it a serial killer after all? Or was it just the drug dealer, who's now sitting in a jail cell somewhere between here and the Mississippi River, using his own skin to play the music his mother taught him? You can't be a man on the highway without going somewhere. You can only hope that the somewhere you're headed to has a sliver of light for you to hold on to. Or was it the man at the Blue Hour who's responsible for all this death? The collector of tears who watched us from afar? Perhaps it was the someone we have always known. The one who makes the spiderwebs or the one who plays the violin. In some ways, it's all of them. River Man was made from a piece of each.

So where am I now? In death have I been reunited with my father? Mamaw Milkweed? My sister? Is Sage Nell laughing with Thursday? Is Violet taking handfuls of the clouds like it's flour? Is Harlow naming the hummingbirds, and is Indigo holding her hand out to me?

Are we all in heaven playing harps, as the old preacher told us we would be when we sat on the pews any given Sunday? What we labored in life, is it truly better fruited here?

Daffy and me used to think that everything in the world was made out of and from a woman. Now I think the universe must be, too, because I feel I am time and space itself. The stars, the planets, pooling in my collarbone until I am energy. Comets are cut by my body, and it is my hands you see when you lay your eyes upon galaxies through the lens of your telescopes set on the heavens. I am the known and the unknown.

Sometimes I think I am with them all. Daffy, our father in his army uniform, and Mamaw Milkweed in yellow scarves as our friends ride by in Cleopatra's time machine. Other times I feel I am alone, just me and the stars gleaming across my skin. Perhaps the only definite thing I can say is that even ghosts shiver in boundless space.

Maybe that's not the answer you wanted. I'm sure you wanted to hear that everything has been righted in the end. That though we are dead, we are blessed in being together. But just as life is a journey, so, too, is death. You don't one day die and wake up having crossed the highway to the white and wild flowers. You've got to do a little journeying before you get there. And maybe in that journey, I can save myself.

This is the journey I failed at in life. It is the journey I must continue in death. I suppose much will circle back around to my life.

So what was my life?

It was lived on the savage side, and it can be said that no heart is safe on the savage side. But I'd like to say something more. I'd like to say that on the savage side, there was love. Love for us, love from us, love between us. We mattered, but no one will much think of that before thinking we were just addicts and prostitutes and weak-minded women who are easily gotten rid of and even easier forgotten.

I reckon you'll forget us, too. But if by chance, you do remember us, we were daughters, sisters, and mothers. Remember us for that. Maybe then, on the old land once called Chala-ka-tha, we will have left the most amazing artifacts of ourselves behind.

Acknowledgments

Thank you always to my family for their love and chocolate cake: My mother Betty. My father Glen. My two sisters, Dina and Jennifer. *Ruff, ruff* to our seventeen-year-old rescue beagle Maggie May, and *meow, meow* to our rescue cats Tabitha, Stella, Sal, Sir Purrington, Ichabod, and Lady Van Tassel. A special thank-you to Loud Ass Rockstar, our ever-energetic woodpecker.

Additional thanks to the following publishers:

Knopf: Timothy O'Connell, Maris Dyer, Nora Reichard, Emily Reardon, Matthew Sciarappa, Kelly Blair, Betty Lew, Reagan Arthur.

Atlantide Edizioni: Simone Caltabellota, Francesco Pedicini, Francesco Sanesi, Enrico Bistazzoni, Gaia Rispoli, Priscilla Caltabellota, Maia Terrinoni, Gianni Miraglia, Flavia Piccinni, Gaetano Carboni, Leonardo Ducros, Luca Briasco.

Weidenfeld & Nicolson: Federico Andornino, Francesca Pearce, Lynsey Sutherland, Esther Waters.

The team at Hachette Australia and Hachette Aotearoa New Zealand.

Oliver Gallmeister and the group at Gallmeister Editions.

And to all other translation publishers sharing this book with their readers, my thanks.

A NOTE ABOUT THE AUTHOR

Tiffany McDaniel is an Ohio native whose writing is inspired by the rolling hills and woods of the land she knows. A novelist, poet, and visual artist, she is the author of *Betty* and *The Summer That Melted Everything*.

AN *OBSERVER* BOOK OF THE YEAR

'Breathtaking'
Vogue

'A girl comes of age against the knife'

So begins the story of Betty Carpenter.
Born in a bathtub in 1954 to a white mother and a Cherokee
father, Betty is the sixth of eight siblings.

Despite the hardships she encounters, Betty is resilient. Her
curiosity about the natural world, her fierce love for her sisters
and her father's brilliant stories are kindling for the fire of her own
imagination, and in the face of all to which she bears witness
Betty discovers an escape: she begins to write.

'I felt consumed by this book. I loved it, you will love it'
Daisy Johnson, author of *Sisters*

READ AN EXTRACT NOW

My mother, Betty, was born February 12, 1954, in Ozark, Arkansas. She was born to a woman as telling as a dream and to a man who was a Cherokee, a moonshiner, and a mythmaker. One of twelve children, my mother came of age in the foothills of the Ohio Appalachians. This book is part dance, part song, and part shine of the moon. Above everything else, this story is, always and forever, the Little Indian's.

I love you, Mom. This book is for you and all your ancient magic.

Author's Note

This novel takes place in the foothills of the Ohio Appalachians in southern Ohio. Ohio Appalachia is a place where families are raised and individuals step into their own light. Southern Ohio has its own beautiful traditions, culture, history, and rich southern drawl and dialect. I have been honored to call this region my home. I hope, after reading this novel, that you love this part of Ohio as much as I do.

I further hope that you enjoy your time with this story, which is inspired by generations of my family. In particular, it is inspired by the strength of my mother and the women who have come before me. In the face of adversity, they rose to their own power. It has been an honor for me to tell such a story.

Prologue

I thank my God upon every remembrance of you.

—PHILIPPIANS 1:3

I'm still a child, only as tall as my father's shotgun. Dad's asking me to bring it with me as I go out to where he is resting on the hood of the car. He lifts the shotgun out of my hands and lays it across his lap. When I sit next to him, I can feel the summer heat coming off his skin like he's just another tin roof on a hot day.

I don't mind that the tomato seeds, left over from his afternoon lunch in the garden, drop off his chin and land on my arm. The tiny seeds cling to my flesh and rise above it like Braille on a page.

"My heart is made of glass," he says as he starts to roll a cigarette. "My heart is made of glass and if I ever lose you, Betty, my heart will break into more hurt than eternity would have time to heal."

I reach into his pouch of tobacco and rub the dry leaves, feeling each as if it were its own animal, alive and moving from fingertip to fingertip.

"What's a glass heart like, Dad?" I ask because I feel like the answer will be greater than I can ever imagine.

"A hollow piece of glass shaped like a heart." His voice seems to soar above the hills around us.

"Is the glass red, Dad?"

"It's as red as the dress you're wearin' right now, Betty."

"But how is a piece of glass inside you?"

"It's hangin' in there from a sweet little string. Within the glass is the bird God caught all the way up in heaven."

"Why'd He put a bird in there?" I ask.

"So a little piece of heaven would always be in our hearts. Safest place for a piece of heaven, I reckon."

"What type of bird, Dad?"

"Well, Little Indian," he says, striking the match against the sandpaper ribbon on his wide-brimmed hat to light his cigarette, "I think she'd be a glitterin' bird and her whole body would shine like little fires of light, the way Dorothy's ruby slippers did in that movie."

"What movie?"

"*The Wizard of Oz.* Remember Toto?" He barks, ending with a long howl.

"The little black dog?"

"That's right." He lays my head against his chest. "Do you hear that? *Thumpity, thump.* Do you know what that sound is? *Thumpity, thump, thump.*"

"It's the beatin' of your heart."

"It's the noise of the little bird flappin' her wings."

"The bird?" I hold my hand over my own chest. "What happens to the bird, Dad?"

"You mean when we die?" He squints at me as if my face has become the sun.

"Yes, when we die, Dad."

"Well, the glass heart opens, like a locket, and the bird flies out to lead us to heaven so we don't get lost. It's very easy to get lost on the way to a place you've never been before."

I keep my ear against his chest, listening to the steady beating.

"Dad?" I ask. "Does everyone have glass hearts?"

"Nope." He takes a drag on his cigarette. "Just me and you, Little Indian. Just me and you."

He tells me to lean back and cover my ears. With the cigarette hanging in the corner of his mouth, he raises the shotgun and fires.

Part One

I Am

1909–1961

1

There shall be weeping and gnashing of teeth.

—MATTHEW 8:12

A girl comes of age against the knife. She must learn to bear its blade. To be cut. To bleed. To scar over and still, somehow, be beautiful and with good enough knees to take the sponge to the kitchen floor every Saturday. You're either lost or you're found. These truths can argue one another for an infinity. And what is infinity but a tangled swear. A cracked circle. A space of fuchsia sky. If we bring it down to earth, infinity is a series of rolling hills. A countryside in Ohio where all the tall-grass snakes know how angels lose their wings.

I remember the fierce love and devotion as much as I remember the violence. When I close my eyes, I see the lime-green clover that grew around our barn in the spring while wild dogs drove away our patience and our tenderness. Times will never be the same, so we give time another beautiful name until it's easier to carry as we go on remembering where it is we've come from. Where I came from was a family of eight children. More than one of us would die in the prizewinning years of youth. Some blamed God for taking too few. Others accused the devil of leaving too many. Between God and devil, our family tree grew with rotten roots, broken branches, and fungus on the leaves.

"It grows bitter and gnarled," Dad would say of the large pin oak in our backyard, "because it doubts the light."

My father was born April 7, 1909, in a Kentucky sorghum field downwind from a slaughterhouse. Because of this, the air smelled of blood and death. I imagine they all looked at him as if he were something born of these two things.

"My boy will need to be dunked in the river," his mother said over his tiny reaching fingers.

My father descended from the Cherokee through both his maternal and paternal lines. When I was a child, I thought to be Cherokee meant to be tethered to the moon, like a sliver of light unraveling from it.

"Tsa-la-gi. A-nv-da-di-s-di."

Following our bloodline back through the generations, we belonged to the Aniwodi clan. Members of this Cherokee clan were responsible for making a special red paint used in sacred ceremonies and at wartime.

"Our clan was the clan of creators," my father would say to me. "Teachers, too. They spoke of life and death, of the sacred fire that lights it all. Our people are keepers of this knowledge. Remember this, Betty. Remember you, too, know how to make red paint and speak of sacred fires."

The Aniwodi clan was also known for its healers and medicine men, those who were said to have "painted" their medicine on the sick or ill. My father, in his own way, would continue this.

"Your daddy's a medicine man," they would tease me in school while flapping feathers in my face. They thought it would make me love my father less, but I only loved him more.

"Tsa-la-gi. A-nv-da-di-s-di."

Throughout my childhood, Dad spoke of our ancestors, making sure we did not forget them.

"Our land used to be this much," he would say, holding his hands out to either side of him as he spoke of the eastern territory that had once belonged to the Cherokee before they were forcibly removed to Oklahoma.

Our Cherokee ancestors who managed to avoid going to this alien land called Oklahoma did so by hiding in the wilderness. But they were told if they wanted to stay, they would have to embrace the way of the white settlers. The higher powers had made it the law of the land that the Cherokee must be "civilized" or be taken from their home. They had little choice but to speak the English of the white man and convert to his religion. They were told Jesus had died for them, too.

Before Christianity, the Cherokee celebrated being a matriarchal and matrilineal society. Women were the head of the household, but Christianity positioned men at the top. In this conversion, Cherokee women were taken from the land they had once owned and worked. They were given aprons and placed inside the kitchen, where they were told they belonged. The Cherokee men, who had always been hunters, were told to now farm the land. The traditional Cherokee way of life was uprooted, along with the gender roles that had allowed women to have a presence equal to that of men.

Between the spinning wheel and the plow, there were Cherokee who fought to preserve their culture, but traditions became diluted. My father did his best to keep the water out of our blood by honoring the wisdom that had been passed down to him, like how to make a spoon from a squash leaf and stem or how to know when it's time to plant corn.

"When the wild gooseberry bush has exploded in leaf," he would say, "because the wild gooseberry is the first to open her eyes from her winter nap and say, 'The earth is warm enough.' Nature speaks to us. We just have to remember how to listen."

My father's soul was from another time. A time when the land was peopled by tribes who heard the earth and respected it. His own respect filled up inside him until he was the greatest man I ever knew. I loved him for this and more, like how he planted violets but never remembered they were purple. I loved him for getting his hair cut like a lopsided hat every Fourth of July and I loved him for holding a light on our coughs when we were sick.

"Can you see the germs?" he'd ask, shining the light beam on the air between us. "They're all playin' violin. Your cough is their song."

Through his stories, I waltzed across the sun without burning my feet.

My father was meant to be a father. And, despite the troubles between him and my mother, he was meant to be a husband, too. My parents met in a cemetery in Joyjug, Ohio, on a day given to the clouds. Dad wasn't wearing a shirt. It was in his hand and fashioned into a sack. Inside it were mushrooms that looked like pieces of a smoker's lung. As he scanned the area for more, he saw her. She was sitting on a quilt. You could tell the quilt had been handmade by a girl still learning. The stitches spaced unevenly. The crookedly cut sheets of fabric in two different shades of cream. In the center of the quilt was a large appliquéd tree made out of scraps of mismatched calico. She was seated on this tree and was eating an apple while facing the headstone of an unknown Civil War soldier.

What a peculiar girl, Dad thought, *to be sitting in a cemetery chomping an apple with all that death beneath her.*

"Excuse me, miss. You seen any of these around?" He held his shirt sack open. She briefly looked in at the mushrooms before glancing up at his face and shaking her head.

"You ever had one of these mushrooms, miss?" he asked. "Fried with butter? Mighty delicious."

She said nothing, so he went on to say she was a girl of many words.

"I bet you're the guardian of a lost language," he said. "That soldier one of your people?" He motioned toward the grave.

"How can he be?" she finally spoke. "No one even knows who he is." She flicked her hand in the direction of the headstone. "THE UNKNOWN SOLDIER. You can read, can't you?" She asked harsher than she meant to.

For a moment, he thought he might leave her be, but part of him existed there better with her so he sat on the grass outside the edge of the quilt. Leaning back, he looked up at the sky and remarked how it looked like rain. He then picked up one of the mushrooms and twirled it between his long fingers.

"They're ugly things, ain't they?" She frowned.

"They're beautiful," Dad said, insulted on the mushroom's behalf. "They call 'em the trumpet of death. It's why they grow so well in graveyards."

He held the small end of the mushroom to his mouth and made the noise of a trumpet.

"Toot-toot-ta-doo." He smiled. "They're more than beautiful. They're a good dose of nature's medicine. Good for all sorts of ailments. Maybe one day I'll fry ya some. Maybe I'll even grow ya an acre all your own."

"I don't want no mushrooms." She made a face. "I'd like lemons, though. A whole grove of 'em."

"You like lemons, do ya?" he asked.

She nodded.

"I like how yellow they are," she said. "How can you not be happy with all that yellow?"

She met his eyes but quickly looked away. For her sake, he turned to the mushroom in his hand. As he studied it, rubbing his fingers over its crinkled flesh, she slowly moved her eyes back to him. He was a tall, sharp-boned man who reminded her of the walking-stick insects that would climb the pane of her bedroom window every summer. His muddy pants were too big for him and were held up by a scuffed leather belt cinched around his thin waist.

He had no chest hair, which surprised her. She was used to seeing the curly coarse hairs on her father's barrel chest and the way they felt like tiny wires in her hands when she grabbed hold of them. She forced the image of her father out of her mind and continued to consider the man in front of her. His thick, black hair was cut short on the sides but left long on the top, where it flopped up as high as her hand, then down in waves.

Pappy would not approve, she said to herself.

She knew the man must have come from a household run by women. It was the way he had sat outside the quilt, rather than sitting on it. She could see both his mother and his grandmother. He held them there in his brown eyes. She trusted this about him. That he should hold women so close.

Something she could not ignore was his skin color.

Not negro dark, she thought in those 1930s, *but not white either, and that is just as dangerous.*

She lowered her stare to his bare feet. They were the feet of a man who traveled the woods and washed in the river.

"He's probably in love with a tree," she said under her breath.

When she raised her eyes, she found him staring at her. She turned back to her apple, which had only a few bites left.

"Excuse the dirt, miss," he said, dusting it from his pants. "But when you're the gravedigger, you can't help but get a little dirty. It ain't bad workin' here. Though it's bad for the folks I'm diggin' the holes for."

He saw her begin to smile from behind her apple, but she caught herself. He wondered what she thought of him. He was twenty-nine. She was eighteen. Her shoulder-length hair hung bagged in a white crocheted snood. The color and texture of her hair reminded him of pale wisps of corn silk in the light of the sun. Her skin was peachy against her mint-green dress while her small waist was girded tightly by a dingy white belt, matching her soiled crocheted wrist gloves. She was a girl of little means up close, but from afar she could look like she was more.

That's what the gloves are for, he thought. *To pretend she's a lady and not another muted beauty expected to rust her way out of creation like some broken-down tractor in a field.*

The apple was nearly at its core, but a patch of red skin was still visible around its stem. When she took a bite, the juice escaped out of the corners of her mouth. As he watched the wind blow the loose strays of hair above her small ears, he felt a gentle rain falling on his bare shoulders. He was surprised he could still feel something so soft and light. Hardness had not yet gotten the better of him. He looked up at the darkening sky.

"You don't get clouds like that unless they aim to prove they got a storm in 'em," he said. "We can either sit here and become part of the flood or seek to save ourselves best we can."

She stood and dropped what was left of the apple to the ground. He noticed her feet. She was barefoot. If she and he were the same in anything, it was the way they walked the earth. He was about to say something he thought would interest her, but the rain fell harder. It beat on the two of them while the sky brightened with lightning. The storm was laying claim to my parents in ways not even they could have understood.

"We'll get some cover under that shagbark hickory," Dad said.

Keeping a grip on his shirt of mushrooms, Dad grabbed the quilt up off the ground to hold over her head. She allowed him to lead her to the tree.

"It won't last long," he said as they found relief beneath the dense canopy of the hickory's branches.

He shook the raindrops off the quilt before touching the shaggy bark of the tree.

"The Cherokee would boil this," he told her. "Sometimes for ailments, but sometimes for food. It's sweet, this bark. If you bubble it in milk, you've got a drink that'll—"

Before he could finish, she laid her lips upon his in the softest kiss he had ever known. She reached up under her dress to pull down her fraying panties. He stared at her and wondered, but he was a man, after all, so he set the mushrooms off to the side. When he spread the quilt on the ground, he did so slowly in case she wanted to change her mind.

Once she lay on the quilt, he lay down, too. In the fields around them, the ears of corn shot up like rocket ships while they smelled of each other and did not fall in love. But you don't need love for something to grow. In a few months' time, she could no longer hide what was developing inside her. Her father—the man I would come to call Grandpappy Lark—noticed her growing belly and struck her several times in the face until her nose bled and she saw small stars in front of her eyes. She cried out for her mother, who stood by but did nothing more than watch.

"You're a whore," her father told her as he removed his heavy leather belt from his pants. "What grows in your belly is sin. I should let the devil eat you alive. This is for your own good. Remember that."

He hit her across her midsection with the belt's metal buckle. She dropped to the floor, doing her best to cradle her stomach.

"Don't die, don't die, don't die," she whispered to the child inside her as her father beat her until he was satisfied.

"God's work has been done here," he said, slipping his belt back into the loops of his pants. "Now, what's for dinner?"

Later that night, she laid her hand upon her belly and felt certain that life continued. The next morning, she walked to find her mushroom man. It was the summer of 1938 and every expecting woman was expected to have a husband.

When she got to the cemetery, she scanned the open expanse before finding a man digging a grave with his back to her.

There he is, she thought to herself as she walked in between the rows of stones.

"Excuse me, sir?"

The man turned and was not him.

"I'm sorry." She looked away. "I thought you were someone I'm lookin' for. He also works here diggin' graves."

"What's his name?" the man asked, not stopping his work.

"I don't know, but I can tell you he's tall and thin. Black hair, dark brown eyes—"

"Dark skin, too?" He stabbed the shovel into the dirt. "I know who you're talkin' 'bout. Last I heard he got hired at the clothespin factory out on the edge of town."

She walked to the clothespin factory, where she stood outside the gates. At noon, when the horn blew, the men emerged from the building with their lunches. She strained to find him in the crowd of blue shirts and even darker blue pants. For a moment, she thought he was not there. Then she saw him. Unlike the other men, he had no lunch tin. He rolled and lit a cigarette, feeding on its smoke as his eyes moved across the treetops.

What is he looking at? she wondered as she, too, looked at the leaves blowing in the wind.

When she lowered her eyes, he was staring at her.

Is that the girl? he asked himself. He couldn't be sure. It had been some time since. Besides that, there were now bruises disguising her features. Her swollen eyes certainly didn't help. Then he saw the way her hair blew like corn silk over her ears and he knew she was the girl from the rain. The girl who had quickly put her panties on after.

He noticed how she rested her hand ever so gently on her stomach, which was not as flat as he had remembered. He exhaled enough smoke to hide his face as he walked back into the factory. The smell of wood, the grating sound of the saw, the fine dust filling the air like constellations of stars all did nothing but take him back to that moment in the cemetery. He thought of the rain and how it had dropped in between the tree branches and splashed against her pupils, the water puddling at the sides of her eyes to run down her cheeks.

When the factory's final horn blew hours later, he walked outside ahead of the other men. He found she had not left. She was sitting on the ground outside the factory's iron gates. She looked weary, as if she'd just marched a million funerals, the sole pallbearer at every one. She stood as he approached her.

"I have to speak with you." Her voice shook as she dusted dirt off the back of her skirt.

"Mine?" He motioned toward her stomach before starting to roll a fresh cigarette.

"Yes." She made sure to answer quickly.

He chased a bird across the sky with his eyes, then turned back to her and said, "It ain't the worst I've done in my life. You got a match by any chance?"

"I don't smoke."

He finished rolling the cigarette only to slide it behind his ear.

"I got work until five every day," he said. "But I get an hour for lunch. We'll go over to the courthouse. It's the best I can do. That okay?"

"Yes." She dug her bare toe into the ground between them.

He began to silently count her bruises.

"Who gave 'em to ya?" he asked.

"My pappy."

"How long the devil been livin' in your daddy's heart?"

"All my life," she said.

"Well, a man who beats a woman leaves me with little more than anger. The type of anger I can taste in the back of my throat. And boy is it a bad taste." He spit on the ground. "Pardon my action, but I can't keep that sort of thing to myself. My momma always said a man who strikes a woman has a crooked walk and a man with a crooked walk leaves behind a crooked footprint. You know what lives in a crooked footprint? Ain't nothin' but things that set fire to the eyes of God. Now I ain't a man of many talents, but I know how to spend my anger. Seein' how he is your daddy, I won't kill him if you don't want me to. I'll yield to your wishes, sure enough. But you're soon to be my wife and I wouldn't be worth a damn as a husband if I didn't raise my hand to the man who raised his to you."

"What would you do to him if you didn't kill him?" she asked, her swollen eyes brightening.

"You know your soul is right here?" He gently touched the bridge of her nose. It felt more intimate than anything they'd done before.

"That really where my soul is?" she asked. "In my nose?"

"Mmm-hmm. It's where everyone's soul is. When God told us to inhale our soul through our nostrils, it stayed right where it first entered."

"So what would you do?" she asked again, more impatient than before.

"I'd cut his soul out," he said. "That's worse than death in my opinion. Without a soul, who are you?"

She smiled. "What's your name, sir?"